Lorelei's Family

Lorelei's Family

Eileen Arthurs

Acknowledgments

The journey from inception to completion of Lorelei's Family has been far from solitary. For the first rendition, I thank the staff, faculty and guest speakers of Carlow University's MFA program, under the able direction of Dr. Ellie Wymard. I am grateful to my mentors at Carlow, who shared their expertise: Jane Candia Coleman, Janice Eidus and Sean Hardie. Also, I must thank my fellow students in the MFA program and my fellow writers in Madwomen in the Attic, especially Kathryn Pepper and Evelyn Pierce.

I am indebted to my former coworkers at Chang Eye Group, particularly Cindy Kelly, Michele Schraeder and Linda Carilli. I am grateful to Deborah Flanigan for the loan of her 'bad guy' library and to Tim Menees for his timely advice. Thanks to my sisters Kathy White, Janice Daley and Jennifer Smallshaw for their support, and to my parents, John and Ellen Daley, for being readers in general, and for catering Sunday dinners so I could write instead of cook.

I offer a heartfelt thanks to my chief mentor at Carlow University, Carlo Gébler, for his guidance, feedback and infinite patience. Without him, this book would still be a dream.

As I release the revised edition, I must add to this list. I thank each member of the Liars' Club for their savvy comments. My friends, Diana and Jim Farley, and my inimitable Uncle Willy, aka Dr. William Tiegel, provided valuable feedback. My father offered constructive analysis, as well as marketing material. Despite transitioning from her earthly role as Sunday cook to that of ethereal cheerleader, my mother has remained a vital inspiration.

Throughout all, my talented and artistic children, Faye, Sam and Ian and their significant others have inspired me by their energy and example. Each has been instrumental in this project in more ways than they can imagine.

Lastly, I could not have embarked on this journey at all without my husband Richard, whose role in the process has ranged from editor, sounding board and proofreader to so much more. His faith in my writing has been unshakable and sustaining.

Prologue

The End of Wishes

The last time Cody ate peas he threw up. His mom knew that. Why hadn't she remembered? Cody poked at the green mound before him.

"Eat your peas," his dad growled.

"I am."

Cody watched out of the corner of his eye as his dad drained a tumbler of whiskey. His Adam's apple bulged twice. "Mona?"

His mom leapt from her place at the dinette and grabbed the two-handled whiskey bottle on the counter. Cody scooped up some peas, shook a few back onto his plate, and shoved what remained into his mouth. Something hitched in the back of his throat. He gagged.

"What the hell is your problem?" his dad yelled.

Cody sat on his hands and held his breath.

"Maybe he's sick," his mom said. She unscrewed the lid and tipped the bottle over his dad's glass. He grabbed it from her hand.

"He's not sick," his dad said. He refilled his glass and banged the bottle down.

Cody stared into his plate. Ketchup from his meatloaf leaked a slimy river into his peas. His mom's hand, soft and warm, pressed against his forehead.

"Go to bed," she said. "Now."

Cody slid out of his chair without pulling it from the table. He had to think of something to fill his brain, fast. He ran down the narrow hall and fixated on the words to the new song from music class yesterday. He sang it in his head while he brushed his teeth and pulled on his striped pajama bottoms. Won't you come home, Bill Bailey? Won't you? Any time he stopped, shouts from the kitchen invaded.

It occurred to him that his mom probably wouldn't remember that he needed fifty cents for the field trip to the beanery tomorrow, but that's what he got for not eating his peas. He would tell Miss Morgan that he'd dropped his quarters down a sewer grate, if tomorrow really came. He ducked his head under his covers, worrying about peas and quarters, wondering where Bill Bailey had gone, and what his parents might do in their cramped kitchen. He shut his eyes and pressed his body into the mattress until everything swirled around him.

The crash that jolted Cody awake was a tyrannosaurus rex, definitely, belched from the flats beneath Glendale and lumbering towards him. When its giant head burst through his door it would probably have bits of his parents still stuck in its teeth, his mom's hand slopped under its chin. Cody sat up and huddled against the wall in his narrow bed. Another crash, then glass shattering against tin walls. He was awake now, and he knew it wasn't a tyrannosaurus rex after all. His eight years had already taught him that he didn't have that sort of luck.

He edged across his bed into the shaft of light and stared at his index fingers. Why wouldn't they grow into enormous plums the way Coyote Bill's did on the Cartoon Jamboree? That way he could stuff them into his ears and never hear that sound again. His father shouted. Some banging. The collision of something breakable against the trailer floor. His mom screamed. Cody smashed both palms against his ears and dove under his pillow. He angled himself so he could breathe. The metal coils poked him in a familiar pattern, the twisted spring under his left rib the worst.

Cody's pajamas felt sticky and his nose was stuffed. He willed himself to remain hidden, but his back arched and his head popped out from under his pillow. The front door slammed and rocked the trailer in shock waves. Cody pulled his knees close to his chest and wound his arms around them. He wondered which of his parents had left this time.

There was the sharp crack of a metal ice tray, followed by the clatter of cubes across the linoleum floor. The television blasted from the living room. Flickers of brightness lit the partitioned space at the back of the trailer that was his room. Cody knew by the sounds that this time his mom had left. After a while, the Star-Spangled Banner blared, followed by the roar of fuzzy static. Cody uncurled his limbs, scooted to the edge of his bed and waited. Only static. He forced his wobbly feet onto the floor, his right hand pressed against his thumping heart. He crept up the narrow hallway. His father lay sprawled in his orange vinyl recliner, mouth twisted open. Tufts of hair poked from his ears and nostrils. His swollen ball of a belly stuck through his half-open shirt. Cody checked to see that it rose with each breath.

Cody imagined that if he lived up on the hill, his house would come with a dad that didn't yell and throw things. One that wasn't so rumpled and wrinkly. One that didn't care about peas and slept in a wide flat bed with sheets tucked tight against the mattress. Probably Glendale was full of dads like that. He stared at his dad. Why had he gotten the one he had?

Cody turned off the television and felt his way back to bed in the darkness. He knew that his mother would return, her face puffy, her make-up wrong. She would take him to Murphy's and buy a box of tall glasses, because most of theirs would be broken again, and maybe a peppermint stick for him. He wished she would let him ride the horse in Murphy's front window. The horse had wild painted eyes and a real leather strap. But he knew that wouldn't happen. She always said that a nickel for a horse ride was robbery.

In the stillness, Cody pulled his blanket up to his chin. He imagined his feet in cowboy boots, his fingers coiled around the reins as the horse lurched its way through the nickel ride. Even though he was too old for that, he wanted it more than anything.

Cody stumbled into the kitchen the next morning to find his father spooning powdered coffee into a mug. Shiny slivers of glass dotted the floor. Cody's empty stomach growled and his throat was raw. He coughed. His father glared at him and turned away. The melmac bowl from last night's peas tilted in the sink. Grayish little orbs floated in the dishwater.

"Can I have a glass of orange juice?" Cody asked.

His father opened the refrigerator and slammed a jug onto the counter. He reached into the cabinet for a coffee mug. Cody picked up the jug with both hands. The glass was cold and slippery. He aimed it at the mug. Orange juice flooded the counter and pooled on the floor. His father scowled at him, then walked out the front door.

Cody drank his juice. It was cold and soothing on his scratchy throat. He didn't feel like facing Miss Morgan and the field trip today. He waited until mid morning, shoved a bag of M&Ms and two tootsie rolls into his pocket and headed to the edge of the clearing just past the trailer. He slipped between a rusted car fender and a stand of milkweed into the shade of the woods. He picked his way through overgrown trails and clambered up outcroppings of gray boulders. It had rained during the night. He could tell by the way the stream rushed across the stones. A still pool had formed where a branch jammed the flow. The water was stained brown from the pine needles that mixed with the fallen beech and maple leaves, but clear enough. He cupped his hands and drank. It surprised him that he hadn't heard raindrops splatting against the roof of the trailer last night. He must have slept some.

When the shadows lengthened along the mossy creek bank, he returned home. He was happy to find the trailer empty. Later, his father stormed through the front door and crashed his keys onto the Formica counter. Within seconds, his father cracked ice cubes from a tray, threw them into a chipped glass, and sloshed his whiskey over them. He unsnaked his belt from its loops and glared at Cody through thick eyelids.

"She'll be back," Cody said. His father swallowed a mouthful of whiskey.

Cody was right. His mother appeared, just in time to take him to Julia Dixon's birthday party. Cody couldn't remember the last time he'd been invited to a party. His mother had bought him a new shirt, stuck with pins onto tissue paper. She unwrapped it in silence, facing away from his father.

"Go ahead. Put it on," she said.

The shirt was itchy and rubbed against the shiny present she tucked under his arm. She walked him up the wide steps to the Dixon's front door and pushed against his back when Julia appeared in a dress shaped like an upside-down flower. His whole third grade class was there, the girls a rainbow of stiff dresses, the boys scrubbed and in neckties. At the party, no one talked to him. His mom was late to pick him up. She tripped over Julia's parlor rug when she reached for his hand.

The next day, when he got home from school, Cody's mother met him at the trailer door with a ball of gray fur cupped in her hands. He focused on her painted red fingernails with big chips on the ends where the white showed through. Her nails were always like that, bright with odd splotches, like the little islands that dotted the oceans in his geography book maps.

"Here," she said. She shoved the gray ball of fur at him. "It's a kitten."

Cody stared at it. It opened its jaws and squeaked. Its mouth was pink and lined with tiny razor-like teeth. He hadn't known that he needed a kitten. The woods were full of rabbits and woodchucks and a few stray cats now and then. He didn't know why his mother wanted to trap a kitten inside the trailer with the rest of them. She made him follow her to the bathroom where a red plastic pan sat wedged between the toilet and the bathtub. She showed him a shovel with slits in it, and told him he had to scoop the kitten's poop out of the litter box, every day. She handed him the squirmy fur ball. "Come on. Let's give him a name." Her green eyes were bright, her voice high. "How about Mittens?"

Cody shook his head. He was just a kid, and even he knew Mittens was a dumb name. The kitten was solid gray, like fog.

The next morning, Cody's mother was gone. Overnight, everything about her vanished, her flowery smell, her lilac bar of soap, her pink can of Aqua Net hair spray from the bathroom shelf. When his mother left, she took all the colors with her. She took all the colors and left the kitten. The kitten remained nameless.

Every day, Cody awakened early and stayed up late waiting for his mother. One afternoon, he answered the door to find his neighbor, Mrs. McCormick. She had never come to the trailer before. She held out a tray of pink-frosted cupcakes while a few of her moon-faced children orbited around her. Cody recognized them, of course, since the two families shared the lowlands beneath Glendale. But they never spoke, unless they crossed paths in the woods by accident, or if one of the creepy, skinny kids lost a ball in the field by his trailer. "I'm sorry about, you know," Mrs. McCormick said. She pushed the tray into his hands and mumbled something about a new Martha Washington cake mix. She left, followed by her pale brood with their whitish hair and eyes that glowed pink in the sunlight when they turned back to stare at him.

Cody ate those cupcakes all week, spitting little nuggets of artificial cherries from his teeth. He no longer expected that every creak or rattle was the sound of his mother's footsteps on the doorstep, her hand on the doorknob. His father drank lots of whiskey and only spoke to yell about the kitten. Cody had no luck when he tried to control it. It careened around the furniture, broke into cabinets, and made frequent, frantic romps to the cat litter until a dusting of pebbly grains covered the entire trailer floor. It leapt from the dinette and clawed jagged streaks into the side of his father's recliner.

The kitten had a thin voice that it rarely used, and a square head with bulging gold eyes. It brushed against Cody's legs, in and out, tripping him when he got up to pee at night. It purred when he threw back his quilt in the morning, like it had waited all night just for the chance to see him again.

One night, the blackness of the trailer tricked Cody into thinking he had fallen into hell itself. He began to cry. The kitten circled him, purring and prancing and kneading. Cody wanted to hold it close, but the kitten wouldn't stop its meaningless dance. Cody lunged at it and grasped it hard. The kitten let out a reedy cry. Cody dug his fingers into its fur and held on until the kitten was soaked through with his tears and snot. It clawed its way out of Cody's grip and scratched his forearm. Cody tried to chase it, but it was lightning fast as it hurled itself from bed to wall and bolted from the dark room. Cody lay awake the rest of the night, his tears streaming, his arm bleeding in a long ragged streak. He didn't want the kitten around anymore.

He wished that it would leave all by itself, but it didn't. It stretched and purred and jumped out at him from odd corners of the trailer. When Cody was outside, it came running toward him and tripped him up, weaving in and out of his legs. Cody would have to kick it and throw rocks at it to make it stop.

One morning, when his father left for work, or to drink, or whatever he did, Cody decided it was time to take matters into his own hands. When the metal door clanked shut, Cody got out of bed and dressed. The kitten jumped out from under the sofa, flecks of cat litter stuck in its fur. It opened its mouth and let out that high-pitched whine that Cody hated. Cody opened a can of food and let the kitten gobble it up, its whiskers slimed with fishy gravy. Then, he watched it bask in a patch of sun and lick the traces of breakfast from its fur. He wondered where it had learned to wash its face like that, licking its paw and rubbing it against its square head. Its tail still had bits of litter and poop stuck in it. Cody shoved it out the front door.

Cody watched it while he made his plan. He didn't know how to get rid of a kitten, but he'd learned to do all kinds of things since his mom left. He would figure it out. He got his bike from the shed in the field behind the trailer. At first he thought he would just run over the cat. But when he hopped onto his bike, the front tire wobbled so much that he couldn't even ride it through the grass. As soon as the spring mud had begun to harden, he had asked his dad to fix it, but his dad hadn't gotten around to it. His dad never got around to anything.

It took Cody a long time to figure out how to fix his bike. By the time he finished, the kitten had disappeared. Cody didn't mind too much. He would wait for it to return.

He was good at waiting. In those first days after his mother left, he had waited for her. He and that frenetic kitten. They had waited inside the trailer, or on its crumbled front step, or down by the gully, filled with water then, because she'd left in early spring when everything was soggy. Then, he went to school and waited there, the oversized clock above the blackboard ticking off minutes and hours. He liked to be at school with that giant clock eating up time in big slices.

He thought about that now, as he waited on his bike for the kitten. How had he been so sure that she would come back? For a while, some of the teachers had fussed about his rumpled clothes, his untouched homework, his lunches of plain bread or a paper bag of Frosted Flakes, or lots of times, no lunch at all. They asked him questions, and he answered them. But mostly he waited. The other kids stayed away from him. He wasn't really from town anyway. The teachers were all women, soft and fragrant and colorful, but none of them were his, and when the bell rang, they disappeared. But that didn't matter any longer. Cody got off his bike and propped it against the trailer. He had learned to take care of himself.

Cody sat on a rock until the sun was high in the sky and his lips tasted salty with sweat. He heard a rustle from the direction of the woods and turned to glimpse the kitten slink from the shade and pick its way through the brush. It bounded from the field beyond the gully, its gray fur now and then hidden by clumps of undergrowth. It rounded the corner of the trailer and stretched itself out on the crumbled cement step. It lolled in the sun and twisted its head almost backwards, as if that patch of cement were its throne. As if it didn't care that life in that trailer was forever ruined. It extended its front paws in a long stretch, closed its bulging eyes, and curled into a small, still ball.

Cody watched it for a while. He wondered how he would kill it, how long it would take. The day seemed purposeful, for a change, as if it mattered. After a bit, he hopped on his bike and headed for it. He chased the kitten and swerved on his bike like the racecar drivers he'd seen on television. He tipped and crashed and fell into the brush a few times. His knees were scuffed by the time he managed to corner the kitten against a pile of cement blocks by the shed. The kitten cowered into the blocks, its sides heaving, its fur torn in spots, streaked with blood. Cody got off his bike. He pried the panting animal from the blocks. His fingers circled the kitten's tiny neck and squeezed until the heaving stopped. He dropped it, wiped his hands on the grass and sat down.

The damp spots along the kitten's side congealed into a brownish ooze. Its gray fur still looked soft in spots. Flies began to boing up and down all over it. How did flies know how to find a dead body, Cody wondered. The dance of the flies transfixed him. Was it a party they were having? He swatted at them when they lit on his arms and the sticky sores on his knees.

Cody's head hurt. Killing the kitten wasn't so bad, just a lot harder than he thought it would be. But he really hated the flies. They hadn't let up in their air strikes, and now it seemed that more bugs had arrived to share in the party. He hadn't thought about that part at all. The kitten might lie there forever, with millions of bugs coming from all directions to do whatever bugs did.

Cody wasn't sure what to do next. Maybe it was best to forget all about it. He stood, picked up his bike and leaned it against the shed. Stones crunched under his feet on his way back to the trailer. He grabbed the front door handle, held now by only one screw, but changed his mind. Inside, the trailer was always too dark and musty.

He walked back to where he'd left the kitten and grabbed it by the tail. He held the limp body away from his legs as he carried it to the gully's edge. It made a whispery rustle when it landed in the brush far below, like all the important stuff had already leaked out of it.

Cody felt better. He looked up. The sun hung lower in the sky. He spread his fingers and held his hands up in front of him, wiped them on his pants and thrust them into his pockets. He trudged back to the trailer. He was thirsty. He wondered if his dad had bought sugar like he'd asked him. He would make some Kool-Aid if they had enough sugar. There was a packet of cherry and one of grape in the kitchen drawer with the knives and scissors and string. He'd seen them earlier when he was looking for some way to kill the kitten. He thought about which flavor he wanted as he pulled the handle of the trailer door, careful so the lone screw wouldn't pop out. He went inside and switched on the television while he searched for sugar.

••

Prologue Part Two

Moving On

Cody kicked at the scrubby vegetation around the trailer. He had failed his algebra test. No surprise in that. He had cut algebra class every day for the past two weeks. And history, too. He hated high school. Maybe he would run away, once and for all. It's not as though anyone would miss him. He grabbed what remained of the trailer door handle and pulled. The door didn't lock, but nothing inside was worth taking anyway. He stepped from the cement slab to the peeling linoleum entry patch and flung his algebra book at his father's empty recliner. Mr. Landon had shoved the book into his arms after sixth period, told him to stay after school, make something of himself. That guy was such an ass. He headed for the kitchen, but froze at the sight before him. His father lay sprawled across the kitchen floor. Cody didn't need to poke or prod him to figure it out. The old man was dead.

Cody eased himself to the floor. The reality of the corpse surprised him. He wasn't sad. He'd often fantasized about killing his father. Still, it was strange. Cody stared, trying to grasp what he saw. His dad looked stiff and awkward, not much different from any dead woodland creatures he'd seen. Had he just keeled over, or had someone killed him? Either way, it didn't really matter. For a moment, Cody was sorry he hadn't done it himself. The image of the gray kitten all those years ago popped into his head. He remembered the way its neck had felt under his fingers. Of course, he hadn't killed much since then, unless he counted the abandoned litter of fox pups that he had found crying in the woods that one summer. He had to tie them in a sack and throw them into the creek. That wasn't murder, that was mercy. And the idiot squirrel with its empty black eyes. But the squirrel had it coming, he thought. And maybe there were a few more. He looked away from his father's body. There had always been a reason.

He returned his gaze to the lumpy form at his feet. It hadn't been there in the morning when he'd left for school. The telephone was on the wall across from the refrigerator. He would have to step over his father to call for help. He didn't want to do that.

Cody rubbed the frayed spot on his jeans that was on its way to becoming another hole. He studied the body, face down on the floor. One elbow was bent as if someone had sawed it off and re-attached it backwards. The unevenly worn soles of his father's shoes loomed huge and purposeless. All dead bodies looked alike in a way, he thought. No matter how still a living being managed to be, the possibility for movement pulsed underneath, an electric current waiting to be switched back on. Dead bodies were permanently disconnected, robbed of that current, more still than a rock. The mocking stillness of his dad filled the yellowed patch of kitchen floor.

How had it been for his dad? The moment of death intrigued him. Again, he recalled the kitten, so long ago. Killing it hadn't been the bad part. Killing was liberation, a release of sorts. The bad part came afterwards. Dead bodies presented problems that Cody did not like. In a way, he was happy that his mother had simply vanished all those years ago. That might have been the nicest thing she'd ever done for him.

Cody wondered if his dad's hidden face held any clues. It was hard to suck the life out of a living body. He knew that. He crawled forward and reached out his hand. He hesitated, took a deep breath and touched the back of his father's head. His father's coarse black hair felt alien, diseased even. Cody jerked his hand back and scooted away, scuttling sideways like a crab. His broken shoelace caught beneath him and he stumbled. He righted himself and willed his jerky heartbeat to return to normal.

Cody's mouth felt dry. He always kept a wide-mouthed jug of water in the refrigerator. Usually, after school he stood with the door of the fridge open and guzzled right from the jug, letting it spill onto his shirt and the floor. Nobody ever yelled at him. Not at home, where he and his father coexisted in their disjointed worlds. Not even at school anymore, most of the time. His throat felt tight. With his father in the way, he couldn't get to the refrigerator.

Cody exhaled, picked himself up, and opened the front door. He walked outside, immediately soothed by the chirping of birds, the low drone of insects and the rumble of trucks on Glendale's Main Street far above him, on the edge of the hill. He cut across the field, surprised at the warmth of the September sun. It occurred to him that even on a regular day, the trailer was a lot like a tomb. His father's body, trapped inside on this glorious day, simply confirmed it.

His only neighbors would be home. They always were. The ever-growing army of near-translucent McCormick children spilled out of their tiny rectangle of a house at all hours. He remembered the plate of cupcakes Mrs. McCormick had brought after his mom had left when he was just a little kid. He wondered if today's events warranted another plate of cupcakes.

When he got close, he could hear the McCormick kids playing in their yard, laughing and yelling. One of them was crying. He smelled cigarette smoke and spotted a few of the older ones huddled behind their garage, puffing and coughing. A plastic wiffle ball sailed across their clothesline, strung with enormous white nylon underpants in a fluttering row. He stopped. He couldn't bear it, the mob of albino-haired kids, the underpants, maybe even another plate of fake cherry cupcakes. He went home.

The idea came to him fully formed. He knew exactly what to do, but he would have to wait for darkness. He switched on the television. Every now and then, Cody got up and checked on his father. After a while, his father began to acquire the familiarity of the tattered sofa or the nicked coffee table. Cody's stomach rumbled with hunger. He decided to eat while he waited for night to fall. He would need his strength. He kicked at his father's legs but they stayed put. Finally, he bent over and pushed hard against them with both hands. His father's legs felt heavy and unreal, like the weighted limbs of an oversized rag doll. With one more shove he wedged them tight against the metal cabinets. Cody straightened up. The refrigerator door cleared the legs just enough. Cody got out the milk and poured himself a big bowl of cereal. He ate the whole thing and poured himself another. He ate that, too.

When twilight fell, he turned off the television and got to work. He filled a bag with every scrap of food that he could find in the pink metal cabinets. He went through his father's belongings and scavenged every bit of loose change in the trailer. He looked for his dad's wallet, but it wasn't in its usual spot, under his socks in the top dresser drawer. He walked back to the kitchen. A telltale square bulged in his dad's back pocket. Apparently, he had been planning to go somewhere. Cody stared at the body and swore. The Frosted Flakes in his stomach lurched as he fumbled with his dad's pocket. He yanked the wallet free and forced his stomach to settle. Three ones and two fives were folded into the worn leather. Cody swore again. How long could that last him? He tore into one last compartment and found three twenties tucked behind his dad's driver's license. Cody smiled. It was a small fortune. The old man had finally redeemed himself.

Cody didn't turn on a lamp. In the fading daylight, he stuffed his few clothes into a duffel bag from under his dad's bed. He opened the trailer door a crack to be sure that no one was around. Not that anyone ever ventured down by the gully. The Dempshers and the McCormicks had sole run of the lowlands.

The McCormicks would be too busy swarming around their own house to come near. And Cody and his father were like two bats holed up in their narrow trailer cave, alone, untouchable. Cody knew what the town kids called him. Cody Dumpster. Cody Dumb Shit. He knew what they called his mother, too, although no one had seen her in years. He had been too little when she left to understand the implications of the flabby white skin that pushed out above her bra when she left the house. But he grew to understand that the word whore and his mother were interchangeable.

He took his stash of food and his duffel bag and hid them at the edge of the woods a few hundred yards from the trailer. Then he began his task. He set a book of matches from Jerry's Pub on the kitchen counter and began to crumple all the paper he could find, starting with a stack of old newspapers. After that, he ripped out every page from his algebra book, every page from his dad's pile of rifle magazines, the worn Playboy and the bass fishing guide it was stuffed inside, every photograph that lay in the bottom drawer of an old chest. As he yanked the glossy photos from the drawer, some of them caught his eye—his father lean and smiling, his mother with her dark hair and freckled chest spilling from her shirt in every shot. She was holding him in one. He had his arm around her neck and they were smiling at each other, his teeth a row of little pearls, his crew cut sticking up. Her green eyes were exactly his. He crunched the glossy paper in his fist, more material for his memento-ridden fuel. He knew how to make fires. He had learned to do a lot in the past seven years.

At midnight, the town up on the hill was dark except for a few circles of brightness under arched metal streetlights and the migrating headlights of the trucks heading for the interstate. Cody picked up the book of matches from the counter and opened it. He broke off a single match and dragged it across the rough strip. It blazed to life.

He was careful to light all corners of the trailer. In the kitchen, he paused to study his father. He imagined how, in a few moments, his father would curl into a cinder and waft into the night sky. Smoke stung Cody's eyes. His lungs burned and he began to choke. He fled the trailer, took cover in the woods with his stash of possessions, and waited. Thin orange spires pierced the top of the trailer and thrust little stabs into the night sky. Cody watched the spires grow fat and bright. They massed into a wall of deafening flames.

Satisfied, Cody slipped through the woods and followed the creek. He would walk by night and sleep by day in the cool woods of western Pennsylvania. When he was far enough away, he would hitchhike. He heard the crescendo of sirens behind him as he embraced the caressing blackness of the night air. His brain was alive with plans. Cody was one with the night.

••

He studied the row of stores before him. It took only a split second to realize that The Butcherie had once been Pete's Meats. He remembered the fine sawdust on the floor, and the women in belted dresses and wrist-length gloves buying their chops and roasts. He remembered how they had lifted their eyes from his as he waited his turn, when his mother had sent him for chop meat because she was too lazy to make it up the hill. They had all been so proper, those town women, asking after each other in solicitous tones. They had reeked of perfume that settled in his nostrils and filled his lungs while he waited for Pete to spot him from behind the counter. He had coughed as his feet made circles in the sawdust floor, but the women never asked after him, never even heard him.

Clarkson thought about getting out of the car, but decided against it. He pulled out from the space and continued to drive. He could almost smell the beery dankness wafting onto the sidewalks from the doorway of the half-lit pub. He could almost feel the hostility in the walk of the unshaven man who sucked the last dregs of a cigarette, flicked the butt onto the ground, and hopped into a dented pickup. As always, Glendale's underbelly lurked. After all these years, Clarkson still knew it well.

Just beyond the parking meters and the stores on the other side of the street, Glendale became country. Stately old brick houses with wide cement steps and awning-covered porches sat back on broad lawns, cheerful with puffs of peonies and kitchen gardens. The road forked to divide their manicured expanse from the lowlands, the shadows of Glendale. He took the lower fork.

There it was. His old world, still tucked beneath the massive hill, etched with the same gully that used to swell in the spring and crack in the heat of summer. He remembered the garish orange glow that had played across his face the last time he stood there, blinding his eyes before he turned his back on it. He had been euphoric that night, stripping himself of his history, shedding the curse of Glendale with every step he took into those cool, black woods.

He drove slowly. Even more than the town, the lowlands had remained unchanged—wild and patchy with weeds, dotted by an occasional stand of wildflowers, gnarled bushes, heavy-limbed trees. He came upon a dusty, gravel-strewn patch, somebody's abandoned driveway perhaps, and cut the engine. A cloud of dust rose and stuck to the car's metallic paint. He stepped out of the plush coolness into air that was too sticky and close. The sun sank low in the sky. He unfastened the top buttons of his oxford shirt, removed his gold cufflinks and dropped them into his pocket. He rolled up his sleeves and stood in the valley where he used to be Cody Dempsher.

His new name had come easily to him. Clarkson, after Clark Kent on the Superman show he used to watch in black and white in his trailer, and Dupree, written in fancy black letters across the first eighteen-wheeler that had picked him up. The new name had been a relief. It had been a long time since he had allowed himself to think of Cody Dempsher, son of Mona and Frank. Mona, the whore who had abandoned her only child, and Frank the drunk who made a pitiful living selling brushes out of a satchel. Mona and Frank and Cody Dempsher.

His old name seemed to emanate from the brush. He rolled the syllables around on his tongue as he walked. The gully still cut a snaky path where it skirted the hillside, as dense as ever with rhododendron and mountain laurel and ropes of leafy vines.

The years of striving and conniving that had led to financial success in his construction company and to the painstaking creation of Clarkson Dupree faded. He wanted to get back inside the car and drive away, but it was impossible. He remembered when he was ten and smashed his finger in the hinges of the shed and didn't want to look at it, but finally did. And once he had, the mangled skin fascinated him. That was exactly how he felt now.

He looked upward to the hill that had once shrouded him, shading the lowlands in summer, prolonging the snow cover in winter. He remembered the gray fur of the kitten that his mother had given him, matted with dark blood. He remembered the taunts, the unbearable loneliness of his school years, the silent evenings with his father, and then his father's body, large and ungainly on the kitchen floor.

He hadn't thought too much about his father in all those intervening years. Even in his childhood, his father had seemed vague to him, lifeless, as if he were viewing him through a glass. His father emerged in his memory as a collage of body parts, unsavory impressions. Ruddy cheeks and a large nose with black hairs inside. Blue eyes, bloodshot, with heavy lids. A thunderous voice. Dark coarse hair, the smell of stale alcohol, his large body bent forward in an awkward stoop.

Aside from his stature, Clarkson thought, he bore no resemblance whatsoever to his father. In fact, all through his adult years women had found him handsome. That had surprised him at first. When he left Glendale, he had been short, overweight, and pasty from hiding out in his trailer where he watched TV and ate boxes of sugary cereals and bags of junk food instead of real meals. If anyone commented on his appearance at all, it was to taunt him. By high school he had taken to wearing tinted glasses, partly because he had lost his regular ones, but mostly because they kept him insulated from the rest of the world. He grew his hair past his shoulders, which he kept hunched forward so he didn't have to look anyone in the eye.

But as soon as he left Glendale and hit the road, his body had snapped to attention. The long hours of hiking along dusty roadsides strengthened his muscles. The sun seared his skin until it was dark gold. He remembered the day he had pinched a pair of scissors from a gas station clerk, and turned his long jeans into cutoffs because they suddenly hit him at mid-shin, and then, as an afterthought, sheared off his long hair. The face that stared back from the filmy mirror in the men's room was almost unrecognizable. More than once, he wondered if he would have remained forever short, pale and flabby had he not escaped Glendale.

Clarkson's skin prickled. The configuration of the grasslands and the hill was exactly familiar. A family of bunnies posed, statue-like, precisely where the Dempsher trailer once sat. Two of them bolted, white tails bouncing. The last seemed intent on feigning invisibility. Clarkson stood beside the frozen rabbit on the little plot of land that used to be his home.

No scar marked the spot where Cody Dempsher had ceased to exist in a raging inferno. No gravestone marked the site of his father's hasty cremation. And yet, he felt its power. His past was contained in that plot of land. His feet were too heavy to move. Clarkson shaded his eyes, and peered in the direction of the McCormick homestead. He half-expected a gaggle of ghost-children with pale hair and pinkish eyes to converge on him. But only a stand of scrubby vegetation and tangled brush extended until it melted into the glare of the waning summer sun. His heart began to beat a little faster. Sweat dripped from his neck and underarms.

He repeated his names. Clarkson Dupree, Cody Dempsher. The two were completely incompatible. He was a different person now. He felt for the wallet in his back pocket, smooth, fine-grained leather, full of credit cards from stores that people in Glendale could only read about, if they knew enough to get their noses out of their claustrophobic, incestuous orbit. It amazed him, as he got older and increasingly successful, that he had once allowed himself to be bullied by such primitive folk. It pleased him to know that the well-heeled citizens of Old Brighton, Connecticut would hold both the Glendale townspeople and their despised lowlanders in equal disdain.

He neared the edge of the woods. Memories surfaced like untreated wounds and seeped into his consciousness. Sheila Herndon, for one. Her dad had taught geometry at Glendale High School, where she and Cody were both misfit students. She had shadowed Cody one day when he had scrambled out the janitor's back entrance after second period. Sheila was a fleshy girl, a spread of red pustules across her cheeks, and knees that faced each other, giving her gait a simultaneous forward and inward slant. At first Cody tried to lose her, but she labored after him, pressing her skewed knees into obedience. Despite himself, Cody began to hope for something, perhaps a glimpse of breast, although he had no doubt that Sheila's breasts would be as deficient as the rest of her. He led her in a descent down the long hill out of town, across the clearing by his trailer, and into the woods. She followed, tripping once or twice. Before they arrived at the flat boulder face that Cody had in mind, Sheila began to cry. She became hysterical, something about being an ugly duckling in a family of swans. When she wouldn't quiet herself, Cody left the woods. She followed him through the clearing and toward the hill to Glendale where he stopped. Sheila shuffled off when Cody started back down the hill.

Out of nowhere, Mr. Herndon appeared and stormed after Cody, his eyes mean slits. "If you touch my daughter again, I'll cut your fingers off one by one, you stinking piece of white trailer trash," he said. He had a cowering Sheila by the hand. He yanked her arm until she screamed.

Sometime that summer, Cody ran into Mr. Herndon, standing in line with a group of teachers at the Tastee-Freeze. Mr. Herndon turned away, his back slope-shouldered in his ill-fitting shirt, a wrinkled, sweat-spotted mess. Clarkson closed his eyes against the heat, the buzzing of the insects, the memories. Why had he been the canker in their world? It occurred to him that they had never let him become otherwise.

The anger that coursed through him was palpable. Its intensity surprised him. He could feel the vein in his forehead pulsating. His breath came faster. His hands trembled. A poisonous rage spread until it consumed and invigorated him. It was a tonic that had awaited him all these years, a potion that he had finally stumbled upon. He thought of the fortuitous and fateful magic cookie that Alice had found in that strange jar in Wonderland, inscribed with the words 'Eat me.' Like Alice, Clarkson chose to partake of it.

He looked to the woods, where he had taken his first steps to freedom so long ago. He picked up a rock and threw it against a decayed stump. Somehow, he had always known that freedom from his past had never been an option. He took a deep breath. The cells in his body tingled, vibrated, resonated with the bleak lowlands that had spawned him. It occurred to him that every fiber within him had longed for this day.

He entered the woods, the late afternoon sun now shredded into fragile shafts. He sat on a felled log by the creek bed until violet shadows pooled around his feet. His vein in his forehead throbbed more. His lips mouthed his old name with a frightening familiarity. Cody Dempsher.

He stood up and walked deeper into the woods, picking his way through half-obscured trails. He felt the weight of the gold cufflinks in his pocket. His steps were sure and heavy. Deeper into the woods, he heard a melodious chanting. He walked towards it. In a small clearing, a woman sat, eyes closed, legs crossed, arms resting in her lap. The candle on a stump in front of her carved out a faint circle of brightness in the dusky light. He stepped closer to her. She opened her eyes and started.

"Hello," she said, her voice small and questioning. He didn't answer. He leaned on the tree nearest her. Her eyes widened. "Do you have a name?" she asked, after a minute.

The question cut deep. "I do," he answered. He wasn't sure which name to claim. His voice was thick, as if it belonged to someone else. He saw the shadow of alarm cross her face. Her hair was long and brown, wispy, ringing her face in a ragged halo. Her skin was pale. Her hands were small and very white on her lap. She was wearing a thin wrap across her chest, tied at the back in a knot. He could see her nipples through its loose weave. At first he thought she was very young, but then realized she had to be in her late thirties, maybe even older. He started to walk away. He heard her sigh with relief. He turned to watch her rise without uncrossing her legs, arms outstretched in front of her. Streaks of paint spattered both arms. A canvas rested against a tree. Jars of paints and a worn leather suitcase were nearby. She began to assemble her paints. She was pretty in a way that surprised him, disheveled, wide open. He walked over to the canvas and pretended to be interested in the washes of color, faintly visible in the fast-diminishing light. She watched him.

"That's not really a painting," she said. Her speech was fast, nervous. He stepped toward her. She stepped backward. "It's just an exercise, a release, you know, a way of working things out." The suitcase and some jars of paint stood between them. She dragged her arm across her face.

"Working things out? What things?" Clarkson made a small, sarcastic laugh. Throwing streaks of paint across a canvas wouldn't begin to work out what had gone wrong in his life.

When she tried to make eye contact, he averted his gaze. "Just, you know." He could feel her looking at him. "Just stuff. That's all." Her voice trailed off. He watched her fingers curl into the palms of her hands.

"Stuff?" he asked. Again, he stepped toward her. Hammered silver wrapped around a turquoise stone on her right ring finger. Her left hand was bare. "So, problems with a friend? Lover?"

She cocked her head to one side. She seemed reluctant to answer. "Something like that," she said, after a silence. "You know how that is," she added, her voice shaky.

"No, I don't," he answered.

"Oh," she said.

He raised his eyes and looked at her. She held his gaze for a few seconds. Her fingers flexed, then relaxed.

"I really must be going," she said. A questioning note in her voice corrupted any sense of resolve she might have meant to convey. Clarkson felt a surge of power. She looked around her, inhaling slowly. He watched her shoulders rise.

"Where do you live?" he asked.

"In town," she answered, pointing vaguely in an upward direction.

"Glendale," Clarkson said. The word spat from his lips.

"Yes, of course."

"Up on the hill, there?" he asked, following her gesture.

"Yes, right above us, on the outskirts these days." She bit her lower lip.

"How is it, living in Glendale?" he asked. He leaned against a tree, feeling the cufflinks against the bark. He adjusted his pocket.

"It's a lovely town," she said. She grabbed two brushes and some jars of paint and began stuffing them into the leather case. A jar of paint tipped. Thick liquid oozed down its side and across her hand. She wiped her hand on a rag from the case. "But where you live doesn't matter. What matters is what's in your own heart."

Clarkson stared at her. Only a fool could say such a thing. If she had kept her mouth shut, ignored him, packed up her paints and left, he later thought, she might have remained only a memory of a pale face and pink nipples visible through her wrap, a cloud of brown hair, a faint jasmine scent. But she didn't. "You believe that?" he asked.

"It's just the truth," she said.

"Have you always lived in Glendale?" he asked, after a short silence.

"Always," she answered. Her tone was the same, confident, superior even.

"That must feel nice," he said, "You have roots. I don't have that."

Her lips curved upward in a slight, guarded smile. Her shoulders let go of some of their tension. "Yes, I suppose it's nice to have roots," she said.

"You're lucky."

She shrugged. "Maybe. Not so lucky lately."

His head cocked sideways. "No?"

"It's nothing," she said. She continued to pack up her paints. She turned her back on him for the first time, but swung her head around to face him every few seconds. He regarded her thin form, her narrow back where her scarf tied in a loopy bow.

"You can talk about it," he said. His fingers traced the arch of a hanging vine. Pink blossoms dripped along its length. "If you want." He took a half-step toward her. He could see that her neck and chest were moist.

She inched away from him. "That's beautiful," she said, pointing at the laden branch where his fingers rested. Her voice shook ever so slightly. "I've always meant to find out what that is." She continued to draw herself away from him.

"I can't help you there. I'm a city dweller." Clarkson plucked a flower. It rested in his open palm. "Here." He stretched his hand toward her.

"Oh no, I can't. I never pick flowers," she said. "I can't bear to. They become so disconnected when you pick them." She didn't move.

"It's just a flower," he said. The blossom in his outstretched palm trembled slightly. She froze. He tucked it behind her ear and began to gather up her paints with her. She had spread them all around her. There were a half dozen or so jars and maybe three times as many silver tubes with bands of color along the sides. Clarkson slid some of the tubes into the notches of the leather case.

"You don't need to help me," she said. Her hand reached up to her ear.

He held up a jar of paint. "What do you call this one?"

"Vermilion," she said.

"It looks almost blood-like."

He heard the sudden intake of her breath. Her voice emerged with a false breeziness, "You can't really see it now, though, at this time of day. Color is light."

The girl's mix of terror, superiority and politeness fascinated him and rankled him at the same time. It was the same Glendale from his youth, the hollow face of cordiality with who knows what lurking beneath. It was the worst kind of dishonesty.

"You're an artist."

She smiled weakly. "I guess you could say that."

"I'm a bit of a collector. I'd like to take a look at your paintings some time."

"That would be nice." She looked around. Clarkson remembered how fast the woods darkened. The faint light that still bathed them was about to be swallowed, he knew. Extinguished. Insects hummed, twigs snapped.

"I could come right now," he said. He stepped so close to her that his leather loafers almost touched her bare toes in their macrame sandals. She looked up at him. Her shoulders rose and fell. "To look at your art work. As I said, I am a bit of a collector." He stepped back and picked up a thick brush and examined the tip. He wondered what she would do—cry, bolt, continue her polite charade?

"I have a lot to do," she said. He caught the fleeting panic in her expression.

"I do, too. It won't take long. I'd like to see a real painting of yours," he said.

She nodded and began to walk away, her steps quickening to a run when she got to the trail from the clearing. In a few long strides he was even with her. "Were you looking for this?" he asked and held up a brush. Her face reddened. He put the brush into the case and smiled at her. "Well, are we ready?" he asked, as if the plan had finalized itself while they weren't looking.

"Okay," she said. Her soft voice quavered. He helped her with the spilled jar of paint, lightly touching her fingers as he handed the lid to her. He saw her neck muscles tighten as she swallowed.

"My car is far away. We'll just take yours, if that's okay. Can you walk to town from your house?" he asked.

She was silent for a moment and then nodded.

"I'm meeting someone later tonight at a restaurant. I forget the name. I'll walk to town and he'll give me a lift to my car."

"You're meeting someone?" He could hear her hopefulness.

"Yes," he said, comfortable with his lie. "So you see, I'll get to see your paintings, have a nice walk on a summer night, meet my friend."

"Okay," she said. "I have plans, you know. Later. I'll just show you a few paintings. If that's what you'd like?"

He carried the leather case to her car.

"As I said, my car is way across the field," he said. "If you'd like, you can drive me there and I'll follow you to your place." She opened her mouth as if to speak, but he continued quickly, "But I suppose that would waste your time. We'll just go quickly. It's no problem for me at all." Her hand reached up to the flower by her ear again.

"No, no, that's no problem. I only have a little while, you understand," she said.

Chapter 2

They got into her car. It started up on the second try. They edged up the hill, away from the lowlands. She fiddled with the radio. Her eyes darted around her.

"It's a very pretty town you have here," Clarkson said.

"Thank you. Look, it's getting late and I'm sure you're busy. Maybe we should do this some other time. I can drive you back to your car and I'll meet you tomorrow, when we'll both have more time."

"Oh, don't worry. Tonight is fine, really. I won't stay long."

She brushed away a few strands of hair that had fallen across her forehead.

"These are really beautiful houses here," Clarkson said.

"I grew up in that one." She slowed the car and pointed to a mansion at the fork of Main and Sycamore. Lights burned from long rows of windows in two stories, and a third story was dark under a steeply pitched slate roof that shone in the sun's afterglow.

Clarkson controlled his reaction. So, that's who she was. One of the town's elite. It didn't really surprise him. Her veneer of manners had already betrayed her. He studied her profile, the cloud of hair, the chiseled cheekbones, the slight upturn of her nose. He wondered if she realized how little she deserved her status. Did any of them? "It's stunning. Really. Does your family still own it?" he asked in a deliberate, even voice.

"Of course. It's been in our family always," she said. "Just my mom lives there now, but that house is a part of me."

Clarkson turned his head away from her.

She pointed out a few other landmarks, and then the lights became scarce. Darkness in the country was darker than elsewhere, he thought. A half-mile or so from town, she pulled into a driveway.

"We're here," she said. They walked up a flight of rounded cement steps and into the ground floor of a brick house. It was small and messy, filled with paintings. She showed him a few, talking a great deal. He towered over her, nodding, answering now and then.

She was especially proud of a canvas where a disjointed mother figure tended a flock of neon sheep, her elasticized arm hugging a fuchsia lamb that floated near the sun. The figure's rippled violet cape snared a yellow lamb that had leapt or fallen from a cliff.

"Yes, that one's very nice," Clarkson said.

"I won a prize for that in the Arts Festival in Pittsburgh," she said.

She held up a series of abstracts done in oranges and mauves in squishy configurations that looked surgical, a few landscapes of the Glendale countryside in bright colors with floating cows and spotted pigs, skies inhabited by fanciful meteors and swollen moons. He studied all of them, asked if she were willing to sell any. Her face reddened. He could see that his insincere flattery pleased her, frightened as she was. Her vulnerability both disgusted and intrigued him.

"Well, that's it, pretty much," she said. "As I said, I have a lot to do. I can direct you to Pamela's. It's not far." She walked to the front door and opened it.

"You live alone?" he asked. "On the edge of town, by yourself?"

"I have neighbors," she said, "across the field where the barn is." She glanced back inside toward the kitchen. "So do you like the paintings?"

"No dog. Not even a cat."

She didn't answer. He followed her furtive glance, down the short hall to the kitchen. At the end of a black cord on the kitchen counter, a cell phone charged.

"Do you like living here? In Glendale?" he asked. He placed his body between hers and the cell phone.

"How can I answer that? It's a part of me."

He walked into the kitchen and fidgeted with the teakettle on her stove. "It sounds perfect," he said. She lingered at the door a minute, then closed it and followed him.

"It's not perfect, it's home. I'll make you tea, if you like," she said. Her eyes shifted to the charging phone on the counter. She paused over it as she filled the kettle. Clarkson saw the flush spread across her cheeks. She cleared her throat a few times. She opened a box and pulled teabags from it. Her hand hesitated over the cell phone. He asked her questions about Glendale, life in the town, how it felt to grow up as a decent member of society in that big house on the hill. With a high society family and no worries about anything. With nothing but the best in life awaiting her. And no thought to those who didn't share her good fortune. The boiling water overflowed one of the mugs when she filled it. Her voice broke a little as she fielded his questions.

"It's funny, we don't even know each other's names," she said at last. He could tell that her breath was coming faster.

"You asked me my name already," Clarkson said. "But we got distracted." He paused, unsure of what would come out of his mouth. He couldn't remember the last time he felt that way, teetering, as if some unaccountable force gripped him. "It's Clarkson Dupree," he finally said. It was the first time that his new name had ever sounded like a lie to him. He thought for a moment that he would leave it at that.

"Clarkson," she said. She tried to smile, as if they had been introduced at a cocktail party.

He regarded the hapless girl before him, the sincere tilt of her head, the way she strained to maintain a level of caring politeness that made no sense under the circumstances. He had never met anyone so lacking in self-preservation. And yet, how would one learn self-preservation from a childhood spent in the gilded cage of a Glendale mansion? He had sensed her entitlement from the second he saw her, so engrained that it was artless, offhand. Dangerous.

The unfamiliar force that gripped him grew. Memories of his childhood swirled. His throat constricted, as if he might suffocate. And there she sat, child-like even though she was clearly middle-aged. Untested. He leaned close to her and continued, "But it wasn't always. I used to be Cody Dempsher. I don't know if you remember that name. I'm not even sure you were born. My mother and father had a trailer down below the hill."

He remembered the words 'down below' all of a sudden. That's how Glendale townspeople used to describe where he lived. He's from down below, they would say. They made it seem like hell. They weren't really wrong, he thought.

She edged away from him. She failed to conceal a quick flash of recognition.

"You know about me," he said.

"Only what people used to say. Stories. From when I was little."

"Stories. What stories?" They were seated now at her small kitchen table. He pushed his chair closer to hers. It scraped the floor. "Tell me."

"I'm sure they meant no harm. People used to think the woods were haunted, that you killed your father, or your father killed you, and both of your spirits lived in the woods. Your trailer burned to a shell." Her hands were limp in her lap.

He nodded. "What do you think?"

"I don't know. That's okay, even if you did kill your father and set him on fire," she said, her eyes filling with tears. "It's not a kid's fault. I won't tell anyone. Everyone has forgotten all about you. I'll never say a word. And don't worry, even if you did kill him, murderers aren't always bad people. Lots of times they're just trying to kill a part of themselves."

He began to laugh. When he stopped, he leaned back. "You try to seem different, don't you? But you're all the same. All of you." He pushed the teacup away and stood up. He rummaged in the kitchen until he found a bottle of vodka in a low corner cabinet. He opened the upper cabinets until he found a glass.

"Want some?" he asked.

"No. I don't like it."

"Your boyfriend drinks it?"

He filled the glass and drained it. He stood up and reached for the bottle yet again. She lunged for the cell phone. The charger wire tangled in her fingers and the plug yanked from the wall. In one movement, Clarkson knocked the phone from her hand and held her by the wrist. She was so small he could have lifted her off the ground.

"We were just having a conversation," he said. Sweat congealed in the lines of his forehead. He took a swig from his half-spilled glass.

With her free hand, she unknotted her wrap, exposing her breasts. "Here, is this what you want? My life isn't perfect either." She twisted in his grip. "My brother died, my father died. I'm in love with a woman in a world that won't let us be what we want to be. Is this what you want? Take it and leave."

"No," he said. He stared at her.

She stared back at him.

His fingers pressed into her skin. She tried to reach for the phone again. Her shoulder cracked with the effort. She kicked at him, but his long arms held her so that her legs made pointless stabs at the air.

"You shouldn't have done that," he said.

She became very still.

"What's your name?"

"Lorelei."

"That's very beautiful."

She looked at him, paralyzed. She seemed to him as if the purpose of her whole life was to die at his hands at that moment. She closed her eyes.

"Whether you know it or not, you are all the same," he said. "I've always wondered, what gives you the right?"

Her eyes remained closed. His question hung in the air, unanswered. His grip tightened.

"Summer," she said, very softly, as her eyes opened and her tears traced two slow rivers against her cheeks. For a fleeting moment, he thought about kissing her.

"You know it's your fault, don't you?"

She didn't answer. Her body was shaking.

He edged his hands up to her neck and circled her throat tightly. He closed his eyes and squeezed until her arms stopped flailing and her body grew limp. He lowered her to the floor. She was small and fragile. He retied her wrap around her breasts and carried her outside to the small courtyard off her kitchen. Her jasmine perfume mingled with the honeysuckle in her garden. He laid her in the hammock. In the blackness, he found his way into town. He paused ever so briefly before her family estate that rose from the shadows on the corner of Main and Sycamore. It was distinctive, magnificent even, in the dim moonlight, with its bricked arch above the door, the corner turret, the porch wrapped sideways around its sprawling asymmetrical footprint. He had a vague memory of that house from his childhood, looming above his, as they all had.

He picked his way back down the hillside to his car on the little square of driveway in his desolate part of the world.

Chapter 3

"Lorelei's gone," Lucy said to no one. She had spent two days coming to grips with this news, two long days for the police to perform whatever tests they required under the circumstances. She couldn't believe that her younger sister was dead. Murdered. Lucy gripped the steering wheel as she made the turn into her mother's driveway.

She wasn't surprised that her mother already waited on the side porch, looking small and old. Her gray silk shirt was buttoned up to her chin and tucked, as usual, too high into baggy black slacks. As Lucy slowed to a stop, her mother raised her hand in a feeble wave, and dropped a wad of Kleenex. She bent down and her handbag slid from her shoulder and scraped the cement. Lucy dabbed her eyes, blew her nose and got out of the car. She reset her mom's purse on her shoulder and guided her to the passenger side of the car. She opened the door for her.

"Okay?" Lucy asked, knowing already that she wasn't. Her mother's attempt at a smile resulted in a grimace. Lucy looked away as she closed the car door.

"Put your seat belt on, Mom," she said and buckled her own. She turned the key in the ignition. Her mother fumbled with the buckle.

The two rode in silence.

"Thanks for understanding," Lucy said, after a minute. "I'm dropping you off first. With Al. Remember?"

Dee didn't answer.

"I have some paperwork to do. The viewing begins at two. I'll be back before then, I promise." Lucy glanced at her mom.

"All right," Dee said.

Lucy pulled into the gravelly parking lot at Al's funeral home, Mancini's. She helped her mom from the car and put her arm around her shoulder as they walked to the door. Lucy wished that Al had replaced the shabby siding, or at least patched the faded canopy over the cracked walkway. Lorelei deserved better. Al met them at the door and whisked Dee into the parlor, away from the viewing rooms.

"I'll be back directly. Thanks for sitting with her," Lucy said to Al in a low voice.

"Sure," he replied. He fidgeted with his tie. His face above his starched white collar was old and lined.

Lucy climbed back into her car, glad for the solitude. She drove past the storefronts of Main Street on her way out of town. Everything was so familiar, the place she bought her new school shoes every September for her whole childhood, the donut shop, the butcher shop. At first, the air of normalcy on Main Street jolted her, but she began to take comfort that others shopped or drank a beer when her own world had collapsed.

Always, Glendale had been there for her. The town had seen changes, everyone said, but they were superficial, like leaves falling and sprouting from the same substantial oaks. She passed the Christian Book Store and Jerry's Pub, open and bustling. She felt a knot in her chest as she passed Rhinehart's, the town's other funeral home. Large and stately, it stood on the left side of Main Street before the road curved up the hill to the hospital. Her brother had spent three days at Rhinehart's after he came back from Vietnam, his casket wrapped in the American flag like an unwanted present. That was so long ago, she thought, amazed that her older brother had already left so many years uninhabited. And her father had followed soon after, ensconced in the same hushed room. Everyone said he died of a broken heart.

Two funeral homes. It had become a town joke over the past few years, ever since Al had branched out from his bowling alley business. "We may be small, but we have two funeral homes," people would say. Glendale was old. Historic. The drugstore specialized in accessories like portable shower seats for withered behinds, and racks of sturdy canes in a rainbow of colors. No wonder Al had looked to death for his latest entrepreneurial venture, Lucy thought. She never imagined Lorelei would be one of his first customers.

Lucy stepped on the gas to make it up the steep hill beyond the hospital. She turned the radio on, then off. She didn't have to do any paperwork, as she had told her mother. That first day, when Lorelei's best friend Summer had telephoned her with the news, Lucy hadn't known what to do. Finally, with swollen eyes and a running nose, she had driven twenty miles to the mall in Clarion to shop for a funeral dress. As she pulled it from her closet this morning, she realized it was wrong. Completely wrong. She had to replace it.

She parked and walked briskly, checking her watch. She knew the mall almost like she knew her own house. On auto-pilot, she navigated the aisles of Fieldstone's until she arrived at women's better dresses and returned the offending garment. The sea of summer pastel dresses had a few somber shades stuck among them. She tried on four, found the right one, bought it, and immediately headed for the ladies room. In the spacious handicapped stall, she set her things on the shelf and stripped. With the miniature collapsible scissors she kept in her handbag, she snipped the tags from her new dress. As the folds of granite silk slipped over her, she was careful to keep her make-up away from the fabric. When she emerged from the stall, she fluffed her hair and looked in the mirror. She touched up her lipstick. That's better, she thought. Lorelei would understand. Lorelei knew how Lucy was. The tears started afresh.

Lucy got back in her car and drove to meet her mother at Al's. Every few minutes she glanced at the dashboard clock. She wondered what they were doing, Al and Dee. What they were talking about. She wasn't sure what had transpired between those two over the years. Sometimes it seemed that everyone else's lives pulsed with hidden mysteries while her own proceeded on its flat, dimensionless path.

She would be in perfect time, she thought, as she drove back into town, past Rhinehart's, past the stores, and back to the fork of Main and Sycamore where she made the turnoff to Al's. She wiped her eyes as she got out of the car, her heels catching in the rutted surface of Al's parking lot.

She opened the funeral home door. Directly inside was an aluminum frame, with Lorelei's name spelled out in magnetic letters, like a movie marquee. Lorelei Armstrong. She worried that someone would bump into it and knock the letters askew. As her eyes adjusted to the dim atmosphere, Al appeared at her side and took her elbow. He guided her into the parlor, where Dee sat on the edge of a burgundy velvet sofa, its plump arms snagged and worn in spots. Lucy sat beside her. Al pulled up a chair across from them.

"You two will go in together, first, in just a few minutes," he said. "Take some time to get adjusted. When you're ready, I'll open the door to your friends. To Lorelei's friends." He patted Dee's hand and nodded encouragingly to Lucy. "Okay?" he asked. Dee looked down. Lucy nodded. The curved clock on the mantel ticked away the seconds.

"I'll be right back," Al said.

Lucy felt for her mother's hand. They didn't speak. Lucy's heart raced.

When Al returned, he was reverential. "She looks really beautiful," he said. His voice caught as he helped Dee to her feet.

Al walked them past the foyer. They paused under the archway of a carpeted chamber, the marquee with Lorelei's name now repositioned at its entrance. The cloying scent of lilies filled the room. Lilies had been Lorelei's favorite flower. Lorelei had once told Lucy they were stars fallen to earth. Lucy clung to her mother's elbow and fought a wave of nausea.

Lucy turned, faced her mother, and took a deep breath. Their eyes met. Her mother looked every bit of her seventy-eight years. She nodded to Lucy, ever so slightly, and squared her frail shoulders.

They crossed the threshold.

Against the far wall sat the casket. A rushing static filled Lucy's ears as they approached it. Lucy remembered other such walks in her life. She remembered her brother. He had been invisible, sealed inside a banner of red, white and blue. Photos of his vibrant self ringed his box, but death had erased the light behind his smile even in those flat likenesses. Then her father, eyeglasses reflecting the bobbing flame of the candle near his head. Aunt Marian, gray-blue hair teased into a netted mound, pursed lips a thin pink line. She thought of the student who had fallen under the wheels of a tractor last year, small and doll-like, more sculpture than child.

Always, it seemed, she'd crossed a padded expanse to face disappointment. The waxy beings before her had never seemed real or unreal, merely impostors who posed unanswerable questions. Death had always left Lucy profoundly perplexed.

Lucy's heart thumped against her ribcage as she neared Lorelei's satin-lined coffin. Linked with her mother by fragile fingers, she stopped.

She peered into the frozen face of her sister.

Lucy felt disembodied as her eyes took in what lay before her. A cloud of soft brown hair across a rose satin pillow. An up-turned nose in pale profile. The orchid floral dress that Lorelei had worn many times was strange in its stillness. Her delicate white hands clasped a lily.

Propped against the open casket lid was one of Lorelei's watercolors. Lucy concentrated on the painting, dreamy and swirly, clouds chasing across a purple sky, an orange sailboat skimming mottled green and gold waters, strange sea creatures popping up here and there. That was Lorelei for you. She had her own view of the world. Half-submerged in the water, Lorelei's curly signature floated. Lucy's tears blurred the childish script. It struck her how unlike her own it was. She wondered how much of Lorelei's world she had ever really shared.

She tried to force her eyes from the painting to Lorelei's pale, immobile face, but at that moment the air around her vibrated with a cry that seemed to come from another world. Lucy turned to her mother. She watched, more than heard, her mother wail, her pale mouth open, wrinkled eyelids shut. Al rushed in with a glass of water and led Dee to an upholstered chair in the corner, tissues and water pitcher within reach on a high-legged table. Dee's clouded eyes drifted above the commotion.

Lucy took over, shaking hands, hugging well-meaning mourners until her hands hurt and her feet were swollen. The whole town filed in over the course of two days, exclaiming over Lorelei's freshness, her spirit, her beauty, the wretchedness of what had happened. Lucy responded to the same words over and over.

"Of all people. She never hurt a soul."

"How could anyone hurt Lorelei?"

"Only forty-two years old. So young, really."

Lucy would shake her head. Only a monster could find it in his heart to harm her younger sister. The whole thing was incomprehensible. She hadn't been the one to find her. She was grateful at least for that. Lorelei's friend Summer had that misfortune. Lucy spotted Summer in the back of the viewing room, Lorelei's room, as she had begun to call it. Summer caught her eye, unexpectedly. Lucy smiled at her. Summer wasn't holding up at all well. Next to her mother, she seemed least capable of handling this act of random evil. Or, was it random? Lucy tried so hard to understand how events had transpired, leaving Lorelei strangled in her fringed hammock. The police were sure that she had been carefully deposited there, as if her murderer couldn't bear to leave her on the cold, hard floor.

Summer raised her hand from across the room to acknowledge Lucy over the sea of acquaintances. Most of them would return home and discuss the tragedy before cooking dinner or turning on the evening news. Only a few in that room bore wounds that wouldn't retreat after today, wounds that would ooze and seep for a lifetime.

Lucy wondered what would happen after today, after the marquee with Lorelei's name had been reconfigured to announce the demise of another, this time someone appropriately old. Expected. The thought took her breath away. She wished they would all convene here forever, Lorelei in her position of honor, Dee in her soft chair by her table and tissues, Al peeking his head in and out, announcing schedules, breaks, and Lucy in control. They had created a world here. It served them well. Why couldn't it simply continue?

Lucy gazed around her at the overdone parlor, its thick gold carpet muting approaching mourners' footsteps. Lorelei would have hated this hushed and heavy room, she thought. She would have made fun of the fabric wallpaper, stains and blotches obfuscating an ornate pattern of cascading rose garlands. The sprays of tiger lilies and baskets of gerbera daisies seemed wildly cheerful, stuck in amid fussy old mahogany furniture. If Lorelei were suddenly to sit up, she would survey the whole scene and grimace, puckering her pretty, pale face in disgust. Funny, how Lucy would never see that expression again. How would she endure that?

Lucy wandered into the vestibule of the funeral home to catch her breath. Young children of some distant cousins had gathered there, lounging on worn damask sofas away from Lorelei's silent presence. The kids talked and laughed, awkwardly formal, the girls in dresses, the boys in suits and ties. Lucy felt comforted by their ability to act like normal kids in the oppressive atmosphere of the funeral home. She walked toward them, but stopped.

"I hope I never get murdered," one little girl told the others.

"If I get murdered, I hope I don't know it," a boy said.

"What do you mean, you hope you don't know it. Of course you would know it."

"No. Someone could just sneak up behind you and kill you and you wouldn't even see them. You would just be dead," the boy insisted. He jumped up and grabbed the kid next to him, encircling his throat with pudgy fingers.

One of the kids noticed Lucy, and poked another one. Abruptly they all fell silent. Before Lucy could control the shaking in her knees, they dispersed, red-faced, eyes downcast.

Lucy didn't blame them, of course. She, too, wondered. Once, the three of them, Lucy, Summer and Lorelei, had speculated about their last words on this earth, while sitting on her mother's front porch, sipping the Argentine Torrontes that Summer insisted went best with honeysuckle-scented nights.

"I bet mine will be 'shit'," Summer said, and they had all laughed.

"Well, it's completely in your power," Lorelei said. "Just remember when you feel everything draining away, say something beautiful."

"Like what?" Lucy asked.

"I don't know. Anything. If you can't think of something yourself, maybe remember John Keats' poem, Ode to a Nightingale," Lorelei said. "Think of that lovely nightingale, so happy and beautiful, 'That I might drink, and leave the world unseen/ and with thee fade away into the forest dim.' Maybe just say that."

Lucy started when she felt a hand on her elbow.

"I'm so sorry, I still can't believe it," sniffed Mrs. Haverton, a widow for as long as Lucy could remember, still living in what everyone in town called the 'big house' at the turnoff to Braden. Mrs. Haverton let go of her elbow and leaned her heavily rouged cheek close before she continued, "If there's anything I can do…"

"Thank you, of course," Lucy answered, wondering what anybody could really do. She watched Mrs. Haverton hobble out the door, hips listing, arthritic left hand one with her ivory-tipped cane.

Lucy wondered if Lorelei had a chance to think of that nightingale, or if she even knew what happened at all. She hoped she didn't, that Lorelei simply ceased to be, like an old vinyl record playing merrily along until someone picked up the needle in mid-song. She wished she weren't able to think about Lorelei's final moments at all. She wished she would imagine herself bursting in, fighting the intruder and saving Lorelei.

But of course, she hadn't. Lorelei was dead. Accepting what had happened to her had opened an escape door. Already, Lucy edged toward it, leaving Lorelei to face eternity while she got on with her life. The thought shamed her. But she wasn't the evil one. No matter how hard she tried, she couldn't imagine anyone diabolical enough to murder Lorelei. She took a deep breath and returned to the muted bustle of Lorelei's room. She glanced to the back corner where Dee sat. The way she held her bent spine upright, snakes of veins purplish in her folded hands, feet crossed at the ankles, made Lucy shiver. Dee looked almost as waxy and immobile as Lorelei.

Chapter 4

Dee brushed the lint from her chenille robe as she sat at the kitchen table. Her coffee had grown tepid, a clotted brown crust congealing overtop. She pushed it away. The last few days had crushed everything left in her old and weary soul. The funeral home seemed a distant dream. Wisps of recollections surfaced, but she couldn't seize any particular image. Her youngest child, her daughter was dead. Not just dead, but murdered. How could life hold joy for her again? It hadn't been all that great even at its best.

Nothing interested her anymore. Her son and husband had died, almost in a row. And now Lorelei. Everyone was gone but Lucy. And Summer, she thought, but she wasn't sure what to think about her. Summer had insinuated herself into the family through Lorelei as some sort of long-lost sister. They had all accepted her nicely enough, but now she was carrying on about Lorelei's last wishes. As if anyone really knew what Lorelei would have preferred, for God's sake. Lorelei was only forty-two years old. Dee didn't believe that Lorelei had spent her spare time obsessing over the disposal of her remains, despite Summer's claims. Why couldn't they just gently fold Lorelei into the ground and be done with it? What was all this cremation talk about?

She shuddered at the thought of the raging inferno of cremation. She couldn't bear to have any more violence unleashed on Lorelei. She wished that Al would just fix everything for her, the way he used to. Lucy had phoned earlier to see if she wanted to stop by the bowling alley and talk to Al, figure out how to lay poor Lorelei to rest once and for all. She didn't. She didn't want to do anything. Lucy should have known that already.

Dee felt empty when she thought about Al. In the old days, just hearing his name had made her warm and weak. Now, everything inside her had dried up, like the cracked skin on her forearms, or the remnants of last night's dinner still stuck to the plates in the sink. Dee couldn't remember what dinner had been. She couldn't remember what it had felt like to be in Al's arms, either, small and receptive against his bare chest. She remembered only that it happened. She had given Al her youngest daughter's body as a parting gift. Glendale was a small town, and everyone from the big houses sent their dead to Rhinehart's. Dee had nothing left to give Al, except for Lorelei.

Dee forced herself to rise. She dumped her coffee into the sink, watching the curdled streaks settle into last night's mess. She could get dressed, she thought, looking at the clock, but she didn't want to be upstairs when Lucy stopped by. Lucy was responsible like that. She would go to the bowling alley, talk to Al, straighten everything out and check in on her. Lucy was as predictable as a human could possibly be, Dee thought, ever since she was born.

Lucy. What a pain that child was. Fifty-one years old and still as odd as she had ever been. Thaddeus, Jr., now there was a child who lit up the hearts of everyone—cheerful, handsome, smart, but not the kind of smart that irritates people. And Lorelei, goofy in her bohemian artistic way, but sweet. Dee had always hoped that Lorelei would give her a grandchild, but she hadn't. She never even had hopes for Lucy. Lucy was different. She had that weird penetrating way of looking at people ever since she was little. She smiled plenty, but her eyes were always appraising, dissecting, like she was trying to get to the bottom of everything. Dee didn't want to think about her part in the way Lucy came out. After all, when it was all said and done, people were just who they were meant to be. Still, Lucy made everyone uncomfortable, Dee included. And now it was just the two of them. Well, the two of them and Summer.

She pictured Lucy at the bowling alley, struggling to find a way around the stalemate. Dee didn't care what she had to do. Lorelei didn't deserve an inferno, after all she'd been through. Who was Summer anyway? Lucy had better fix things. Dee knew that Al would listen to Lucy. She pictured Lucy, her hair perfectly styled, her nails polished to match some tasteful and expensive outfit. How she ever afforded all that upkeep on a teacher's salary amazed Dee. If Lucy had put half that energy into finding a husband, raising a family, maybe they wouldn't be so alone. Dee had done everything she could, marrying, raising three children. Now she had only one left. Even with medical advances, Lucy was way too old to ever have children now, and probably too selfish to think of adopting one of those little Chinese babies or whatever nationality they were giving away these days.

Dee glanced at the dirty dishes again. She picked up the dish-cloth but dropped it back onto the crusty plates. She didn't have to clean up. She didn't have to do anything. Her only guest had left last week. She had converted her house, stately and huge, into a guesthouse more than a decade ago. She had been in her sixties then, finally rebounding after the losses of her son and then her husband so many years before. Everyone said it would do her good, and it had, for a while. Lucy had encouraged her, even helped out when she could. But she took that damned teaching job so seriously. Dee imagined that there were brain surgeons who took their jobs more lightly than Lucy did. She turned away from the sink. Lucy could clean up when she stopped by.

Dee looked at the mess around her. She didn't think she would re-open the house for guests ever again. As soon as the word about Lorelei had reached her, Dee had hung the closed sign inside the front door and switched off the answering machine. She no longer cared what happened. She certainly wouldn't starve. She still had the Navy pension from Thaddeus,

Sr., and her house was inherited from way back. There was money in the bank from the oil rights her great grandfather had been smart enough to snap up long ago. She never shopped anymore. And there was the meager social security, although security was way too strong a word for that check. She looked down at her robe, powder blue and worn thin. She didn't even want a new one. She imagined how horrified Lucy would be to see that robe.

But Lucy didn't understand what it was like to be seventy-eight. Could she possibly be that old? She looked at her hands, all spotted and veiny. Definitely. She didn't look in the mirror much anymore, but she knew that she bore the wrinkles and scars to prove it.

Lucy was at that weird stage, Dee thought, all the while wondering why she was directing her irritation at Lucy. That weird stage, where she was fighting every advancing year. She was always getting her hair cut, streaked, dyed, putting crazy face creams on day and night. Her bathroom looked like a laboratory. There wasn't a condition that existed that Lucy hadn't already bought its antidote—spots, wrinkling, sagging. And still, Lucy was fifty-one. Anyway. Despite her efforts. Not only that, but she was alone, and there weren't even any grandchildren for Dee to bounce on her knees. Dee winced. At this age, her friends had grandchildren that were graduating, heading off to Ivy League colleges, becoming doctors and lawyers. It seemed like every grandkid her friends had produced was a genius. How could that be? She had raised three kids, and she knew that they didn't all automatically learn to read at two-and-a-half and get into the University of Pennsylvania at age seventeen on a full scholarship. She wondered if the old ladies who gathered Thursday mornings at Pamela's were really telling the truth. How could you ever know?

And then the searing pain hit her gut again. Lorelei. Just when she had herself all distracted, it had swooped down and taken her breath away. And now she hurt so much that she wanted to die. She sat, eyes closed, waiting for the pain to subside. She knew it would, having been through this so many times before. She wished the phone would ring. She wished Lucy would knock on her door. Rising, she walked to the front window. Her usually bustling corner was quiet. She craned her neck, trying to see around the sharp curve toward Sycamore Street, toward the bowling alley. She squinted, hoping for a glimpse of Lucy's red Honda. Lucy would fix everything with Al and stop in. Dee was sure of it.

She waited at the window. Somewhere out there, the person who murdered Lorelei walked, talked, ate, maybe laughed. A tear filled the criss-cross of furrows in her cheeks on its jagged downward course. She fumbled for the handkerchief stuck in the sleeve of her robe, found it, and dabbed at her nose. Damn that Lucy, where was she?

Chapter 5

"One more minute, Lucy," Al said. He sprayed the inside of a pair of rental shoes with a cloud of disinfectant.

Lucy tried to smile as she pulled an orange plastic chair from under the aluminum table. Al looked strange, dressed in his short-sleeved cotton shirt instead of his funeral suit. In a way, it was a relief to see Al in a different setting. He seemed younger, despite his years, and more alive.

A bowling ball collided with pins. The staccato crash echoed in the narrow, windowless building. What was it about that sound that set her teeth on edge? The stale smell of spilled beer and greasy snacks didn't help. She peered down the blue and tan strip of carpet, lined with video games and dotted with metal furniture purposely constructed to jab one's flesh. Someone rolled a strike and the din of the collision sparked a barrage of cheers.

"Damn it, mother," Lucy said under her breath. She thought about Lorelei, still lying somewhere in Al's hushed funeral home, although they had all said their final farewells. Why was Summer so adamant that Lorelei wanted to be cremated? And Dee. She had hardly spoken at all throughout the long vigil only to emerge to insist that Lorelei be buried properly, next to the other Armstrongs. The funeral had drained the last vestiges of sense right out of everyone.

On top of that, fresh-faced Officer McMahon was making noises about forensic considerations before disposal of the remains, his term for Lorelei's tiny body. She guessed that everyone in town had already heard the gossip, that the Glendale police had botched the on-site investigation. By the time the Oil City detective squad had arrived, the damage had been done, according to some. Lucy wasn't sure what was true and what was simply small town politics. What did anyone expect? There hadn't been a murder in Glendale in seventy-five years. At any rate, the police had already had their time with Lorelei, Lucy thought. Leave her alone.

Lucy cringed when she thought of Officer McMahon's relentless questioning. He seemed tireless, enthusiastic even. She supposed he couldn't help it. He was barely more than a child, certainly young enough to be her son, if life had ever blessed her with children. Or, for that matter, a man. Lucy pushed the melmac ashtray to the edge of the metal table.

The least they could have done was to allow Lorelei to rest peacefully at Rhinehart's up on Main Street. Rhinehart's had beautiful rooms, a chapel, gold-encased tissue boxes, rose plush carpeting. And after the viewing, what did it matter what happened to Lorelei? Al was a family friend, Lucy realized, but even so. Lucy looked at her shoes. She remembered how that weird squishy gold rug in Lorelei's chamber had sucked at her heels like quicksand. She closed her eyes for a moment until the memory disappeared.

Lucy resettled herself in her chair. Even in her half-comatose state, Dee could be stubborn, she thought. A little selfish. Of all the siblings, it seemed to Lucy that she had tried the hardest to please her. It had never made a difference. Lucy felt ashamed by the thought. She was the only one alive now. A skinny girl in tight jeans weaved through the tables, waved her cigarette and blew a long exhale out of the side of her mouth as she passed. The afternoon was beginning to feel like hell itself.

Lucy looked around for Al. To his credit, every time he saw her, he tried his best to trade his bowling alley persona for a more somber countenance. "Sorry, Lucy, business is business, I can't do anything about it," Al had said on the phone earlier that day, by way of apology. She caught his eye as he squeezed his belly between a row of bolted down chairs and a rack of black bowling balls. He gave her an apologetic look and shrugged. A splash of beer lurched from the plastic pitcher he was on the way to deliver to a chain-smoking foursome. Lucy tried to smile back.

She had to acknowledge a genuine fondness for Al. He had been around her family for a long time, even before her brother Thaddeus returned from Vietnam in a box. Al had shoveled snow from their sidewalk in winter, mowed their lawn in summer, brought the newspaper in from the rain. Lots of times when she was younger, she had come home to find him sitting in the kitchen, drinking tea with her mother. Her mother had laughed with Al until her cheeks flushed. She had looked different with him, not pinched and weary like she had with her husband. Lucy tried not to think about that.

"Lorelei will finally be with her father and brother," lots of people told Lucy at the funeral home all week. But Lorelei had only been six when Thad died and seven when her father followed. Lucy couldn't help but wonder if Lorelei would remember them at all. Anyway, the idea of a big happy reunion of the dead seemed a bit creepy.

Lucy had been sixteen when a band of smartly dressed soldiers knocked on their door and handed her parents a letter. She remembered it well. But when she tried to resurrect Thad Jr.'s image, his toothy smile beaming from the frame in the den usurped her recollections. In her mind, her brother was decked out in military clothes one day and shipped home under the American flag the next.

Her dad was proud of Thad's decision to serve his country. For some reason, he'd never imagined that serving included the possibility of dying. That lack of foresight literally killed Thaddeus, Sr., which seemed awfully naïve to Lucy, now that she was older.

And now Lorelei, the most shocking death of all. Murder. Even the word was hideous.

Another crash of a ball exploding into pins. Lucy covered her face with her hands. She couldn't believe she was waiting for the bowlers to give Al a break so she could talk to him about getting Lorelei out of storage and eternally deposited somewhere. Anywhere. Frankly, she hardly cared what happened at this point. Lorelei was just dead. She had even said that to her mom and Summer, but her mom got all grim-lipped and wouldn't answer and Summer had cried. Again.

How her mom and Summer figured they had the market cornered on missing Lorelei, she hadn't a clue. She was the sister, technically genetically the closest. She had read that factoid in the science for schoolteachers magazine she subscribed to so she could keep her fourth graders abreast of the latest advances. Lucy had played with Lorelei, counseled her, cared for her when their mother was reeling from the losses of her son and husband.

And Summer, why she hadn't even met Lorelei until about ten years ago. Lucy felt indignant. Where were Summer and Dee right now? What gave those two the right to retreat and act like their worlds were torn apart? She was the one waiting patiently for Al to eradicate athlete's foot fungus, the one trying to orchestrate a truce.

"Al, you know, I think I'll give you a call later," Lucy said, rising from her chair.

"No, no, I'm on it, one sec." Al rang up something on the cash register and wiped his hands on his pants as he approached her.

"So, what can I do for you?" he asked. He pulled a yellow plastic chair from under the table and sat across from her. His elbows rested on the table.

"Whatever you can." Lucy flipped her dyed blonde hair away from her face. "Summer and Mom are having fits. Summer is positive that Lorelei wanted to be cremated and Mom is positive she hates the idea. I half-expect Lorelei to rise from the dead soon and clobber both of them." Her face reddened. "I'm just so frustrated. And that Officer McMahon…"

"Here's what we do. Don't worry about Officer McMahon. He can't help it. The police stuff is about over," Al said. He leaned closer. The center furrow in his forehead cut into both eyebrows. "You give Dee and Summer twenty-four hours. That's all. I'll get you a brochure."

He walked to the counter past a young girl standing in her socks and pulled a glossy pamphlet from under the display of wristbands and bowling gloves. He sat back down, the buttons of his short-sleeved orange shirt straining across his belly.

"Give this to Dee and tell her we can put Lorelei's ashes in a really nice container and bury her right next to your dad and brother. That way, everybody wins. Tell Summer none of this scattering the ashes over the hills or rivers or out of airplanes or whatever artistic nonsense she may think Lorelei wanted. Tell her Dee has had enough of this crap."

Lucy nodded, taking the brochure of assorted cremation accessories from his big hand. The wiry hair that sprang from his knuckles was gray.

"It's not so bad to be cremated," Al continued. "It makes sense. I can believe that Lorelei wouldn't want to take up too much space now. Tell Dee it's another one of those Lorelei causes she can't do a thing about." Al tilted back in his chair.

Lucy's shoulders started to shake. She laughed until a tear edged down her cheek. "I'm sorry," she said, trying to get herself under control. "All of a sudden, this is just so damned funny. If only Lorelei were here, she'd be in hysterics."

Someone bowled a strike again. When the cheering stopped, Al put his big hand on top of Lucy's. "I'm really sorry about your sister. She was a nice person," he said. Lucy blinked and nodded. She stood and pushed her plastic chair back under the table.

"She was the best."

"Anything new in the investigation? Any leads?" Al asked as she headed toward the door.

She faced him. "Nothing." She took a deep breath. "I know what people are saying about the investigation, that it was sloppy and all, but lately Officer McMahon has been working almost around the clock. Still, no witnesses. It's like whoever did it had no motive at all. And she must have let him in. Why would she do that?" Lucy didn't expect an answer.

Al shook his head. "The police have talked to everybody in town. Some people a few times."

Lucy nodded. When she went to buy milk at Mike's Market yesterday, Lorelei stared out from *The Sentinel* on the wire news rack by the counter. She had dropped her wallet, spraying loose change across the floor. The clerk, a former student of hers, had raced to help.

"I'm sorry," the young girl had stammered. "I hope they catch him," she added.

The few places Lucy had ventured into over the past few days were abuzz with talk about the murder. Maybe it was no wonder Dee and Summer had gone into hibernation.

"So, what do you say, Lucy? You think you can convince them?" Al asked, his voice soft as he brought her back to the present. He struggled out of his plastic chair. The chair tilted precipitously as he stood. "Let's put your sister to rest."

"Yes," Lucy answered, wiping her eyes, glossy brochure in hand.

"Don't give them more than twenty-four hours. If you can't reach me, stop in at the bowling alley. I'm usually here, even if I don't answer the phone. And if there's anything else I can do for you…" His voice trailed off.

"I know. Thanks, Al."

"Dee?" he asked, softly, just as she was about to lean into the tinted glass door.

"She's not doing too well," Lucy answered.

Al nodded. He looked down.

The sun blinded Lucy as she stepped outside. She squinted and pulled her sunglasses from her purse. The sky was blue. A breeze rustled the sycamores. Lucy was amazed to notice that it was a stunning July afternoon. She looked at her watch. There was time to check on Dee, give her the scoop and then head over to Summer's apartment. She would get the whole mess straightened out today.

Chapter 6

Summer motioned toward the kitchen table. Officer McMahon sat down and edged backwards in his seat. Crumbs from her morning toast littered the glass top.

"Coffee?" she asked.

"No, thanks."

Summer pulled out the chair across from him and sat. She remembered his big-shoulders. He had driven her home from the station the night she discovered Lorelei's body. He had walked her up the steps and settled her onto her tan leather couch, brought her a glass of water and two Advils from her medicine cupboard. She hadn't been able to talk that night. He had questioned her the day after and she had little to say then either. She had nothing to add today.

Summer focused her gray eyes on the young cop. She knew she was pretty, even with her eyes puffy and red-rimmed. It usually helped her deal with men. "Do you have a cigarette?" she asked.

His florid face reddened a little more. "I don't smoke."

"I don't either." She shrugged. "I just wanted something to do."

"I understand."

Summer ran her fingers through her straight black hair and slumped back in her chair. She saw him glimpse her belly-button ring as she shifted position. It surprised her that he didn't know how to check out a woman and pretend otherwise. She sat up straight again.

"So, you were the first person to enter the crime scene?" he asked.

"We've been through that before. The answer is still yes, as far as I know." She waited for him to say more, but silence hung between them. "Is this part of the everyone's guilty until proven innocent approach?" she asked after a minute. She stretched both arms in front of her and watched the predictable flush rise from his neck again. He cleared his throat and pulled at his collar. "I'm sorry. Look, you know if I could help you at all, I would," she said.

The past week had been extraordinarily difficult, maybe even worse than the night she had found Lorelei. The numbness that had enabled her to function in those first few days had dissipated. In its wake came an unbearable pain that awakened her at night from a sound sleep. Lately, it had begun to transform itself into a constant, crushing weariness.

Lorelei was dead. Gone. That was her everlasting reality.

And now, it seemed that everyone had an agenda. Officer McMahon wanted to waste her time with his pointless questions. She had heard rumors about a faulty investigation, so maybe he was simply working doubly hard to make up for it. And Dee was even worse. She had developed an intense hankering to arrange her family's corpses in a neat little row, as if she were planting tomatoes or string beans. Lucy was her usual self, trying to salvage peace and normalcy from something so grievously twisted that even the thought of it made Summer ill. Nobody cared about Lorelei anymore, Summer thought. And nobody cared at all about her. How could they? People weren't aware of her true relationship with Lorelei. If the two of them had lived as husbands and wives did, everything would be different. People would be sympathetic.

"Summer, I know this is difficult. I realize you've been through this already. You'll have to bear with me one last time. It's really important for you to try to remember everything you can. Did Lorelei seem different in any way in the days before her murder?"

Summer looked away. She wanted to answer him, but there was no way to convey what had happened between her and Lorelei in those last days. Yes, she wanted to say. But that had nothing to do with any murderous psychopath. She picked up a paper napkin and began to twist it until a scrap fluttered to the floor. It landed on her pink-polished toenails. She leaned down and fidgeted with her toe ring, smoothed her white stretch pants and stood up. She faced away from Officer McMahon, the bit of napkin still at her feet. She felt his eyes on her back.

"You called 911 at approximately 3 A.M. Sunday morning," he said.

"I don't remember what time it was. I told you before. I called as soon as I found her." Summer didn't turn around.

"You dropped by Lorelei's house at three in the morning?"

Summer turned to face him. "Yes." How could she explain anything to this cop, this kid? She was still reeling from everything that had happened.

"Was that routine for you and Lorelei? Did you drop in on her at that hour often?"

"No," she answered. Bright July sunshine lit the kitchen. This whole day was a nightmare. She wished it were winter.

"So what made you decide to visit her that night?"

Summer narrowed her eyes and stared down at Officer McMahon. He should know just by looking at her that she had no guilt, at least in the estimation of the police. He should be able to see that Lorelei's murder had ruined her life.

"I don't know, I just did," she said.

It was a lie. She knew exactly why she had visited Lorelei at that hour. Normally, she would have been staying there. With Lorelei. A few days before the murder, she and Lorelei had talked about going public at last. They both hated the phrase, 'coming out of the closet.' They weren't in a closet. Together, their lives had become lighter, clearer, expanded. Lorelei had tried to talk her into making an official announcement, had even bought a dress for the occasion. She had tried it on for her, its lace-edged neckline low. Summer remembered the little hollows under her collarbones. "If we act like we're doing something wrong, things will never change," Lorelei had insisted, twirling to show her the way the fabric moved. But Lorelei was like that, impulsive, naïve, not always sensible. Summer had told her that it wasn't as easy as all that. She had tried to explain to Lorelei that sometimes 'coming out' was as suffocating as remaining hidden. It wasn't the right time. Not yet. That's what she had believed at the time. But that wasn't the reason they had quarreled that night.

She had managed to convince Lorelei that in a town like Glendale, life moved at its own pace. Change was slow, and people had to be careful. What would the neighbors think? Her co-workers at the radio station? And certainly, Dee had enough calamities in her life already, and always complaining about no grandchildren. And Lucy. What would Lucy think?

Lorelei had agreed to wait a bit longer. She had hung up the dress, and they made love for the last time in their lives. Summer hadn't sensed that it would be the last time.

She remembered the first time. They hadn't discussed sexual orientation, but Lorelei had been supremely confident. They were at a party. Lorelei grabbed her hand and told Summer she needed help getting home, she was a little trashed. They didn't even get home. They walked to the empty playground down by the dam. It was closed, no admittance after sundown. Lorelei declared the sun shining in South America, the North Pole, maybe even Saudi Arabia. She said as long as the sun shone somewhere, they were cool. She stripped, letting her clothes fall onto the soft pine needles beneath them. "Well," she had asked Summer. Summer had only waited a moment before she reached for her, touched her hair, her lips, the curve of her bare back. Lorelei had taken both of Summer's hands in her own and placed them against the velvety softness of her breasts.

Officer McMahon's voice seemed to come from far away. She realized that he was repeating himself. "You stopped by

Lorelei's house for no good reason at three in the morning." He phrased it as a statement.

The image of young Lorelei, naked at the dam, evaporated. "Pretty much," Summer answered. She didn't feel talkative. The quarrel that had separated her from Lorelei forever had been all her fault.

Officer McMahon's radio buzzed.

"I see," he said. More garbled voices came from his radio. Whatever the voices had said made him stand up. "Look, I have to go. But this is important, and if you don't try to think and cooperate a little more, things won't get any easier," he said. He started to walk toward the door, and then turned to her with a forced smile that she guessed was supposed to convey sympathy. "Really, Summer. I mean it. I'm trying to catch a murderer here."

"I want to catch him as much as you do," Summer said. She wondered as soon as she said it if that were true. What would that accomplish? Lorelei would still be gone.

"If you think of anything at all, call me," he said. He held out a card between his fleshy thumb and forefinger. She took it. His name was written in ink above the precinct address and phone number. They faced each other. She didn't know what she was supposed to do, shake hands, maybe thank him?

"I will," she said. She didn't even try to manage a smile.

She turned away and let him find the front door on his own. When she heard it shut behind him, she sat down at the kitchen table. She pushed the crumbs around. Her hands began to shake. She tried to make herself stand up, do something. But she couldn't.

Her conversation with Lorelei after they had made love for the last time was still fresh in her memory. "I have to tell you something," she had said to Lorelei. "I got a letter from someone. She's coming to meet me. This might be the hardest thing I've ever had to say. I think it's better if you and I stay apart for a while. We're not breaking up. I just don't know what to tell her. It's just that, well, she's my daughter." Those words had taken all of Summer's nerve. Her heart had nearly stopped beating.

"You have a daughter?"

"She wants to meet me."

"What's her name? What's your daughter's name?"

"I didn't name her. She tells me it's Megan."

"Megan," Lorelei had repeated.

They had argued. Summer said she didn't know what to expect, that she needed to take time to deal with this unknown girl. It was painful, personal. Lorelei said she understood. That wasn't the problem. In all their hours of talking, sharing, loving, she couldn't believe that Summer had never mentioned her daughter. Never. "If you really loved me, you would have trusted me. I would have already known about Megan. It's as simple as that."

"She's not someone I can talk about."

"Why not? What, you forgot about her?" Lorelei had asked, tears welling up. "In all our time together, it simply slipped your mind that you had a child living somewhere in this world?"

"Lorelei, she was a part of a past that I shut out long ago. I'm sorry," she had said.

Lorelei shrank from Summer's touch. "That's not enough."

"Lorelei, please. It's not easy for me."

"That's why you have someone else in your life," Lorelei said. "It's never easy."

Summer had reached out to her with one hand, the other at her side, clenching Megan's letter, rose-scented on pale pink stationery.

"I understand that, for now, you'd prefer to hide me from the world. But I can't understand why you needed to hide yourself from me," Lorelei had said at last, her voice soft and quiet. "Leave me alone."

And Summer did. She hadn't seen, called, or talked to her for days. Finally, Summer had gone to Lorelei's at three A.M. to apologize.

Summer wished the July sunshine would stop streaming through the kitchen window. She wished that Megan hadn't suddenly needed closure. Mostly, she wished that Lorelei would walk into the kitchen, throw her burlap satchel over the back of the chair, and touch her shoulder on the way to the refrigerator to grab a yogurt.

Chapter 7

After the incident with the girl, Clarkson was unsettled. The fact that he had killed her was not the root of his restlessness. Although he preferred not to dredge up history, he had killed before. Only when necessary, of course. As Old Brighton's hot July melted into August, his unease grew. Later in the month, the diminishing daylight brought the surprise of nocturnal crispness, something that usually refreshed him. But this year, his edginess grew. When the bright clouds and fresh breezes of September in Connecticut made way for October's gaudy palette, he figured it out.

The manicured crimson maples, the mulched pathways dotted with mounds of chrysanthemums, the signs in the windows of local bistros hawking calvados martinis and pumpkin lattes—all of these left him cold. For Clarkson, Old Brighton had become like a worn out love affair. It had lost its charm.

The memory of Glendale and its surrounding countryside lured him. He longed to breathe in Glendale's dank air, tinged with wild honeysuckle in summer, perfumed with sweetly acrid wood smoke in the fall. He wanted to bask in the mind-numbing opacity of its dark nights. He wasn't sure precisely when these images had become more vibrant than the picturesque world where he conducted his daily affairs.

On an especially bright October morning, he drove to work along the sleek commercial strip lined with Saks-inspired storefronts. As always, the pedestrians were less perfect than fashion models only because of minor genetic flaws and surgical limitations. He viewed the human swarm on the sidewalks as if for the first time, their fine haircuts and toned bodies, their lambskin briefcases and shoulder bags. He no longer congratulated himself for having fit into this rarefied mold. He saw the mold for what it was, a fabrication by people who required such things. Now, he was not one of them.

The golden sunlight evaporated as he pulled into the subterranean garage and turned left into the space reserved with his name. He exited the car, straightened his collar and walked the few steps to a bank of gleaming elevators. Without thinking, he punched his code into the board and stepped inside. When the door slid open, the floor guard greeted him with the usual "Good morning, Mr. Dupree." Clarkson nodded and headed for the wing where Elite Construction had its office. He swiped his card in the strip by the door. Jeanette, his receptionist, wasn't due in for another half hour. He passed her desk and closed his office door behind him. He turned to the window that framed a gurgling stream and an arched concrete span that would fill up by mid afternoon with pretty mothers pushing pretty children in fancy strollers.

He stared at the scene before him without pleasure. That Glendale house where the girl had grown up would not leave his mind. The house and the girl. His background in construction led him to categorize the house by its design, a monstrous Queen Anne, a concoction of spindles and turrets, archways and cornices, surprise and excess at every turn. The architects he worked with these days would not understand such a house, accustomed as they were to their precious concepts of harmony and musicality. What, were they all composing sonatas? Diluted descendants of Frank Lloyd Wright, that's all they were. Most of them aspired to tuck behemoths of mansions into the countryside the way a housewife folded nuts into a cake batter. To Clarkson, that policy was disingenuous, producing mirthless creations that despoiled the landscape with a series of apologetic disruptions. Clarkson wondered if he were the only one who saw the underlying flaw. Whoever had built the homes of the Glendale elite so long ago had understood the truth. People did not build to hide. They built to conquer.

It annoyed him that he had only glimpsed the girl's house in shadows. He longed to see it in raw daylight, to examine every detail of its careless majesty. He imagined that on this bright October morning, its half-paned windows would gleam above the sprawling porch that wrapped sideways along the house, beginning just under the bricked arch of the doorway, and running in the opposite direction from the corner turret. The randomness of the house thrilled him, its lack of symmetry jarring, original. It wasn't a house that struggled for harmony. It was a house that shouted victory. And he wanted it.

He wanted it for himself and for what it had meant to the girl. That girl. As time went on, the girl and the house had merged for him, both such unlikely creatures. At odd moments he would see her unruly tangle of hair, the looped bow of the scarf that barely covered her breasts, her eyes, wide and innocent despite the crinkly crow's feet at their corners. He would hear her polite, quivering voice. He remembered her paint-streaked arms and especially, her dignified surrender in his arms.

He imagined her childhood. She must have awakened on Christmas mornings in that splendid gem of a house in a bedroom with draped windows and thick coverlets. She must have tiptoed from her room into a grand hall that led to a magnificent staircase, with machine-turned newel posts and stained glass at the landing. The girl must have squealed with joy as she skipped down the stairs into the front parlor where a mountain of presents waited under the bejeweled limbs of a stately fir.

Clarkson knew about such things. Was he in fifth grade when his entire class went to Chockey's tree lot on a snowy December afternoon? That seemed right. One of those dreadful school field trips. They had all filed into the cabin at the gate to the evergreen farm where Mrs. Chockey stirred a pot of hot chocolate on a black stove. Mr. Chockey seemed to know everyone in the class. "Why Nancy Johnson! Your mummy and daddy were in last weekend for that lovely Norwegian spruce," or, "Stephen, did your father have to cut much off the Scotch pine when he got it home?" He patted some of them on the head. His classmates ran excitedly around the tree lots, calling to the dogs by name, asking Mrs. Chockey for seconds on the steaming cocoa. Clarkson had hung back. His dad hadn't bothered with a Christmas tree since his mom left. Even before that, they had only hacked a seedling from the lowland woods and plunked it in a bucket of water. His dad swore while he strung it with a few lights so that Clarkson could hang the ornaments he had made at school.

Mr. Chockey had noticed him as he wandered solo through the fields and asked if he were new in town. Clarkson had nodded yes, too ashamed to admit that he wasn't, that Christmas at his house didn't include the customary town pilgrimage. "Well, be sure to have your family stop by. I'll have a tree with your name on it." A group of his classmates ran by at that moment and burst into laughter. "A Cody tree. A Coodies tree," they had called. That girl in the woods, Lorelei, couldn't hide her dismay when he had plucked the blossom from the laden vine. He remembered her stillness as he had tucked it behind her ear. In her childhood, would she have taunted him with cruel names? Just because his life had no stately parlor doors, no grand archways, no two-handled vases tucked into swirled plaster niches?

Clarkson heard Jeanette enter, the running of water as she filled the carafe, the hiss of the coffee pot. A smoky aroma infiltrated his office, the pricey Costa Rican blend sent by a grateful client, he guessed. He wondered what Jeanette was wearing today, if she had on her high-heeled red shoes. She had worn those the first time he had had her, right in this office, in the glow of the gaslights that lined the concrete bridge beyond the window. He had dallied with Jeanette on and off for a year or two with intermittent, lustful assignations, until the night she had dissolved into an inexplicable fit, when she held her blouse over her bare breasts after they had finished, and cried until her eyes were swollen puffs and her nose was wet and red. It wasn't that she didn't want him anymore, she had sobbed. She had become engaged. The whole scene was absurd, her offer to resign from her job, her certainty that their entanglement had a life of its own that demanded a sudden and violent end.

Some years later, he still couldn't understand it. If she believed that the ring on her finger meant the loss of their carnal nights, then they were over. Simple as that. Clarkson had found her histrionics much harder to bear than their supposed break-up. What had been broken? And now, he was fairly certain that she was sleeping with Edward, the associate he hired some five years ago. With the ring still on her finger. Who could understand?

He leafed through a stack of orders on his desk without enthusiasm. It occurred to him that it was time to take Edward up on his offer. Edward was in a position to buy Elite Construction, if they could structure it the right way. It was something he had mentioned several times over too many cocktails at Isabella's. In his defense, Edward had tried to be delicate when he pointed out that Clarkson wasn't getting any younger. Clarkson made a note on one of the forms and tidied the rest into a folder for Edward.

He heard the front door open, then Edward's purposeful steps in the hall. Clarkson turned his attention again to the concrete span beyond the window, already alive with the first squadron of identical young mothers, their hair gleaming in the early October sunlight as they jogged behind huge-wheeled strollers. He sat at his desk. If all went as planned, Clarkson would be on his way to Glendale by the end of the month. He could haggle over the details with Edward at his leisure.

The thought calmed him. For the first time in a long time, his nagging restlessness gave way to anticipation. He stood and stretched, then opened the door to his office. Jeanette passed him and smiled, bright lipstick gaudy and purplish against her over-whitened teeth. He glanced at her feet. She wore her straw platforms today. They weren't his favorite.

He really didn't need to be in the office at all, he realized, what with Edward's capable presence. Why wait? If he went home and packed, he could be in Glendale by tomorrow, just to scout things out. The plan invigorated him.

"Jeanette," he called to her back.

She turned. Was it his imagination or did she suck in her already flat midsection and thrust her breasts toward him? He thought he saw a hopeful glimmer in her eye. The flush of red from her cheeks to her cleavage confirmed that it was not his imagination. He cleared his throat. It didn't matter, anyway.

"I have urgent business out of town. I won't be in the office for the next week or so," he said.

Chapter 8

A chill invaded the mild October afternoon. Lucy pulled at the edges of her knit sweater, one of her favorites, a Lorelei creation. Yellow and scarlet streaked the maples overhead. A handful of leaves skittered across the path before her. She marveled that autumn had erupted all over the Glendale countryside in colors that Lorelei would have loved to paint. How relentlessly time passed, she thought. She had already made it through the start of the new school year. It hadn't been easy, with the whispers following her down every hall, but she had made it. She was happy that it was Friday, relieved to be alone in the sanctuary of the cemetery. These graveside visits were the only peaceful moments of her life.

Lucy followed the path through Glendale Cemetery, past headstones with names almost as familiar to her as her own. The Schneiders, the Thompsons, the Cooks, families so rooted in Glendale history that she felt among friends. The path turned alongside Blake's creek, site of the Parker family plot. She remembered old Mrs. Parker, ensconced in her bedroom for most of the last decade of her life. The three of them, Lucy, Lorelei and Dee, had climbed the stairs to drop off a birthday or Christmas card for her for years. When Mrs. Parker died last year at the age of 102, it seemed anticlimactic. It wasn't fair. Lorelei didn't get to practice how to lie motionless for a whole decade before she quit breathing completely. Lucy turned onto the path that followed the gentle rise of the hill.

She halted briefly just before the Armstrong family plot came into view, braced herself, and then trudged forward. Past the hillcrest, the tombstone rose before her, shiny and new, Lorelei's name and fateful dates etched into the pinkish marble with a glaring clarity. She rummaged through her purse for a tissue. Maybe one of these days the hot tears wouldn't come, she thought. She wasn't sure if that would be a relief. The bright thatch of flowers that had covered Lorelei's plot had mostly decomposed, leaving only remnants of a brownish tangled web, bare now in spots. Through the spots, Lucy noticed that the spongy mound had sunk almost level with the Thads, Lorelei's nickname for the departed men of the family.

Dee had won the battle over Lorelei's remains. She had fainted in her kitchen when Summer and Lucy had met with her to resolve the cremation issue. The sight of Dee on the floor, pale and wrinkled had softened Summer's resolve. She said that enough tragedy and drama surrounded all of them already. Dee could have her garden of bodies.

Lucy sat on the concrete bench just off the path, her usual spot for the last few months. She liked it here. Passers-by were rare, and she was free from the awkward horror and sympathy of her co-workers, neighbors and friends. She understood now why people knocked down houses that were the sites of heinous crimes. She felt similarly tainted, that it would be easier for others if she just disappeared. She was the sister of the murdered. There wasn't a place for her in society. She thought of Dee, mother of the murdered. She was not faring at all well these days, either.

Lucy wondered what Dee was doing on this crisp October afternoon. For as big a deal as she had made over the whole burial issue, Dee hadn't even been to Lorelei's gravesite. In fact, she hadn't been much of anywhere, and she hadn't mentioned reopening the house for boarders. Lucy and Summer had talked about broaching the subject with her, but neither wanted to intrude on Dee's silent, tortured world just yet. In fact, conversations with Summer were still strained. Lucy had enough to do handling her own pain, she thought, without tackling Summer's, or her mother's.

She imagined that Lorelei would have handled the situation much better if she had been the surviving sibling. Lorelei would have rallied the family. She would have painted one of her crazy scenes, written poetry, plunged herself into a mourning wardrobe, but probably not black. She smiled. If their roles were reversed, Lorelei would certainly declare her own color of mourning. What would it be? White for the clouds and angels? Blue for the sky? Gold? Lucy tried to guess, but her brain didn't work the way that Lorelei's did.

Nobody's did. Lucy stared at the tombstone. Lorelei was irreplaceable. No one else had her spark.

That's what's wrong with me, Lucy thought. Fifty-one, single, and desperately lonely. Why? No spark. None. She remembered the year the other fourth grade teacher had invited her to Paris for spring break. Kate Willoughby was her name. Kate's older brother had rented a house just outside the city.

"It will be a blast," Kate had said, grasping Lucy's wrists with both hands. "The Louvre, the Eiffel Tower, the Champs Elysees." Lucy never forgot the way Kate had held her wrists, so natural, so easy. She wondered why she couldn't reach out like that, why she always felt so walled-in from everyone. Lucy had agreed that it would be a blast. But she didn't go. She tried to remember exactly why not, but now she couldn't.

"It was the most romantic place in the world," Kate had told her in the teacher's lounge afterwards, her skin glowing, her face transformed from plain to pretty through the magic of love and Paris. She left Glendale soon after to marry the lawyer she'd met there. Lucy winced, remembering the regret that had bubbled up inside her at the time. She had quit corresponding with Kate after the birth of Kate and Alec's second child, blaming her lapse on her impossibly hectic schedule. Penniless and intrepid, Lorelei had gone backpacking in Paris when she had the chance, Lucy remembered.

The shadow fell across her without warning. Lucy jumped.

"I didn't mean to upset you," a man said.

"You surprised me, that's all," Lucy answered. She didn't recognize him. He was wearing jogging pants and a gray T-shirt. He looked about her age, his face lined but handsome. He was extremely tall.

"I was just passing through. A little jogging, you know." He patted his midsection, which appeared to Lucy to be lean enough already.

Lucy didn't answer. Someone actually visits a cemetery for recreational purposes, she thought. She waited for him to leave, so she could get back to her thoughts. He stopped and leaned forward. His breath came in gasps. His presence crowded Lucy, as when someone fails to head for a distant corner in an elevator.

"You're just sitting here? In the cemetery?" the man asked. He straightened up, his breath still ragged.

Lucy looked up at him. His pale green eyes stood out from his tanned face. They seemed lit from behind. "Not exactly," she said.

"Forgive me for not introducing myself to such a lovely lady. I'm Clarkson Dupree," he said. "And you are?"

Lucy couldn't bring herself to speak. She had never been good at meeting men, and current circumstances hadn't added to her charm. Just leave Lorelei and me alone, she thought. And with a jolt, she caught herself. Lorelei had already left her alone. That's what she had just been thinking about. The way she was going, Dee's life of pathetic solitude was only a heartbeat away. Lucy tried to recall the last time she took a chance in life, but nothing surfaced. She had a sudden vision of herself, old and decrepit after the creams and lotions failed her completely. She saw herself in Dee's chenille robe, padding through a quiet house filled with piles of school papers awaiting correction with her customary fine line red marker. She had been using that exact marker for twenty-four years, even though she had to special order it now. She gulped.

"I'm Lucy. Lucy Armstrong." She thought her voice sounded small.

Clarkson looked from the bench to the plots in front of them. "Armstrong," he said. Clearly, he had made the connection. Lorelei's fresh grave stood out like a beacon.

"My sister," Lucy said.

Clarkson nodded. "I see. Recent, it looks like."

"Yes. July."

"Looks like she was pretty young. What happened?"

Lucy was silent. She blew her nose. She managed to shrug, but didn't look up. Clarkson took a few steps and seemed about to jog on, but instead made a little half-circle and planted himself on the far end of Lucy's bench. He fussed with his shoelaces. "Car accident?"

"Worse." Lucy was surprised that she could answer at all.

"God. Do you want to talk about it?"

Lucy couldn't believe her ears. It occurred to her that this handsome stranger was the first person to ask her that question. Everyone else tiptoed around her as if she were made of glass. Memories of Lorelei swirled through her brain, too raw to share with Dee and Summer. She felt weak, as if she might faint. Did she want to talk about it? She wasn't sure. She didn't know if she could. She shrugged and a funny sound emerged from her that wasn't a yes or a no. Apparently, she couldn't talk at all.

Clarkson's voice was soothing. "Maybe another time. I bet you come here a lot."

Lucy collected herself a bit. "Almost every day."

"I have business in town on Wednesday. I'll probably jog afterwards. Maybe if you're here, we can sit and talk. About anything."

"Okay."

"I mean, if you want to, if you wouldn't mind. We could have a drink afterwards, if you have time. No pressure. I'll be in town for a few days. There's only so much to do in Glendale. It's not like it's Paris, you know."

Lucy hoped he didn't notice the way her spine stiffened. Paris. Of all cities to mention. It was a sign. She was sure of it.

"No, I was planning to be right here anyway," she said, feeling shakier than she sounded.

"All right. It's a date. See you then, Lucy."

Lucy felt her heart pound. She looked up and he was gone. She watched him jog up the hill, past the departed Hendersons and Ridleys. She watched him until he disappeared from view.

Lucy felt panicky. She didn't know anything about him. He could be anyone. Strangers just didn't show up randomly in Glendale. She fought her panic. Hadn't she just been counting all the lost opportunities in her life? Of course she couldn't be rash or careless, Lucy thought, but maybe it was time she lived a little.

Lucy straightened the neckline of her sweater and ran her fingers through her hair. Clarkson Dupree was actually a very handsome man.

Chapter 9

Lucy entered through the side door of Dee's house. How many times had she mentioned to Dee that she ought to lock the door? After all that had happened.

"Mom?"

Lucy didn't wait for an answer. She and Summer hadn't expected Dee to participate in their meeting tonight to talk about Dee's relentless slide into what seemed to be a living coma, but they did hope she would at least put in an appearance. Lucy was glad she had arrived first. Maybe she could convince her.

"Mom?" she called again. The first floor was empty. She walked upstairs. Dee sat on top of the floral coverlet on her bed. The television blared in front of her. She hadn't switched on the lamp, even though the room was already shadowed.

"Hello, Mom," Lucy said, kissing her cheek. Dee's skin felt cool and too soft.

"Lucy," Dee said. She turned briefly before the television again absorbed her attention. Lucy regarded Dee's uncombed hair, her bent spine. She switched on the lamp beside Dee's bed and got a hairbrush from the dresser.

"Don't," Dee said.

"Maybe if I just brush your hair a minute. Summer's coming over…"

Dee turned away. She stretched out her wrinkled arm and switched off the lamp. Lucy set the hairbrush back on the dresser.

"I'll be downstairs," Lucy said.

Lucy was relieved to get into the kitchen. She rummaged through Dee's pantry. She found a tin of cashews, opened it, and rinsed the bunch of grapes she'd picked up at Mike's Market on the way over. She arranged them on a platter with some cheese. The thought of seeing Summer again made her nervous. She could count on one hand the times they'd gotten together since Lorelei's death. Things weren't the same anymore.

But there was more to it than that. Ever since yesterday, the whole world looked different. Was it really only yesterday? Thoughts of Clarkson obsessed her. Over the past twenty-four hours, he had popped up in her thoughts constantly. At first she had tried to make excuses. She was alone, sad, grasping for anything that might make the hurt go away. But she couldn't stop herself. Those eyes, that voice. And he had seemed so concerned for her. What if she had at last met someone? Maybe she was too old, and it was just silly, but she couldn't help herself. Would Summer look at her and instantly know that something was up?

Summer had initiated today's meeting with a phone call earlier in the week. She had sounded awkward and tentative, and tripped over her attempts at small talk.

"Summer, what's wrong?" Lucy had finally asked.

"It's Dee, Lucy," Summer had said, after a pause. "Maybe it's time we did something." Summer described how she had dropped by Dee's house that afternoon with a plate of ham and scalloped potatoes. After ringing the doorbell for what seemed an eternity, Dee had finally appeared, hair sticking up, arms stringy inside the sleeves of her nightshirt. She had looked into Summer's face for a few long seconds before greeting her. "It was weird. I don't think she even knew me at first," Summer said.

"I've been hoping she would snap out of it." Lucy said. She told Summer that she had brought Dee a bag of groceries earlier in the week only to discover the food from the previous week completely untouched. "So I lined up the new box of All Bran right beside the old one. I threw out the old milk, unopened and expired. She just stood there and watched me. And she was wearing that god-awful robe and those gold slippers with the holes in the toes."

They decided to meet at Dee's to come up with a plan to try to rekindle Dee's interest in life. "If we're right there, in her house, maybe we can get her to join us, actually talk," Lucy had suggested.

"That's true. It's been awhile since we've all been together," Summer had said.

Silence followed.

"Yes, well, thanks for calling. See you Saturday, then, around five or so." They hung up.

Neither had mentioned how much they had missed sitting on Dee's porch on lazy summer evenings, while Lorelei told her stories and Dee fussed over them, serving up old-lady foods like melba toast and nut-studded cheese balls on a silver tray. Neither mentioned how utterly different life was without Lorelei.

Lucy set the food on the table between the lounge chairs flanking the hearth in Dee's spacious kitchen and then walked down the hall to the bottom of the staircase.

"Mom, Summer will be here in a few minutes. Come on down and say hello for a bit," Lucy called upstairs.

"I'm watching my program," Dee answered.

"When it's over then," Lucy said.

Dee didn't answer.

The doorbell rang. In the old days, Summer wouldn't have rung the bell.

"Summer, thanks so much for coming," Lucy said as she opened the carved wooden door.

The two women hugged each other, at once tender and tentative.

"You look wonderful," Summer said.

Lucy smoothed her gray tweed skirt and tugged at her cashmere sweater. "Thanks, so do you."

"I look like shit." Summer brushed at her blue jeans and adjusted the clip in her hair.

They both laughed, a little nervously, as Lucy motioned Summer to the far end of the kitchen.

"I love this kitchen," Summer said as she settled into one of the chairs beside the bricked hearth.

Lucy nodded. "Me, too. It's grand, I think. That's the word for it. So what's new?"

They talked a bit, about the bright early October sunshine and what awaited them as fall edged into winter. They asked after a few mutual acquaintances.

"So, you're okay?" Lucy asked.

Summer shrugged. "My life is full of complications as always. What about you?"

"I don't know," Lucy began.

Lucy realized that she was bursting with the need to tell somebody about Clarkson. She smiled and looked down.

"What?" Summer asked.

"What do you mean?"

"Look at you. What happened? Did you win the teacher of the year award? The lottery? Something good has finally happened for you, hasn't it?"

Lucy raised one shoulder and smiled. "Maybe, I'm not sure. Maybe it's nothing. At my age, I'm probably behaving like a silly schoolgirl. Well, if you really want to know…" She couldn't have stopped herself if she tried. She told Summer about meeting Clarkson at the cemetery, his surprising kindness. She omitted the part where he had invited her to talk about Lorelei.

"I'm seeing him on Wednesday. It's sort of a date."

"That's nice," Summer said, without enthusiasm.

"No, really, he seems like he cares."

"I'm sure he does. That's wonderful. It's just a little unusual, that's all, finding the man of your dreams at…at your sister's grave. No, I'm sorry, that's a terrible thing to say. I mean, what a strange 'how we met' story that could be some day."

Lucy laughed a little too hard.

Summer reached for a handful of nuts and jostled the table with her knee as she leaned forward. "I'm happy for you, Lucy," she said. Lucy reached out and steadied the plates.

"You would like him if you met him," she said after a pause.

Summer nodded. "Okay."

From across the high-ceilinged room, the stainless steel refrigerator began to hum. Lucy fidgeted with the hemline of her skirt.

"I have to get this skirt hemmed or else retire it," she said, turning the edge so that Summer could see the offending wisps of thread.

Summer barely nodded.

"Want a glass of wine?" Lucy asked.

"Sure."

Lucy got up from her chair. Her heels sank into the braided rug under her feet. Summer leaned forward as if to rise.

"No, sit, I have it."

Lucy crossed the rug. When she hit the tiled part of the floor, her heels clattered. She pulled a bottle of merlot from the wine rack in the corner.

"Red okay?"

"Sure."

The creak of the floorboards overhead made them both look upward. Lucy tilted her head and set down the corkscrew.

"Dee's up," she said.

"Let's try to get her down here," Summer said. She seemed as relieved as Lucy by Dee's stirrings.

Lucy hurried through the front hallway to the main staircase. "Mom, your program must be over by now. Summer and I are about to have a glass of wine. Come join us for a bit," Lucy called. She heard a squeak and the creaking of a door.

"No, thanks, I'm a little tired." Dee's voice was flat. Lucy heard the door shut, the floorboards creak and then silence. She waited a moment.

"Are you sure, Mom?"

No answer came. Lucy walked back to the kitchen. "She doesn't want to."

"Surprise," Summer said.

Lucy poured two glasses of wine. She crossed the room and handed one to Summer. When Lorelei was there, they had always clinked glasses in a toast. It was a Lorelei tradition. She toasted anything, the new moon, the opening of a movie they wanted to see at the Cineplex in Clarion, the patch of grape hyacinths she had just painted. Once they toasted the fact that water swirled down the drain the opposite way in the southern hemisphere. Lorelei loved that idea.

Lucy raised her glass, wracking her brains for anything toast-worthy.

"To your date," Summer said, clinking her glass against Lucy's.

"To my date," Lucy said.

They clinked glasses and sipped their wine.

"It's nothing formal, you know, we're just meeting at..." Lucy stopped. She didn't want to say, "we're meeting at Lorelei's grave." It was all so odd sounding, she knew. She felt Summer's eyes on her.

"To your encounter then," Summer said.

Lucy cleared her throat. "So, about Dee. What if we just advertise and reopen the house for boarders? We can do it for a while, and hope that Dee wakes up and helps," Lucy said, glad to get off the subject of Clarkson and on to business.

"We could. You and I both know that Dee is useless right now. I could help on and off, but I can't promise to dive in and run things. The timing is a little difficult for me," Summer said.

"You're busy at work?" Lucy asked.

Summer shook her head. "Kind of. Really, I just have a lot on my mind right now."

"Oh?"

"It's nothing." Summer waved her arm. Lucy could tell it was something.

Lucy nodded. "Anything you want to talk about?" She was surprised as soon as she said it. She wasn't usually like that. She remembered how Clarkson had invited her to talk about Lorelei. Something about meeting him had already opened her up a little, she realized with a bit of a shock.

Summer lifted her eyes. "Thanks. I don't know. It's personal, I guess you could say."

Lucy fussed with the food on the platter. "I've finally settled into the new school year," she said. She sliced herself a wedge of cheese. "The house is ready, and we might as well take advantage of leaf season. I could get things up and running here. I guess I should move in here for a while. It wouldn't hurt to keep an eye on Mom, anyway."

"That's for sure."

"And anytime you can help, that would be great."

"I'll do what I can, you know that," Summer said.

They talked a while, about little things, the new coat of olive paint on the drug store and whether it should have remained the bright blue they'd always known. The new produce section at Mike's Market, with actually interesting mushrooms, like shiitake for goodness sake, loose by the pound. They didn't mention Clarkson again, or Summer's personal issues. Lucy walked Summer to the door and watched her climb into her Volkswagen.

Chapter 10

On the short drive home from Dee's, the change in Lucy possessed Summer. She had seen the excitement in her eyes. And something else, too. Sensuality. Even more than that. Sexuality. For the first time in the ten years she had known her, Lucy reeked of it.

Summer slammed the car door hard. She unlocked the front door to her duplex and switched on the lights. Her feet dragged as she mounted the staircase to her bedroom. She threw her keys onto her dresser, purposely avoiding the pale pink envelope beside her jewel box. She looked in the mirror. Flat gray eyes peered back at her from circles of darkness. Summer pulled first at the skin along her temples, then her cheeks. The circles stayed. She undressed, regarding her full breasts in the mirror with indifference. Her body had remained untouched by another for so long that it had become unresponsive. It used to be a playground, she thought. She turned from the mirror and pulled on a gray t-shirt and flannel drawstring pants.

Clarkson, she thought, as she headed for the bathroom. What kind of a name is that? She turned on the water and washed her face. She looked into the mirror and again caught the reflection of her expressionless eyes. She remembered Lucy's shining eyes. She wasn't sure why she was so annoyed with Lucy for having met a man. She had tried to be generous, of course. Hadn't she dedicated their toast to Lucy's upcoming date? She turned the faucet off, dabbed at her face and tossed the towel into the wicker basket in the hall. Droplets of moisture still clung to her face and neck. How could Lucy meet someone at Lorelei's grave?

Back in the silence of her bedroom, she studied the handwriting on the rose-scented envelope. The letter had arrived in yesterday's mail. She had recognized that pale pink stationery immediately, Megan's ominous, gentle calling card. Summer picked it up, then set it back down. She started to walk away, but could not. She pulled the letter from the envelope, unfolded it, and read it again.

> *"I've been waiting to hear from you. I hope you don't mind. I am making plans to see you. I understand how difficult this is for you, but please allow us to meet at long last. I will be free at the end of October. Let me know if that's all right. Don't worry, I just want to meet you, see your face, see if I have your eyes or hair or hands or anything. And then we can part ways again, if you like."*

Summer held the letter in her hands, staring at the rounded script. It all seemed so desperate to Summer. Megan was twenty-five years old. Her eyes should already be her own. Why did she need to compare them now? But that's unfair, Summer thought. Of course Megan would be curious about her. It was only natural. First Lucy, now Megan, Summer thought, ashamed of herself. Why was she so devoid of kindness these days? Lorelei would be appalled at her hard-heartedness.

Summer dropped the letter back on the dresser and lay across the bed. She stared at the ceiling. Megan had been a consequence, not a choice for her. Summer had been young at the time, so young that she hadn't yet learned that everything wasn't her fault.

In those days, she had been certain that choosing the correct sexual orientation was a matter of behaving, like not biting one's nails or doing one's homework. The other girls in her class were giddy over the boys' skinny legs sticking out of baggy basketball shorts, their budding masculinity. She remembered exclaiming over them, too, with her best friend Jessica. But Jessica's long straight ponytail kissed with highlights interested her far more.

By the time Summer was a junior in high school, she had it all figured out. Even though her mother and grandmother sincerely believed that Liberace, a flamboyant male entertainer with puffy hair and ruffled blouses was merely eccentric, Summer understood. Not everyone's lives complied with her mother's innocent beliefs.

She had tried her best to change herself. Aware of her looks, and what they provoked in high school boys, she flaunted her long legs in short skirts. She flipped her waist-length black hair as she talked. The boys had pursued her relentlessly. Summer let them do whatever they wanted, trying to figure out how to enjoy it, how to transform herself into what they desired, what her mother desired for her. She remembered their hands more than their faces, the way their fingers trembled as they fumbled with her bra hooks or the zipper of her skin-tight skirt.

The night she resolved to give up the whole charade for good was the night she conceived Megan. It wasn't her first time. She wasn't exactly sure when her first time was. Sex for her was a continuum of messy, squishy encounters with escalating degrees of penetration.

It was with a quiet boy named Rob. He was in her World Cultures class, and anytime she looked at him, he was staring at her through a tousled mane of sun-streaked hair, half obliterating his dark blue eyes. He sat with his feet up on the desk in front of him. Nobody challenged him. Not even Miss Curran, their teacher. Someone said his grandfather had served time in the Oil City prison, that his dad knew somebody in the real Mafia. True or not, people left him alone.

Summer could identify with his isolation. They ended up together, awkwardly, over prom weekend at somebody's parents' cottage near Lake George, north of Albany. Summer's date had abandoned her for a cute redhead who actually wanted him. Rob was alone, and offered to drive Summer home.

That's all she had wanted. A ride home. But they ended up in the back seat of his car, on the dark shore of the lake, the cottage a pinpoint of light in the distance. She couldn't bring herself to refuse him. He fumbled with her clothes, moaning as he exposed her breasts, running his hands over them. He pulled off her jeans, bumping her into the back of the seat as he freed her legs. Finally, he unbelted his own jeans, pulling them only as far down as freedom of movement required. He entered her, sharp and hard. The metal door handle jabbed her with every thrust. She bit her lip until it bled.

"I'm not on the pill," she had said.

"It's okay. I won't come inside," he managed to answer, tossing his golden hair out of his eyes with a jerk of his neck.

"Okay."

She resolved right there that she would never inflict this pain on herself again. When she got back to Schodack, she would hop on Interstate 90 and head to New York City, or even San Francisco. She would find a home where people understood that Liberace didn't buy women's clothes simply because of his unusual taste. Life would be less complicated elsewhere.

The next month she realized that Rob had either lied or miscalculated. She never knew, because she never asked or told him anything. That fall, he left for some sort of construction job in the Alaskan wilderness. She allowed denial to stretch into an unwelcome pregnancy. She refused to participate in any sort of childbirth education classes, despite heart-felt appeals from the young women at the family planning clinic in town. Her father, long divorced from her mother, quit visiting her. Her mother cried a lot and consulted a therapist to sort through, as she told Summer, the ruination of her life at her daughter's hand.

Summer remembered those months as a time of mind-numbing loneliness, culminating in the messy and frenetic birth of her daughter. The baby emerged with fine pale hair—Rob's hair, not hers. She had no memory of her eyes.

And now, she had a pale pink letter claiming that this girl needed to know if their eyes were the same.

Chapter 11

Lucy awoke before the alarm sounded. She swung her legs over the side of the bed and stretched her feet in front of her. Her toenails gleamed crimson with a glossy topcoat. Her fingernails matched. She smiled and slid her feet into her slippers.

Her plan was to go straight to the cemetery after school. Clarkson hadn't set a time to meet. What if he got an early start on his jog, and she missed him by seconds? She couldn't risk it. She would get all ready, teach, and hurry over to Lorelei's grave.

She grabbed a towel on the way to the bathroom, hung it on the door hook and stripped off her nightgown and slippers. She ran the water until it steamed and lathered herself in the rose-scented gel that had decorated the bathroom shelf since last Christmas. She washed her hair with the jasmine shampoo and conditioner from the salon. She shaved her legs and under her arms. When she shut the faucets off, she inspected her dripping body. She wished she had done those fifty sit-ups every morning like she had promised herself, but it was too late now. She blow-dried her hair, then turned her head upside down for a few seconds for a looser, sexier look. She remembered that trick from a magazine article she'd read long ago.

She couldn't decide last night, so two choices waited on the hook on her closet door. One was a black suit, smooth and classic, with a gray silk sweater. The school principal had once told her she looked nice in it. The other was a scarlet dress she had bought while shopping with Lorelei. "Lucy it looks great. Buy it, wear it, live a little," Lorelei had told her. But she never had. The neckline was too low, the ruffled hemline flirtatious. She had tried it on lots of times, imagining herself to be the kind of woman who wore scarlet and showed a hint of cleavage. But the tags still dangled from the sleeve.

Lucy wiggled her toes in her white slippers as she touched the sleeve of the dress, then let it fall. She zipped herself into the black skirt. The gray silk sweater was in her hand when she caught her reflection in the mirror. The principal was right, she thought. She looked nice. Fifty-one with no significant other was a direct result of nice.

It had to be the red dress. She took off her bra and switched to the one she had worn to the New Year's Eve party two years ago when she thought the new third grade teacher wasn't married. It was the kind that squeezed your breasts together. She had worn a woolen turtleneck to that party anyway, so married or not, he wouldn't have known. She pulled on the center of the bra to even out her cleavage. The folds of red chiffon fell around her, light and soft against her skin. She felt reckless, new.

She slipped her feet into the red sling-back heels she had bought last Sunday afternoon. At the mall she had told herself that everyone needs a pair of red shoes, just in case. She posed before the mirror. Despite her age, she looked nice. No, she looked good, she thought, like those young teachers that she usually frowned on as they strutted down the halls in their sexy shoes. She wondered if anyone at school would mention her attire. Then she remembered. She was the sister of the murdered. No one would say anything.

The day felt long. When the dismissal bell rang, Lucy felt her stomach tighten. She imagined Clarkson's face when he saw her. She ducked into the faculty ladies' room to touch up her hair and her lipstick. Carolyn Hirsch, the art teacher, touched her shoulder as she passed and asked if she had lost weight. Lucy smiled. She felt better than she had in months.

At the cemetery, she followed the paved path. The ground was spongy from last night's rain, but the sky was clear. She picked her way to the bench by Lorelei's grave, relieved to find it dry. She sat and smoothed her dress. It looked pretty, she thought, hitting her knee just so, the shoes a perfect match. She crossed her legs and arranged the ruffle of her skirt to show off the curve of her calf. Her legs were still good.

She looked up. "Oh, my God, Lorelei, I'm sorry."

For the first time ever, the sight of Lorelei's grave had failed to pierce her heart. No tears, not even a pang. Had she moved on? She looked hard at the tombstone, so familiar that she hardly needed to see it to know the shape of the etched letters. She told herself that she hadn't really moved on, and anyway, even if she had, Lorelei would understand. Lucy noticed a gangly weed emerging from the center of Lorelei's plot. She decided to pull it, to prove her devotion to her sister. She took a step toward the grave, but her sling-back heels sank into the wet grass. She picked her way back to the bench and lifted both feet to inspect her heels for damage. They were unscathed.

She heard a rustle behind her and her stomach lurched a little. Heat overtook her body. Two squirrels sprang from the thicket nearby. They chased each other with arching leaps across the green. Lucy felt the irritation rise in her chest. Where was Clarkson? She looked at her watch. He would come. Hadn't he been the one to say, "It's a date"?

A date. She remembered Summer's coolness when she'd mentioned her date. Summer had seemed okay by the time they parted, but still... What was Summer's problem? Meeting someone at your sister's gravesite wasn't illegal or even immoral. And what mysterious personal business was taking up so much of Summer's time lately? Summer probably wished that she had been the one to meet Clarkson, Lucy thought. She strained her eyes in all directions, hoping to catch sight of him as he strode toward her, in a hurry because he'd kept her waiting.

The silence of the graveyard weighed on her. For the first time, she felt lonely there. The realization unleashed a crushing sense of guilt. Lorelei was so alone in that quiet green expanse. Had she been lonely when she was alive, Lucy wondered? Had she ever met anyone special? Summer and Lorelei had been ridiculously inseparable. Even Dee used to tease them that they would end up old maids together if they weren't careful. Probably Lorelei would have met someone in her young life if it hadn't been for Summer hanging around all the time. Now it was too late. Lucy felt the crease deepen between her eyebrows, the one that only used to appear when she got cross. She massaged the crease with her index finger.

After a while, she stood up. She peered as far as she could up the hill where the path meandered in loops, gently parsing Glendale's dead. No Clarkson. She turned and searched as far as she could in all directions. Nothing.

"Lorelei, where is he?" Her voice seemed thin in the open air. She leaned forward to stand, but she remembered that her new red heels would sink into the grass. She sat back and crossed one leg over the other and removed her shoes. She brushed them off carefully and set them beside her.

Her feet felt strange in her pantyhose without shoes. She stared at her toes, stuck like little sausages in the tight nylon. They looked unbearably stupid. She tried to be inconspicuous as she reached under her dress and pulled at the waistband of her pantyhose. She leaned back on the bench and wriggled the waistband past her hips. She rolled down both nylon legs at the same time, looking up every few seconds to see if she were caught in the act. With both hands, she pinched the seams at her toes and yanked them from her feet, almost falling backwards off the bench. She caught herself by gripping the edge of the concrete bench. Her manicured nails scraped its rough underside. "Damn it," she said. She checked each nail carefully. No damage. She balled up the stretched-out beige mess and threw it into her purse. With a shudder, she picked her way across the chilly grass to Lorelei's plot and grasped the errant weed with both hands. She pulled with all her might. It emerged too easily from the soggy ground and she lost her balance. Righting herself, she retreated, and tossed the weed into the thicket. She plucked bits of grass from the hem of her dress and arranged herself once again on the bench.

She waited.

She imagined that his business had detained him, that at any minute now he would jog up the hill, breathless and apologetic. She would tell him that it was okay, that she hadn't really expected him anyway. As usual, she was just in the vicinity. They would laugh at her bare feet, flecked with grass and mud.

Dusk began to soften the edges of the silent army of headstones. The October air went from crisp to chilly. Her jacket was back in the car, because it hadn't matched her dress. She hugged her arms close, and rubbed her shoulders to stay warm. Her toes felt icy.

Lorelei's tombstone turned from pink to gray.

Lucy had known all along he wouldn't show, she lied to herself. She grabbed her shoes and trudged barefoot back along the cemetery path. She paused and looked behind her to the spot where the path widened. All quiet. She walked down the three steps at the pavement's end and out through the angel gates. Her car waited, solitary, in the parking lot.

Her hand shook as she unlocked the door. She climbed in and slammed the door behind her. Her tears were not for Lorelei, but for herself.

"Lorelei, I'm so sorry," she whispered. She straightened up, dabbed her eyes with a tissue and started the car. She saw no beauty in the streaks of indigo and magenta above the horizon.

When she got home, she turned on the fluorescent light over the bathroom mirror and stared at her face. Mascara caked in the folds under both eyes. Her runny nose had made her lipstick bleed into the feathery lines above her lips. Her hair was matted. How could she have believed that anyone was out there for her? She had missed that part of life. Forever.

She uttered his name, "Clarkson Dupree."

The muffled cocoon of grief she had inhabited for the last three months split apart. Lorelei was more distant than ever, and Clarkson had been nothing more than a figment of her imagination. Lucy felt naked, exposed.

"I hate you Clarkson Dupree," she screamed.

When Lucy's alarm sounded the next morning, she opened her eyes to the red dress that lay rumpled on her bedroom floor, bright and accusatory.

Chapter 12

Clarkson Dupree consulted his watch. He was certain that Lucy was already making her way to her sister's grave. That had been an amazing stroke of luck, finding Lorelei's grave in the first place, meeting her sister to top it off.

He opened the screen door, walked onto his front porch, and inhaled deeply. The air, fresh from last night's rain, smelled of pine and wildflowers. Clarkson ran his fingers along the smooth knotted post at the porch's front corner.

He liked the cabin. He had happened on it last week almost immediately after he had fled the constraints of Old Brighton for the Glendale countryside. It was far enough from town that he could stay invisible, but close enough so that he could drive by the Armstrong house whenever he felt like it. Just last night he had driven by it again, to take another look at the wonderful surprise of the oriel window that jutted from the southern face of the house. It was a magnificent window, a true homage to the mashrabiya one finds in the Middle East, those elevated containments that allow women to view the world and yet remain undetected, invisible. He wondered if Lorelei had sat there often, hidden with her secret, watching a world that did not know her at all.

Lorelei. He was so close to her here. He thought about her often, her openness, her desire to please. He remembered her quivering body at that last instant, the tear that traced her cheek as she closed her eyes. She had been beautiful in her surrender. What had transpired between them was so much more intimate than sex. Even being first was nothing compared with the enormity of what they had shared. More and more, he understood that Lorelei was his, completely.

Clarkson tried to picture Lucy as she sat and waited for him. He knew she would be patient and vigilant, but he couldn't quite remember her face. He thought about getting into his car to meet her, but he wasn't ready. The fragrant afternoon air transfixed him. He wondered if he had time for a stroll along the creek before the ten-mile drive into Glendale. Yesterday, he had walked as far as he could along the creek's edge without encountering a trace of human habitation. He had followed the watershed as it twisted through the woods until it disappeared under an angular pile of dull gray boulders. He had lingered there to listen to the soft trickle as the stream dropped from sight. He had imagined its muffled and invisible subterranean course.

The property pleased him. He thought he might buy it from the old man who had rented it to him, if events in Glendale progressed to his liking. He had already opened the negotiation process with Edward over the sale of Elite Construction. Clarkson knew Edward too well. The choked enthusiasm in Edward's voice was apparent, despite his attempts to conceal it. Clarkson would be in a very good position to choose his future, and he had made up his mind that his future was in Glendale. Now that he had actually returned, it surprised him at how easy and natural it felt. He would not leave again. And this time, things would be different.

He held onto the railing and looked out onto the vista of pines. The afternoon sun was beginning to pale in the soft October sky. He decided against a walk. The idea of Lucy waiting for him began to interest him. He tried to picture her again. He remembered her blonde hair, streaked, and her thin hands with long polished fingernails. She was older than Lorelei by a lot. That much he remembered. She had that same vulnerable air.

It amazed him, always, the weaknesses of those who were born into pampered lives. He had watched such families, complete with well-meaning parents who toiled at their jobs and returned home to wash dishes, tidy the house and kiss each other good night. He had seen their endless efforts to wrap their children in a protected world. To Clarkson, such well-intentioned pains rendered their children soft and vulnerable far into adulthood. Clarkson had discovered that few ever managed to shake the constraints of such civilized upbringings.

He thought of the way Lorelei had pointed out her childhood home to him as if it were a living part of her. Blood, family and tradition shackled those people to each other with gently crippling bonds. Only he knew those bonds for what they were. Only he understood that one's entrance to life was the result of the luck of the draw, nothing more, nothing less. He was free to understand what they could not, that life was an individual activity, not a team effort.

A herd of deer emerged from the woods and stopped to graze on the cleared patch in front of his porch. He watched as they fed and edged onward, lifting their heads at intervals. He turned away and went inside.

He opened the refrigerator and reached for the jar of water on the top shelf. As he filled his glass, he decided he would arrive at the cemetery as if he had emerged from a business meeting. That would impress Lucy. He understood her already, partly from her fragile and forlorn demeanor at her sister's grave, but mostly because she had grown up on the hill in Glendale in the stately house on the corner of Main and Sycamore.

He changed his shirt and pants and grabbed his gray sports jacket in case their encounter extended into dinner. As he was about to shut the door, he paused. He decided to wear the cufflinks, molded of eighteen karat gold, engraved with his initials. He had bought them with one of his first substantial profits twenty years ago. He walked back to the bedroom, where his calfskin shaving kit sat on top of the maple dresser. He opened the zippered side pouch, where he always kept his watch and his cufflinks when he traveled. The cufflinks weren't there.

He shrugged and headed out the door. He would find them, or he would have new ones made, he thought. But their absence irked him. He went back inside and looked around the floor. He opened the top drawer of the high chest in the corner where he kept his clothes. The drawer stuck as usual. He swore as he lifted it back onto its rickety track. He rummaged through his belongings. Nothing. It was unlike him to misplace anything. He prided himself on his ability to be spontaneous and yet always in control. He straightened the mess he had made with his clothes and shut the drawer.

He stood in the center of the room and thought. When had he last worn them? A sudden alarm possessed him. Could it have been that night, with the girl? But that was impossible. He had carefully accounted for the cufflinks after that night, he was sure. In his mind, he retraced his steps that night in the dim moonlight, his slow descent down the hill, the smell of Lorelei on his hands, the cufflinks heavy in his pocket. He remembered the long drive back to Connecticut, broken by a night under a soft comforter in a roadside hotel. He remembered removing the cufflinks from his pocket and zipping them inside the leather pouch before he washed his hands and face. He remembered his face in the hotel mirror, his eyes bright as they looked back at him. He could almost feel the excitement that had pulsed through his body in shudders and waves.

Where else could those cufflinks be? He emptied the contents of the shaving kit onto his bed. Not there. He replaced the items and zipped the kit, returning it to the dresser.

He walked to the living room and sat on the upholstered chair by the back wall, closest to the hearth. The cabin wasn't large, and his possessions were neatly contained. The missing cufflinks were inexcusable. Logic was the only way to resolve the problem. He walked to the kitchen and poured himself a vodka.

He sipped it. He thought about Lucy, by now certainly wondering about his whereabouts. He was sure she had already thought a lot about him. It brought him satisfaction to remember how effortlessly he'd conquered a woman so obviously in need of attention. He had looked at her with undivided gaze. He had spoken to her with a caring voice. He had orchestrated their chance meeting to be simultaneously intense and brief. He was aware that he had left her reeling. Even better, wanting.

She would wait, or she would return, that wasn't the problem. He would not leave the cabin until he had sorted out the problem. He did not lose, forget or misplace things. He took another sip of his vodka. He listened to the pre-dusk chatter of the birds outside. He rose to shut the windows over the screens as the autumn chill seeped into the cabin.

At length, with absolute confidence, he walked straight to the bedroom closet, reached his hand onto the top shelf and plucked the cufflinks from the ledge above his hanging shirts. He remembered, clearly, that he had removed them from the tan pinstripe after he had met with the landlord's son over the possibility of acquiring timber rights in the region. He had set them on the ledge when his cell phone rang. He had forgotten them in the long conversation that had ensued with Edward over their ongoing negotiations.

He looked at his watch again. He wasn't sure that he wanted to meet Lucy now, when he was hungry for dinner. He didn't want to make excuses, apologize for his lateness. The other evening, on his way to drive by the Armstrong house, he had noticed an attractive hunting lodge about halfway into town. He decided to treat himself to a relaxing dinner there. He threaded the cufflinks through the buttonholes at his wrists, pulled on his sports coat and headed for his car. His stomach reminded him that he was ravenous. He hoped that the menu had genuine country food, venison maybe, with juniper berry glaze, and earthy potatoes dug right out of the Glendale soil.

Chapter 13

Lucy adjusted the crystal vases flanking the mantle in her mother's front parlor. She stood back, hands on her hips. The mirror above the mantle doubled the bright sprays of yellow and rust chrysanthemums. Her reflected face surprised her with its irregularities, the pouches under her eyes, the slight droop in the skin alongside her mouth. Would she ever again believe she could look attractive? The last time she thought so she had been left waiting in her scarlet dress. Was that only weeks ago? It seemed to belong to another lifetime. She looked away. No time for that. The Owens could be arriving at any moment.

Lucy brushed a few stray yellow petals into her palm. She headed for the kitchen. Everything was ready. The baseboards gleamed, the furniture shone. Summer had offered to help as much as possible, but Lucy hadn't wanted help. The preparations were a timely diversion for her. A godsend, in fact. Anything to avoid thinking about Clarkson. As many times as she had tried to unravel what had happened, she still couldn't understand. That day at the cemetery he had been so gentle and solicitous, clearly drawn to her. She was the first to admit that she didn't know much about these things, but still she could feel it. Yet only a few days later, he had left her stranded in the chill of twilight at Lorelei's grave. Why?

She stepped on the pedal of the stainless steel wastebasket and brushed off the yellow slivers, then ran both hands under the faucet. The clock above the sink showed almost noon. High time to check on Dee. She wiped her hands on the towel and hurried upstairs.

"Mom, are you awake?" she called.

Dee opened her door on the second knock. Her outfit was tattered and mismatched. At least she had dressed.

"Mom, come downstairs and I'll make you lunch. I have the makings of your favorite, cream cheese and olives on wheat."

Dee didn't answer.

"The Owens should be here within the hour. You remember, right? Their names are Walter and Carla, and they'll be with us until Tuesday." Lucy straightened the quilt on Dee's bed and fluffed her pillows as she talked. "I'll stay with you the whole time, of course, so you won't have to worry about a thing. I'll have to teach on Monday and Tuesday, but we'll work it out. At least we have the weekend to get things settled." Lucy waited for Dee to respond, shrugged, and then continued. "They seemed very nice on the phone. Just married, although it's the second time around for both of them. They're on their honeymoon. They drove up to New England and now they just want to relax for a few days before they go home to their jobs in Pittsburgh. Enjoy the leaves, walk in the woods, you know." Dee stared out the window. "Where's your brush? Want me to fix your hair for you?"

"No, I'll do it." Dee frowned. "I'm not hungry."

"Okay." Lucy put a hand on her mother's shoulder. "If you need me, I'll be downstairs. I'll introduce you to the Owens later."

Lucy hurried downstairs and pulled up the window shades in the side hall and set her great-uncle's Audubon book on the coffee table in the parlor. Thank heaven it was Saturday. She'd had time to make everything perfect. The sound of tires on gravel set her heart thumping. She hurried to the side door.

"You must be Walter," she said as a man climbed out of the driver's side of a Volvo station wagon. He smiled at her and gave her a wave that was part salute, then turned to pull one large suitcase and a smaller tote from the back of the car. His showy wristwatch caught the sun. A woman emerged from the passenger side with a slouchy leather bag and a plastic litterbag filled with Starbucks empties.

"And Carla," Lucy said.

Carla fumbled with the litterbag, flung a length of brown hair over her shoulder and shook Lucy's hand.

"Hi," she said. "Any way to get rid of this?"

Lucy held the door open for Walter and relieved Carla of her accumulated trash.

"We're happy you had room for us," Walter said. "It's leaf season, and you know how these places fill up around here."

"It's our honeymoon," Carla added.

Hands full, Walter bent down and kissed Carla on the cheek.

"Congratulations to you both," Lucy said. "We're delighted to have you. It's a beautiful fall. The leaves are spectacular." She didn't mention that she had only just decided to open Dee's house as a lifeline from the sinking depression that had lately threatened to overwhelm her. Or that this year, the lush autumn colors irritated her. Especially, she didn't mention that she hoped that the Owens were the first step toward some semblance of sanity for her and Dee both, and maybe Summer, too.

"Let's settle your suitcases upstairs in your room first, and then I'll give you a tour of the house," Lucy said. She led them up the wide staircase.

"I love this old stained glass," Walter said. He paused on the landing. The sunlight through the leaded panes splotched the rug with rose, gold and cobalt. They continued up the second set of steps.

"Right here," Lucy said. She stopped at the end of the hall.

Walter set the bags down. Dee poked her head out of her bedroom and then emerged into the hallway. Her hair was uncombed. Her plaid woolen pants and yellow print blouse seemed too large for her. She ducked back into her bedroom.

"Another guest?" Walter asked.

"No. That's my mother." Lucy didn't look up as she showed Walter how to use the key in the old-fashioned lock.

After they had settled in, Lucy brought them tea and biscuits in the parlor.

"Do you have Splenda?" Carla asked, poking through the sugar cubes in the cut crystal bowl.

"I'm sorry. I'll pick up some before tomorrow," Lucy said.

"That's okay. It's really fine. I'm in the country, right? I'll walk it off," Carla said. She sat back, her lower lip in a pout.

Walter had heard of a lodge on the river that served what he called, "real country dinners." Lucy knew the place, and called for reservations for later that evening. By the time the Owens left for the restaurant, Lucy was drained. She wished she could talk to someone. Summer was the only one who understood any part of what she was going through these days. The prospect of eating alone, or worse, cajoling Dee to eat with her, was intolerable. Even though things were still awkward between them, maybe Summer would join her for dinner. If she didn't find someone to talk to soon, she feared she would lose her grip. How could that be? Nobody had a tighter grip on life than Lucy. What was happening to her?

She would see what she had in the refrigerator and call Summer.

Chapter 14

Summer threw the knotted pile of yarn into the basket and stood up. The sales lady at Knits and Knots had promised her that knitting reduced stress. She was mistaken. The basket fell off the sofa and rolled under the couch, long needles clattering.

Was it too early for a glass of wine? Summer arose, walked to the kitchen and opened the refrigerator. She grabbed the jug of pomegranate and acai juice. Rich in anti-oxidants, the label said. Just what she needed, Summer thought, bonus years to her already empty life. She put the jug back on the shelf.

Learning to knit had been a silly idea. The array of dyed yarns in the store window had reminded her of Lorelei and all her colors. When the saleswoman had spoken about the zen of weaving a bright world with two needles and a skein of yarn, Summer had fallen for it in spite of herself. It had all smacked of Lorelei. The truth was, Lorelei was gone, and Summer didn't know how to imagine the world as a colorful tangle.

She walked back to the living room, knelt and poked around under the couch. The needles rolled farther into the dust balls. "Shit," she cried, and her voice echoed in the quiet. What was she doing in Glendale, anyway? Anymore, nothing made sense. Until Lorelei's murder, the path to Glendale from her childhood town of Schodack in upstate New York had seemed providential. Now, it seemed merely improbable.

She sat cross legged on the floor. That bus trip from Schodack to San Francisco had been so long ago. How old had she been?

Eighteen, maybe. She remembered that she hadn't been afraid. It had been enough to own her body once again. The interloper baby that had swelled inside of her was newly, thankfully absent. That alone had sustained her through the bumpy bus miles, broken only by cheap meals and bathroom breaks across America. She could still envision the neon soap oozing from sticky dispensers, the way she'd held her breath against strange odors as she brushed her teeth in hair-flecked sinks, backpack wedged between her feet.

Summer dove under the couch again, and this time retrieved the errant needles, gathered up the yarn and basket, and plopped onto the couch, basket on her lap. How little she had thought about those early days in San Francisco. She had to hustle for work, move around a lot. And then, one night, at her job as a waitress at a health food café, she met a girl. "My name's Venus," the girl had said, leaning into her as Summer served her a squat pot of jasmine tea. "Arlene just wasn't working for me anymore."

Summer remembered carrying crates of clothes down the street as she moved into Venus' rundown house with its revolving cast of roommates, all female. Posters of mysterious deities with more breasts than fingers filled the walls. The bookshelves were crammed with stories about Sacagawea, female orgasms, the secrets of vaginas. Lively debates about goddess poetry, Gloria Steinem, genetic determinism kept them busy in the evening. One night someone brought up St. Paul's only biblical reference to a woman, the mysterious Apphia. Venus turned to Summer. "Someday we'll have a daughter and name her Apphia," she had said. Summer set the basket on the table next to her. That had been so long ago.

She had felt liberated at first, when she and Venus held hands and touched each other's hair in public. For the first time in her life, she had been happy. And then, she wasn't. Summer stood up and picked at a piece of yarn that had come unwrapped from the ball. Had she simply awakened one morning and yearned for a life that didn't broadcast her sexuality? No, it had happened slowly, she decided, breaking the bit of yarn in two. The endless drama of the women in the house had become wearisome—the spats, the crying, the cluttered shared bathroom. Summer had wanted to move out, hang pictures of landscapes, walk in the park with Venus without ensuring that strangers knew what they meant to each other. But for Venus, the quest for acceptance of their sexual orientation dwarfed everything.

Summer stuffed the basket, needles and all, into the hall closet. She headed for the kitchen. It had been so long since she thought of the evening when she'd bought the hinged silver locket for Venus' birthday. She'd first considered something with diamonds. They were too expensive, but even if they weren't, Venus had principles. She believed that diamonds were yet another symbol of a culture that had rejected them. At that precise moment, locket in hand, Summer realized that she was sick and tired of assigning significance to everything. That night, she packed a few belongings into a bag and left Venus a farewell note, the silver locket tucked inside.

Summer opened the cabinet and reached for a glass. The bottle of Shiraz on the counter wasn't her favorite, but it would have to do. She rummaged in the top drawer for the corkscrew as she recalled her long, slow journey back east from San Francisco. She hadn't been sure at the time what her final destination might be. She had supposed that she would end up back in her hometown of Schodack, if only because it was familiar. She would find out if it were as claustrophobic as it had seemed when she was a pregnant teenager.

It was funny now, to think that Glendale was supposed to be only a stopover on her long trip home. But her money and energy ran out right about then. She was stuck at least until she got herself flush again. The job she lucked into at the radio station was an easier way to make a living than waiting tables or clerking. And over time, she became accustomed to Glendale's rolling hills, its sense of history. Especially, she appreciated the peculiar arms-length welcome that the townspeople reserved for strangers.

And then, she met Lorelei. They fell in love, just the two of them, without anyone's sanction or rejection. They were happy. They should have stayed that way. Summer looked around the kitchen, quiet and empty. Why had Lorelei decided that public recognition was so important to her? Had she been wrong to explain to Lorelei that public exposure wasn't always worth the price? She hadn't thought so at the time. She'd only wanted to be free to live her life, in love with a person, not a cause. Was that too much to ask? Apparently it was. Summer ran the foil cutter around the edge of the bottle. It wasn't too early for that glass of wine.

The phone rang.

Chapter 15

Lucy was relieved that Summer answered on the first ring. "I know it's short notice, but I could use the company. Any chance you want to run over here for dinner? I have everything. Nothing fancy." She looked to the counter where she had piled a pack of organic chicken breasts, a bag of green beans that could pass for fresh, some romaine lettuce, a few potatoes, a head of garlic, and a bunch of limp basil from Mike's Market. Lucy's palm was moist on the telephone receiver.

"Aren't the Owens there?"

"They went to the Huntsman's Inn for dinner. It's me and Dee." She tried not to sound too desperate.

"I'll pick up bread, grab a bottle of wine and see you in half an hour," Summer said. Lucy barely had time to chop the romaine lettuce into bits and sliver some garlic for the chicken marinade before she heard Summer pull into the side driveway. She met her at the door and took the bottle of wine from her arms.

"Thanks for coming," Lucy said.

"You have no idea how much I needed to get out." They were silent for a moment. "So, how are the Owens?" Summer asked. She set the loaf of bread onto the cutting board that Lucy handed her.

"Casual, maybe. I don't know, okay. Younger than I expected. Chicken okay?"

Summer nodded, her fingers tracing the frame of a painting of inflated asparagus and elongated beets that hung by the refrigerator. Her hand rested right below Lorelei's curly signature.

Lucy turned the chicken breasts in the glass dish. The olive oil glistened, flecked with basil. The kitchen was warm and fragrant.

"When they said they were celebrating their second marriage, I pictured an older couple. They can't be more than early forties," Lucy said. She transferred the chicken into the already sizzling skillet on the stove.

"Early forties is old enough for a lot of missteps." Summer and Lucy looked at each other for a moment. "I guess you haven't heard from your friend yet. Clarkson."

Lucy adjusted the burner and pushed her hair away from her face. The pale flesh of the chicken whitened, then browned. Steam poured from the tilted lid of a saucepan. She shook her head. "I don't think he's my friend." Olive oil spattered.

Summer drew her hands to her side. "Hey, let's bring Dee downstairs. It would be good for her," she said.

"It would. She hasn't even met the Owens. At least not formally." Lucy was happy to change the subject.

Together, they half-coaxed, half-pulled Dee from her bedroom. Summer commented on the lovely shade of Dee's white hair, so much more beautiful than the usual dirty gray, and infinitely more becoming on older women. Dee patted her unruly nest of hair. Lucy led the way while Summer held Dee's elbow.

"I've missed you, Dee," Summer said.

They settled Dee into her chair in the dining room. Summer dimmed the chandelier and Lucy picked up Dee's plate. "Chicken, Mom?" She didn't wait for an answer. "I wish the potatoes and beans were as good as the ones from Mrs. Haverton's son. He has that lovely garden every year. But it's a little late for that now." She plopped a chicken breast onto Dee's plate. Dee reached for the plate, tilted it, and the chicken slid across the table. A snail trail of grease streaked the tablecloth.

Lucy stabbed the chicken with a fork and returned it to Dee's plate. "It's all right, mother, these things happen," Lucy said.

"Everything happens," Dee said.

"The weekend weather is supposed to be wonderful," Summer said.

"Maybe the Owens should rent a canoe. Remember, mother, how we used to do that? You would pack us ham salad sandwiches and iced tea."

"I did," Dee said. Lucy couldn't tell if it was a question or a statement.

At the end of the meal, Dee rose. "I'm very tired."

"Of course you are," Lucy said.

The rope of bells on the front doorknob jingled and Carla burst around the corner. Backlit by the bright prism chandelier, Carla's features were invisible. She looked small, thin, with a halo of dark hair.

"Lorelei," Dee whispered. She hurried toward her and pointed a bony finger at Carla's face. "God in heaven, I can't believe it's you."

"I'm Carla."

Carla backed away, slowly, her arms folded across her chest.

Dee edged toward her, arms outstretched. "Please don't go away again," she begged.

"Stop it, whoever you think I am..." Carla felt behind her for the wall.

Lucy touched Dee's shoulder. "Mom—"

"Shh. It's Lorelei, honey," Dee said, her voice quiet.

"Please stop. I'm Carla." Carla looked from side to side. "Walter?" she called.

"She thinks you're someone else," Lucy said. "She's not Lorelei, Mom."

Dee's hands fell to her side. "No," she said. She began to cry. Her nose dripped. She dragged her sleeve across her face. Splotches of moisture darkened the worn yellow silk. Walter's footsteps echoed from the entryway. He reached them and halted. Carla looked at him, wild-eyed.

"Lorelei's gone," Dee said, turning to Walter. She addressed him as if he were the only person in the room, as if they were old friends. "Dead. Murdered, you know. Strangled and left in her hammock."

"I'm very sorry," Walter said. He took Carla's arm. They spoke in hushed voices on their way upstairs.

Summer insisted on helping Lucy with the dishes after they settled Dee into her bed, their silence broken only by the sound of the water running, the refrigerator door opening and closing. When they were through, Summer touched Lucy's shoulder and left.

Lucy lay awake in her room, unable to sleep. She heard the creak of floorboards and threw on her robe to find Dee wandering through the hall in her nightdress, toes sticking through the holes in her gold slippers. Dee didn't resist as Lucy guided her back to bed.

"Mom, I'll just sit here a minute, okay?" She tucked Dee into bed. From the green velvet chair in the corner, Lucy watched until Dee fell asleep.

In the morning, Lucy heard the flurry of activity from the Owens' guestroom. She didn't need to be told they were packing up their belongings. Walter appeared in the kitchen as Lucy was about to grind beans for coffee.

"We can't stay here, after all," he said.

"I know," Lucy answered.

By the time she brought them breakfast, Lucy had found space for them in a bed and breakfast near the river, run by long-time friends of the family.

"They're expecting you. As luck would have it, they had a cancellation."

"Thank you," Walter said. Lucy handed him the slip of paper with the address and phone number, written in her best school-teacher script.

"I'm sorry," Lucy said. She set a tray of muffins and coffee in front of them, the lavish country spread she had planned no longer appropriate.

"It's our honeymoon," Carla said. Her lower lip protruded and she tossed her hair over her shoulders.

Lucy watched from the window as they loaded their Volvo and drove up Main Street. As she walked through the front parlor, she avoided her reflection in the long mirror.

Chapter 16

Clarkson took the sharp turn by the hospital and descended into Glendale. He was glad to be back, finished more or less with the sale of Elite Construction to Edward. Edward had offered to conduct the whole affair long distance, but Clarkson was aware that it was in his best interests to oversee the final details in person.

He hadn't expected the sendoff party in the office, people he had passed every day for years without expectation or camaraderie, laughing, mingling, sharing trays of halved red-skinned potatoes with crème fraiche and bacon, gorgonzola and figs drizzled with ruby port, panko coated squash blossoms, blood-red slices of filet mignon rolled and skewered with silver picks. The party filled every corner of the place, extending into his office, where the caterer had set up a martini bar in front of the window where he and Jeanette used to have sex. Even the security guard stationed by the elevator bank dropped by with a farewell card.

It all seemed strange. He hadn't had a real conversation with any of them over the course of his many years as head of Elite Construction, including Jeanette, who drank way too many martinis and eventually pulled him by the sleeve into his old office after everyone had left. Edward had been waiting for her, but she sent him away under the pretext that her husband was on his way to pick her up. Edward had seemed a little miffed, muttering to himself with the shiny brass plaque engraved with Edward Kingsley Construction tucked under his arm.

After Edward finally disappeared, Jeanette cried a little, pressed herself against Clarkson and unbuttoned his shirt. He reciprocated with the unbuttoning, hiked up her skirt and leaned her face down over the window ledge behind the martini bar in the half-light from the gas lamps that arched over the concrete span beyond. Her body was soft and full, her legs smooth, her ass voluptuous. He had forgotten how vocal she was. She screamed and moaned in utter surrender as he clutched her hips and entered her from behind. It was a fitting end to all, especially since he wouldn't be around the next day to entertain Jeanette's sobbing regret that he knew would ensue.

While Jeanette sniffled and arranged herself, he looked around his office one last time. There were farewell cards piled on his desk. He opened a few, stuffed the whole mess into a folder and presented it to Jeanette to hold for him until he sent for his things, knowing of course that he never would. He didn't want such mementos and didn't relish the bother of throwing them away. She would be thrilled to guard the meaningless stash, believing he had chosen her to maintain vigil over his memory as life shifted in new directions. That was the sort of drama that fed her, and he didn't begrudge her that. He left her seated on the window ledge, clutching the folder beneath her bosom, half-buttoned into a skewed mass of silk with misaligned edges.

All in all, he was happy to escape into his car parked for the last time in the reserved space in the underground garage. Without regret, he departed the garage and left behind the sleek commercial district, the civilized invention of Old Brighton. It was a smooth, peaceful exit in the dark of night onto the freeway that would reconnect him once and for all with his past.

After he made the turn by the hospital, he opened his car's moon roof and let the Glendale night envelop his body. The chill invigorated him, and the crispness of the air tingled his nostrils. The scent of pine and wood smoke and whatever constituted that intangible wildness in the Glendale air intoxicated him. He was home. Instead of taking the route toward the cabin, he decided he would drive by the girl's house. Tonight the moon was almost full and he knew that the steep pitch of the slate roof would shine just a little, that the rings of fish scale shingles around the turret would appear raised and shadowed in precise rows. He followed Main Street to the end where it met Sycamore, and slowed his car. No traffic shared the street with him.

There it stood, unlit. The house was majestic as always, no hint of apology, no servant to tradition with its unpredictable, meandering silhouette. Unlike so many things in life, it dared to be original. From its very first brick, it had been built to dominate the ground beneath it, where Sycamore curved around to Glendale's outer reaches and Jefferson cut upwards to the terraced streets on the hill. That house was Glendale's sentry, its guardian, its soul. He pulled over to the curb across the street and drank in every glorious detail.

Chapter 17

"This must be the worst Halloween ever. Don't you think so, Miss Armstrong? I mean, Lucy. I know you told me to call you Lucy." The window at the end of the empty elementary school hallway framed the bent sycamore tops. A few crinkled leaves battled the wind. The country kids were loaded into school buses. The last students had dispersed onto the wide town sidewalks. Purplish clouds thickened the sky.

"Quite possibly," Lucy said. She wasn't in the mood for chit-chat. Either her new student teacher hadn't understood her mood this year, or she was relentlessly cheerful. Lucy guessed it was the latter.

"Any plans?" Casey asked. Her lively brown eyes lined with her customary teal eye pencil made Lucy weary.

"Plans for what?" Lucy asked, her voice sharp even to her own ears.

"It's Halloween. It's Friday. People do things." Casey raised both arms to the ceiling and looked at Lucy before continuing. "Bryan and I are going to a costume party. I'm always a witch, but this is a princess year for me. I asked Bryan to go as a prince so we can practice for our wedding, but he'd rather be a Ninja. So, no plans?"

"Not really. I need to grade the Language Arts tests." Lucy's voice trailed off. "Look, Casey, I'll see you Monday." Lucy pivoted and headed down the hall in the opposite direction.

"Where are you going?" Casey called.

"I forgot something back in the classroom. Go on without me."

"Okay, Miss Armstrong, I mean, Lucy. Happy Halloween."

Lucy waited until Casey had disappeared down the flight of steps. As irritating as she was, Casey was right. It was Halloween and Friday, and people really did 'do things.' Except for Lucy. She leaned against the painted brick wall of the old school hallway. She didn't care if Casey knew she hadn't forgotten anything back in the classroom. Another word about Casey's princess year might send her completely off the deep end.

Lucy wished that it weren't Halloween at all, and that she didn't have to go home to Dee's huge, echoing house. Since the Owens' visit, she had been afraid to leave Dee alone. She hadn't had any choice but to continue to stay with her. Lately, in the middle of the night she had awakened in her childhood bedroom, her heart pounding, her body in a sweat. Fifty-one years old, and her life was almost the same as it had been when she was twelve, or fifteen, or twenty. She would sit up and try to quiet the beating of her heart. And she would remember things.

Like the time in sixth grade, when Jim Cooper had written her a love letter. She had crinkled it into a ball and thrown it away, insulted by his unworthy pale eyes and freckled skin. It had shocked her, years later, when he couldn't remember her name to sign her high school yearbook. She had seen Jim and his wife Darlene a few months ago. They were taking a pair of freckled, light-eyed grandsons for ice cream.

She remembered how everyone in health class had snickered and passed notes during Miss Kingsley's stilted sex lecture, as if the whole thing were an inside joke. No one had passed a note to her. No one had grabbed her arm afterwards on the way to the cafeteria.

Mostly, she remembered Lorelei, planted in Dee's family garden up the hill from the angel-wing gates. She could scarcely visualize Lorelei's upturned nose, her fair skin, or her head thrown back in laughter. In the stillness of those nights, all she saw was Lorelei's pinkish stone, rising from the hush of the cemetery. She would lie awake and think of Lorelei, underground in a world gone mute. The same fate that awaited her.

On the worst of these nights, she would sit up in bed until the blackness lifted, until the interlocking green stems of the daisy wallpaper became visible. She felt better then, in the light, and would manage at last to huddle under her top sheet and surrender her exhausted body to sleep. And then her alarm would shriek. At school, no one commented on her drawn appearance.

Lucy wished she had someone to talk to, but the other teachers at school were caught up in their own comfortable worlds. Summer was the only possibility. Clanging from the end of the hallway startled her. William, the school janitor, pulled his metal bucket and mop contraption slowly toward her. Lucy straightened up and walked down the hall. She wondered if she should call Summer again.

The last few times she had tried to talk to Summer, things were awkward. Neither brought up the debacle of the Owens visit, other than to agree that Dee was not up for houseguests. Summer and Lucy behaved as though each feared the other would break. Lucy had mentioned her disastrous non-date with Clarkson, how she had waited for him until twilight fell, but she hadn't confessed how her body longed for the touch of a man before she was too old. Maybe she had made lighter of it than it was, but Summer had readily allowed the conversation to drop. Once, last week, Summer had stopped in to check on Dee. As she was leaving, she mentioned to Lucy that she was drowning in personal problems. "Shit beyond measure," she'd told her. Lucy hadn't pressed her.

"Are you all right? Better get home for the trick-or-treaters, Miss Armstrong." William paused as he dragged his bucket past her in the empty hallway. She smelled the acrid vinegar and germicidal solution that sloshed in the brownish water. "If any kids even go out in this weather. But you know kids, they don't care."

"No, I suppose not. Good night, William."

The wind pounded the door as Lucy exited the school building and she had to fight to close it. Leaves and sticks skidded around her feet. She looked up at the childish drawings of jack-o-lanterns and ghosts in the classroom windows. Her own class had read poems about dark nights, the smell of chocolate, candy apples. Life felt so promising for a child. Life felt promising for Casey, Lucy thought. Lucy wished Casey would finish her enthusiastic student teaching elsewhere. She wished she would gush about her upcoming wedding, and should she buy strapless like every other bride these days or go with three quarter length sleeves, to someone else. Or at least quit calling her Miss Armstrong. She hurried to her car, jumping as thunder cracked and growled.

Miss Armstrong. Why did everyone have to call her that? Lucy pulled into the parking lot at Mike's Market. It was a label, a banner that meant she never loved anyone and no one had ever loved her. She didn't even have a life. She skated on the surface of one, perfectly groomed and poised to jump in when the moment seemed right. Only so far, it never had. The one time she thought it might, she had been left to sit, humiliated, by her sister's grave.

She ducked her head as the rain began to fall in big, heavy drops that splatted as they hit the pavement. She ran into the store and headed directly to the candy aisle. Without deliberation, she threw a few bags of chocolate bars into her cart. Pumpkins lined the floor alongside the candy shelves. She could at least buy a pumpkin, she thought, and picked up the nearest one. On the way back to her car, the wind whipped her hair. She fought the urge to protect it from the now pelting rain. Maybe if she quit acting like prissy Miss Armstrong, her life would change.

She started to drive to Dee's house. On an impulse, she veered up the hill and headed for her own home. Before she could change her mind, she left her car running and braved the rain. She skipped steps on her way to the door. Once inside, she pushed her closet door open, and grabbed the scarlet dress, hanging in the very back. Almost as an afterthought, she rooted through the carefully stacked shoeboxes until she found the one with the red heels inside. She doubled the dress over her arm so it wouldn't drag on the ground and threw it into the back seat of her car. The shoebox opened as it hit the floor of the back seat. She didn't bother to check her mailbox.

Back at Dee's house, she called to her mother. The creak of the floorboards told her that Dee was where she always was, upstairs somewhere, padding about in her holey slippers. Lucy filled a crystal bowl with candy and set it in the front window. She set the uncarved pumpkin beside it, and a candle in a bronze-footed stand. The rain that pelted the front of the house blurred her view of the street. Everything outside seemed deserted.

Mounting the stairs to her childhood bedroom, she held the dress against her chest. Ralph Lauren's Romance wafted from the soft scarlet folds. More than anything else, that fragrance weakened her. Tears gathered in her eyes. She didn't want to cry.

She wouldn't cry. She threw off her jacket and sopping shoes, her rain-spotted skirt, her wool sweater. She removed her demure schoolteacher underwear and stood naked in front of her dresser. The only thong that she owned was at the bottom of her drawer, wrapped in white tissue paper. She unwrapped it and slipped it on, the black lace surprisingly soft. She dug for the bra that she had now worn twice, the one that accentuated her curves, hooked it and adjusted her breasts against the satin. Bare-legged, she eased the dress over her head and reached around to zip it. The red shoes had been untouched since that day. She flexed her toes and then slid her feet into them. She scrunched her hair a bit and put on red lipstick and a little eyeliner. She dispensed with her usual layers of serum and creams. What did it matter? No one would see her anyway. It was Halloween. She could be whatever she wanted to be.

She emerged from her room to find Dee standing in the hallway.

"Mom, it's Halloween," Lucy said to Dee. For once, she didn't ask Dee if she were hungry or thirsty, or if she could comb her hair. Lucy headed downstairs. Dee followed her. Lucy poured them each a glass of claret and motioned for Dee to sit in the front parlor. She lit the candle. Its reflection danced in the rivers of rain that cascaded down the tall windows.

Lucy didn't speak as they sat. She didn't feel like expending every ounce of her energy to extract a response from Dee's grizzled body and soul. It was Halloween. She would do as she pleased tonight. Where no one else could see her.

Dee sipped her wine and stared at Lucy.

"You look beautiful," Dee said, after a while.

As Lucy turned her head toward her mother, the doorbell rang.

"It's probably trick-or-treaters," Lucy said, rattled by Dee's uncharacteristic compliment. She picked up the crystal bowl and opened the door. The wind swooped up her skirt. With her free hand she tried to hold the ruffled edge down, but to no avail. In the driving rain, a tall man stood. In one hand, he held a black umbrella that threatened to upend itself. In the other, a bouquet of blood-red roses.

"Happy Halloween, Lucy," he said. "I hope I'm not interrupting anything."

She stared at the man as if he were an apparition. A growl of thunder eclipsed the gasp that Lucy was unable to stifle. She gulped and hoped that her voice would emerge from her body.

Chapter 18

The pale pink note lay unfolded on Summer's lap as she sat at the end of her leather couch. The untouched bowl of candy rested on the table next to her, full of Twizzlers, Jolly Ranchers and Peanut Butter Cups. Rain and wind made scratching sounds at her door. Was that a knock she heard? She folded the letter in half at the crease, set it on the couch next to her, and picked up the bowl of candy. She opened the door. Her porch was empty. Water and wind gusted inside, dotting the carpet with dark spots. She closed the door, set the bowl back on the table and sat down again. She picked up the letter, unfolded it without glancing at it, and let it drop into her lap. She looked at the cordless phone that lay mute on the couch. For once, she wished that someone would call her. Anyone. Anyone but Megan.

That delicate stationery and the feminine script had terrified her from the moment she caught sight of it in her mail box today, slid innocently between her electric bill and the dry cleaner's half-price coupon. Her first inclination had been to throw it away, but she hadn't. If I were to dress for Halloween, I'd be a witch, she thought. An evil, heartless witch.

Megan's arrival was only days away, according to the letter. Summer imagined their meeting. She saw herself answering an insistent knock, opening the door to face a young woman. No matter how hard she tried, she couldn't fill in the details of the young woman's face, or decide whether she was short or tall, fat or thin. Summer imagined sending the woman away, and watching as the woman turned and retreated into the distance. Even as she pictured the blurred back of the retreating girl, she knew it was wrong. Summer replayed the fantasy. This time, she tried to envision the girl's face, the face of her daughter. Still, no success. Was it odd, she wondered, that she had never tried to conjure up what sort of life her child was living, or at least what her face looked like. Or even her name. It was, she thought. But she didn't care.

The truth was, throughout the twenty-some years since she had given birth, her child had remained utterly without an identity. In fact, each passing year had added a little more distance, making the child's very existence a little less real, more on the order of a recurring but well-repressed nightmare than a slice of actual history until out of nowhere, Megan's girlish script had arrived on scented stationery. Megan slid into reality, a clean and bloodless birth, on pale pink paper.

Summer remembered her pregnancy, so many years before, neither clean nor bloodless. It had usurped her body, severed her ties to her parents, altered her standing with her friends. Summer had survived by counting the days until she was free of her burden. The actual birth had been painful and messy. Summer remembered the sound of her own cries, the earthy smell of her insides suddenly exposed. The child seemed incidental, its arrival significant only as the conclusion of her ordeal. The child had survived because Summer hadn't figured out how to wish it away. She still hadn't.

Summer wondered what Lorelei would think of her now. She ran her fingers through her straight black hair. That is, what Lorelei would think if some faceless monster hadn't drained the life from her body.

Summer's stomach felt queasy. She stood up. The leather couch held her imprint in a soft depression. She stared at it. One depression, one spot worn into the couch. Again, the scratching at the door became insistent. This time, surely, they were the sounds of children, someone's legitimate, cheerful children out to trick-or-treat on a miserable night. Summer opened the door again. Rain poured in. The newspaper on the coffee table fluttered across the room. The doorway framed only blackness. Summer shut the door.

Without further deliberation, she grabbed her jacket and keys. She stopped and picked up Megan's letter that had dropped to the couch, folded it and tucked it into her purse, ran down the cement steps to the sidewalk, through the torrents of water, and slopped through puddles and rushing rivulets to the driver's side. She hopped in, slammed the door and inserted her key into the ignition before she knew where she was going. It was Friday night, Halloween. At the radio station today, her coworkers had invited her to go out with them, first to Pamela's Restaurant on Main Street, and afterwards to the pub. In the light of day, she hadn't given the invitation a moment's consideration. She could join them now, she thought.

She eased her car down the hill, windshield wipers losing against the downpour. From the flatness of Main Street's center, she could see the warm glow of the restaurant's front window. She could barely make out the lit pumpkin that shone under the lace valance. Summer slowed her car, but the ache in her chest told her that joining her coworkers wouldn't help her, might in fact make her feel worse. She passed by without turning into one of the angled spaces.

Lucy would be at Dee's house, she thought. She followed Main Street to the Sycamore fork. Lucy never went anywhere else, Summer was sure of it. As odd as Lucy was, they understood each other in their unspoken, tentative way. Both of them had become rudderless. Time heals all, Summer had heard. At Lorelei's funeral, a lot of people had said that, to her and to Dee and Lucy. From what she could see, time hadn't healed any of them. Summer knew that time had become her enemy, thick and sluggish, squeezing fresh pain from every long, slow day. If she could bring herself to really talk to Lucy for once, Summer suspected that she would say the same. She couldn't even imagine what Dee would say.

As she pulled into the driveway, Summer decided to show Lucy the letter tonight. Megan wouldn't be a secret much longer, anyway. A newly vicious wave of rain pounded the roof of her Volkswagen. She waited in her car by the side door of Dee's house. In the past, that door had always been open. In Glendale, no one locked their doors unless they were away on vacation. Had that changed for Dee?

When Lorelei was alive, the two of them would burst in together. They would follow the long hallway to the arch that opened into the kitchen. Dee would pop from the kitchen, damp towel over her shoulder, to greet them with kisses. Summer remembered Dee's crinkly-eyed smile, the papery feel of her cheek as she tilted her face. The few times Summer had been to Dee's house since the murder, she had gone around to the front and knocked. Like a stranger. Dee had long since abandoned her kitchen. She didn't dole out kisses anymore.

Summer listened to the rain. When the rain let up, she decided, she would take a chance that Dee's house was unlocked, still vulnerable to the outside world. She would walk right in, through the side door, the way she used to with Lorelei. It was Halloween, a night of ghosts. Maybe Lorelei ghosted around somewhere nearby, and her invisible presence would burst into the old Armstrong estate with her. And Dee would emerge from her kitchen to greet them and offer her powdered cheek. These are crazy thoughts, I'm having, she thought. I'm thinking like Lorelei.

A softer cadence of storm played across the car's roof.

"Let's go, Lorelei," Summer said. She leapt out, slammed the driver's door behind and raced to the side door of Dee's house.

The curved brass handle turned easily.

Chapter 19

"Clarkson."

The crystal bowl of candy in Lucy's right hand drooped as her wrist went slack. Clarkson dropped his umbrella and put his hand under the bowl. In a fluid motion, he kicked his umbrella to the side of the porch and traded Lucy the bouquet of roses for the bowl. Lucy felt the brush of his hand and then the sudden lightness of the bouquet in her arms. She stood in the doorway, a rain-spotted, aged beauty queen with her swirling chiffon dress and spray of flowers. Clarkson hunched his shoulders in his trench coat and held the crystal bowl with both hands. The rain and wind whipped around them.

"Well?" Clarkson asked.

"Yes, of course, come inside," Lucy said.

She took a step backward. With one hand, Clarkson pulled the door closed after him. Sudden silence wrapped them both. They faced each other. Clarkson's green eyes sent heat through her body.

"This way," she said. She turned and walked down the tiled hallway. Clarkson followed, still holding the bowl of candy.

Lucy led them to the front parlor, where Dee sat with her glass of claret. Dee looked up. Clarkson set the bowl of candy on the table nearest her.

"Who might this lovely lady be?" he asked. He directed his gaze at Dee, who continued to stare at him. She didn't answer.

"Mom, this is Clarkson," Lucy said, deliberately addressing her mother first. "Clarkson, uh..." Lucy pretended to have forgotten his last name.

"Dupree," Clarkson said.

Dee sipped her wine. Her gray eyes locked on Clarkson.

"This is my mother. Dee," Lucy said. She steeled herself when she looked at him this time. She tried to remember, had she refilled her wine once already? Twice? However many times she had, she wished now that she hadn't. There was a rushing sound in her ears. Heat rose from her neck and chest.

"Delighted to meet you," Clarkson said. He bowed ever so slightly to Dee.

Dee nodded. She lifted her glass a smidgeon.

"Please, sit down," Lucy heard herself say in a strained voice.

"I wouldn't dream of it. This elegant upholstery... " Clarkson gestured first toward the sofa and then to the droplets of water still running from his coat.

"Oh, let me take that," Lucy said. She set the flowers on an end table.

Clarkson slid his long arms out of the sleeves, folded the coat neatly over his arm and handed it to Lucy. Again, she felt the slight brush of his hand. She turned her head from him and took a deep breath.

"I'll go hang this," she said. The roses sat on the table, cradled in rain-spotted silver tissue paper. "These are beautiful. I'll put them in water in a minute."

Alone in the hallway, she willed herself to calm down. His smell was on his coat, masculine and unfamiliar. It made her a little dizzy. She hung his coat next to hers. She walked to the kitchen and pulled a cloisonné vase from a corner cabinet, filled it with water and started to walk back to the parlor.

She wanted to duck into the powder room off the kitchen to check her face. Her lips felt dry, as if her lipstick had worn off. She worried that her mascara had flaked. For some reason the idea of occupying the powder room with him so near embarrassed her. She licked her lips, squared her shoulders and walked back into the front parlor with the water-filled vase.

Clarkson was already sitting.

"So your family has owned this house for that long?" he asked Dee. He had a glass of claret in one hand, and gestured with the other. Dee watched him, a half-smile on her lips. Lucy untied the ribbon on the wilted tissue and set the flowers in the vase. She wasn't sure what to do with them, so she stuck them in the front window next to the pumpkin. She picked up the bowl of candy from the end table and set it back in the front window on the other side of the pumpkin. The candle flame leaned sideways.

"I was telling your mother how lovely this house is. Quite the family legacy," Clarkson said.

He had sat on one end of the sofa. Dee was in the chair nearest him, flanking the window. Lucy wasn't sure whether to sit in the far chair, with befuddled Dee between her and Clarkson, or at the other end of the sofa. She stood awkwardly. If I were Lorelei, I would just sit somewhere, anywhere and not worry about it, she thought. She hovered uncertainly.

"The architecture is wonderful, so many details," Clarkson said.

"Thank you," Lucy said. "The house has been in our family since 1890, when it was built, as mother must have told you." She wondered if Dee had managed to tell him anything. She shifted her weight. The red heel of her left shoe wobbled slightly. She really ought to make a decision about where to sit.

Clarkson rose and swept his arm toward the sofa. Gratefully, Lucy followed his gesture. She settled herself on its far end. Clarkson handed her the glass of wine that she had abandoned.

"There's no need to wait on me," he said. "Dee has already seen to my wine."

Lucy was sure that Dee had done nothing of the sort. She could scarcely get herself a glass of water. Lucy opened her eyes wide. Clarkson winked at her and lifted his glass.

"Cheers," he said. "Happy Halloween."

"Yes, Happy Halloween."

Dee watched them silently. Lucy took a sip of her wine and then set it down. Her head was fuzzy. She folded her hands on her lap. Then, worried that she appeared too prim, she let them fall to the sofa. After a moment, she drew them in and fingered the chiffon folds of her dress.

"I didn't mean to intrude. Perhaps you were going some-where..." Clarkson leaned toward her. His brow furrowed. He seemed apologetic.

"No," Lucy answered. She thought of more words to say, but they stuck in her throat.

"Then perhaps I'll stay just a minute?" It seemed only part question as he leaned back into the sofa.

"Yes, by all means," Lucy said.

Lucy focused on Clarkson's feet, large and clad in expensive black loafers. She had imagined this scene so many times. She and Clarkson, in her own house, even in this house, together. But she had usually pictured him in his jogging clothes. Or, lying alone in the dark, she had imagined him intangibly naked, like the men in the romance novels she occasionally read, an ambig-uous mass of warmth, protrusion and pressure. It occurred to her that she couldn't fill in that image with the appropriate de-tails anyway. She worried that Clarkson might be able to read her thoughts. She cleared her throat.

"Are you coming down with something, dear. You look a little flushed," Dee said.

Lucy glared at Dee. Of all times to remember how to speak, she thought.

"I'm fine, mother," Lucy said. "Thank you for asking."

Clarkson adjusted his position. He looked from Dee to Lucy.

"Terrible out there tonight," Lucy said, and then immedi-ately wondered if it would have been possible to volunteer a more vacuous comment. She hadn't a clue how to engage in conversation with this man, with any man. Her mother, now perched on the edge of her seat, irked her. Lucy didn't want any witnesses to her incompetence, even the shell of a human that was her mother.

A door slammed and they all jumped. A flurry of footsteps followed. Wet and breathless, Summer rounded the archway from the hall.

"Lucy? Dee?" Summer called. "I'm sorry I should have knocked. I forgot to even call first."

"I guess there's a lot of that going around tonight," Clarkson said, on his feet at once.

Summer halted. Her eyes widened.

"Summer, this is Clarkson, Clarkson Dupree," Lucy said. She paused before she said Dupree, as if she weren't quite sure she had it right. She hoped that Summer wouldn't give her away.

"Oh. I'm Summer." Summer dropped her hand to her side. She held a thin pink note in her hand.

Clarkson became animated. "Summer," he repeated. "A beautiful name."

Lucy looked at Summer. Even wet and disheveled, Summer was pretty, almost beautiful. She had that nicely chiseled jaw-line that eluded Lucy these days despite the neck exercises. And Summer was tall, thin, long-legged with dark shiny hair that never seemed to frizz. Lucy watched Clarkson. She already imagined him showing up at Summer's door tomorrow with a bouquet of flowers. Would they be red roses, too, she wondered. She felt an intense need to escape the room.

"I'll get us a snack," Lucy said. "Summer, have a seat."

"Let me help."

"No, please, sit." Lucy wanted to be alone, catch her breath.

Summer kissed Dee on the cheek and then sat down.

"I'll help you," Clarkson said to Lucy. He followed her down the hall and into the kitchen. Summer's raincoat, draped over a kitchen chair, slipped until one wet sleeve grazed the floor. Lucy started to pick it up at the same time that Clarkson reached for it. His hand closed over hers. She swallowed hard and trained her eyes on the coat.

Clarkson's hand tightened over hers. "Lucy, you look beautiful tonight," he said.

Lucy looked up. He was staring down at her. She didn't mean to, but she looked directly into his eyes. They went right through her. No man had looked at her that way. Ever. She imagined throwing herself into his arms, pressing her breasts against his chest.

"It's the dress," she said, after a pause, stammering a bit, and immediately regretted her words.

He released the grip on her hand. Lucy exhaled. He took both of her shoulders in his hands. His touch was gentle. "No. It's you."

The sound of footsteps in the hall jarred Lucy. She turned away from Clarkson, brushed her hair off her face and opened the refrigerator. She fumbled with the pull-out wire shelf. A block of cheese in saran wrap tumbled onto the floor.

"Hey," Summer said, "Look, I don't want you to go to any trouble. I didn't realize you were busy," she said. "Really, I just dropped in."

"No, Summer, please stay, it's fine," Lucy said, straightening up, the refrigerator door still open.

"By all means. It's a Halloween party," Clarkson said. He picked up the block of cheese from the floor and set it on the counter. "I'm a bit of a chef. Or maybe a sous-chef. Or at least a cook. I see we have cheese. Let's see what else we can find here." He opened the pantry door.

"Really, Summer, that's a grand idea," Lucy said. She closed the refrigerator. She didn't know how to behave, how to be alone with Clarkson. With Clarkson's back to her, Lucy mouthed the words 'Please stay.'

Summer nodded.

Clarkson rifled through the packages in the pantry.

"So, what's new?" Lucy asked Summer, straining for nonchalance.

Summer opened her eyes wide, then swallowed. "Nothing much," she said.

Lucy looked at Clarkson's back as he browsed the pantry. She smoothed her red chiffon dress, the claret still coloring her world.

"Same with me," she said.

Summer and Lucy both burst out laughing. Clarkson turned around.

"Okay if we use these crackers?" he asked.

Lucy shrugged. "Anything you want." She opened a jar of olives and drained the juice. "Summer, I think there's still a loaf of Mrs. Engel's date bread on the cutting board. Do you want to grab that?"

"Your mother will think we got lost in here," Summer said. She picked up the cutting board and took a knife from the rack in the corner.

"We're almost ready. She probably won't even notice," Lucy said. She leaned over Clarkson to reach the frilled toothpicks on a high shelf in the corner. She saw that he glanced at her cleavage. The rush of pleasure surprised her. When she retrieved the silver tray from the lower cabinet, she leaned over just a little more than necessary.

Chapter 20

Dee looked around. She was alone in the front parlor with the bowl of candy, the flickering candle and the uncarved pumpkin. And the roses. She sipped her wine.

Now and then, a faint hint of voices carried from the kitchen. Even if she could have heard them clearly, she didn't need to decipher the words that drifted her way. Already, she knew what was happening. The night had the smell of sex. She had known it as soon as he walked in. She was old, but she remembered the feeling that a man gives a woman. She had felt the tension instantly, stirring up the air in the parlor more than tonight's storm had buffeted the sycamores.

Dee remembered well how these things worked. She wished that Lucy had dressed herself in siren red and sat in the front parlor like a beacon when she was younger, when it could have made a difference. Now it was only a sputter for Lucy, meaningless, really.

Dee picked at the raveled hem of her blouse. A few spots of wine had dripped down her front. The purplish splotches invaded the weave of the fabric. She counted them. There were three large splotches and two smaller ones. If she were younger and still cared, she would jump up and strip off her blouse. She pictured herself spreading the stained cloth under a stream of running water in the sink while she stood in her bra. It seemed almost a memory to her, as if it had in fact happened.

Maybe it had. When she was much younger, of course. She pictured Al next to her by the sink, curly black hairs showing above his white T-shirt. She was in her bra, white, because in those days she didn't have any other color. They were laughing. She was rinsing a cotton shirt printed with big purple orchids under the faucet. The spray had wet her bra, making her nipples stand up. Al had touched her. Where had Thaddeus been that night? Maybe that had happened, long ago, in her kitchen.

She picked at the stain by her lower button and sipped her wine again. She was relieved that her shirt was already damaged, because now she didn't have to be careful not to spill.

The bottle of claret was on the sideboard. That man, Clarkson was his name, had helped himself to it and refilled hers as coolly as could be. Dee stood up. Her legs were a little stiff, so she waited until they were more solid under her. She walked to the sideboard and poured herself another splash. Burgundy droplets shimmered on the mahogany surface as she set the bottle back down. Dee ran her fingers across them and then wiped her hands on her wool pants. She wondered where he had come from, this Clarkson. He felt masculine to her. There was something different about a man. A man wanted without pretending he didn't, without explaining why he did.

She walked to the door and listened for a minute, hearing only the urgency in the voices that drifted her way. She plopped herself back into her chair. She tried to remember urgency. Wanting.

It was funny, what happened to old people, how the want part of life faded away. Everything faded when you were old, she thought. She remembered having had waves of chestnut hair and pink lips even without lipstick, and a closet full of clothes that were crimson, turquoise, the orange of burning lava. Her eyes used to be steel gray. Now, the eyes that looked back at her from the mirror had the dull sheen of an overcast sky.

Pale. That's what getting old was. Growing ever paler. Dee thought about when church let out on summer Sundays, how the old people flooded the sidewalks in their white pants and skirts and soft pastel shirts, aged ankles rising from bone or cream or white shoes, aged heads frosted with thin thatches of snow, or dusted with the gray of powdery ashes from a long-spent fire.

But old people still knew the smell of a night like tonight. Dee knew that for sure. That's why the ladies in book club chose the novels they did, steamy, blatant. She pictured her book club friends, even though she never went anymore. She saw them, curled under their soft comforters, wrinkled arms warmed by quilted pastel bed jackets. She knew what they read, stories about women with mounds for breasts and pointed rose-colored nipples and men in scarlet capes with rippling, bronzed torsos and muscular loins. The old ladies read their vivid stories until their colorless lips parted with the peaceful breathing of sleep.

And in the morning, she pictured them awakening once again to their unpigmented worlds, just like she did. Like all old people did. Dee tried to remember if white was the absence of all color or the union of all colors. It seemed important, but she didn't have it straight anymore. She had read accounts of near deaths, survivors who described their imminent demises as rushing toward a white light. Maybe the ever-increasing paleness of the elderly was preparation for the ultimate whiteout. Dee sipped her wine. A shimmering ruby drop slid down the stem, traced a path across the base and dripped onto her blouse. She didn't try to wipe it.

White had to be the union of all colors, because wasn't God white light? That's what she had learned. But really, if there was a God at all, would he have let her life happen to her, the way it had?

Still, there might be a God, Dee thought. And maybe he was older than anything imaginable, paler than anything Dee could envision, paler than the albino boa she had seen at the county fair in her childhood that still haunted her dreams. Maybe God had started out long ago just like herself, like all old people. Pale. And over the eons he had gradually become a glowing mass of whiteness.

And maybe the older and paler he got, the more keenly he could smell what was really happening, and how little he ought to do about it. At a certain age, Dee thought, one understands to let things be.

Sounds from the kitchen became louder, nearer. Voices edged with want. Dee was glad she had refilled her wine. She took another sip and waited. She watched the wax drip from the candle into a soft puddle around the bronze-footed base.

Chapter 21

"Here you are. Happy Halloween." Summer handed Dee a plate of cheese and a slice of date bread. Dee took the plate without speaking. Summer settled herself into the far chair in the parlor. She balanced her own plate on her lap and tilted her head. Lucy and Clarkson had been right behind her a moment ago, but there was no sign of them now. She turned to see Dee staring at her.

"Eat up, Dee. It's a Halloween party." Summer tried to sound cheerful. She smiled at Dee, and reached for her glass. Her plate wobbled on her knees and began to tip. She had to catch it with both hands.

"Let me help you with that," Clarkson said, striding into the room. He picked up Summer's glass and handed it to her.

"Thank you," Summer said. She looked up. His eyes never met hers.

Lucy entered the parlor. Her face was flushed. She checked her earrings with one hand and handed Clarkson a stack of rice paper cocktail napkins with the other. Summer saw that Clarkson held Lucy's hand in his for a split-second as he took the napkins. He handed one to Summer.

"Lucy found these in the kitchen. We thought we should use them," he said, turning away from her.

"One for you, my dear." He picked up Dee's glass, placed a napkin where the glass had been, and then centered her glass on the square.

"There," he said, as though he had just completed a masterpiece.

Dee murmured something that approximated a thank you. Her attempt at manners surprised Summer. She realized how accustomed she'd become to Dee's new habit of not responding.

"And for you," he said to Lucy. Summer saw that he managed to touch Lucy's hand in the process of arranging her cocktail napkin. Again.

The doorbell rang. Summer made a move to get up, but Lucy had already risen from her seat, as if spring-loaded. She picked up the crystal bowl of candy and left the parlor. After a moment, she returned.

"That was the Delaney father and his two boys, I can never tell them apart. One was a pirate, and I don't know what the other one was. In wet stripes. Maybe a bug of some sort, or a convict. I can't believe they're out in this weather."

Lucy set the bowl back in the front window. Summer noticed that her skirt brushed Clarkson's knees on the way to her seat.

"Think of it, out in this weather," she said as she sat.

"Yes, think of it," Summer said.

"Mom, this is Mrs. Engel's date bread that you like so well," Lucy said, after a minute. Her cheeks almost matched the red of her dress.

Dee took a bite of it. "Mmm," she said in a bland voice.

"Mrs. Engel brings one to Mom every fall. It's sort of a tradition. I'm not sure why." Lucy sat back. She looked to Summer, as if she expected Summer to comment.

"It's very good," Summer said. She felt that Lucy wanted her to say more. "Really quite good," she added.

"It's always been a favorite of ours," Lucy said. Summer thought that Lucy's voice sounded high and tentative. For once, she didn't sound like a schoolteacher.

"Very good," Clarkson said. He wiped his mouth with a rice paper napkin.

The stilted conversation lapsed. Summer peered into her plate, as if the bits of cheese, bread and olives were more absorbing than she could fathom. With each passing second, the lull transformed itself into a presence.

"Well," Lucy said.

Summer looked up. Lucy turned her head toward the candle in the front window. Summer followed her gaze. The candle had burned unevenly, leaving a fat glob of wax on one side. Summer looked at Clarkson. He seemed relaxed, nonchalant, his legs stretched out in front of him, thin trouser socks visible above shiny loafers. He crossed his feet at the ankles and leaned back, like a cat readjusting his position.

"What brings you here, tonight?" Summer asked Clarkson.

Clarkson uncrossed his ankles and shifted his long legs. He leaned forward a bit. "Oh, the vagaries of business. I've only just returned. I remembered this lovely lady here," he smiled at Lucy, "and thought I'd look her up. I asked around. Everyone seems to know the Armstrong house. So, I thought I'd give it a try."

"Well, the family house, anyway," Lucy said.

He turned to face Lucy, beside him on the sofa. Summer noticed that Lucy was no longer at the very opposite end. "That's what's nice about a small town." Clarkson stretched his arms across the reach of the upholstery. His fingers were inches from Lucy's shoulder. "People are connected."

Summer opened her mouth to speak, but Lucy beat her to it. "It is," she said.

Silence engulfed them again. Lucy cleared her throat and continued, "There was a time when Glendale seemed on the verge of turning into a city, but it just didn't happen. That was generations ago, of course."

Clarkson smiled. "I, for one, am happy it didn't. This town is charming, historic, set in these rolling green hills."

"Where are you from, Clarkson?" Summer asked.

Clarkson seemed to force himself to drag his eyes from Lucy. "A little here, a little there," he answered. "But I must say, nowhere as beautiful as Glendale."

Lucy smiled. "It's home," she said.

The doorbell rang again.

"Rush hour," Lucy said.

"Let me get it." Summer stood, picked up the candy bowl and walked to the front door. Three young girls shivered, huddled together, a dark haired girl with a crown and two towheads with pink sequins sticking out from under coats that smelled like wet wool.

"Trick-or-treat."

"Here, take handfuls," Summer said. "There aren't many of you out tonight. What are you?"

"I'm the queen and they're the fairy princesses," the dark haired girl answered. Her nose was running.

"You're very brave," Summer said. She threw another handful of candy into each bag.

"Thank you," each girl said, in turn. They raced back down the steps. Summer watched the queen, hanging onto her crown with one hand, candy bag swinging from the other. So that's what little girls look like on Halloween, she thought. She had never wondered what costume her daughter might have worn, or if she had joined her friends in a high-pitched chorus of thanks on a chilly Halloween night.

Rounding the corner into the parlor, Summer felt Clarkson's eyes on her.

"Just a queen and her fairy princesses," she said.

She set the bowl back in the front window and sat down. When she looked up again, he was facing Lucy, smiling. Summer studied Clarkson's face. He hadn't really answered her, about where he was from. A little here, a little there? What does that mean? And how can someone not show up for a date, then appear weeks later without explaining himself. Maybe he already had, Summer thought, before she arrived. It had gotten so that she never saw the good in anyone these days. She looked to her purse on the floor and thought about the letter inside. Ever since she'd lost Lorelei, she had felt so much less generous. And now, with Megan, things had become even worse. She was always on edge these days. Even so, something about Clarkson made her just a bit uncomfortable. She looked up to catch his eyes on her. They were so green, almost illuminated. He turned away.

"We have new Victorian lamps all along Main Street," Lucy said. "Summer, have you noticed how cheerful they make these fall evenings?"

"I have," Summer said. She wasn't sure, but it seemed that Clarkson still watched her out of the corner of his eye.

Summer and Lucy chatted about Glendale, whether the town should have pruned back the shade trees along Main Street quite so drastically this year, how the new Christmas garlands for the courthouse would look when they were unveiled after Thanksgiving. Summer watched Clarkson while they talked. He was charming in a way, certainly, but so far she hadn't learned a thing about him. She wished Lorelei were here. Lorelei would have known how to question him, how to find the human behind that practiced exterior. There was something about her that always brought out what was real in a person. Clarkson leaned forward. His gray slacks had a perfect crease. His gold wristwatch flashed just under the cuff of his loden cashmere sweater. He reached for a bit of cheese. She couldn't pinpoint what it was about him that disconcerted her.

"Summer?"

Lucy was looking right at her.

"I'm sorry, what?"

"Quite all right," Clarkson said. "You seem deep in thought."

"Yes, I guess I was."

"Clarkson needs to leave, he was saying."

Clarkson stood up and smiled at Summer, the practiced smile of a game show host or a TV news anchor. She couldn't make herself smile back.

"Even though tomorrow's Saturday, I have a packed schedule. I'm still sorting things out. Business, you know," Clarkson said.

Summer nodded. She didn't know at all, but she was certain that no questioning on her part would help. "It was nice to meet you," she said. She hoped she sounded more convincing than she felt.

"Very nice to have spent Halloween with you," Clarkson said. "I'm so glad you stayed."

"I am too." Summer managed a smile.

Clarkson walked over to Dee. He clasped her wrinkled, bony hand in both of his. "I see where your daughter gets her good looks," he said. Dee smiled. "I'm sure we'll meet again," Clarkson said, catching Summer's eyes as he turned from Dee.

"Yes," Summer answered.

"I'll get your coat," Lucy said. She followed him out of the parlor. Her voice sounded happy, animated even, as it faded into the distance.

Summer picked up her purse, wondering whether to leave, or to stay and tell Lucy about Megan. She took the letter out and read it automatically. She knew every word already.

Chapter 22

Lucy watched from the doorway as Clarkson got into his car. The rain had stopped and a misty fog clogged the air. The nighttime chill raised the skin on her arms in little bumps. She lingered there, holding her arms in her hands against the cold. A gust of wind lifted the edge of her dress. She didn't move. She wondered if he had looked back at her, if he had seen a hint of her black thong in the thick darkness. When the red taillights of his car melted into the night, she turned away and closed the door.

She started for the parlor, but went straight to the powder room instead. She switched on the bright light over the mirror. Thank heaven, she thought. Her mascara hadn't flaked, and her lips still held a reddish stain. He hadn't kissed her, but she was sure he wanted to. She switched off the light. She touched one hand to her lips as she rounded the corner into the parlor. She collapsed onto the sofa.

Dee stood up and walked over to Lucy. She stared at her a moment. "I'm going to bed," she said. She rubbed her blouse where the wine had left its mark.

"I'll help you upstairs," Lucy said, struggling to her feet.

"No," Dee said.

Lucy kissed Dee on the cheek.

"Good night, Dee. Happy Halloween."

"Call down if you need anything, Mom," Lucy said. The sound of Dee's footsteps faded from the long hallway.

Summer blew out the candle in the front window. She poked at the congealing wax.

"What a night of surprises," Lucy said.

Summer nodded. They were silent for a moment. Lucy was about to ask Summer what she thought about Clarkson. Her shoulders still tingled where he had held them before he had bent down, picked up his umbrella, and left.

"Can you stand one more?" Summer asked.

"One more what?"

"Surprise."

From her voice, Lucy knew it wasn't a good surprise. She felt her insides twist. "What? You know him? He's married?"

"No, I don't know him at all. It's not about Clarkson. It's about me. I need to tell someone, Lucy. I don't want to spoil your night, but...read this."

The twist in Lucy's stomach relaxed. As long as it wasn't bad news about Clarkson, nothing could spoil her night.

Summer's fingers trembled as she handed over the letter. The curly script on the pink paper seemed childish. Lucy read the whole thing through twice. "Summer. You have a child? A daughter?"

"I did. I do, I guess."

"You never said. I had no idea."

"I don't talk about her. She's from a part of my life I don't want to remember. I know that makes me sound like a monster." Summer took the letter back from Lucy. She folded it and put it in her purse. Lucy saw that her hands still shook.

"The father?" Lucy asked.

Summer shook her head. "We were in high school. I don't know where he is, whatever happened to him. I don't know if Megan is looking for him. I don't know anything." Summer put her face in her hands.

"Oh, Summer, please. It can't be that bad. How old is she? She's an adult, right? She just wants to see you. To see who you are. She'll be here and then she'll leave and your life will be just the way it's always been."

"Oh God, Lucy."

Lucy took Summer in her arms. The feel of Clarkson's strong arm around her shoulder was fresh in her mind. "It will be all right. She only wants to meet you, she says. Maybe something good will come of that. You must wonder about her, now and then. How could you not?"

Summer shrugged.

"It's not the end of the world."

Summer disengaged herself from Lucy. She stepped back. "I'll be all right," she said.

Lucy smiled. "Of course you will."

"It's late. I should be going."

"Wait. Let me make you a cup of tea. We could both use one."

They walked to the kitchen. Summer sat at the table while Lucy lit the burner and filled the copper kettle.

"Herbal okay?" Lucy looked over her shoulder. She took two china mugs from the cabinet, and opened a box of chamomile sachets. She wanted to ask Summer more about her daughter. All at once, Summer had acquired an altogether new dimension. She was one of those girls. Unwed and pregnant. In trouble. Lucy imagined Summer as a young girl. She had been beautiful, she was sure. Beautiful and loose, apparently. Lucy felt a little ashamed of her thoughts.

She cleared her throat. "So, we have Megan in your life. And Clarkson in mine. Maybe we needed more people around. It's been hard lately. Lonely." Saying something nice made her feel better. Summer didn't have to know how ungenerous she could be in her heart. Lucy set two spoons and a jar of honey on the table. She tried to give Summer a reassuring smile.

"I remember when I was little. Any time we were sick, or sad, Mom always made us a cup of tea," Lucy said. "Dee believed it was the answer to everything."

"I hope she was right," Summer said.

The kettle whistle lowered to a whine as Lucy lifted it from the stove. She poured water into the mugs, set them on the table and sat down. Wisps of steam curled between them.

"I know this isn't the time to ask, considering what you're going through over your daughter...Megan..." Lucy said the name slowly, "but I can't help myself. What did you think of him?"

Summer fidgeted in her chair. She didn't answer.

"I know it's a funny time to ask, but tonight was, for me...a lot. Just off the top of your head, what did you think of Clarkson?"

Summer squeezed the excess water from her tea bag with her spoon.

"I didn't really get a chance to form an opinion," Summer said after a moment. "Where can I put this teabag?"

Lucy took the teabag from Summer. It made a plunking sound as it hit the trash.

"Maybe not an opinion, I guess. What was your impression of him?" Lucy felt a little put out that Summer hadn't answered her question more directly. She understood that Summer was in distress tonight, but still... Anyone would have enjoyed meeting Clarkson. She remembered his soft green sweater, the smell of his coat.

"He was okay. Charming. Handsome." Summer looked at the pantry. "He seemed to know his way around a kitchen."

"Yes, he did." Lucy didn't try to disguise her hurt. The least Summer could do was admit that Clarkson was like a breath of fresh air in their battered lives. He had turned a dismal evening into a Halloween party. It was as if he belonged with them. And certainly it was fate that had made her wear that red dress meant for his eyes all those weeks ago. "Summer, I can't believe you don't have more to say about him."

"I'm sorry, Lucy. For one thing, he seemed a little..." She paused. "Evasive."

"Evasive about what? He just returned from a business trip. He was tired. He thought to look me up. He brought flowers, for goodness sakes."

"A business trip from where, Lucy? What kind of business? Where is he from? 'A little here, a little there,' what did that mean?" Summer sat back. She looked down.

"Oh."

"Look, Lucy, I'm really sorry. I'm out of sorts tonight. Maybe it's just me. He seemed perfectly fine, I guess."

"No, you don't mean that."

"I would just be a little leery of him, that's all. Make him open up, tell you things. The least he can do it is say where he's from."

"It's not like you ever opened up and mentioned Megan. Everybody doesn't have to be wide open all the time." As soon as Lucy saw Summer's face, she realized she had gone too far. "I didn't mean that," she said.

They were silent. Summer sipped her tea.

"No, you're right," Summer said. "It's not like I've been that forthcoming either. I'm sure he's fine. He seems to like you, Lucy."

He does, Lucy thought. Again, she remembered the way he looked at her, the way no man had ever looked at her before. The thought of Clarkson liking her, wanting her, made everything better.

Chapter 23

Clarkson pulled into the rock-strewn space that served as the driveway next to his cabin. The fog swathed everything. He stepped out of his car and stretched his calves. The drive from the Armstrong house had taken twice as long as it should have. That might have bothered him had the night gone less swimmingly. He closed the car door, the sound of the impact flat in the thick atmosphere. The scent of wet pine permeated all. He picked his way to the varnished pine porch, the old floorboards soaked through even where the roof covered. He stood on the edge of the porch, keys in hand, and peered into the soupy distance. The night air felt heavy in his lungs, and cold. It was not unpleasant. He turned away, unlocked his front door and entered the cabin. He switched on the lamp by the door.

That had been a stroke of brilliance, he thought, showing up at the house in town with an armful of roses. When he had first mounted those wide steps to the Armstrong's front entry, he had no idea who or what he might find. What luck it was when Lucy answered the bell. She had seemed oddly unsurprised to see him. He considered that as he hung his coat in the closet. And the house did not disappoint. What a magnificent structure, with two staircases, recessed alcoves and leaded stained glass. Every mantle he glimpsed was a work of art. He had wanted desperately to climb the stairs, to find the room with the oriel window. But that would come in time. Of course, it all needed work, but the bones were there. It was a royal Queen Anne treasure, down to the original sidewalk bricking around the front, signed and documented as first-fired brick, and the date of construction, 1890, emblazoned over the carved front door. This wasn't just a house, it was a signed artwork, a bona fide first edition. Already, he felt a proprietary pride. He went to the kitchen and poured himself a glass of vodka from the bottle on the far corner of the counter.

Tonight called for some background music. He switched on the radio, tuned as usual to the classical station. The signal was a little weak, so he adjusted the dial. Still slightly fuzzy, the soft piano concerto pleased him. It was infinitely better than country music, or oldies, the only other local options. Country music was insufferable, of course, but the oldies stations particularly irked him. Did everyone in these parts want to relive dancing cheek to cheek in high school proms? He sipped his vodka. Did all of them need their pasts oozing into the present all the time?

He sat by the hearth in the upholstered chair that had become his favorite, listening to the radio as the piano's high notes tripped over each other in a frenzied, fluid path before the deeper chords swallowed them. He closed his eyes and leaned his head back. Tonight had been perfect, no question.

After the house, most magnificent of all was meeting Summer. He pictured her, willowy, regal almost, her steel-gray eyes ringed underneath with a bluish shadow. He remembered Lorelei's brown eyes, wide and pleading. He had looked into Lorelei's eyes and known that she knew all about him. She had tried to bargain with him, to let him know that he wasn't alone in his isolation. She had told him how imperfect her life was, that she was in love with a woman and unable to divulge that forbidden secret in the town of Glendale. In a way, it was a shame that she had left him with no choice. He could see her even now, that tear shimmering on her pale cheek, sliding slowly downward as he encircled her neck with his bare hands. 'Summer' she had said. He hadn't been sure what that meant at the time.

When he met Summer tonight, he knew. He had watched her, as much as he dared. She was beautiful, but those gray eyes had a deadness. There was no lightness in her graceful movements. Summer had been crushed under a weight.

A kinship existed between them, even if she didn't know it. They both shared Lorelei, of course. But it was much more than that. Each of them lived a life that others hadn't imagined, couldn't allow. He had watched Summer as she laughed and talked with Lucy. There was something brittle about her, as if she existed within a shell that was in danger of cracking. Surely, Lucy must have known about Summer and Lorelei, he thought. But even so, Lucy wasn't the sort of woman who understood these things, who appreciated what it was to live a fragmented life, to hide so much of oneself.

Lucy. What to do about Lucy? For some odd reason, Lucy had already given herself to him completely, in spirit at least. That could be useful. There would be no need to bargain, flirt, cajole. As had happened after the first time they met, her face had already faded in his mind. She wasn't unattractive, to be sure. For a woman her age, she was a model of perfect grooming. In the streets of his Connecticut town, she would fit in without too much trouble, unlike most of the women around here. He liked that in the middle of backward Glendale, on a stormy Halloween night, Lucy had dressed in red chiffon and heels to hand out candy from a crystal bowl. In a way, that excited him. Also, if he looked into her eyes, he could see something of Lorelei. Of course, when he looked into her eyes, she practically swooned, so he had to be careful. There would be time for such things, if required.

All in all, tonight had been a revelation for him, intoxicating, in fact. It had felt so natural to sit on an upholstered damask sofa inside a house on the hill in Glendale as an equal, a guest. In his childhood, he had set foot in a few. Once, at a birthday party that his whole class had been invited to attend, when his mother had bought him a new shirt and walked him up the steps herself, right before she'd left forever. No one had talked to him and he'd ended up alone in the back yard throwing sticks for the dog while the other children played silly games they all seemed to know. In junior high, for a whole summer, he had mown the lawn for a rich old lady who allowed him into her foyer while she paid him. He had seen a piano in the room beyond that his fingers had ached to touch, and paintings in gilded frames. One of the times that his father was drunk and missing, Jerry the bartender had suggested he ask Mr. Hartley if he knew what happened to him. Mrs. Hartley had invited him to wait inside their entry while she ran to find her husband. The splintered light from a crystal chandelier had seemed magical until Mr. Hartley appeared, ushered him outside and dismissed him with a savage curtness.

But tonight had proved how different his life now was. Ever since his arrival in Glendale, it was as though events had unfolded in a way that seemed preordained, as if the hand of fate had intervened. He sipped his vodka.

Others, he knew, might have been deceived by such an illusion. But he knew the perils of trusting to fate. There was no such thing. Maybe a random bit of luck started the ball rolling. But real results came from a well-constructed plan and its careful, but flexible execution. It amazed him that so few people understood this simple truth.

He thought of Lorelei, her soft hair, her desperate pleas to him that could only have been meaningless. He had learned long ago to follow through with the logical and appropriate action even when it was difficult. Most were buffeted by life, he thought. Only a few sought to engineer its course.

He was young when he began to understand how life worked. It was shortly after he had left Glendale, when he was just a teenager. He had hitchhiked halfway across the country, laboring at odd construction jobs to fund each hard-won day. He had enough money in his pocket for a fried egg sandwich at a roadside diner. As he waited for his food, inhaling the greasy diner air, thick with the smell of bacon, coffee and cigarettes, he watched the people around him. A young woman with shiny black hair and a black armband was involved in an argument about the war in Vietnam with a pig-faced man, whose fat rear drooped over the sides of his diner stool. She was telling him that the war was immoral, that villages scorched by napalm assaults were unacceptable. That no war could be fought in a way that killed innocent people. She was tearful, incensed for dead children she didn't know, in a country she had likely never seen.

The pig-faced man had focused on his soup as he argued, his eyes small-looking because his fat cheeks had squeezed them to slits. Clarkson had listened to them both. He had wanted to agree with the girl, mostly because he wanted to have sex with her, which he did, later. But before that, when they were still arguing, the man had looked up from his soup and said, "It's not just war, honey. Life is a battle. Life causes collateral damage. Get used to it."

The girl had cried. After Clarkson figured out how he could get the girl alone to remove all of her clothes except the armband, he thought about his own life. He had left a wake of damage already. The man's statement comforted him. The moment a baby toddled across a green lawn, a bug or two certainly had died under the child's lurching steps while the parents shrieked with joy. No good ever emerged without destruction of some sort. A cow was slaughtered to prepare a feast. A flower was plucked to make a bouquet. Life caused collateral damage.

Clarkson was pleased he'd been able to fashion himself into the sort of man who didn't flinch when a decision demanded a wake of inevitable destruction. He wouldn't be in his position today if he were otherwise. His first construction partner in the early days had never learned this skill. It was an accident, of course, that day at the quarry when Scott slipped from the steep edge of the cliff. Clarkson had sought help, just as he had promised Scott, who lay thirty feet below, ashen and bleeding against a flat face of rock. But Clarkson knew that it would have been quicker to lead the rescue team over the east side of the hill. He hadn't murdered Scott. He simply had allowed him to lie unattended just long enough so that survival was all but impossible. No one blamed him, not even the widow. And if they were still partners today, the business would have long dissolved into bankruptcy.

And old Mrs. Calhoun with her heart medication. He had given her a pill, just not the right one. She hadn't long to live anyway, and who knew if her son from Georgia would show up and pressure her to remove Clarkson from her will? After all he'd done for her. He couldn't take that chance. These decisions became easier each time they were necessary.

Clarkson stood up, walked to the kitchen and refilled his vodka. He stood at the window. He watched the fog settle in layers on the forest floor, soft and rolling. He wondered what the upstairs rooms looked like in the Armstrong house. He had yet to go upstairs in one of the big houses on the hill. He wondered if the wallpaper was floral and fussy, if the bedrooms bore any trace of masculinity at all.

Chapter 24

Lucy's pulse quickened at the sound of the ringing phone, but Al Mancini's voice instead of Clarkson's disappointed her. Her cheeks burned. When she hung up, she stared at the phone as if it were responsible for its calls.

Al's words echoed. "Lucy, there may be a break. The police have information about Lorelei's possible... assailant." A few months ago that statement would have made her heart race. Her eyes filled with tears. What was wrong with her?

Things really were happening too fast, she thought, starting with Halloween, starting with Clarkson. All week, she had relived those moments with him. The desire between them on Halloween was undeniable. That was only four days ago, no time at all, really. He was a busy man. He would call her at the first opportunity. She didn't want to admit that she would rather have heard from Clarkson than anyone else. Even Al, with his shattering news. Could the mystery of Lorelei's killer be solved at last? Al seemed to think so. Would it do any good?

Lucy hadn't seen Al much since the funeral, partly by design. She couldn't look at him without remembering the perfume of lilies, the thick gold carpet, the muted atmosphere of Lorelei's chamber. She had run into him on the street a few times, recently at the bakery. They had chatted a bit, about the picture of Lucy's fourth graders in *The Sentinel*, about Al's extended Saturday night hours at the bowling alley. They had stood in front of the glass cases filled with cream-topped tarts and sheet cakes until they ran out of all the unimportant words they could think to say. She had left without Dee's sandwich rolls.

Al would be here shortly. Her shakiness surprised her, although Al had seemed to expect it. He had set up everything, called Officer McMahon, offered to drive her to the police station. She mounted the staircase, not pausing at the landing to admire the morning light that filtered through the stained glass.

"Mom?" Lucy called, aware that Dee wouldn't answer. She knocked and entered Dee's room. Dee sat on the edge of her bed. Her television was on, tuned to a game show.

"Mom, I have to run out for a while."

Dee didn't look at her.

"Al is picking me up. We're riding over to the police station. They might have news for us, you know, about what happened." Lucy waited to see if Dee understood what she was trying to say.

She dropped her voice until it was soft, almost a whisper. "With Lorelei."

Dee turned away from the game show and faced her. Her eyes looked a million years old.

"It won't make any difference," Dee said after a minute.

Lucy shrugged. "I don't know, Mom. Al wondered if maybe you wanted to come along."

Dee shook her head.

"I could help you get dressed."

Dee pulled her robe tighter around her.

"Maybe just ride along with us. It's not cold out."

"No. I'm sorry. I can't." Dee hit the volume-up button on the television remote control. A contestant on the game show shrieked with joy and jerked from side to side. Balloons and confetti hit her head. The contestant didn't duck.

"Okay. I'll be back in a bit. I'll let you know what we learn. Did you hear me, Mom?" Lucy wasn't sure if Dee nodded in answer or if she just imagined it. Not that it matters, she thought, as she headed into her childhood bedroom.

The day would be sunny. The morning light was still soft where it seeped through the curtains. She sat on her bed. News about Lorelei's murderer, at long last. Her eyes focused on the wallpaper, peeling off at some of the seams. She remembered choosing it at the paint store in Clarion when she was still in grade school. Dee had helped her pore over samples in wide, heavy books. They had laughed, compared colors, put markers in a few pages. It was one of the few times that Lucy had felt special. At the time, Lucy thought the delicate chain of daisies was surely the right backdrop for a country princess, which was what she wanted to be. That had been so long ago.

She decided to slip into a skirt and heels. Her face in the mirror over her dresser seemed pale, so she dabbed on blush and fresh lipstick. She grabbed her purse, went downstairs and stood outside on the side porch by the driveway to wait for Al. To find out what the police knew about the murderer of her sister.

She hadn't waited long when Al pulled up in his red Monte Carlo. He opened his door and stuck out one leg. His shoulders lurched from side to side. Lucy could see that his belly was wedged under the steering wheel.

"No, stay, Al, I have it." Lucy opened the passenger door and smoothed her skirt as she settled into the seat. She patted him on the shoulder. Al pulled onto the street and veered right along the fork, down Main Street. He checked his side-mirror.

"Thanks for offering to come along with me," Lucy said.

"You shouldn't go alone," he said.

"No." Lucy had to clear her throat before she could get more words out.

"What do you know about this?"

"Not much. Bruce called me the other day to say they were working on things. You know, the young guy, Officer McMahon. Nice kid. He bowls on Thursday nights. He tried your house, even left a message. They didn't have your cell. Called your mom's, but you must have been at work. Dee doesn't answer the phone, you know."

"I know. She even turns off the answering machine."

"Anyway, he called me to see if I knew how to find you."

"Thanks. I would have been at school today, but it's an in-service. Not mandatory for me, so I thought I'd keep Dee company. I usually stop by my own place and check messages every day or so." Lucy felt her face flush. Ever since Halloween, she had stayed at Dee's every possible second, hoping that Clarkson would return. She hadn't even been home to check her mail.

"Have they arrested someone?" she asked. All of a sudden, the idea of identifying the murderer was worse than her current ignorance.

"No, it's not that definite. I think Bruce said the guy is dead."

"Dead. Oh." Lucy felt confused, then disappointed, then wondered why.

Lucy glanced sideways at Al. He had aged a lot. Before the funeral, her memories of him were mostly from her childhood. He had had a lot of black hair, on his head, his arms, his knuckles, poking out in tufts above his shirt collars. He would sit in the kitchen with her mother after he shoveled the snow on their walkway. Sometimes Lucy would sit with them while she ate her after-school snack. Al would talk about Italy, how to cook tomato sauce with real tomatoes, about his Uncle Gino who ran his own Italian restaurant in Pittsburgh. Now, all over he had become a soft silver.

They parked in front of the station. Al held the door for her. Inside, Officer McMahon rose from a desk and greeted them.

"I'll wait for you here, Lucy," Al said. He started to lower himself into one of a row of spoke-backed chairs.

"No, Al, if you don't mind, please...I'd rather have you with me." The tightness in Lucy's chest wouldn't ease up.

"This way," Officer McMahon said.

They followed him past a counter with a half-filled coffee pot that smelled burnt and stale. Styrofoam cups, powdered creamer, packets of sweetener and plastic stirrers littered a stained plastic tray.

"Coffee?" he asked.

"No, thanks," Lucy said. Al held up a hand in response. They gathered around a wooden desk and arranged their chairs to face each other.

"So Bruce, what's the deal?" Al asked.

"We can't prove anything right now, so before I tell you, understand that closure isn't what I'm offering today."

Lucy nodded.

"We found a guy, dead, where 22 intersects the train tracks just south of Crestview. Three days ago. We've been talking to lots of people. Seems the guy had a long history. Was in mental institutions on and off for the past twenty years."

Officer McMahon sat back and watched them.

"That doesn't make him a murderer," Lucy said. She could tell that he wanted to be coaxed into unfolding his story.

"No. But it turns out he's threatened a few people, women mainly. Recently, a woman about your sister's age said he confronted her in the alley behind the Food-o-Rama and followed her home. She managed to get away, called the police on her cell. He was gone before the Crestview force got there." Officer McMahon paused. He took a sip of coffee. Lucy noticed that he had his own ceramic mug, smudged with dark fingerprints. 'Managed to get away,' she thought, what did that mean? Why hadn't Lorelei done that?

"What's his name?" Lucy asked, surprised that she could find her voice.

"Danny Rillo. Seems he went mostly by D.R., though."

After all this time, Lorelei's killer had a name, a label. Lucy wasn't sure that she wanted to know that, to link Lorelei forever with Danny Rillo. He didn't deserve that.

"Anyway, people around him say he talked a lot about strangling women, wanting to see somebody die," he said.

Lucy felt ill. She wondered if Officer McMahon had a picture of the dead man. She didn't want to ask. She refused to think of him by name.

"You say he's dead? What happened?" Al asked.

"Hit and run, it seems. Another mystery. Maybe we'll figure it out. But with a low-life like that, it doesn't rank as high as finding the guy who killed Lorelei Armstrong."

Lucy felt her stomach turn again. She started to cough. Officer McMahon disappeared and returned with a Styrofoam cup filled with warmish water. She took a sip.

"You said you can't prove anything right now. Does that mean that you can, later?" Lucy asked.

Officer McMahon's eyes seemed glued to his shoes. When he raised them, they didn't meet hers. "There's a way. But we'd have to do some more tests."

Lucy couldn't believe her ears. "On Lorelei?"

"I'm sorry. I know word has gotten around town. Somehow, between the Glendale investigation and the Oil City department coming in, there's a problem with retrieving some vital material." He stopped.

"You lost something," Lucy said.

"No. I'm not sure if it was ever done. It's her..." he looked down, then continued quietly, "her fingernail clippings, what was under her nails. Maybe, we can get back in there. It would require filing some paperwork, an order. I'm sorry."

Lucy nodded. "I see."

"Look, we haven't had a murder in Glendale in seventy-five years. I'd have to look up the procedure. But say the word and we'll get started."

Lucy shuddered. She thought about Dee and Summer, squared off over Lorelei's frail body all those months ago. How could Dee endure an exhumation, with its fresh set of atrocities? Could they bear to go through it again? Could she? She felt faint.

"I don't think that's a good idea," Lucy said.

Officer McMahon nodded. "I'm sorry."

They were all quiet.

"Anything else?" Al asked.

"No. If we come up with anything else, I'll let you know." Officer McMahon focused his eyes on Lucy. "I'll call your friend, the one that found her. Think about it. If you change your mind about anything…"

"No, I don't think I will." Lucy thought about Summer, at this moment waiting for the arrival of the daughter that she hadn't wanted, still didn't, really. "That's all right, I'll tell Summer. Thanks."

Al opened the door for Lucy and followed her outside. The slats of the Venetian blind hit the wood frame as it swung shut.

"Are you all right?" Al asked. He put a hand on Lucy's shoulder.

"I guess." She looked up at Al. "So, what do you think?"

"I'm not sure. There's a damned good chance that they've already found the guy. But then again, you could know for sure…"

Lucy nodded. "Or not. The older I get, the less I believe in closure. What if something else goes wrong? It's so frustrating. So much of life is just not knowing things."

They got into Al's car. Al didn't start the motor.

"You're right," he said.

Lucy waited for Al to start the car. "Lucy, this is hard for me to say, but it's been on my mind, and, well, you deserve closure about something, at least. I'm not going to apologize. Things happen because, well, they just do."

"Al, what is it?"

"Dee and I always thought you knew. I'm sure you've always wondered. You might as well know the truth. The older I get, the more I realize that what you've done in your past is all a part of you. Good or bad, right or wrong, it's you and you better own up to it before you die."

Lucy scraped her heel on the floor mat of Al's Monte Carlo. She wanted to get out of the car and run.

"Your mom was a fun-loving lady back then. And your dad, well, he was just who he was. Sort of more serious. I was new in town and your mom and I hit it off. I guess that's how to put it. And then, after your dad died, Dee didn't want anyone to see us together. They might have talked, known that we had been, you know, while he was still alive. Out of respect. Of course, that was all years ago. I never wanted to cause your family any pain. I was crazy about your mom. You know that."

Lucy searched for the right words, any words.

"I'm sorry if you've held this against me for all these years."

"No, Al, I didn't. Really."

Al started the motor and pulled out of the space. They rode silently to Dee's house. He pulled up at the side door.

"I hope I didn't upset you. I mean, more than you already were."

"No, not at all."

"Closure for both of us, I guess."

"Yes, it is."

Al's shoulders lurched. Lucy knew that he wanted to walk her into Dee's house.

"Please, don't get out. Thank you for everything. Don't worry, Al, I understand."

"Thank you," Al said.

Lucy hurried inside and shut the door behind her. Inside, the whole house looked different to her. Would Lorelei want to be dug up, just to prove the guilt of someone who was already dead? And, God, what about Dee and Al?

Everyone in the world, it seemed, had an undercurrent, an alternate existence. Her own mother, for God's sake. Maybe Al was right, a part of her knew, or at least suspected. She used to sit with them, it's true, but she liked to hear Al's stories, see her mom laugh for a change. Even when she had wondered about them, it was in that theoretical way, where the truth is the furthest thing from one's mind. Lucy held her hands together. Everyone, with their secrets. Dee and Al. Summer and Megan. Lucy felt like the only transparent soul on earth. At least she had met Clarkson. She walked to the kitchen and dropped her purse on the table. Wasn't it her turn for some intrigue for a change? She looked at the phone, willing it to ring. Was it too much to hope?

Chapter 25

The clothes strewn across her bed proved it. Summer was a mess. If she could skip today completely, she would. She had no desire to forge a connection with the girl who was at this moment driving from Virginia to meet her. She picked up the navy skirt from her bed and hung it in the closet. Why had she made such a big deal out of what to wear to meet a daughter who should remain unmet?

She pushed aside the silk blouse and sat on the bed. All because of Lorelei. It had started with Lorelei's rainbow scarf, after the Columbine shootings in Colorado left a wake of schoolchildren dead.

They had sat in front of the television in shock, Lorelei pale, biting her lip. After a bit, Lorelei left the room. She returned with her neck wrapped in her rainbow scarf, the one woven and sold by former prostitutes in Thailand to fund a new life for themselves and their children. Lorelei wore the scarf all week, around her neck, knotted at her waist or turban-like around her head, throughout the long days of televised funerals of teenagers. "It's the only thing I can do," Lorelei told her. "It's a positive scarf." Summer surveyed the heap of clothes on the bed. Unlike Lorelei, she didn't have any magic clothes.

She glanced at the clock on her nightstand. Megan was late. For a moment, Summer allowed herself to believe that Megan had come to her senses and realized that a birth mother was only that—a vehicle for entrance into this world. How horrified Lorelei would have been by that idea. Summer envied

Lorelei's relentless optimism. She no longer felt connected to anything. Some days, even Lorelei, especially Lorelei, seemed to belong to a different lifetime. She picked up the silk blouse and slipped it back onto its hanger.

As she shut the closet door, Summer wondered if she still had Lorelei's rainbow scarf. She was sure she'd kept it. Had she put it on the top shelf of her closet, or in a dresser drawer? The need to find it possessed her. She scoured the closet first, with no luck. She rummaged through her dresser and at last pulled it from the bottom drawer. The scarf was soft. A faint smell of Lorelei clung to it.

The doorbell rang.

Summer threw the scarf onto her bed and got as far as her bedroom door. She stopped. She returned to the bed, picked up the scarf, and draped it around her neck. Its fringed edges grazed her jeans as she hurried from her room. She took a deep breath and walked down the steps to the front door.

The doorbell chimed a second time. Summer opened the door.

"Oh, I'm so sorry," said a young woman, her hand poised in midair, index finger extended toward the doorbell. She had deep blue eyes and brown hair with a few random stripes of crayon red. Summer was about to respond, but the girl continued in a high, excited voice, "I thought maybe you didn't hear me, or you weren't home, or something. I'm Megan, of course. But you already know that, I'm sure. Well, not positive, like a million percent sure, but almost. Actually, I am sure."

Her face was elastic. While she was talking, it morphed too quickly for Summer to get a fix on. A flash of white teeth pushed up her round cheeks. Her forehead folded into a worried pout that split her eyebrows with a deep crease, then unfolded and stretched until her brows almost disappeared into her hairline. She switched her purple leather handbag from her right side to her left. A hand with short fingernails thrust toward Summer and almost in the same motion, fluttered to her side. And then she was quiet.

"No, I did, I mean, I am home, of course…come in." Summer stepped back and allowed Megan to enter. She was tall, almost as tall as Summer. She tilted her head to the side and stared at Summer's face until Summer looked away. When Summer looked back, she saw that Megan's cheeks had turned bright pink. The pinkness spread and organized itself into all-over blotches that traveled into the neckline of her coat. Her full lower lip began to quiver.

"Hello, Megan. Call me Summer, please," Summer said. She stepped back. She had trouble believing that her body had participated in conjuring up the girl that stood before her.

"Okay," Megan said. Her blue eyes reddened around the rims and seemed lost in unspilled tears.

"Did you have any trouble finding your way?" Summer asked, embarrassed by Megan's fever-pitch emotions, and her own lack of them. Summer feared that Megan would keel over, break down, or erupt into more colors.

Megan shook her head, little movements, side to side, as if she were too overcome to answer. Spiral silver earrings wobbled in her earlobes. She put a hand to her forehead, then let it fall, where it remained, limp, at her side. Tears jumped from her eyes and splashed onto her cheeks. Her histrionics were outrageous, contagious. If they faced each other for one more second, the sheer force of Megan's expectations would require Summer to wrap her arms around the girl in some sort of maternal hug. But then what? Summer turned away so abruptly that Lorelei's rainbow scarf snagged on the chain handle of Megan's handbag.

"Oh. We're caught," Megan said.

Summer turned back around. Megan worked to extricate the scarf from her bag. "There," Megan said, as the scarf floated free. "I hope it isn't snagged or something." She picked up an end with her trembling fingers. Summer could tell that she bit her nails.

"It's fine," Summer said.

"It's very pretty." Megan let the end go.

"Thank you." Summer almost added that it was Lorelei's. The stranger before her had no idea who Lorelei was, what that meant.

"Things like that always happen to me," Megan said.

"Really, don't give it a second thought."

Megan nodded. Summer watched her take a deep breath. The pink splotches migrated to just her cheeks. Her expression settled. Her face was round and soft. Youthful.

Summer led Megan into the living room, partitioned from the entry only by the square of slate by the front door. "It's pretty small. This is most of it." Summer gestured toward the couch and tried to smile.

"It's nice," Megan said. She stood in her puffy coat, still buttoned.

"I guess you have things to bring in," Summer said.

"They're in my car. I wanted to meet you first."

"Yes," Summer said. She hoped she had injected a little enthusiasm into her voice. She felt as though a stray puppy had found its way to her doorstep. "We'll get your things in a minute."

Megan nodded and began to unbutton her coat. The doorbell rang.

"Oh, dear. Excuse me. I wasn't expecting anyone."

Summer opened the door to find Lucy.

"Summer, I wouldn't have stopped by if I didn't think it was important. I saw the car. I guess Megan got here safely. I'm so sorry to intrude. Is it all right?"

"Lucy, hello. Yes, she's only just walked in. It's fine. Come in." The interruption was not unwelcome.

Lucy entered and gave a half-wave to Megan while she removed her gloves, loosening each finger before pulling them from her hands. "You must be Megan. I'm Lucy. I'm so sorry to barge in on you like this. It's nice to meet you, of course."

"Nice to meet you." Megan pushed an arm toward Lucy, but it was trapped in the sleeve of her coat. Lucy didn't appear to notice.

"I'll only stay a minute, really," Lucy said. She opened her handbag and dropped her gloves inside. She removed a packet of pink tissues and peeled off one with her long polished nails. She folded the tissue and dabbed underneath her lined lower lids. Summer was surprised to see that Lucy's hair wasn't picture-perfect, that her nose was red and shiny.

Megan took off her coat and draped it over the back of the couch. She drifted over to the dining area, touched the backs of the dining chairs, then clasped her hands behind her back and looked at the paintings on the walls.

"I just got back from the police station a little while ago," Lucy said. She sniffled a little and blew her nose. She lowered her voice. "I would wait, but I'm afraid Officer McMahon might call you anyway, and I wanted to tell you first. In person. Is that okay?"

Summer felt her face grow warm. "What is it?"

"The bathroom is upstairs, right?" Megan asked.

Summer nodded. Megan headed upstairs, her purple handbag swinging from her shoulder.

"It's about Lorelei," Lucy said.

Summer put an arm on Lucy's elbow and led her to the couch. Lucy sat as if her body operated without her knowledge, her back stiff. Summer sat across from her.

"Lucy, are you all right? What is it?"

"I don't know, yes, I mean it's just sort of everything right now." She fidgeted with the clasp on her handbag. "The police think they've found him. It's not certain, but it seems that a homeless former mental patient may have... done it. He's dead now, but Officer McMahon thinks it's a good possibility." Summer was speechless. How many times had she wondered whose hands had encircled Lorelei's neck? She leaned over and let her head fall forward into her hands.

"I know. It was almost better before, wasn't it?"

"He's dead?" Summer tried to take it all in.

"Yes, hit and run, it seems. There was no confession or anything. From the homeless man. We don't know for sure that he did it. Unless… Well, there are more tests they can do." She paused and looked down. "On Lorelei."

"Oh." Summer sat back. Dead, she thought.

They were silent.

"I told them to leave her alone."

"Oh," Summer said again. This was all too much to absorb. She envisioned Lorelei's coffin as it broke through the newly settled earth above it, followed by a lonely journey to a cold morgue. She felt a little faint.

"There's something else, too," Lucy said. She blotted her eyes. A sooty strand of mascara streaked one cheek.

"What?"

Megan's footsteps creaked in the upstairs hall and then became louder.

"Oh, never mind, it's nothing," Lucy said.

"More news about Lorelei?"

"Oh, no. I don't know why I brought it up, even. Just something Al and I were talking about. He drove me to the police station. About Dee. It can wait," Lucy said. "I just wanted to tell you before Officer McMahon did. He mentioned that he might call you. I'll be going." She stood up.

"Okay." Summer stroked the fringe of the rainbow scarf as she stood. "Lucy, I don't even know what to say." The news was disturbing, inconclusive.

Lucy dabbed at her eyes again. She crumpled her tissue into a ball and fished in her bag for another. Summer had never seen Lucy like this. Her hair stuck up on top, and the remnants of her make-up congealed in the creases under her eyes, lining the folds alongside her nose. The Lucy before her was almost as foreign as the improbable Megan.

"I understand," Lucy said.

Summer stood up, and walked with Lucy to the door. So, they found him, she thought. Maybe. What did that really meant to her, to any of them? And now, they proposed to inflict further indignities on Lorelei. She looked at Lucy. Lucy's shoulders hunched over and her hair was caught in her coat collar.

Summer swallowed hard. As long as Lucy had held up, the rest of them had been free to melt down, she thought. That was Lucy's role, to hold up, to smooth things over, to make things right for everyone else. Lucy turned to her and waved a little. Her red eyes and her lips, pale and pinched without her lipstick, struck something deep within Summer.

"Lucy, we can think about this. We don't have to decide right away. How certain are they?" She didn't wait for Lucy to answer. She reached out and patted Lucy's arm. "We'll get through this. Thanks for telling me in person. It's a lot to handle. For both of us." Summer realized how rusty she'd become at reaching out to someone. At caring.

Megan burst into the living room. "Summer, it's amazing, we use the same brand of toothpaste," she said.

Summer looked at Megan. For a moment she had almost forgotten about this strange creature that had wedged herself into her life. Megan stood with her hands in the air, as if witness to a miracle. The leather belt on her skirt was slung low over her slightly wide hips.

"Really?" Summer said. She tried to remember what brand of toothpaste she had bought.

"I mean, it may be just a coincidence, but then again," Megan said. "It's only toothpaste, but that's something. I know it doesn't seem important." She looked from Summer to Lucy, elation on her face. "I'm sorry. Is something wrong?" she asked.

"No, not at all. Again, nice to meet you, Megan."

"Likewise," Megan answered. "I wonder if we have other coincidences," Megan said, as the door shut behind Lucy. "I'll be right back. I have a photo album that I brought. This might be a good time for us to look through it."

While Megan ran, coatless, to her car for her photo album, Summer collapsed onto the couch. She slumped forward. She tried to recapture that split second of caring that Lucy's distress had sparked, but it was lost. What had it felt like? Connected, was all she could think, but the feeling had disappeared. Inside, she felt hollow. It occurred to her that she hadn't even asked the name of Lorelei's killer. It didn't matter. She didn't care to know it.

She stood up, picked up Megan's coat from the back of the couch, and hung it in the closet. It seemed alien, unlikely, in line next to her own. She sat again and waited for Megan to return with a book of photographs she had no interest in seeing.

Chapter 26

Clarkson poured a glass of orange juice and set it next to his cereal. He sat in the high stool at the counter, glad for the sunshine that filtered through the window over the kitchen sink. If it were a bit warmer, he would open the window to smell the pine. He checked his watch. Plenty of time to relax and read the paper before he drove into Glendale to meet with the realtor over the sale of the old Fox's Pizza building. It was in such disrepair, he would get it for a song.

He opened the new weekly edition of *The Sentinel*, stuffed as always into his mailbox by the road in the early morning hours. He unfolded the paper. Lorelei's picture on the front page surprised him so much that he knocked his spoon to the floor. He left it there as he read that a new break in the case had pointed to the identity of Lorelei's killer. He skimmed the article. The loose ends of the hastily conducted investigation could be neatly tied if the police could obtain a DNA sample from the suspect, identified as Daniel Rillo. Lorelei was not unreachable from her grave. He read the article again, this time carefully. He disliked the sweat that broke across his brow when he refolded the paper.

The details of that July night returned, still crisp in his memory—the surprising potency of his childhood memories, his subsequent rage, his chance meeting with Lorelei in the woods. But mostly, Lorelei's impossible vulnerability. Hadn't she practically given herself to him? Really, as time went on, it seemed almost as if she had wished to atone for his past suffering at the hands of the Glendale citizenry.

He reached for his orange juice. Maybe he had erred when he drove through Glendale before he was prepared. Of course, if he hadn't met the girl, things would have gone quite differently, especially if he hadn't divulged his true identity to her. He remembered the moment that his real name had slipped from his lips. There had been a reason for that. Something about her naïve openness provoked honesty. That was what had killed her, really, her insatiable innocence. She had left him no choice. He could not return to Glendale as Cody Dempsher. Cody was dead, and so Lorelei had to be as well. He had no regrets, other than the uncharacteristic impulsiveness of the deed. Impulsive behavior always led to sloppiness. He had learned that lesson long ago. Until now he had been lucky. He simply had to insure that his luck held. And, really, if he hadn't strangled the girl, perhaps his subsequent good fortune in Glendale would not have occurred at all.

He picked up the spoon from under his chair, rinsed it, dried it, and took a bite of his cereal. When he thought about it, the issue was simple. There could be no further testing on Lorelei. Daniel Rillo had to be guilty of Lorelei's murder. Already, in the eyes of the police and the Glendale populace, the unfortunate man was as good as convicted. As long as Lorelei remained undisturbed, of course.

The obvious key to this end was Lucy. He pictured her, practically swooning every time he glanced her way. Her capitulation to him was so blatant that he had deemed it prudent to avoid her since their encounter on Halloween. A desperate woman, even one as staid as Lucy, had the potential for volatility under careless management. Now, he needed to think how to adjust his strategy, intrude into her life without committing himself unless it was completely unavoidable. He would figure it out. Yes, Lucy was his to shape as he wished.

Much heartened, he finished his cereal as he read the report of Thursday's meeting regarding drilling prospects in the

Marcellus shale. He drained the rest of his orange juice and made a mental note to buy the fresh squeezed from Mike's the next time he shopped. It was so much better.

When he stopped at the coffee shop on his way to meet with the realtor, the girl behind the counter handed him his usual, a twelve ounce Columbian extra-bold with a trace of cream. She asked him if he'd seen the news, and without waiting for his reply, told him that Lucy wouldn't hear of any further atrocities to Lorelei's resting corpse, and she could understand that. She said that everyone in town remembered how Dee had obsessed over planting her youngest daughter in the ground.

Clarkson smiled disinterestedly and wished her a good day. He hoped the young cashier was right. But he knew how these things went. No matter what Lucy said now, in a week, or a month, the possibility of confirming the identity of Lorelei's killer would become more and more tantalizing. People who lost loved ones couldn't help themselves. It was unlikely, perhaps, but certainly possible that Lucy would mull it over, decide it was her duty to her sister, and eventually give the go-ahead to unearth Lorelei. And what about Summer? She had no real claim on Lorelei, but if she wanted to, she could pressure Lucy. When Rillo was discovered to be innocent, the case would not merely remain unsolved. It would be newly opened, a gash on the town psyche yet again. Obviously, Clarkson wouldn't become a suspect, but on the other hand, a closed case was the only acceptable outcome.

Clarkson passed the police station and glanced inside. The crooked slats of the Venetian blinds afforded a view of the musty interior, the worn linoleum floor. He continued along Main Street toward the corner where Fox's stood in disrepair. He only needed to get closer to Lucy, where he could monitor what she was thinking. That way, he could do what was necessary, either help her accept the ambiguity of Rillo's guilt, or if that approach proved difficult, convince her that Rillo was, in fact, the only possible perpetrator.

Either way, he had to persuade Lucy that it was best to leave Lorelei alone. In a moment of epiphany, he had it. He would assuage her guilt by offering a donation in Lorelei's name to the struggling Glendale police department. They could use it for training and resources. Dee, Lucy and Summer would love the idea of Lorelei resting in peace, knowing that her death had made a difference. Glendale would be a safer place with a better police force. Lucy, especially, would appreciate that. She could dress up in one of her schoolteacher outfits and present the check with him. They would have their picture in the *The Sentinel*.

That's all he needed to do. He glanced at his watch. He was on time for his meeting with the realtor. How fortuitous that he had arrived at a plan before he made an offer on the building. Now, he knew to offer a little less, so that he would have funds left over for the Lorelei memorial donation. No sense in dipping into his personal savings for that.

"Mr. Dupree," the realtor called, as he neared. He reached out to shake Clarkson's hand.

"Call me Clarkson." He shook the young man's hand and then laid his arm across his shoulder. "No need for such formality in this town. In the short time that I've been here, I've learned that in Glendale, we're all practically family."

Chapter 27

Lucy pulled her leopard hat tighter over her ears. The mid-November wind cut through her coat and the thin leather of her boots as soon as she stepped from her car. She was later than she'd expected. She looked up. The moon bulged full and ice-white against the sky. Dee's stately old house, slate roof glinting in the moonlight, looked picture perfect, a given and not a comfort these days.

The windows glowed yellow. More than usual, Lucy thought, and wondered why so many lights blazed. Dee had made it her habit to confine herself to her bedroom, alone with the glow of her television until Lucy returned from work. Maybe Dee was actually looking after herself, for a change, Lucy thought, but dismissed the notion almost immediately. She would find out in a minute.

Lucy headed to the curb to retrieve the empty trashcans. She wondered what she would make for dinner, annoyed that she had to think about it at all. The pale squares of crustless chicken salad sandwiches and half-dry celery and carrot sticks at tonight's meeting to save the YMCA had been enough for her. She would have preferred to take a hot shower, flop onto the sofa with a magazine and relax. Maybe she could throw together a tuna casserole. Dee hardly ate anyway. Lucy shivered as a gust of wind set the edges of her coat flapping.

She stopped. Where were the garbage cans? She had definitely placed them on their usual spot, that same cracked patch of cement as always, late last night. She remembered it well.

She had flung an old jacket over her bathrobe, her feet freezing in her slippers. Tears of anger and self-pity had blurred her vision as she hauled the cans, bouncing and scraping across the sidewalk, while Dee sat upstairs in what had become her strike against life. Sure, Dee had more than her share of troubles, tragedies really, but at least once, long ago, she'd had a life complete with a husband, children. A lover even, for God's sake. But these days, Dee just sat around and stared, answering if she felt like it, while Lucy made breakfast, taught school, attended community meetings, made dinner and put her to bed. Everybody's servant, that's what she was. As always.

Lucy stood rooted to the spot where she'd left the garbage cans. The thought of Dee emerging from her self-absorption to save Lucy any effort was incomprehensible. Maybe the cans had blown away, swept into the street by the chill autumn gusts. Or maybe Al had come over and carried them from the curb. She hadn't seen Al since his confession, or whatever it was. She didn't blame him for anything other than for telling her. Why had he thought she needed to know?

Lucy approached the side door. She glanced along the side of the house. The empty trashcans were neatly arranged on the cement slab near the back garden. She opened the door, surprised that the hall light was on. Her forehead creased as she walked to the kitchen and set her purse on the table. "Mom?" she called. She took off her hat and gloves and listened for a response as she unbuttoned her coat on her way to the hall closet.

Heavy footsteps sounded in the hall and a long shadow passed across her. "Lucy?"

Lucy jumped. One of her gloves fell to her feet. "Clarkson."

"I see I've startled you," Clarkson said.

Lucy bent to retrieve the glove. She stayed bent for a moment, composing her face as she picked up the glove, then slowly straightened, gloves and hat in hand. Her heart raced.

"You did." She worried that her face looked pinched from the cold, her nose, no doubt, red and running. She hoped that the heat that started low in her body and rose from her neck to her face wasn't visible.

"I'm sorry. May I?" He took her gloves and hat from her, and lifted her hair as he helped her out of her coat.

Lucy didn't want her body to feel the way it did when his fingertips grazed her neck. He opened the closet, hung her coat and put her hat and gloves on the top shelf. He seemed utterly comfortable, as if he had lived there his whole life.

"I didn't notice a car," Lucy said.

"Oh, I'm parked up the street. I was working on some business, thought I'd amble down this way since I was right in your neighborhood."

"How nice."

"Your mother and I were just chatting in the parlor. I've made a pot of tea," he said as he closed the closet door.

Dee and Clarkson chatting? Lucy followed him into the parlor, speechless. She hadn't heard from him since Halloween, over two weeks ago now, and he had a sudden need to drop by to chat with Dee? Lucy doubted that Dee had so much as answered the doorbell. She followed Clarkson through the archway into the parlor, his scent already familiar, welcome, in spite of herself. The archway framed his wide shoulders. His body fitted the proportions of Dee's big house. She remembered the way his hands had felt on her shoulders as he pulled her close on Halloween, his eyes looking into hers. She wanted him to look at her that way again. Was he here because he felt the same way?

Dee sat in the chair by the window, wrapped in the unicorn tapestry blanket that Lorelei had brought back from France a few summers ago. The blanket cocooned Dee, and her wrinkled hands seemed to spring, disembodied, from its middle to hold a steaming bone china cup. Dee smiled.

Lucy looked from Dee to Clarkson. The room felt settled, peaceful. For a second, she imagined that they were a real family, huddled together on a frosty November night.

"I'm not sure how this happened," Lucy said, inclining her neck toward Dee. She tried to sound normal, casual. "Mom, you look cozy." She walked over and kissed Dee on the forehead.

"We've had quite a nice time. She's probably getting tired now," Clarkson said. "Tea?"

"Please." Lucy watched him tilt the teapot. His hands looked strong, elegant, she thought, as he tipped it with one hand and steadied the cup with the other. She tried to think of something to say. The gurgle of the pouring liquid filled the room.

"Are you tired, Dee?" Clarkson asked as he replaced the teapot on the trivet.

Dee nodded.

Lucy studied her mother. She looked different. Even her wrinkled face couldn't dispel her transformation into a contented, obedient child.

"We've been talking about things," Clarkson said to Lucy. He turned to Dee with a smile that made the skin around his eyes crinkle in a fan from his temples to his cheek.

Lucy would have preferred jealousy instead of the inadequacy that gripped her. How had he done that? Clarkson had waltzed in sometime today and managed to swaddle Dee in a cozy wrap and ply her with steaming tea. The hurt and hunted expression on Dee's face had lifted. She looked like someone finding a little comfort on a cold night. It took a kinder soul than her own, Lucy thought, to grant her mother a moment of peace at last.

"Cream and sugar?" Clarkson turned to Lucy, focusing his crinkle-eyed smile on her.

"Neither. Thank you." The shame that had squeezed her stomach began to dissipate. Maybe she and her mother both needed some attention, some kindness. Lucy took the cup and saucer that he offered. How had he known it was her favorite? He didn't touch her as he passed the cup, delicate, gold-rimmed, hand-painted with a hummingbird alit on a gilded branch that curved around into a stylized handle. She wished he had.

"You took in the trash cans," Lucy said.

"Yes, well, it was windy, they might have blown into the street." Clarkson seated himself in the chair by the window, the way that men sit, knees apart, relaxed, unguarded. Lucy had seen the male teachers at school sit with the same unstudied ease, but Clarkson made it seem so elegant. Intimate.

Lucy nodded.

"Dee and I were thinking about how difficult it must be for you," he said. He sipped his tea. "By the way, we've already eaten. I can get you a plate of leftovers while we talk, if you like. Dee was hungry."

Hungry, Lucy thought, amazed. With coaxing, Dee had scarcely managed to eat enough to stay alive since the funeral. Lucy's teacup rattled in the saucer as she edged forward to examine Dee's face. Dee sat, beatific as a young dalai lama.

"No, thanks, they fed us at the YMCA meeting."

Clarkson asked about her day at school, whether she believed the campaign to save the YMCA was going well. She answered, distracted, mostly wondering if that's what having a husband felt like. Did the other teachers at school come home to a cozy tea party and conversation? Jealousy stabbed at her.

Clarkson leaned forward. He put his hands on his knees. "We've decided, if it's all right with you, of course, that it might be a fine idea if I were to move in and help both of you out," he said. He sat back again and sipped his tea, as calm as if he had just commented on the weather.

Lucy backed away from her teacup. She swallowed the sip she had taken without choking. She wanted to appear casual, the way he had. She fidgeted with the gilded branch handle.

"If you like, that is," Clarkson continued. "It's just a thought. Maybe you could stay here, too, for a while, until I get the lay of the land, you know, and then, depending on how things go, you can go back to your own place."

His mention of returning to her own place deflated her. She wished that he wanted to move in to be close to her. But maybe he did. After all, what interest could he have in Dee?

"Well, I'm really not sure," Lucy said. That heat that happened when he was near began to bubble up inside her again, exacerbated by the hot tea. She set her cup and saucer on the table and stood up. She needed air.

"You don't have to decide right now. I'll call you tomorrow."

"Yes, tomorrow," Lucy said. She picked at an imaginary spot on her skirt. "I'm at school, you know, in the day."

"Tomorrow evening, then. You and Dee can discuss it and we'll talk."

"Yes," Lucy said. She wondered if he knew that Dee rarely spoke at all. Had Dee actually conversed with him?

"I'll let you two get back to your business. Shall I help you clean up in here, first?" he asked.

"No, thank you, it's nothing. Thanks for the tea. And the offer."

He retrieved his coat from the closet. It occurred to Lucy that he could disappear again, the way he had before. "So you'll call tomorrow?" she asked, as he slipped his arms, both at once, into his black cashmere coat. She wasn't sure if she'd avoided sounding desperate.

"Shall I stop by, instead?"

"No, calling is fine."

Lucy walked to the front door with him. She folded her hands across her chest. He opened the door and stepped into the darkness.

"Oh, by the way," he said.

"Yes?" Lucy asked. Her heartbeat was too fast. Was he reluctant to leave? Maybe he would kiss her goodnight, the way she'd imagined so many times since Halloween.

"The light bulb on the front porch was out. I replaced it for you. Also, I think you need some insulation around your windows. Especially in the upstairs bedrooms. But we'll get to those, as we need to. That is, if you and Dee decide it's a good idea."

"Yes," Lucy said. She closed the door.

Chapter 28

Lucy glanced at the clock once again as she set the tray of Dee's half-eaten dinner on the kitchen counter. After six and still Clarkson hadn't called. Where was he, and more to the point, how could he do this to her one more time? She thought of her fourth-graders, mooning over their silly crushes. At her age, she was just like them, but without their resilience. She was way too old for this game.

What did she expect from Clarkson, anyway? Lucy had no real hope that he could help Dee. Her mom was so far gone at this point that Lucy had begun to consider alternative arrangements. The brochure from Golden Years Sunshine Suites had arrived in yesterday's mail. Lucy had stuffed it between the pages of the new Vogue magazine, not that Dee would have noticed. Anyway, at this juncture in life, Dee wasn't the one who needed Clarkson's help. She pulled at the skin that was beginning to crepe at the folds of her elbows. There was still a chance that he would call.

Lucy ripped a page from a tablet on the kitchen counter. She would use her time to compose a grocery list. She opened Dee's refrigerator and poked around. A tub of cream cheese had sprouted a bloom of reddish mold. She pitched it, and added it to her list. She checked the expiration dates on the milk and eggs. Still good. She flung the pantry doors wide to count the boxes of cereal and pop tarts, which Dee had expressed a fondness for and then ignored. When the phone rang, she nearly hit her head on a cabinet in her race to grab it.

"Lucy? I'm glad you answered. I got a bit detained today. I wonder if you could meet me at Pamela's for dinner. We can relax, grab a bite, sort things out."

Her heart rate ratcheted up at the sound of his voice. "Clarkson. Yes, I could do that. I've only just finished feeding Dee, not that she ate, really."

"Shall I pick you up?"

"No, that's all right. I'll be there as soon as I can."

Lucy hung up the phone. Why hadn't she accepted his invitation to pick her up? She couldn't be too hard on herself, though. She had done well just to make sense. Thank heavens she had worn her new sweater today. The blue was exactly right with her eyes. She ran into the bathroom, fixed her make-up and called upstairs to Dee.

"Mom, I'm meeting Clarkson at Pamela's. I won't be too long. Call my cell if you need me." The polish on her middle fingernail had worn thin, so she touched it up, making her other nails dull by comparison. She slapped a quick coat on the rest and paced the house while she waved her fingers in a frenetic dance.

When she got to Pamela's, Clarkson was already seated, a drink in front of him. He stood when she approached. She wasn't sure how to greet him, a wave, a handshake, air kisses? She lowered her head and fumbled with her purse and gloves. Clarkson appeared not to notice and helped her with her coat.

"Please, have a seat," he said.

The leather squeaked as Lucy slid into the booth. She was mortified. Did Clarkson misconstrue the source of that sound? Her face burned with embarrassment. Oh God, what if she had a hot flash now? She thought she might suffocate in her sweater. Why hadn't she worn her paisley blouse? Her purse caught on the edge of the table and the clasp opened, sending its innards clattering to the floor. She backed out of the booth, leaned over and gathered up a tube of lipstick, eyeliner, a vial of herbal vitamins, Advil and her folding scissors. Her cashmere turtleneck dampened under her arms.

"Oh my God, I can't believe I did that."

"It's all right. Let me help you." Clarkson bent down, collected a handful of change and slipped it into her outstretched palm. His hand grazed her fingertips.

She took a deep breath. "Thank you."

It was all she could do to order, and once her salad arrived she was horrified at the contortions required to chew it. Why had she ordered such a crunchy meal with Clarkson across the table? She was relieved when Clarkson launched into a long story, something about the history of Drake's Well in Titusville he'd learned the other day. She nodded at appropriate points between self-conscious bites.

"Shall we head over to Dee's house?" Clarkson asked after he paid the check. "We can look around and make sure there's room for me somewhere inside that grand-dame of a house you and your mom rattle around in. You must be anxious to get back to your own place at some point."

"Yes," Lucy said, her throat very tight.

Inside the house, Lucy called to her mom who didn't answer. "I should check on her," she said.

"I'll come with you."

They walked upstairs. "I might as well give you the tour on the way to Mom's room. She's okay, I'm sure. She just never answers anymore." Lucy led him down the hall. At the door to her room with the daisy chain wallpaper, she didn't switch on the overhead light. She hoped the darkness would conceal her prim existence. When she got to Lorelei's childhood room, she stood in the doorway, still unable to cross the threshold without a stab of pain. The room exuded Lorelei. All those years when she rented rooms to guests, Dee only used Lorelei's room as a last resort. Right up until her death, Lorelei would occasionally declare a sleepover night and stay, much to Dee's delight. Clarkson strode forward and stood in its middle.

"So Lorelei had the room with the oriel window," he said.

"Excuse me?"

"This window." He walked to the wall where a window jutted over the side street.

"Yes."

"This is a fantastic example of an oriel window. You'll find them in some of these old Queen Anne's. Some cultures use them as reverse birdcages for their women. You know, for their harems or kept women. Trapped in the confines of their rooms, they could look outside without being seen."

"A window for prisoners," Lucy said.

Clarkson laughed. "A window for women who weren't permitted to bare their faces to the outside world."

Lucy stepped across the threshold and rubbed her arms. A wave of shivers pulsed from her spine to her shoulders. "She loved to sit there," Lucy said.

Clarkson gave a little laugh. "Yes, I suppose so."

Lucy turned to him.

"Anyone would," he said.

The television was on, soundless, in Dee's room. Dee sat on the edge of her bed, peering at it. Clarkson waited in the doorway while Lucy entered and smoothed Dee's wild wisps of hair.

"Mom, turn the sound on so you can hear it," Lucy said. Without waiting, Lucy picked up the remote and adjusted the volume.

"That's better," Dee said.

"Clarkson is here, mom. He's thinking about moving in for a bit to take care of things for us."

Dee turned away from the TV. Clarkson strode into the room and put his arm around Dee's shoulder. "You look lovely today, Dee," he said. Dee smiled.

Lucy showed him all the bedrooms along the second floor, the recessed window seat at the landing where she used to sit and read as a child, the triptych of bird prints above the velvet chaise in the alcove between the main bathroom and the largest guest room. Clarkson remarked the spots that needed fixing, some frayed wires, loose boards, cracked windowpanes, peeling paint. "I guess we let things go a bit," Lucy said.

"It's okay. It's obvious that this house has been full of women who didn't care about details like that for a long time," Clarkson said. He pointed to a half open door that led to a staircase. "What's up there?"

"It's dreadful," Lucy said.

"How so?" Clarkson started up the flight.

"I don't know. I haven't been up there in ages. It used to be creepy, that's all."

"Mind if I check it out?"

Lucy shrugged. She waited on the second floor and listened to the floorboards groan under Clarkson's weight.

He returned after a bit. "I can move in as early as next week, part-time of course. I'll start with some of the minor repairs—the peeling paint, broken latches, outdated electrical. Lucy, this house needs a lot of repairs. While I work on it, I'll fix up the third floor for me. You can see how things go, stick around until you're comfortable with the situation. I'll stay out of your way."

"You won't be in my way," Lucy said, then worried what her words might imply. "I mean this house is big enough for a platoon."

"It is. So, do we have a deal?"

Lucy struggled to maintain control. He would live here, with her, in Dee's house. They would be together every day. Maybe not every day. Hadn't he said something about part-time? And before, hadn't he mentioned that she could move back to her own place? Still, it was her chance to be with him.

She cleared her throat. "I can't see why not. Mom seemed okay with the idea."

"Great. I need to get going," Clarkson said. "I still have a few chores to take care of this evening."

Lucy followed him down the stairs. He paused on the landing and traced the flourish of a scroll in the stained glass window.

"Thank you Clarkson," Lucy said at the front door. Again, she worried how to say farewell. Maybe she should put her hand on his forearm. At the very least. Then, squeeze it with a little force. Not too much, though.

While she contemplated her strategy, he smiled at her and was off.

Chapter 29

Summer walked up the wide cement steps to Dee's front door. Ever since Clarkson had moved in, the house seemed transformed, remote. No more side door entrances, that's for sure. She paused. Lucy should be home, and with any luck, Clarkson would be out. Attending to his business, whatever that meant.

Summer knocked. Within seconds, the door opened.

"Why, Summer. How nice to see you."

"Is Lucy in?" she asked.

"Is that any way to greet a friend?" Clarkson made a sweeping gesture. "Come in, please."

Summer crossed the threshold. "I only have a minute. I was just hoping to talk to Lucy." She tossed her hair back.

"Yes, of course." Clarkson led her into the parlor.

"It's become quite chilly," Clarkson said. "Allow me." He helped her with her coat and motioned for her to sit.

"Well, it's November." Summer didn't try to disguise the edge in her voice. He left the room with her coat. Summer heard the scrape of hangers sliding across the closet rod.

"Lucy tells me your daughter is visiting," Clarkson said, from around the corner. He made it sound as if it were a festive occasion.

"Yes."

"What's her name again? I'm afraid I've forgotten." He returned and sat in the chair across from her. His forehead creased, his eyes narrowed. He crossed his legs and put a finger to his temple.

"Megan."

"Yes." His forehead relaxed. He folded his arms across his chest. "Well, how is Megan?"

Summer listened for the clatter of Lucy's heels on the tiled hall, but there was only stillness. She tilted her head and stared at Clarkson. She had come to talk to Lucy. "Okay," she said. She concentrated on an uneven edge of a thumbnail.

She wished that Lucy would appear. She needed to vent. Megan was driving her insane. It had been two weeks already, and Summer had viewed Megan's life from infancy to adulthood— school field trips, proms, vacations and holidays with her adoptive parents, Nancy and Joe, and two large stepbrothers, Dan and Pete. All of them, healthy-looking with wide smiles. The life that Megan had rolled out in endless pages of flat photographs looked fine to Summer, stable, idyllic. But Megan showed no signs of wanting to return to it. Yesterday, she had mentioned that she would so enjoy a Thanksgiving feast in Glendale. It would be special, she had said. Summer had pretended not to hear.

"I'm sure it's a change for you, having her here," Clarkson persisted.

"Yes, well. She's young. Is Lucy here?"

"Oh, I'm sorry. Didn't I mention that? She should be back any moment. Dee's napping, so it seemed like a good time. She's gone shopping. You know Lucy and her shopping."

"Oh." The familiar tone in his voice irritated her. Already he was an expert on Lucy's habits. And he had certainly failed to mention that Lucy was out shopping. Summer moved forward and shifted her weight to her feet. "Perhaps I'll come back another time."

"Young," Clarkson said. "Living with a young person in a small space must be an adventure." He smiled at her. "I can only imagine."

"Yes, it is." Summer half-perched on the edge of her seat. She kept her weight shifted forward.

Clarkson leaned back and spread his arms across the back of his chair. He chuckled, as if he had told himself a joke. "We get set in our ways as we get older," he said. "Not that you're old, of course."

"I feel it sometimes." Summer wondered why she had answered him. He had a way about him, she thought. She balanced her weight between sitting and standing. If only she hadn't let him take her coat. She felt for her handbag at her feet.

"So what is young Megan doing that has you feeling so elderly?"

"Nothing really. I'm just not used to living with another person." Summer shrugged. She looked to the archway. How much longer could Lucy shop?

"Really, I don't want to take up your time."

"Oh, don't worry at all. I need the break. Lucy will be here directly."

"Well, for a minute then," Summer said.

"So, you've always lived alone?" Clarkson asked. He leaned forward and fixed his eyes on Summer. The way he said the word alone made her feel unbearably lonely.

"My whole adult life." The words came out of her mouth before she could stop them. Even she could hear the sadness underlying her words.

She fidgeted in her seat. That had been the mistake of her life, not moving in with Lorelei. She had a thousand excuses at the time, and now, not one of them seemed important. When Lorelei had pleaded with her to go public, overcome her inhibitions, Summer had assumed that she had forever to decide, to be with Lorelei. And now it was too late. She looked up to find Clarkson's green eyes locked onto hers. A flash of something between them unsettled her. It vanished so quickly that she thought maybe she had imagined it. Why did that always seem to happen between them?

"I'm used to it, being alone," Summer said. She tried to sound casual, to erase any despair.

"Yes, well. Change is difficult. I know." He paused. "We're learning to adjust to our new living arrangements here, Lucy, Dee and me." He looked down and then raised his head abruptly, as if he had just realized the ceiling held the answer to something. "Why don't you and Megan join us for dinner tonight? I told Lucy that I would throw something together for us after her long day of bargain-hunting at the mall. It would be no trouble to add two more."

His gaze moved from the ceiling back to her.

"That's very kind of you to ask, but—"

"Lucy would love it. She was just saying how she hadn't had a chance to get to know Megan."

At least Lucy would be there. And even Dee. What was her choice? Another dinner with Megan to endure her long stories about her stepbrothers, Dan and Pete, and how it was to be the adopted child with two biological siblings, two 'real' children, as she had put it?

"That might work," Summer said, "I'm not sure. I'd have to check with Megan…" Her voice trailed off. Did he know that Megan never had other plans? Megan loved nothing better than to follow Summer wherever she went, whatever she did.

"While you think about it, if you don't mind, I'd like your advice on something." He stood up and hurried from the room. The jump in his step surprised her. He returned shortly with paint samples.

"I don't know when the hall was last painted, but the scuff marks make me think it's been a while. I'm considering this one." He held a paint chip up to the light, then handed it to Summer. "It's called 'Summer Sandalwood.' Who do you suppose names these colors?"

Summer took the sample from his hands. Had he brushed her hand deliberately, the way she had seen him touch Lucy? She wasn't sure.

"What do you think?" He studied the paint chip. "I'd like your opinion."

Summer nodded.

"Or, what about this one? I think it matches the house." He pointed to the green vein that snaked through the marble mantle. "But what do I know about decorating?"

Summer was careful to avoid touching his hand as she took the second sample. She walked to the hallway and held the greenish one to the wall.

"That's called 'Breath of Cactus.' That name is even better. I can't imagine those marketing sessions were conducted soberly." Clarkson laughed at his own comment. "So?"

He walked over and stood near her. When she tried to look into his eyes, he focused on the paint chip, as if it were the most important decision he had ever made. He confused her. Maybe she had imagined things on Halloween, when she'd felt his eyes on her even while he seemed intent on Lucy. She looked at him now, absorbed by the dilemma of the paint chip. He seemed so much less enigmatic than he had. Usually, she had found him evasive, a bit creepy even. Was he merely obtuse? Most men were, she guessed. She didn't know that much about men. And Megan did have her unsettled these days. Megan and everything else in her life. She wasn't sure about anything anymore.

"Maybe the green. The cactus breath or whatever it's called. Cleaner, more modern, maybe, than the other," Summer said. She hoped she sounded conversational, decisive.

"Yes. Could be." The tiled hallway reverberated with the deep pitch of his voice.

"Will you do the work yourself?" Summer asked. She dropped the paint chip in his hand, careful again not to touch him. Were they having a mundane, casual conversation?

"I'll certainly do a lot of it. See how things go. The downstairs at least. The upstairs bedrooms could use some work, too. Seven bedrooms. Some of them look worn out. I don't know how the two of them managed such a huge house."

"Dee ran it for a while as a guesthouse, you know," Summer said. Before Lorelei was murdered, she thought, but she couldn't bring herself to say it.

"Well that makes perfect sense. And it gives me an idea." He touched her lightly on the shoulder. "No, maybe it won't work."

Summer looked at him.

"No, it was just a thought." The lines around his temples went from jovial crinkles to mere creases.

"What?" Summer asked. She asked because she knew that he wanted her to, and it was easier to play along. She was suddenly very tired.

"I really don't mean to intrude, but what if Megan didn't have to stay at your place? What if she moved in here with us? Just for a while."

"Hello!" Lucy's voice floated down the hallway.

The side door slammed, and Summer heard Lucy's heels cross the kitchen floor.

"Lucy, Summer's here to see you." Clarkson looked past Summer and raised his voice. He tilted his head in the direction of the footsteps.

Lucy emerged from the hall, smiling, one large shopping bag in each hand.

"Summer, so nice to see you," Lucy said.

She set her bags down and gave Summer a hug. Not the robotic hug that Summer and Lorelei used to make fun of, but a real hug. She flashed a smile at Clarkson, a little shy and sweet, her face flushed. Summer knew that for Lucy, that smile was downright flirtatious. Lucy was a new person. The realization made Summer even more tired.

"Lucy, Megan and Summer are joining us for dinner," Clarkson said.

Summer was about to say she hadn't decided for sure. While she was thinking of an excuse to decline, Lucy squeezed her hand.

"That is such a good idea. I've been meaning to come over to see you. And Megan, of course. I've been so busy."

"It's all right, we have been, too," Summer said.

"Lucy, Summer was explaining to me how difficult it is to live in confined quarters with Megan. We thought it might work if Megan were to move in here, with us, for a while." Clarkson picked up Lucy's shopping bags and set them on the table.

"Summer, is that what you want?" Lucy asked. She had blushed a little more when Clarkson had said 'with us.'

"I don't know. Clarkson only just mentioned it to me. I haven't had a chance to think about it."

"We certainly have enough room," Lucy said.

"I propose we talk about it at dinner tonight," Clarkson said.

Summer shrugged. At this point, she couldn't refuse the invitation even if she had wanted to. "What time?" She directed her question to Lucy.

"Ask him. He's the cook." Lucy threw up her arms. Summer had never seen her move so loosely.

"Seven okay?" Clarkson asked.

Summer nodded. Lucy took her shopping bags in her hands. "Summer, I'll see you later. I want to make sure this skirt fits right. You know those mirrors at Fieldstone's. I don't trust them." She headed down the hall.

Clarkson walked Summer to the door.

"I'm looking forward to tonight with you and your charming daughter," he said to her. He bent and kissed her hand in a most gentlemanly manner.

"Yes, of course," Summer said.

The door closed behind her. Summer stood on the porch for a moment before returning to her car. Clarkson was not an easy person to figure out.

Chapter 30

Dee's snore was the only sound in the house. Clarkson relaxed. He liked the house best that way, just Dee and him. Having Dee around was almost better than being alone. Her nearly comatose presence reminded him to go after what he wanted in life while he still could.

His keys clattered as they hit the silver tray that Lucy kept on the sideboard so the wood didn't scratch. He set his leather gloves next to the tray, took off his coat and hung it in the hall closet. He stopped at the doorway of the downstairs powder room. It had been the right decision to invite Megan to live with them, he knew that. But why that girl could not wrap her tampons more carefully escaped him. He had never expected to live in a house of women. Lucy was bad enough, with her stash of creams, in tubes and jars, and vials of scented oils tucked in various corners about the house. But Megan was worse, with her blood-tinged trash and those glittery squares of eye shadows that she left on sink corners. Were all women vivid and slippery? Dee sputtered and coughed from her chair in the parlor. Even Dee had her share of potions and ointments.

His mind flashed to his mother's things, bits of ribbon, pots of rouge, little brushes with creamy cobalt flecks stuck to them. Her soft lilac bar of soap that his childish fingers had glided across. His mother had been that same way, all moist and colorful.

It was funny. The longer he lived in Glendale, the more he remembered from his past. As a young man, he had worked in construction in California with an older man who claimed that when he traveled back east to his childhood roots, his brain would light up with forgotten phone numbers, radio station call letters, television channels that he couldn't remember when he was away, even if he tried. He swore that once he breathed in the familiar air of his hometown, the memories rushed back.

Was that it, Clarkson wondered? Had Glendale always resonated within him, so that now he only required the wind blowing from the north with its faint fragrance of pine to resurrect his youth? Youth. That wasn't exactly the word to describe his childhood. Youth brought with it images of vitality and carefree existence. He couldn't remember a carefree time no matter how hard he tried, no matter how many recollections pieced themselves together, borne on the heels of a pine-laced breeze. And he wasn't sure that he had ever been attuned to Glendale.

Still, he had to admit that his memories of Glendale grew all the time. More and more, he recalled the houses, the families, the names of the shops on Main Street, things he hadn't even tried to know when he was young. By his junior high school days, he had made it a point to separate from his surroundings. He had strived not to register details of the lives of those more fortunate around him, smug in their Glendale world while he struggled beneath them in his own.

He hadn't succeeded. Sometimes, when he turned a corner onto a hilly street, a wide front porch and a particular facade would attach itself to a name that arose unbidden from his subconscious. And the name would open a world of images. Liddie Hamilton with her straight blonde hair as she raced across the lawn with her friends, her arms loaded with books, her voice high and clear, her laugh surprisingly throaty. He remembered that his heart had jumped a little every time he saw her. And that he had been invisible to her.

He could recall exact incidents. In those first years, after his mother had left and his father stared, drank, and slept, no one had helped him with the small things that he hadn't known to do. He remembered one day walking to the front of his classroom with his homework paper, late and half-finished. He had expected the lecture about his poor academic performance from the teacher, and that part hadn't bothered him at all. He had shrugged and returned to his seat in the rear of the classroom. But as he passed, the kids in both rows pinched their noses with their fingers. Some of them made quiet gagging sounds. The teacher hadn't bothered to look up from her desk. At home, he found his mother's plastic wash basket and demanded that his father take him to the Laundromat on Jefferson. The next day at recess he stuck out his leg just enough for it to appear accidental and tripped one of his tormenters on the playground.

The other day, he came upon the photo of the Armstrong son killed in Vietnam. He had seen it many times, propped in the corner in the den, behind a lamp, the glass over it coated with dust. This time, when he saw it, he realized that he remembered Thaddeus. Thad had been older than Clarkson, quite handsome and popular. Maybe it had happened the summer before his father dropped dead and he had incinerated his childhood trappings. He wasn't sure. He remembered only that the whole town had convened to weep over the loss of one of their finest. Clarkson hadn't wept. He had felt removed from the whole thing. And jealous. He had imagined himself as the one who lay in state in Rhinehart's under the American flag, while the town of Glendale spiraled into sadness around him. The memory had stabbed him, made him wish he could shatter the glass and shred the photo. Instead, he slid the family album from under the den table and removed the picture of Lorelei after she had won some silly art prize in Pittsburgh. She had mentioned it that day to him, before events had taken their fatal turn. He slipped her photograph under his sweater, carried it upstairs, and hid it in his file cabinet. The Armstrongs could have their heroes, their history. Lorelei was his.

He switched off the hall light and ascended the staircase to his third floor bastion. He didn't care what disaster the women created on the lower two floors as long as he had his own space. And at least, with all her mess, Megan was a distraction from Lucy's swooning adoration. She had also accomplished his goal of defusing Summer's coldness toward him. Summer was hesitant still, of course, but she always would be. Her life of secrets hadn't prepared her to trust anyone. Cautious, reserved appreciation was all he needed from her. He unclasped his watch and set it on his dresser.

"Clarkson. Are you up there?"

"One moment." What on earth was Lucy doing? He hadn't credited her with the nerve to call upstairs after him. He wondered what event had precipitated such audacity. He picked up his watch from the dresser and took his time on his way downstairs.

Lucy leaned on the wall across from the staircase to his room. She had her face in her hands and looked at him above her palms.

"What is it, Lucy?" Clarkson slid the clasp shut on his wristwatch.

She took a deep breath. "I'm sorry to bother you, truly. It's just that, well, I've been thinking. This is the first holiday season without Lorelei and I don't know how I can stand it. We did our Thanksgiving unit in school today, you know, all about giving. And it made me realize something. I've decided that maybe I've been selfish, that maybe I need to let Officer McMahon, you know, do whatever he needs, to confirm the identity of her..." Her shoulders began to shake. "It's the only thing I can give her."

"Oh, Lucy." Clarkson put a firm hand on her shoulder. He needed this plan to come to an immediate halt. "That's very kind of you, to want to do something for your sister," he said. He made sure his voice was soothing.

Lucy looked up at him, her eyes tear-filmed, her nose red.

"What did Officer McMahon say?" Clarkson was careful to sound solicitous.

"I haven't told him yet."

Clarkson withdrew his hand from her shoulder. He controlled his breathing to mask his relief. "And Summer?"

"I thought I would talk to her tomorrow."

"I'm sure she'll stand by you whatever you decide. The one I'm concerned about is Dee. Have you thought about how your mother will handle this?"

"I have. I don't think I'll tell her. At least not until it's over. It's not like she's aware of all that much anymore."

"I see." Clarkson folded his arms and dropped his chin to his chest. "Lucy, we both know that your mother is very fragile right now. She's slipped away, but she hasn't disappeared into her own world completely. You see how she emerges now and then, with a smile, a word?"

"She does," Lucy said.

"If you go through with this, the news will be all over town, in the paper, everywhere. Think what it would do to Dee if her fog lifts at the wrong moment. What if she emerges to discover her Lorelei in the process of being ripped from the ground? Heaven forbid, of course."

Lucy flinched.

"I don't mean to be so harsh, but I'm putting it into words that Dee would understand. The nightmare of that experience might upset Dee for the rest of her days. I'm thinking out loud here. Is there something else you could do for your sister without the potential to tear your mother's heart to shreds?"

"I don't know." Lucy's hands hung by her sides.

Clarkson's forehead contracted into folds. He almost had her where he needed her. Should he let her sleep on it, or should he solve her problem for her right here?

"Unless you're convinced that exhuming your sister is the right thing to do."

"I'm not convinced of anything. I just want to do something for her. It breaks my heart that I can't open a bottle of champagne at Thanksgiving dinner with her, or place her present under the tree at Christmas." Lucy leaned back into the wall behind her.

Clarkson took both of her shoulders in his hands. "Why don't you let me do something for her? We'll do it together. I've noticed that the hard-working Glendale police department is in dire need of funds. Why don't I make a substantial donation in Lorelei's name? We can do it together, present a check, a plaque even. From what I understand, that would make your sister very happy. And your mother." He let go of her shoulders. "I don't know. Maybe that's silly, but it's an idea. Who knows, the donation may even help prevent this sort of crime from happening here in Glendale ever again. But it's your decision."

"Clarkson. Would you consider doing that for Lorelei?"

"It would be an honor."

Lucy squared her shoulders. "Lorelei would want to help someone else. That was Lorelei."

Clarkson allowed silence to consume them. After a moment, he touched Lucy's shoulder. "You've done enough thinking for the night. Why not sleep on it?"

Lucy smiled, her cheeks blotchy. "Yes, of course."

Clarkson made sure to converse a while longer, about Megan, the house renovations, anything. He needed Lucy to feel calm and confident, all thoughts of revisiting Lorelei's murder banished. When he was satisfied, he walked down the hall with her. They paused in the alcove beneath the triptych of the bird pictures.

"Thank you for allowing me to help you," he said to Lucy. The gratitude in her eyes was unmistakable, but he didn't dare linger. "Good night," he said, and headed back down the hall to the staircase to his sanctuary.

He would wait until February to present the check, he thought as he climbed the steps to his room. Over the holidays, Glendale had enough activities and charitable events, the nativity play at the Sawmill Playhouse, the Elks Club clothing drive, the Ladies' Auxiliary food for the needy collection. By late February, when only President's Day filled the barren calendar, his beneficence would be front-page news. He took off his watch and set it on the dresser once again. All in all, despite the complications from the women in the house, things in Glendale were going quite well.

Chapter 31

Wrapped in the unicorn tapestry blanket, Dee sat in the high-backed chair in the parlor. She turned her gaze to the front window. Spindly flurries lit on the curved glass and then slid in fine wet lines until they disappeared. Dee watched them for a while and made a game of them. The rules had something to do with where they landed and how far they slid before they were gone, but it became too much for her to follow. She let it go and turned her attention to the intricate weave of the blanket.

The front door slammed and a flurry of footsteps followed. Dee knew those steps—fast, disorganized, the way the girl seemed to be. Megan, the other new person in the house. There were four of them now, Megan and Clarkson and Lucy and herself. Lots of times, Al was there, too. And Summer. The sound of the girl's steps faded.

Dee felt drowsy. Her head dropped back. She wouldn't fight it. Her eyes closed and a thick stillness crept over her. A snorting noise came from somewhere inside of her and her head jerked. Had she slept?

She wondered if she should feel guilty about the way nothing mattered to her now. Was it true, what her pastor had once said, that the dead puttered around in some heavenly world, all the while watching those still on earth? Dee thought about those ghostly eyes on her. Maybe they knew that she no longer cared about them.

Thaddeus, Sr., or even Thad, Jr. had been dead for so long that they had already tired of her, anyway, she thought. She pictured Lorelei, still newly dead, her wide brown eyes, watching, knowing. Did Lorelei care that she didn't miss her anymore?

Dee thought about that for a moment, how she didn't miss Lorelei. When did that happen, she wondered. When she had gotten the call about Lorelei's murder, the pain was so bad that she had dropped the phone. She had lost her breath and a force had crushed her insides so tightly that it amazed her that she hadn't dropped dead on the spot. It had been that way, every day, for a long time. But little by little, the pain had released its grip. Small things began to acquire meaning again. Who won the grand prize in Family Feud. Whether her feet were too cold on the hard tile of the bathroom floor when she got up at night and couldn't find her slippers. If Lucy remembered to put olives on her cream cheese sandwich. While a part of her drifted away from the pointless busyness of the people around her, a different part of her had reawakened, weary it seemed, of the relentless agony that life had pushed on her. Yes, little by little, the pain had receded. She still remembered it, of course. Could she make it return? She tried to resurrect it, inviting it to cut through her body again. She knew the spot in the center of her stomach where it used to be, but that was all. It felt the same as the pearl ribbon that snaked across her abdomen from Lucy's caesarian delivery, spent and historic.

She looked back to the window, where the snowflakes were now whiter and fatter. She wasn't sure what had changed her. Maybe it was as simple as the passage of time. Whatever it was, lots of things were more tolerable now, sometimes even pleasurable. The unicorn blanket, for example. She pulled a corner of it close to her face and admired its rose color and the marching parade of white unicorns, their raised threads shiny against the rose background. She stroked it with her fingers, then let it go and held up both hands. She turned them, first palms out and then in. Even her fingertips were shriveled. That used to upset her, but not now. She remembered licking her fingertips this morning after she ate the two triangles of toast that Clarkson had brought her. The toast was warm and shiny with butter and dark specks of cinnamon.

An irregular cadence of footsteps clattered nearby. Megan bounced into the parlor. She looked at Dee, but didn't say anything. Dee looked back at her. Megan left, her discordant footsteps again echoing for a moment. She hadn't bothered to nod, or even to smile at her. With no one else around, Megan made no distinction between Dee and the furniture.

That wasn't exactly it, though. Megan appeared to treat her as a piece of furniture, but that was just natural. Young people did that with the very old, only because they didn't know what else to do. Or maybe because they understood the truth, that the old had no interest in them or anyone else. Dee remembered that wrinkled faces and bent frames used to puzzle her, too, when her arms were still smooth and her cheeks were soft. When she longed for the softness of someone else. Now, she didn't long for anyone.

That was it. People had become interchangeable for her. Was it just a consequence of living as long as she had? Megan's face didn't look at all like Lorelei's and yet, there was something about them that was the same. And Clarkson could just as easily be Thaddeus, Sr., or Thad. Or Al. When the ladies from her book club dropped by last week with a card and a basket of cookies, they had thought her addled when she couldn't sort out their names. Dee could tell. But that wasn't the problem at all. Dee blurred them only because she could see the truth clearly, that it didn't matter. One of them was only a variation of the other. If everyone ended up stuck in the wrong house for a night, it would make no real difference.

You just need to live long enough to understand. And once you do, the pain stops, and you can get to the next step of appreciating the world at long last. Dee moved until the pillow behind her back hit just the right spot. A unicorn blanket. A wet snowfall. Breakfast. Finally, the beauty of life sets in and your senses do what they were made to do without the distraction of other people and their endless catastrophes. Peace at last. Dee heard herself murmur, a sound like her infants used to make all those years ago.

The front doorbell rang. Maybe it was Summer. Or Al. He had been spending a lot of time at the house these days. Not because of her anymore. He thought she existed in another world, that she had forgotten how to decode the spoken word. Of course, he was wrong. She knew what was going on, even though Al and all the rest of them thought she didn't. She could have explained it to them if she had wanted, but it wasn't worth the trouble. They wouldn't understand. Their days of not caring were still ahead of them. She heard Megan's voice and Al's. Their footsteps went down the hallway and into the kitchen.

Clarkson was helping Al turn his funeral home into something like the grand palace that was Rhinehart's on the upper half of Main Street. The two of them were sure that the next important person to drop dead would choose Al's place now. And Al was helping Clarkson with Dupree's, the restaurant on the corner where Fox's pizza had been crumbling away for decades. Clarkson said that as long as he was here in Glendale, he might as well make his mark. Al wanted to name the restaurant after his Italian family that ran the one in Pittsburgh, but Clarkson thought his own last name was as good as any.

At dinner last night, Al had said that Dupree's had a real shot at becoming the finest restaurant that Glendale had ever seen. The judges from the courthouse would eat there. And the lawyers. And the young girls who wore high heels on the sidewalks of Glendale at lunchtime. Lucy had brought Clarkson a bottle of wine to open and her cheeks were very pink. Summer had come, too. She had dressed up and combed her hair the way she used to. She had worn lipstick.

Dee's eyes came into focus on Al and Megan standing together in the parlor doorway. She hadn't heard them in the hall. She wondered why she hadn't. Megan smiled at her now. Al walked over and touched her shoulder.

"How are you, Dee?" His voice dropped at the end. Dee knew he didn't expect an answer to his question. She thought she would explain everything to him, let him know that she understood things better even, now, than when she'd appeared to be competent. She looked into his eyes and opened her mouth to begin, but the words floated out of order. There was no way to explain this to someone who didn't feel it. And she was right. When she looked into his eyes, he could be anyone, just a bit of life trapped in a body. He could be Clarkson, or Thad, or even that butcher that she used to talk to on Thursday afternoons when she bought her meat. What was his name?

"Pete," Dee said.

Al patted her hand again and put his arm around Megan.

Chapter 32

Lucy peered out Dee's kitchen window. She hoped that Clarkson would arrive before she left for Summer's house. Her black sweater hid the beginnings of a droop in her upper arms. She smoothed her gray skirt, the tightest one she had in her closet. She felt curvy. Available. She looked around for any last task that would delay her just a bit longer. The dishes were already in the dishwasher. She straightened the kitchen towel that hung on the oven door handle. Probably Clarkson was still with Al, painting or tearing out walls or whatever they did.

Clarkson had such ambition, she thought. Last week, at Thanksgiving dinner, he had announced his purchase of the old Fox's Pizza on the corner of Main and Jefferson. He said he'd gotten it for practically nothing, since it was a shambles, and that he knew how to make something out of nothing.

Clarkson had caught her eye while everyone congratulated him, held her gaze for a split second and then raised his glass to Al. Al knew food, he said. Al had smiled, patted his considerable belly and said they should name their new venture after his Italian uncle who ran the pasta place in Pittsburgh. Clarkson had shrugged. He thought that Glendale had enough Italian connections, what with Mrs. Garibaldi's bakery. Dupree's seemed as good a name as any. Al had sat back and said, "sure, yes, sure." Clarkson was right, Lucy thought. He was a rarity in Glendale, new blood in the town's stodgy old veins. Yes, Dupree's time had come, Al had finally said.

Good old Al. Lucy leaned against the kitchen counter, pulling her skirt so the seams lined up properly. Right after his confession, she had been uncomfortable around him. She couldn't see him without wondering how it had happened, who had initiated things. Had it been Dee, married and older than he, or Al, fresh-faced, fearless? She pictured them eyeing each other knowingly while the attraction between them acquired a life of its own. She shuddered at the thought of how wrenching it must have been for Dee to turn her back on him.

But Al had that steady way about him. He was comfortable with Lucy, as if things hadn't changed between them at all. He breezed into Dee's house the way he had when Lucy was young, only now it was to see Clarkson. Even Summer was less critical of Clarkson, Lucy thought, since he had invited Megan to live with them. Lucy wished she knew how Clarkson felt about her. She looked at her watch. She had stretched out her preparations as long as she could. Summer would be waiting for her.

"Are you okay here with Dee while I'm out?" she called upstairs to Megan from the hallway.

A door opened and Megan spilled down the steps, skipping one here and there. Her sweatshirt slid off one shoulder and she tugged at it. "Sure, hey to Summer for me."

"Will do. If you need anything, call my cell or Summer's."

Megan tilted her can of ultra-caffeinated energy drink, took a gulp, smiled at Lucy and headed into the kitchen. Lucy heard the refrigerator open as she headed for the hall closet.

The tweed pea coat Lucy pulled out seemed old, teacherly. She would have to do something about that. If Lorelei were here, she would help her pick out something more daring. She picked up her handbag and keys and headed for the side door.

The late afternoon sun cast blue shadows across yesterday's snowfall. Lucy dug in her purse for her sunglasses, so her crow's feet wouldn't deepen. She heard a motor and looked up as Clarkson maneuvered his car into the space next to hers on the side driveway.

"Why, Lucy, I thought you and Summer had plans today, or do I have that wrong?" Clarkson climbed out of his car and dropped his keys into his pocket. The sunshine lit the gray at his temples turning them silver. His jacket was open, and his scarf hung loose in two parts along the zipper.

Lucy slid her sunglasses onto her face. "Oh, hello Clarkson. I was running a little late," she said. "You know how that goes." Did he suspect that she had dallied, hoping to cross his path? Her stomach rearranged itself. Did that always happen to people in love?

Clarkson paused as they passed each other. He put a hand on her shoulder and let it fall to her elbow. "Have a nice time," he said. She looked up at him and smiled. His eyes were already focused ahead. He was busy, as always, she thought.

"Thanks. We will." Lucy opened her car door. She turned sideways to Clarkson and sucked in her stomach as she waved to him.

Lucy steadied her hand as she turned the key in the ignition. She relived the feeling of his hand on her shoulder, the way it slid to her elbow. How long could she let things go on this way? Maybe tonight she would confide in Summer. She pulled onto Main Street.

Summer had agreed to get together to make a plan about Megan, Dee and the upcoming Christmas holidays. Before Clarkson moved in, and then Megan, they had discussed putting Dee into a home where someone could watch her all the time.

Now, they weren't sure. Dee seemed more content these days. Lucy adjusted the visor over the windshield to block the low sun and took the fork toward Summer's hilltop street. She supposed that it was a good sign that Dee had taken to sitting in the parlor, wrapped in that blanket most of the time, dozing and staring. Smiling, even. Still, Dee seemed less connected to the outside world than ever. The sadness at that realization failed to squash Lucy's spirits. As long as Clarkson was around, nothing could.

Summer was waiting inside her front door when Lucy pulled up at the curb. She hurried down her apartment steps and hopped into the passenger seat.

"Did we decide on Pamela's?" Summer asked. She slammed the door shut.

"Fine with me. Dupree's is still a dream at this point."

Summer laughed. "I have a feeling it won't be for long."

"So what's new?" Lucy asked.

"We're busy at the radio station. You know, holiday stuff. What are the fourth graders up to?"

"Same stuff," Lucy said.

"Same stuff? Miss teacher of the year? I've never heard you answer that way before." Lucy didn't answer. "Whatever you're doing, it's agreeing with you, I must say."

"Really? You think so?"

"You look fabulous. So, what is it?"

Lucy shrugged. She wanted to tell Summer, right there in the car, about her escalating feelings for Clarkson. Maybe she would. She pulled into the space in front of Pamela's and opened her mouth to speak, but Summer opened the passenger door. "I didn't have lunch today. I am famished." Summer was already halfway out the passenger door.

They knew the waitress at Pamela's. She asked about Dee, said she had heard about a flurry of visitors at the Armstrong residence, even a rumor about a new restaurant somehow connected to the family. Lucy laughed. "It's not competition for you yet, Josie," she said.

Josie led them to a table in the front window, took their orders and left. Summer and Lucy talked about Dee, how she'd emerged from her room every day. "Clarkson makes her breakfast," Lucy said, "and she eats every bite." She told Summer that the downstairs of the Armstrong house had become a new place altogether with his painting and sanding and whatever else he did. Lucy pictured him when she came home from school, working at something in his paint-splattered pants, fine dust in his hair, and then later, at the dinner table in his pressed pants, cashmere sweater and gleaming wristwatch.

Over salads and wine, they talked about Megan. Summer said that Megan was adamant about remaining in Glendale to spend Christmas with her. Clarkson had promised Summer that he would keep Megan busy, put her to work organizing the paperwork when construction on the restaurant heated up.

"Thank goodness he thought of something for her to do," Summer said.

They split a slice of chocolate cake. Summer picked at it while she told Lucy that things were going better than she had expected with Megan. "I don't mind having her around, as long as she doesn't live with me," Summer said. "I guess, in a way, it feels like it was meant to be." Summer pushed her plate away and stroked the iron base of the candleholder in the center of the table. "She just wants to see who I am. Eventually, I expect her family will miss her, or she'll miss them."

When Josie brought the check, darkness had fallen and Lucy still hadn't brought up her feelings for Clarkson.

"So, for now, we'll just see what happens," Lucy said, pulling up in front of Summer's house to drop her off. "Looks like we'll have our big dinner on Christmas Eve at Dee's, with Al, Megan, you and me," she paused and tried to sound casual, "and Clarkson, I suppose."

"Well, of course Clarkson," Summer said. She didn't open her car door.

"Yes, I guess so, for dinner at least," Lucy said. She let out a heavy breath. "He has that rental cabin he keeps. He goes out there every few days, something about negotiating timber rights in the countryside. If he didn't have his own place, I would already have moved out from Dee's house and back into my own. But with his comings and goings, I think I better stay at Dee's for a while longer. You know, in case Dee needs me." Lucy stopped. If she moved out now, would Clarkson forget about her?

"I see," Summer said.

Lucy took her hands off the steering wheel and turned to Summer. "He seems to talk to Megan some, I thought maybe she knew something about his plans for the future." Lucy hoped the darkness hid her face.

"Not that I know of," Summer said. She opened her car door and then half-closed it and turned to Lucy. "Look, Lucy, it's still early. I'm still celebrating having Megan out on her own, at Dee's you know. I bought a mojito mix. Just add rum. Come on in and have one with me."

"Mojitos?"

"It wouldn't kill you. Step out, a little, Lucy. Why not?"

"Why not?" Lucy said.

Inside Summer's apartment, Lucy watched Summer mix together the greenish concoction in a glass pitcher. She poured it over crushed ice in tall glasses, adding little sprigs of mint at the tops. "Fresh from the produce section at Mike's," Summer said. "Who would have thought? Fresh mint in Glendale in December."

"It's a new world," Lucy said.

"We need to toast something. In memory of Lorelei," Summer said, and handed Lucy a glass, already frosting up on the outside.

"She always had something to toast, didn't she? How about to Megan," Lucy said, and then, feeling braver, "and maybe to Clarkson."

"To Megan and Clarkson, it is," Summer said. They clinked glasses and took sips.

"Look at me. Drinking mojitos. What will I do next?" Lucy said. Her insides felt warm.

"It's good for you now and then." They were silent.

"Do you know that I have never even smoked a cigarette?" Lucy said. She laughed a little. The rum made her warm all over.

"Never? Good God, Lucy."

"Summer, I can't believe I'm about to say this." Lucy took a deep breath, then a long gulp, and set her glass down.

"What?"

"I've become like everyone else at last. Like you. I've fallen in love." She paused a minute. "With Clarkson." His name felt intimate on her tongue. "I'm in love with Clarkson." A great heaviness fell away, leaving her free. Naked, in a way.

Summer put her drink down and stood up. Lucy brought herself to her feet next to Summer. "Can you believe it?" She hugged Summer. The hug acquired its own momentum and the two of them listed toward Summer's refrigerator before Summer separated from Lucy, turned away and sat, her hands cupped across her nose, eyes closed.

Lucy sat across from her. "I'm sorry. I didn't mean to be insensitive. I mean, I guess you were in love. You had Megan, after all. You must have loved him to have his baby."

"Oh," Summer said. She opened her eyes and reached for her mojito. Lucy watched her. The muscles in Summer's neck tightened.

"I don't blame you for it," Lucy said. "In fact, I envy you. Everyone has been in love at least once," she continued. "Some lots of times. Except for me, until now. I'm so afraid that he doesn't feel the same way. Sometimes I think he does, sometimes I'm almost sure. But he stays away. God, I sound like such a schoolgirl."

"It's okay," Summer said.

"We haven't, you know…" Lucy looked down, leaving her fingers interlocked in the air in front of her. She looked up at Summer, sure that her face was red.

"Had sex?" Summer asked.

"Oh, God, no." Lucy's hands fell into her lap. "We haven't even kissed. He held my hand before I went upstairs last night, and I wanted him so much. Sometimes I think he would. Kiss me that is, if I didn't seem so nervous or whatever it is I am. Maybe he's waiting for a sign from me."

Summer nodded. "Try to relax, Lucy. If the moment seems right, things will take care of themselves."

"Really?" Lucy tried to feel hopeful. "I don't know. I'm not sure how to let him know how I feel."

"Come on, Lucy. I know it's probably been a long time for you, but don't think so hard. Let yourself go. It will all come back to you."

"There's nothing to come back," Lucy said. The words dropped from her mouth before she could stop them.

Silence engulfed the room.

"Never? With anyone?" Summer's voice was gentle.

Lucy couldn't bring herself to speak. Never, she thought. Really, she had wanted to, when she was younger. There had been a few times that she'd come close. But things were never quite right. She used to resurrect memories of those almost-experiences at night, mulling over each detail—a row of loosened buttons, a hand slipped between her legs. They were proof of her desirability. Over the years, those memories had become worn thin from too much examination. The last time she had tried to dredge them up, they were vague snippets of sweaty, fumbling misconnections. She was a virgin, a fifty-one year old virgin. One of those terminally good girls. No, not even that, she thought, the cruelty in her self-recrimination painful. She hadn't been terminally good, only terminally particular, isolated. She looked up at Summer.

"No," she said. "I've never done it."

Summer nodded and stood up. Greenish flecks swirled in the pitcher as she tilted it, refilling both of their glasses.

"Oh, Summer, I wish I had. If only because it would be easier for me now. I understand how you could have, you know, given in, even though you were young, even though you risked getting pregnant. I understand. I envy you. Oh God, you have no idea what a relief it is to say this. I walk around all the time, with his face in my mind. I don't know what to do. I want to tell him, but I'm so afraid."

The tears that fell from Summer's eyes came fast. They wet her eyelashes and landed on her shirt.

"Summer, I'm sorry," Lucy said. "I didn't know it was so sensitive for you."

"Lucy, it's not that. You don't understand at all."

"Understand what?"

"Lucy, what you just said, about needing to talk about Clarkson. I understand that. And about being in love. I understand that, too. But I wasn't in love with Megan's father. I hardly knew him. I was in love with…"

"Summer, it doesn't matter who," Lucy said. She pictured Clarkson's green eyes, the way his face erupted into a smile and then turned serious all of a sudden.

Summer took a sip of her drink. "Lucy, it does matter who. Think about Clarkson, how you feel about him. It matters a lot."

Lucy nodded. They were quiet. "Well, who was it from your past? Do you want to talk about him?"

"Lucy, I can't believe you never knew. I'm only telling you because I feel the same way you do. I need to tell someone. It's…"

Summer sat down and raised her tearful eyes to Lucy's. They were red, overwhelmed with sadness.

"It was Lorelei." Summer's voice was barely a whisper.

Lucy gasped. That was impossible. Lorelei was her sister, Summer's friend. The three of them had spent so much time together. And then, she remembered—Lorelei and Summer bursting into Dee's house, laughing together, Summer's remote sadness at the funeral, oddly proprietary. It had all been right in front of her. Why hadn't she figured it out? Had she been so removed from the world of sexuality, that she could stare right at it and fail to see it? "Lorelei?" she asked, although she knew it was true.

"Yes," Summer said, her voice almost inaudible.

"And she loved you, too," Lucy said, her tone flat.

Chapter 33

Lucy's second cup of coffee did nothing to penetrate her grogginess. She set the half-empty mug on the counter. She hadn't made much progress in her efforts to come to terms with Summer's revelation last night. One moment she wondered how she had never figured it out on her own, and the next she wondered if it were really true. She had nothing against couples of the same sex. She simply never bothered to think about them. Gays and lesbians were the same as those starving children in Africa. Important to someone, but not relevant to her immediate world. No wonder Lorelei had kept her sexuality a secret from her.

She drove to work on autopilot. Summer and Lorelei as a couple made sense when she thought about it. Lucy pictured them, walking side by side with the ease of married couples, their inside jokes and wordless communication, in retrospect, obvious. For what seemed like the hundredth time that morning, she wondered how she had never guessed. She pulled into her usual space in the school parking lot and braced herself for the day. After lunch, when her fourth-graders proposed that they devote the afternoon to planning the upcoming holiday program, Lucy gave in. For once, she didn't have the energy to direct. As the day wore on, she rolled Summer's news over in her mind. When the dismissal bell rang, her liveliest student, Nathan Cole, stopped at her desk, his backpack dragging on the floor. "Can we not do anything tomorrow, too?" he asked.

On the drive home, Lucy began to see things in a new light. The bottom line was that Lorelei and Summer had been in love. Since meeting Clarkson, she could understand what that meant. Love injects the familiar with a new vibrancy, makes the world deliciously palpable. Real. How could she judge Summer and Lorelei? How could she judge anyone who found love? Would she at last find love with Clarkson? Last night, Summer had said that when the time was right, things would happen naturally. Lucy hoped it was true. At her age, the sooner the better.

She was so intent on her thoughts that the stillness of the house escaped her when she threw her purse on the kitchen counter. A large sheet of bright yellow paper was stuck on the refrigerator underneath a scuffed 'Best Teacher' magnet. Lucy lifted the magnet. Megan had drawn a smiley face on the paper. Below it, she wrote that she had convinced Summer to take her to dinner at the new Chinese restaurant and afterwards, a movie at the Crestview Cineplex.

Lucy checked on Dee, made them both dinner, and settled Dee into her chair. She switched on the television and thought some more about Lorelei and Summer, and Clarkson and herself while Dee dozed and woke beside her. After a while, she took Dee upstairs and put her to bed. Al hadn't come over for dinner, and by now, wouldn't. Clarkson had been at one of his meetings this evening, but she had heard his car pull in while she was putting Dee to bed, and then his footsteps as he made his way to his third floor. Would he come downstairs and discover that the two of them were alone in the house? A sudden anticipation electrified her.

She ground her coffee beans, measured four scoops into the filter basket, and programmed the brewing for six-thirty, as always. She ran cold water from the faucet into the carafe and began to fill the plastic reservoir. What if he were to walk right into the kitchen? How would it happen between them, she wondered. She didn't know how to picture herself with Clarkson, or with anyone, sexually. The romance novels she read were vague and metaphorical when it came down to the actual mechanics of these things. Her imagination ran away with her in the small details—Clarkson smoothing a highlighted strand from her cheek, lifting her at the waist, twirling her around the room in a balletic pas de deux. She could even imagine the pressure of his lips on hers. She knew there was more, much more, but she couldn't envision herself with a man, in the act. Would she know what to do? Heavy footsteps approached. Masculine footsteps. Her hand jerked. Water from the carafe splashed, then puddled onto the granite counter. Lucy reached for the dishcloth.

"Still cleaning up?" Clarkson asked. The kitchen air buzzed around her. Her ears rang. He took a glass from the cabinet and pressed the automatic ice dispenser on the refrigerator door. Cubes clinked into his glass.

"No, just getting things ready for tomorrow. The morning routine, you know." She had no idea if her voice sounded normal.

Clarkson pressed the water lever and a stream trickled into his glass. Had he wandered into the kitchen to find her?

"Yes, I expect you have an early wake-up call. Good night, Lucy. Sleep well," he said. The pulse in her lower body was enough to drive her mad. How could he not sense it? Clarkson took a pen from the counter and jotted down something on a tablet by the sink. His wrists looked strong.

"Good night." Lucy tried to think of something to say that would detain him. She cleared her throat. "Yes, tomorrow comes early," she said, instantly disappointed in herself. She took a deep breath and tried to center herself. That's what Lorelei would have done.

"Good thing I remembered that," he said, half to himself. He ripped the page from the tablet, folded it and put it in his pocket. "Where's Megan tonight?" he asked, looking around the kitchen.

"Oh, that's right, she's not here." Lucy creased her brow as if she had to think. She remembered that the lines on her forehead made her look old and relaxed her face.

"The house is quiet without her," Clarkson said.

"Yes, you two seem to talk a lot." Why had she said that?

"I guess we have something in common. Megan and I are both Glendale outsiders," he said.

Lucy laughed a bit too loudly and worried that her amusement seemed exaggerated. Remember, center yourself, she thought. "Don't feel that way at all. You belong here," Lucy said. She meant it.

Clarkson smiled. Lucy imagined herself melting in front of him. She tossed her hair and squared her shoulders. This was the night, she thought. She couldn't go another day without touching him. What would his body feel like against hers?

"You think so?" Clarkson asked.

"I do," she said.

Clarkson nodded. He shifted his weight. He lifted his glass of water in a sort of salute. "Sleep well," he said and headed toward the kitchen door.

"That's right. Summer took Megan to a movie," Lucy said to his retreating back, as if she had just remembered.

"Really?" He stopped and turned around. He seemed surprised.

"I'm not sure Summer was very enthusiastic. It was some juvenile comedy, I think." Oh, no. Had she sounded old, stuffy? Overly critical of Megan? She turned so that her good side faced Clarkson. She was relieved to see Clarkson's flash of white teeth, the crinkling of the fan of lines at his temples.

"It's an interesting relationship those two have, isn't it?" Lucy continued. She sat at the kitchen table, as if they had both decided that a conversation about Megan and Summer was in order. She crossed and then uncrossed her legs, wondering which way she looked more attractive.

Clarkson paused and then migrated toward her. He put a hand on the back of the chair across from hers. Please sit, Lucy thought. She smiled up at him.

Clarkson pulled out the chair and sat. "Yes, it is."

Lucy tried to think of something to say, but everything that came to mind had to do with sexual attraction. Summer and Lorelei. Clarkson and herself. She felt her forehead wrinkle again and lifted her hand to smooth it. "Megan seems like a nice girl. And I'm sure Summer appreciates what you've done for her," Lucy said after what seemed like an infinite silence. With a burst of courage, she reached out to pat his hand. She retracted her fingers as soon as her skin met his, as if they were attached to an elastic band.

"It was no problem at all," Clarkson said.

"Summer has nowhere to turn. She doesn't have a man in her life," Lucy said. She looked at Clarkson's arm right near hers and wondered if she dared touch him again. She lifted her hand, lost her nerve and let it fall back onto the table.

Clarkson chuckled, just a bit. "No, I don't suppose she would," he said.

Lucy drew back. He might as well have slapped her. What did he mean by that? Did he know? She imagined Summer crying into Clarkson's shoulder, confessing her love for Lorelei to him. The image upset her. Lucy collected herself, stood, then walked to the sink with her back toward him. She didn't want him to see her face. She took the dishcloth and ran it across the already clean counter.

"I suppose everyone knows," Lucy said when her heart stopped pounding. I can't believe it's happened again, she thought. Everyone else was plugged into some secret sex network. She tried to look casual as she turned to face him. "I mean, just looking at Summer, I suppose, you would know." She was in over her head, claiming insight she didn't have.

Clarkson shrugged. He took the note out of his pocket, unfolded it and looked at it again for a moment before putting it away.

Lucy watched him. He knew. Clarkson was clued in, like everyone else in her life. Dee and Al sneaking around right under her nose when she was a child. Summer and Lorelei sitting right next to her on the glider on Dee's front porch, probably pressing their thighs together and laughing at her while she poured them wine and chatted about nonsense.

"It's okay, I mean, there's nothing wrong with Summer being, you know, more fond of women…" She tried to sound offhand, as if the realization that Summer had broached such a delicate subject with him hadn't made her jealous to the point of distraction. She couldn't bring herself to look at Clarkson.

She pictured Summer's tearful confession, Clarkson's hands stroking Summer's shiny black hair, wiping tears from those unlined gray eyes. Beautiful Summer. And what else had occurred between them? After all, Summer had a child. It wasn't like she was a virgin. How could Clarkson have resisted her? Despite her bravado tonight, Lucy didn't understand anything about sexuality. Why hadn't Summer mentioned that she had already confided in Clarkson? Lucy's cheeks felt hot. Maybe Summer had tried, and Lucy had been her usual obtuse self.

"No, of course not," Clarkson said.

This was definitely not the night of her dreams, Lucy thought. The way she was, there never would be one. She threw the dishcloth over the faucet and dried her hands on the towel. Why was she never in the know?

"I've been thinking," she said, not knowing what she would say next. "You have things under control here. I think it's time I moved back into my own place." She hoped he didn't hear the crack in her voice. "Good night."

She put her head down and hurried from the kitchen. Her fantasy of living out the rest of her days with Clarkson seemed suddenly adolescent, no more reasonable than her teenage longing to marry Paul McCartney, or her history teacher, or the kid in high school who smoked cigarettes under the stairwell after fifth period.

Chapter 34

Clarkson stared at Lucy's hunched shoulders as she raced from the kitchen. What had just transpired, he wondered. She was the one who had done all the talking. He stood, paused, then hurried after her. The first order of business was to fix whatever had just gone wrong.

"Lucy," Clarkson said. His tone was calm, commanding.

He followed her up the steps to the second floor of Dee's house and caught up with her as her hand gripped the doorknob to her room.

"Wait."

Lucy gave the doorknob a half-turn, then stopped. She tilted her head downward, resting her forehead on her door. He put his hand on top of hers.

"You're not yourself, Lucy," he said softly. "Do you want to talk about it?"

She shook her head and didn't answer. She had seemed jumpy tonight, he thought, from the time he had walked into the kitchen.

"No," she said.

He left his hand on hers and with the other, lifted her face from the door. He tilted her chin toward him. Her eyes found his. Her lips parted and the effort of her breathing was visible. A good sign.

"Lucy, I don't like to see you upset."

She nodded. He would figure out exactly what had occurred. He did not lose control of his surroundings.

The hall light cast shadows against Dee's closed door. Megan's door was half-open, her room dark and empty. He would smooth things over now, before there was any real damage.

"Lucy, before you left the kitchen, I had been about to invite you to come upstairs with me to see what I've done with the third floor. We've been so busy, I haven't been able to show you."

Clarkson detected a flicker of interest before she turned away.

"It won't take long. I really want you to see it."

Her fingers on the doorknob relaxed under his. A blush spread over her cheeks.

"Al and I have been working up there on and off, for the last two weeks. You'll like it."

"I have to get up early."

"It will only take a minute."

He released his hand from hers, took her wrist and guided her to the staircase at the end of the hall. Her wrist was limp in his hand. "We have to be careful not to wake Dee," he said. They passed the row of darkened bedrooms, the velvet chaise in the alcove. He gripped her wrist a little tighter as they mounted the flight up to the third floor.

He paused at the top of the steps and Lucy paused with him. The stairs opened into a vestibule that led to an archway.

"Here, look," Clarkson said. He dropped Lucy's wrist and put his arm around her waist. They passed under the archway. He didn't switch on the light.

He had revamped the entire third floor. Most of it was still under construction, but his bedroom area was finished. It was uncluttered—a nightstand next to the old four-poster bed that he had found in pieces in the back room, an armoire and a table that he used as a TV stand. Beyond his bed were three floor-to-ceiling windows, now scraped clean of decades of paint and soot. The original wavy glass framed a sparkling Glendale beneath them in the clear December night.

He let go of Lucy's waist. She walked past his bed and looked out.

He followed her and put his hand on the small of her back. "You can see all the way to the bend in Main Street this way." He turned her body slightly, "and down to Sycamore if you look that way."

She let him maneuver her body. He bent forward. Their mingled breath fogged the window.

"I haven't been up here in years," she said. "Has anyone..." Lucy half turned, her lips inches from his. Her question died on her lips.

"Has anyone what?" Clarkson asked. He edged his hand up her back. His fingers almost reached around to her breast. He let his hand drop back to the small of her back. Her breathing was audible.

"Has anyone else been up here? I mean, besides you and Al?"

"No."

"No one?"

"Only you."

She nodded and exhaled. Her back was warm under his hand.

"Look," he said. "Up that way. From way up here you can see the lights of half the stores on Main Street. There's Mrs. Garibaldi's bakery, the donut store, Pamela's, Fox's which is soon to be Dupree's, Jerry's Pub, Pete's Meats. We can see it all."

"We can," she said.

She let him turn her body so she faced him. He put both hands on her waist and pulled her close. She lifted her face to his and closed her eyes. He leaned down and kissed her, lightly on her lips, then pulled back and looked at her. Her gaze dropped. He put his hand under her chin.

"It's all right, Lucy," he said. Her whole body trembled as he bent toward her again. This time she parted her lips. It was obvious that she had no idea what to do next. He kissed her and ran his fingers along her cheek, her neck, her collarbone, barely grazing the softness of her breasts through her sweater and rested his hands on her waist. Her breathing was shallow. He pulled away and held her shoulders in his arms.

"You have to get up early tomorrow," he said. He let her shoulders go. She rubbed her arms where his hands had been.

Clarkson relaxed. Whatever had happened earlier, it was all right now. She wanted to be his. He would proceed slowly, keep her unbalanced. "Let's put you to bed. You have to be ready for that room full of wild fourth-graders."

She let him lead her downstairs. At the door to her bedroom he kissed the top of her head. "Good night Lucy."

"Good night," she whispered before she slipped into her room and closed the door.

Alone in the hallway, Clarkson relaxed. The situation was under control. Over the course of the last few weeks, it had become obvious that romantic overtures were inevitable, but tonight was sooner than he'd planned.

He walked past Dee's door, then peeked into Megan's empty room. He needed to replace that cracked windowpane sometime soon. He tried to recall his conversation in the kitchen with Lucy. Apparently, he'd slipped up. Was Summer's sexual orientation a huge secret? He had known about Summer from the moment he heard her name. The image of Lorelei's fragile body in his hands, the tear coursing down her cheek as she whispered her lover's name was indelible. He was the bridge between Summer's past and present. It excited him that Summer was completely unaware of that. But he had to be very careful. More careful than he'd been, obviously.

He looked down the hall to make sure that Lucy's door was shut, and turned the doorknob into Lorelei's room. He stepped inside and shut the door behind him. Her childhood room fascinated him. He visited it often while Lucy was at school. Once, Lucy had caught him in the act. She had stood, frozen, in the doorway, the color draining from her cheeks. But tonight, he didn't have to worry. Lucy would be preoccupied with her own thoughts.

Within this room it was easy to picture tiny, frail Lorelei, the gateway to everything he had attained in Glendale. He walked to the oriel window, sidestepping the floorboards that creaked to the left of Lorelei's drawing table. Had Lorelei often gazed through these aged panes, her view framed by ice-crusted pine needles sharp in the moonlight, while she lived her secret life? Had she believed herself to be protected within the high ceilings and solid walls of this room? She had told him that this house was a part of her. But the truth was, he and Lorelei were both casualties of Glendale's unrelenting smugness.

But tonight's issue was not Lorelei. It was Lucy. Transparent, responsible Lucy. Surely, Lucy had known about Summer and Lorelei's relationship. She was naïve, but could she really be so obtuse as all that? It was incomprehensible, but perhaps she was. He tried to remember exactly what he'd said to Lucy in the kitchen, but he hadn't paid enough attention. He turned away from the window and let himself out of Lorelei's room, his touch sure and silent on the doorknob.

He climbed the stairs to his room. In the future, he would pay closer attention to Lucy and her ramblings, but it was all right now. Lucy wasn't a complicated woman. He guessed that she was now huddled in her childhood bed, still trembling from his touch. As long as he kept her in a state of agitation, love, whatever it was, she would be no problem. He would not make another mistake.

He walked through the dark vestibule, through the archway and into his room, still dark. The lights on Main Street twinkled. Toward Sycamore, the streetlights lit the manicured yards of the big houses that extended in a winding row toward the countryside. He tried to look over the edge of the hill, but the lowlands that lay just below Main Street were invisible in the night.

Chapter 35

Lucy leaned against her bedroom door until she heard Clarkson's footsteps retreat. She locked her door, walked over to her bed and perched on the edge. It had happened at last, she thought. Well, maybe everything hadn't happened, but enough. She shut her eyes and leaned forward to let the blood rush to her head. She straightened and inhaled deeply. She removed her pumps. Her hands trembled as she arranged them in the box, toe to heel in the pink tissue wrapping.

She slipped off her jacket and sweater, unzipped her skirt and let it fall to the floor. He had been gentle, she thought. Did he love her? She picked up her skirt and jacket and hung them. She smelled her sweater before she folded it. Clarkson's scent, woodsy and masculine, lingered on the soft wool. Her body shivered at the thought of his hand on her back, his fingertips grazing her breasts through her sweater.

She unhooked her bra and took off her panties. How would she feel to be exposed this way in his presence? She had come so close, she thought, pausing before the mirror. Her body looked the same to her. It didn't feel the same. She cupped her bare breasts in her hands, and wondered what they would feel like to him. Were they desirable? She reached into her drawer for clean panties, but changed her mind. She pulled her nightgown over her naked body, got into bed and switched off the lamp on the stand next to her. In the darkness, she pictured Clarkson just upstairs from her.

She was a changed person, she thought, sliding her hands over her nightgown, freed by Clarkson's kiss, and the feel of her naked body under the thin cotton. Had she finally become one with everyone else? Was she at last a member of that mysterious adult web of sexual beings, or was it too soon to claim membership? She didn't know. If he had made love to her tonight, she would have been certain. She wished that he had, that she would now fall asleep in her childhood bed, her virginity a part of her past. She imagined climbing the stairs to his room, her body naked under her nightgown, but she knew she couldn't bring herself to do it. What would it feel like? Why had he stopped? Had she seemed too tentative, wary? Too much herself?

She relived everything in her imagination. The pressure of his hand on her back. A flush of embarrassment overwhelmed her when she remembered how stiffly her lips had met his the first time. The second time, when he had lifted her face to his, was better. A shiver ran the whole way through her. That had been the real kiss, when something within her had reached out and yearned to pull him deep inside her. She had been ready, braced for whatever came next. And yet, he stopped. Tenderly, but still, he'd stopped. Why?

Had she been too much herself, she wondered, too Lucy-like. That had to be the reason. Would there ever come a time when she would let herself go, when she would be sensual, erotic, without a trace of the prim Miss Armstrong that everyone knew?

She turned to her nightstand, and in the dark, checked her alarm to make sure it was set. She pulled her extra pillow close to her chest. It would have been amazing to walk into the classroom tomorrow morning without her virginity. How would that feel? Would others know what was missing by looking at her, as if she had left one glove at home, or one shoe? Had Clarkson sensed that she was a virgin, that she didn't know what to do next? Lorelei would have known what to do, Lucy thought. That is, of course, if Lorelei were interested in men.

She wasn't certain how these things worked. Still, Lorelei would have known.

Lucy took the pillow from her chest and ran her hands over her breasts. They were soft, womanly. Her whole body seemed so. The next time she was alone with Clarkson things would be different. She would show him she was no longer the Lucy that watched while others lived. She put her fingers to her lips, remembering the feel of his mouth against hers. She had changed.

Was Clarkson lying awake this minute thinking about her? Did his body pulse with desire the way hers did? She sat up for a moment, readjusted her daisy comforter and settled back into her pillow. Had she really changed? Tonight, in the dark, behind her closed door, she could imagine herself with Clarkson. But what about tomorrow? Would she awaken once again as Lucy Armstrong, virgin, spinster, teacher? Clarkson might reconsider the whole thing. Or she would. Maybe she didn't have it in her to be anyone's lover.

What was wrong with her? Was she prudish? Lucy disliked that word. Even though she had never heard anyone describe her that way, she supposed they had. Prudish wasn't her problem, though. She thought for a moment. Her problem wasn't just sexual. It was far more general. Early on, she'd erected a wall between her and everyone else. Yes, that was more like it.

In childhood, she had clung to her isolation, as surely as Lorelei had clung to her striped baby blanket. Lucy couldn't remember a time when it wasn't there. When she was young, she shrank from the hugs of well-meaning relatives, teachers, her friends' mothers. She dreaded holiday visits from adults who wanted to enfold her in strange arms. Lorelei hadn't been that way at all.

Lucy had been ten when Lorelei was born. She'd been proud, honored even, to retrieve whatever Dee needed, a diaper and talcum powder, or a rag to wipe up the milky spew that was forever dribbling from Lorelei's lips. Dee had called her 'my little helper' and patted her head.

That had been enough for Lucy. She stood by as Dee held Lorelei, kissed her, buried her face in Lorelei's plump tummy. Lucy had wondered at the time if Dee had behaved that way with her. She had assumed that Dee had, but it was impossible to think of herself as part of such games. "Did I do that?" Lucy would ask Dee. She watched her mother tuck Lorelei into her crib, lingering for a moment, her face rapt, fingers resting lightly on the edge of Lorelei's crib rail. "That was so long ago," Dee would say, without answering her question. Dee didn't reach her arm around her shoulder, or give her a little squeeze.

Years later, Lucy had watched as Lorelei, now a sturdy and confident child, climbed into Dee's lap, her limbs too long to fit comfortably. Still, Dee wrapped her arms around Lorelei's dimpled knees and they would cuddle together, their bodies almost one. Lucy would watch them for a moment, and then retreat to her room, listen to the radio, experiment with the Cover Girl foundation and Maybelline lipstick from Murphy's. She would think about what her life would be as a grown-up, riding beside a dashing husband in a convertible. Alone in her room, she didn't have to watch Dee and Lorelei play their silly games. She knew for a fact that Dee hadn't played those games with her.

Every now and then, Lucy had wondered why Dee treated her so differently. Even Thaddeus, a boy, got his share of hugs and squeezes. Lucy had spent some time wondering whose fault it was. She couldn't ask her mother, and her father didn't talk about personal problems, only schoolwork and chores. She could have asked Thaddeus, but he would have shrugged and thrown his ball against the wall. She had to figure it out for herself.

And she did. She decided that she'd been born without that magic that Lorelei had, that most babies apparently had. She would look at her eyes in the mirror. They looked back at her, watchful and appraising. She had the kind of eyes that told people to stay away. Lucy wondered if she had a birth defect, if there was a name for what was wrong with her.

Clarkson didn't know these things about her, she hoped. But what if he did? Panic arose in her chest. What if Clarkson had figured out what Dee and everyone else knew from the time she was born?

Lucy got up from the bed. She switched on the light and looked into the mirror. She expected the worst, but was amazed at what she saw. Her face looked alive, lit somehow, her eyes searching. Maybe it was the ruffled edge of the nightgown against her chest, she thought, but she knew it wasn't. For once, she looked animated, almost pretty, even without her makeup and her hairspray. Tears spilled down her cheeks.

A plan took shape. Tomorrow, when the alarm went off, she would call in sick. The last time she'd done that was fifteen years ago, when she had that stomach flu that raged through school. Then she would wash her hair, shave her legs and rub her body all over with the new tea tree massage oil she'd bought on impulse and stashed in her underwear drawer. She would put on her makeup, get dressed, and find Clarkson. Maybe he would be at work on his upstairs space. She would climb the stairs to find him, busy hammering or sawing or painting, and they would finish what they started.

She switched off the light and got back in bed, pulling her comforter under her chin, imagining. He would turn and see her, the way she looked tonight, her eyes bright, her skin glowing. At first she pictured him discarding his tools, reaching out for her. He would wrap her in his strong arms and slowly unfasten her blouse, his fingers sure as each pearl clasp gave way. But she revised her fantasy.

She would be the Lucy that no one had ever known. She would walk up behind him, and he would turn to her in surprise. She would place her hand on his chest, that triangle below his neck that she caught sight of sometimes at the dinner table, when his shirt collar folded open. She would touch him there, and pull him close to her. She would run her hands across his chest and unbutton his shirt, feel his bare skin with her fingers.

That's what she would do. Wouldn't she? Doubts crept in. She took a deep breath. She didn't think she could.

She sat up and glanced at her clock. Dawn wasn't far off. She lay down again and allowed herself to hope. For a moment, in the dark, all things seemed possible. She'd been able to imagine herself as a changed person, hadn't she? Please wake up tomorrow as that Lucy, she thought. Please.

Chapter 36

Lucy was awake when the alarm sounded. She slept some, she knew, because wispy bits of dreams stuck in her head. She tried to get a handle on them, scenes of strange places, odd people, but they dissolved completely with only a disturbing aftertaste. She turned off the alarm.

Recollections of her evening with Clarkson didn't come rushing back, mostly because they hadn't left her all night. Even the bizarre remnants of her dreams had somehow evoked Clarkson. Last night she imagined that today she wouldn't go to school, that she would climb the flight of stairs to the third floor to be with him. To become a woman, at last. But that was last night.

She threw the covers back. Her head ached. The empty hook on the closet door seemed like a witness to a crime. She got up, walked to the closet and reached for a plain gray skirt and white blouse. She hung them on the hook and headed for the shower. She would go to school, take attendance, put her hand over her heart and lead her fourth graders in the Pledge of Allegiance. Chairs would scrape the floor, children would cough, someone would drop a book and they would all open to chapter seven in that new math book the district had thrust upon her this year.

The hot water hit her body the way it always had, but it felt different. She turned the water off and reached for a towel. Her body was tired, not tight and expectant as it had been last night. Her stomach was queasy. She stepped out of the shower and rubbed a clear spot in the fogged mirror. Puffy eyes stared back at her. She dressed and put on her makeup.

In the kitchen, her mug and plate sat next to the gurgling coffee pot, on the counter where she placed them what seemed light years ago. The events of the previous evening were a jumble. She poured her coffee, stirred in the cream, deposited her spoon in the dishwasher and took a sip. He had kissed her, though. She closed her eyes. That much was real.

Last night in bed, alone with her desire, she'd made everything too complicated. Clarkson had invited her upstairs to his room. He had held her. He had kissed her. That had been enough. The cellophane bread bag crumpled loudly as she took out two slices and dropped them into the toaster. She watched the coils redden, sipped her coffee, buttered her toast and ate a few bites. Her head cleared and the queasiness in her stomach quieted. Tossing and turning in her bed last night, why had she fixated on what was wrong with her, the parts of her that Clarkson didn't want? He was a gentleman, that's all. A thoughtful, caring gentleman. She rinsed her plate and wiped the counter. What if he were already awake, wondering what she was doing right now?

She walked to the bottom of the stairs and listened. Silence. She opened the hall closet to get her coat and hat. She thought of Clarkson, still sleeping upstairs, as she pulled the door shut. Or maybe he was awake, watching from his window to catch a glimpse of her as she left for school. On the way to her car, she resisted the urge to look up.

Soft winter daylight streaked the sky as she drove up Main Street, past the row of stores that she and Clarkson had viewed from his window, when he had put his arm around her and shown her Glendale twinkling beneath them.

She switched on her radio, but forgot to listen to the weather forecast. She thought of Clarkson, and how their faces had nearly touched as he pointed out the stores on the sparkling street below. That had been right before he kissed her, when she had still been tentative, uncertain. When she'd still been angry with him, and hurt, because it was clear that Clarkson already knew about Summer's sexual preferences. No flicker of surprise had lit his face, not even a lifted eyebrow. Why had that upset her so much?

Now, today, in daylight, it didn't seem so terrible. So what if he and Summer had talked. Summer was lonely. Lucy felt enormous guilt at her lack of generosity. She was devastated to lose her sister. But Summer had lost her lover. How could she have begrudged Clarkson a conversation with Summer? Clarkson was such a gentleman. Certainly, Summer would have told her if something more, something intimate, had transpired between them.

Lucy pulled into her faculty space in the parking lot. She took her keys out of the ignition, locked the door and then checked again to make sure it was locked. She was the one invited to Clarkson's room last night. When she'd asked if anyone else had been upstairs before, he hadn't hesitated with his answer. She was the one he had kissed.

Last night, she'd analyzed everything way too much, as she so often did. At the height of her desperation, when she examined her face in the mirror, the eyes looking back at her hadn't been watchful and guarded. They were alive. She was pretty. She opened the heavy glass door to Glendale Elementary, energized.

Her step was spritely as she turned down the hall to the office. She checked the wooden cubbyhole with her name on it. Miss Armstrong. A stack of papers waited. She leafed through them. The fire drill was canceled for Thursday. The Christmas food drive would kick off this week. Another year of collecting bags of creamed corn and kidney beans, she thought. But this year, maybe someone loved her.

With Clarkson at her side last night, Glendale had never looked so magnificent. He'd shown her everything, Fox's Pizza, soon to be Dupree's. He had turned her body so she could look way up Main, to where it began its uphill curve, pointing out Mrs. Garibaldi's, Pete's Meats. Glendale, in his eyes, was a shimmering sea of possibilities. He made it all so new.

She let the papers she was sorting through fall from her hands. Pete's Meats? Had he said that? She must have been mistaken. Pete's Meats hadn't been around in ages, not since she was a child. She had only vague recollections of Dee dragging her there. The floor had been covered with sawdust, and it had smelled of fresh blood. Dee had stood in front of the counter and ordered chops wrapped in paper from a smiling man in a blood-streaked white apron. For some years, Dee and her friends would bring up his name, wonder how he was doing in his Florida retirement. Then it had been Stan's, although Stan and his son hadn't run it for long before Stan died. The son had left town soon after. It had been empty for a while, 'Stan and Son' still emblazoned over the storefront glass for years until the letters faded. Then the youth club had met there, hoisting a banner across the window, blaring music for bored teenagers in the summer. Finally, the Coles from Oil City had arrived and turned it into The Butcherie. Only the old timers knew about Pete's Meats.

Clarkson couldn't have said that. She headed upstairs to her classroom. She switched on the fluorescent lights and took her pen out of the top drawer of her desk. Clarkson's voice echoed in her mind. Everything he said was etched into her memory. He had definitely said Pete's Meats.

Chapter 37

"Here, pull the cord around this way," Megan said.

"That way? I don't think it will reach. If we use this outlet, we'll be in better shape." Summer examined the polished baseboards of Dee's parlor. "These old houses aren't well-wired."

"It'll reach," Megan said.

Summer rolled her eyes. That Megan. So sure of herself in her half-bumbling way. Those pale pink letters with the girlish script hadn't given much of a preview of Megan's stubborn streak. Summer was just beginning to know the real Megan, a woman who could pick up and leave the only family she knew to meet a reluctant birth mother. She watched Megan fuss with the long cord. She couldn't help but feel a bit fond of the girl.

The road hadn't been easy. When Summer took Clarkson up on his offer to ship her off to Dee's house, Megan had pouted for a week. "That's how you get rid of your problems," she'd told Summer, "you give them to other people."

Summer had invited her to dinner to make peace, a truce. They cooked spaghetti together, arguing over everything, whether to add bay leaves, whether to mound the ground beef into balls or sauté it Bolognese style, how many cloves of garlic, how to slice the onions, how much olive oil was too much on the salad. After a while, Megan pulled out a chair and planted herself at Summer's kitchen table, a stripe of tomato sauce across her shirt. "If you kept your daughter at home, you wouldn't have to fight about these things. You would both know them. When you give up a daughter, you give up the right to call the shots on dinner."

It was the first time Summer understood Megan's pain. It was genuine, whether she liked it or not. Summer had thought of a million things to say, "I was a child myself," or "Get over it," but she didn't say anything. She pulled out the other chair, sat across from Megan and said, "I'm sorry." For once, she didn't need to be right. It was the best she could do.

Megan pulled the cord around, looped it under the low branch of the Christmas tree and plugged it in. The lights blazed. "Aha," she said.

Summer laughed. "Okay, you're right. Good work." They stood back. Megan had chosen the tree. It was tall, full and now dotted with tiny multi-colored lights. Summer had wanted clear lights. She thought Lucy would prefer them, but Megan had insisted.

"It's beautiful, positively dreamy," Megan said.

Summer watched her. Was she thinking about her family at home, those smiling parents and large brothers? Megan had a framed photograph of them on her dresser upstairs. Summer had seen it when she helped Megan put the new sheets and comforter on her bed, the ones they bought at the mall last week. Summer put a hand on her shoulder. Megan looked up and smiled.

"Hey, kiddo, really, it was nice work today. Right, Dee?"

Dee sat in her chair in the corner, huddled in her unicorn blanket. She smiled.

"We needed a tree," Megan said. "Every family needs a tree."

They heard the side door open, then shut. There was a clatter of heels, and Lucy stepped into the parlor. "Lucy, we hoped to be all finished here, so you would walk into a surprise." Summer gathered up a few empty ornament boxes and looked at her watch. "It's later than I thought. How was school?"

"It was fine, you know, the usual," Lucy said. Her face was pale.

"I took the day off," Summer said. "Megan talked me into setting up a Christmas tree for you guys. I figured it would be all right."

"It's beautiful. Thank you both," Lucy said. She unbuttoned her coat.

Summer watched her. She hadn't talked to her in a few days, not since the night they shared their secrets. She wished Lorelei were here to see Lucy now. Lorelei would be shocked to see the softness in Lucy's face, the vulnerability in her eyes. But Lucy looked a bit off today. The bluish shadows under her eyes showed through the obvious layer of concealer.

Summer stacked the boxes in a corner closet. "Well, my work is done. I should be leaving," she said to Megan and Lucy.

"Sounds good. And I probably won't see you later tonight. I have to take a shower and get ready," Megan said.

"Plans?" Summer asked.

Megan shrugged. "I signed up to help with the Elk's Club annual clothing drive. We're meeting in the basement of the Methodist church tonight. Sort of a party and work thing mixed up together."

Summer nodded. "Sounds like fun." Megan was a little intense at times, awkward even, but she knew how to go after what she wanted. What she thought was important.

"Should be great," Megan said. "Hot chocolate and hopefully a few cute guys." She paused a moment, blushed and wiggled her foot in its red Christmas sock. "Thanks, Summer. I had a blast today. And thanks for letting me do the multi-color lights. They're sort of a tradition for me."

"I like them," Summer said.

Megan turned to Lucy. "Glad you like the tree." She ran upstairs, the fleshy tags of her earlobes weighted down by her long sleigh bell earrings that jingled when she moved.

Lucy walked over to Dee and adjusted her blanket. Dee's eyes were closed and she snored evenly.

"So, things are okay with you, Lucy?" Summer asked.

"I guess," Lucy said, after a minute.

"It's the season," Summer said. "Holiday magic of childhood turns into holiday stress of adulthood."

"No, it's not that," Lucy said. "Where's Clarkson, have you seen him today?"

"Megan said he went out to his country place, wherever that is. Had to check up on some business. I don't think he'll be back until tomorrow."

"Oh." Lucy looked as though she'd been blindsided.

"Lucy?"

"It's nothing." She sat down on the sofa. "Well maybe not exactly nothing."

"I have time, Lucy. Come on. Let's talk." Summer led her into Dee's kitchen. "Tea? Our usual?" Summer asked. She knew where everything was. Lucy looked exhausted.

"Not for me. Help yourself."

They sat at the table. Summer waited for Lucy to talk. Lucy's eyes looked past her. The clock over the kitchen sink ticked rhythmically.

"How many conversations has this kitchen table seen?" Summer asked.

The tightness around Lucy's lips eased a little. "There's a reason these old houses have a mystique to them, isn't there?" She pushed her hair from her face. "Everything that happens within these walls somehow becomes a part of the house. Oh my God, I sound like Lorelei."

Summer smiled. "Just think, Lucy. Generations from now, when we're long gone, someone will sit right here in this kitchen, maybe even at this table, and wonder about us. Feel our presence."

"We both sound like Lorelei," Lucy said.

"Yes." It was a relief that Lucy knew exactly what Lorelei meant to her. "So. How is it going with Clarkson? Any news?"

Lucy took a deep breath. "I guess you could call it that."

"Well?"

"I don't know." Lucy threw up her hands. After a minute, she added in a soft voice, "He kissed me."

"Lucy, that's wonderful."

Lucy nodded. From the look of her, things didn't appear to be wonderful.

"Well, isn't it?"

"Yes, oh yes, it is." Lucy shook her head. "I think it's just me, Summer, you know how I am. I can make everything into a major complication."

"Anyone can, Lucy."

"Thanks. But I get the medal for it."

"How so?"

Lucy shrugged. "I mean it's okay, it's great even." She leaned forward, her elbows on the table. "Did you tell Clarkson about you and Lorelei? I don't want to be rude. Summer, really, forgive me for prying. But, did you two ever talk about that?"

"Oh, God, no, Lucy. I've never talked about that with anyone. Until the other night, with you. Clarkson and I manage to talk about the weather, the news, but nothing personal."

Lucy wrinkled her forehead. "Have you told Megan?"

"No. I should have. Now, it seems funny. Do I tell her all of a sudden? I've thought about it. I know she doesn't have a clue. She told me about a guy my age at the bank who she thinks would be perfect for me. Why are you asking me this? Did you tell him?"

"I don't know. I don't think so. Maybe by accident."

Summer looked at her. What did that mean? And anyway, maybe it was time for all of this to come out, once and for all. It wasn't as if she had hurt anyone. Loving someone was not a crime. But how do you tell someone news of that sort by accident?

"I'm not sure what you mean," Summer said.

"No, I'm not either," Lucy said.

"Lucy, it's okay, whatever you told him."

Lucy didn't answer.

"I mean it. In fact, it's probably for the best. The other day, when we were talking, there was one more thing I wanted to tell you. If Lorelei and I had been open about our relationship, or if I had told her about Megan from the beginning... if we hadn't tiptoed around so many secrets, Lorelei would be alive today."

Lucy didn't say anything.

"She wouldn't have been alone that night. She would have been with me. It's my fault. Me and my buried past. My secret present."

Lucy reached out to her. "Summer, it's not your fault. I promise. We're all the same. Not one of us is walking around, our lives an open book."

"You mean that?"

"With all my heart," Lucy said.

"You don't know what you've just done for me."

"Summer, this is going to sound like a funny question. Have you ever heard of Pete's Meats?" Lucy said.

"It sounds like one of the bands Megan listens to. Why, what is it?"

"It's just a place. A really old place." Lucy put her face in her hands. "How long have you lived in Glendale?"

"Oh, my. I guess probably ten years, no, longer than that. Closer to fifteen now. Why, do I qualify as a lifer? I didn't think you could be that in Glendale unless you were descended from one of the founding families. You're an Armstrong. One of the elite. You know how that goes."

"I do," Lucy said.

Summer wondered what Lucy was trying to say. She thought about Megan, mostly growing up without any blood relatives at all. But as long as someone loves you, does anything else matter? It wasn't only Lucy who tried to complicate things. It was everyone. Humans with their need for history and dynasties and sexual preferences that had to fit into some specific framework, between some carefully drawn lines. Summer wasn't sure who drew the lines in the first place. God? Not in this mess of a world. She didn't believe in anything. It was easier that way.

"Lucy, is there something you're trying to ask me, or tell me?"

Dee stirred in the parlor.

"No," Lucy said. "Thanks for the tree. Megan's right. She's a smart kid. Every family needs a tree."

Chapter 38

Lucy leaned against the door after Summer left. Her words echoed, "He kissed you, Lucy. Isn't that what you wanted?" It was. It was and it is, she thought as she walked back to the parlor, where Dee dozed. She turned the main lamp off. The twinkling tree lights softened the darkness. She sat, thinking, in the half-lit room until Dee stirred and opened her eyes.

"Bedtime, Mom," Lucy said. She unplugged the lights and helped Dee from the chair. Dee leaned on her a little as they headed upstairs. Lucy switched on the lamp by Dee's bed, opened her dresser drawer and set out her nightclothes.

"I'll be right back with your water," she said.

Lucy rinsed Dee's crystal carafe in the bathroom sink. She looked in the mirror. Her face wasn't beautiful, but she was still attractive enough. Clarkson must think so.

"Lucy?"

"I'm coming." She refilled the carafe, dried her hands on the fingertip towel and hurried into Dee's room. She poured a little water into the glass on Dee's nightstand and smoothed the back of Dee's flannel gown. While Dee sipped, Lucy plumped her pillows and turned down the covers. Dee handed her the glass and edged into bed, one bony leg at a time. Lucy pulled the blankets over Dee's loose and spotted skin. Dee had grown so old.

"Good night, Mom," she said. "Sleep well."

Lucy walked back down the stairway to the main floor and looked out the front parlor window. Snowflakes haloed each lamppost as far up Main Street as she could see. The view from

Clarkson's window would be magical tonight, she thought, as she entered the quiet kitchen. She wished she were upstairs with him right now, Glendale aglow beneath them, his arms around her. Without warning, that new, open sensation overcame her.

She set out her mug and plate for the next morning, measured four scoops of ground beans into the coffee maker, and poured cold water into the reservoir, just as she had last night. Had it only been last night that Clarkson had changed her life?

She still didn't understand how it had all happened, and especially, where she and Clarkson now stood. They were a couple, weren't they? Last night, the thought of Clarkson and Summer confiding in each other had provoked such jealousy she'd almost fainted. But today, she saw how silly that was. She had to learn to be generous in love.

Clarkson was clearly a wonderful man. She remembered his kiss on the top of her head when he'd said, 'Let's put you to bed.' Another man might not have been so restrained, so polite, so gentlemanly. Still, there were some things that didn't add up. Clearly, he'd known about Summer's sexuality. Could men sense these things? Probably that was it. But if men intuitively knew such things, then no one could ever harbor this sort of secret, and that obviously wasn't the case.

And how had Clarkson known that The Butcherie had once been Pete's Meats? That wasn't just odd, that was disturbing. If she really stopped to think about him, there were lots of little, well, irregularities about him. She shivered. Maybe instead of feeling disappointed, she should be relieved that Clarkson wouldn't amble into the kitchen tonight. She needed to think. The side door slammed. Lucy jumped, but right away recognized the quick footsteps in the hallway as Megan's. With any luck, Megan would race upstairs to her room and leave Lucy to her thoughts.

"Hey," Megan said, bouncing into the kitchen.

Lucy straightened her shoulders and attempted a smile. "How was the clothing drive?" she asked.

"Okay. I might even have managed to get a date out of it."
Megan fiddled with a jingle bell earring. "His name is Steven.
He lives outside of town, on one of the turnoffs beyond the
road to the dam."

Megan stood in the kitchen, rocking back and forth on her
heels. She didn't seem to be in any hurry to leave.

"One of the Rogers boys?" Lucy asked after a minute.

"God, is anybody anonymous in this town?"

"Probably not," Lucy said. She wondered if Clarkson might
be that, the only anonymous person in Glendale. Who was he?

Megan grabbed an apple from the fruit bowl on the counter.
"Mind if I take this upstairs?"

"Help yourself."

"Good night, Lucy."

"See you in the morning, Megan."

Megan turned to Lucy from the doorway. "Oh, Lucy. I forgot to tell you. Clarkson said to be sure to let you know he'll be
at his country place tonight, checking on things or something.
He'll see you tomorrow."

"Thanks. It's okay, Summer already told me."

"Sure."

Megan stood there, biting her apple. Lucy had the feeling
that Megan was waiting for her to say something.

"So, you like the tree?" Megan asked. A bit of apple clung
to her lower lip.

So that was it. Of course. The tree had been Megan's idea.
She had worked all day on it. "Oh my goodness, I can't thank
you enough," Lucy said, embarrassed at her uncharacteristic
lack of manners. She'd already thanked Megan, of course, but
with everything on her mind, she had neglected to make enough
of a fuss over it. Lucy was a teacher. She understood the need
for acknowledgment. And truly, Megan deserved more than
a passing thanks. Without her efforts, the rest of them would
never have had the heart to even think about a tree. "It's wonderful. You and Summer must have had your hands full with
that. It's huge," Lucy said.

"Oh, not Summer. She had a few errands to run in the morning, so Clarkson took me to get the tree. He said he wanted to. He tried to find some farm, Chockey's or something weird like that. We drove all over, but he couldn't find it. So we went to the lot up the street by the gas station. But I picked it out. And I helped him tie it to the car. He set it up for us, but he said it was up to me and Summer to decorate it."

"Oh." Lucy couldn't believe her ears. "Well, it's beautiful," she said, struggling to maintain her composure.

"I picked a good one, didn't I?"

"Perfect," Lucy said.

Megan smiled, bit into her apple again and turned.

"'Night," she called as she hurried from the kitchen and bounded up the steps.

Lucy sat, stunned. Chockey's. She hadn't heard that name in years. Chockey's had been a huge farm south of Glendale. When she was little, the whole town got their trees at Chockey's. Most people brought axes and made a day of scouting the hillside for the perfect tree. A few bought the pre-cut ones the Chockeys sold by the cabin at the farm's entrance. Either way, people stopped to chat a bit with Jim Chockey and his wife. Lucy couldn't remember his wife's name, but she remembered her smudged white apron and her smile as she ladled hot chocolate into two-handled paper cups and sold them for a nickel. The Chockeys had shut down their Christmas tree operation thirty years ago, maybe more. Their kids had divided the hillside land into lots for hunting camps and sold them off long ago.

Lucy shut off the kitchen lights and climbed the stairs. So Clarkson went searching today for Chockey's. Who was Clarkson, anyway? It was as if he had a big secret. What was it? She walked to the doorway of her room, started to open it and then stopped. The house was still. She crept to the end of the hallway, past Megan's closed door, past Dee's. She hovered at the bottom of the staircase to Clarkson's room. Were there clues to his past somewhere in his room? Did she dare go upstairs? Megan had said he would return tomorrow. In all likelihood, he was already asleep in his country cabin. She put her foot on the bottom step. The creak echoed in the silent hallway. Lucy froze. What if Dee heard her? Or worse, Megan? Megan was not the kind of person to keep her mouth shut about anything. She perched for what seemed an eternity, one foot on the wooden stair and one in the carpeted hallway. Her heart pounded. Carefully, she lifted her foot from the step and brought it back down. Her heartbeat eased. What was she, a common thief? She couldn't go rummaging around in his room. So what if he did have secrets. Everyone had at least one, she had come to realize.

Even her. She stepped softly, past Dee's room, past Megan's and opened her bedroom door. Before last night, she thought she was the only one without a secret, a hidden life. She'd been wrong. The last twenty-four hours had taught her that much. For so many years now, she'd thought of herself as the proper lady, groomed, articulate, dependable. Never shocking, never out of line.

Clarkson had kissed her and unlocked a complete stranger. All those years, she'd been nothing more than an actress in a very boring play. Why had she pretended that she'd chosen the course of her empty life? The charade had gone on for so long that she had almost believed it. She'd gone to heroics to keep her misery a secret, even from herself. She looked around her pristine bedroom. The daisy comforter adorned her virginal bed.

But last night, in the throes of her distress, the face shining from the mirror was alive. She wasn't playing a role anymore. The charade of perfection was over. She was like the rest of them at long last.

Even Megan, embarrassingly forward and unkempt in Lucy's opinion, knew how to live. When Megan had resolved to meet her birth mother, she had arrived, unwanted, on Summer's doorstep. Now, even Summer had softened toward her. When you decide to take a hand in shaping the events of your life, others seem to open up and give you room. People respect the need to live.

She undressed, remembering her body last night. For once, her head hadn't been completely in charge. She slipped her nightgown over her nakedness. Was Clarkson thinking about her tonight, alone in his bed? She tried to picture him in his country home. She hadn't seen it, of course. He hadn't described it to her. He hadn't really described much of anything to her.

She remembered, on Halloween, when he had shown up at her door with flowers. Summer had wondered why he hadn't answered her questions. They had been simple questions about his past. Nothing prying. And today, months later, Lucy knew no more about him than she did that night. Aside from his occasional references to his construction business and some unspecified town in Connecticut, she knew nothing at all.

Nothing. She laid her head on her pillow, but her eyes wouldn't close. All of a sudden, it hit her. She threw the comforter back and jumped out of bed. Quick, before she changed her mind, she told herself. Hadn't she just derided herself for living within self-imposed boundaries? Hadn't she just shed the lies of her past? Megan had wondered about her birth mother, and went searching for her. Lucy had good reason to wonder about Clarkson. The old Lucy would have gone to bed and wished she knew more. Powerless, restricted. She wasn't the old Lucy anymore.

Dressed in her nightgown, Lucy stole past Megan's door. She heard music playing softly from the radio she knew Megan kept on her dresser. The crack under her door was a sliver of light against the hall carpet. Please don't come out, Lucy thought. Dee's room was dark, quiet, sealed.

Lucy placed her foot on the first step. She looked at it, as if it belonged to someone else. In her haste, she hadn't worn her slippers. Her bare foot was pale, her toes polished a dark rose. The wood was cold against her skin. Her hand shook a little as she gripped the railing of the flight of stairs to Clarkson's room.

Chapter 39

Lucy counted the steps to Clarkson's room as she mounted them. The wood creaked under her. She stopped. If she lost her nerve now, Clarkson's mysteries might remain forever hidden, his secrets forever kept. Her breath came too fast. She pressed forward. One more step and she would be in the vestibule, the gateway to Clarkson's third floor sanctuary. She climbed the last step and stood still.

The darkness of the vestibule engulfed her. She hurried through the archway and into Clarkson's bedroom. The glow from the lampposts and Christmas lights on the street below filtered through the wavy glass and cast the room in shadowed relief. She stood motionless by the window while her eyes adjusted to the dimness. She was afraid to turn on any lights.

The room had his smell, that mixture of outdoors and clean soap and leather and whatever it was that resulted in the scent of a man. It wasn't just his smell that made the room reek of him. It was the room itself, spare, controlled.

Last night she hadn't had the composure to examine her surroundings. Now, in the half-light, she could make out that his bed was neatly made. Two large pillows sat on top of a dark comforter, tucked tight. She imagined him in this room, glancing out the window as he loosened the clasp on his wristwatch and set it on his nightstand. She wondered what he looked like when he pulled that dark comforter over him, when he closed his eyes and slept. The thought was intimate, invasive, as if she peered through a secret peephole.

She stepped away from the window. Her eyes had adjusted enough so she could make out things fairly well. On his nightstand was a magazine. In the corner, a wastebasket held a few crumpled bits of paper and an empty battery package. A sport jacket that she recognized hung on the front of the closet in a dry cleaning bag. She opened the closet door to see a row of pressed shirts, some hangers with pants folded over their wooden slats, four pairs of shoes. She half-expected to see Clarkson emerge from the shadows. Something cracked in the night and she jumped. It's nothing, she told herself, just the wind against the windows, the beams settling. She shut the closet door. Even as her heart stopped racing, she couldn't shake the feeling that Clarkson lurked in a corner and watched her every move. That's ridiculous, she thought. He was at his country home, fast asleep in another bed.

She walked to the door at the rear of his bedroom. In her childhood, the door had led to a storage room, dark and dusty, with a lion's claw table in a corner that used to terrify Lorelei, shelves with rows of Ball jars, moth-eaten linens. She hadn't been inside in years. She pushed against the door and stepped into the room. It was dark, with small, high windows that didn't overlook Main Street. She closed the door behind her. Sudden blackness suffocated her. She opened her eyes wide but could only make out more or less solid forms of blackness. Her fingers groped until she found a switch by the door. The sudden illumination of the overhead fixture stunned her. She blinked.

What was she looking for, anyway? Something she didn't want to admit. She shivered and rubbed her arms. Maybe she would go back into his bedroom, sit on his bed a moment, lean her head against his pillow, and then creep back downstairs. Yes, that's what she would do. She started for the door, but as she turned she noticed the file cabinets in the back corner. Clarkson had turned the space into a sort of office, she realized. What might Clarkson keep in his file cabinets? Was it possible that the answer to the mystery of Clarkson was right under her nose?

To her left was a mahogany table that he obviously used as a desk. Neatly stacked in its center were three notebooks. The silver ball-point pen she had seen him pull from his pocket so many times was apparently one of several that he kept in a Lucite square on the corner of the table. She picked up the notebooks and leafed through them. Business names, phone numbers, transactions, dates of deliveries. She shrugged and returned them to their exact position.

She continued, halting once, until she reached the file cabinets, one with two drawers and one with four. She placed her hand on top of the taller one. Each of its drawers had a label, marked with dates. She bent down. The smaller cabinet had one drawer labeled 'Glendale construction' and one 'current projects.' She wasn't sure where to start, if she should start at all.

The top drawer of the large cabinet screeched as she pulled it out. She waited. Silence. She shuffled through the folders. They were old, their tabs soft. Lucy leafed through them. Only yellowed invoices and receipts. She pulled out a paper here and there, but other than recognizing a few town names in New York and Connecticut, she learned nothing. The next drawers were the same. She sat on the floor to reach the lowest drawer. By the time she had rifled through the entire large file cabinet she felt foolish, sullied even. What was she doing?

There was nothing up here. His life was orderly. He was a businessman, just as she had told Summer from the beginning. The relief that overcame her surprised her. What dark thoughts she had harbored, she realized. She shuddered, her cotton nightgown too thin to shield her from the cold hardwood floor. She wrapped her legs up in her nightgown as best she could and closed her eyes. She would never admit what she had suspected, she told herself. Clarkson wasn't hiding anything. He was simply contained, reticent. Probably it was her Glendale upbringing that had caused her to doubt him in the first place. In Glendale, reticence was evasion, and evasion implied guilt. Even family secrets in Glendale were common knowledge, although rules of etiquette governed how and when to mention them. Her suspicions were her own fault, not Clarkson's.

She opened her eyes. Now that she had released him from suspicion, she could relax, she thought. She sat on the cold floor, stiff and anything but relaxed. Who was she kidding? She no longer believed in life without mysteries, secrets. And Glendale, with all of its familiarity, harbored more secrets than she'd dreamed possible. Recent experience had taught her that. And something about his room bothered her. It wasn't innocent. It was antiseptic, lifeless and there were still too many unanswered questions. Obviously, he knew Glendale. Pete's Meats. Chockey's. No amount of historic interest would have enabled him to come up with those names. He had lived here, or nearby, she was sure of that. But nothing in his files confirmed a family connection, a sordid love story, anything.

She surveyed the room. Who or what was he? Anyone would have a personal note, records of some past association, a card from a relative, an old address book, a trinket from a vacation, photo of a loved one, piece of art, a goldfish, anything. Anyone would own something besides folders with columns of numbers, stacks of neat notebooks, a Lucite square of identical silver pens, business receipts. Her heart pounded. Sweat gathered on her upper lip and between her breasts. Everything about his room seemed cold and inhuman. Heartless.

Now she was just being silly, she thought. She had found nothing, so she was turning nothing into something. Admit it, a voice inside her said. Admit that you just don't feel special enough to have someone like Clarkson walk past Lorelei's grave one day and into your heart. A tear threatened. She had never felt special enough for anything.

She remembered that afternoon, when he had sat beside her on the bench in the cemetery. Lorelei's gravestone had been the center of her world until he had jogged up the hill and planted himself right there on the bench. No one had looked at her the way he did. Ever.

But what was he doing jogging through the cemetery? Lucy ran her hand through her hair. Summer had found that creepy at the time. Why hadn't he jogged on the path that circled the dam? People had used that path for strolls, bike rides, hikes, since Lucy could remember. And there were other things. The questions Clarkson had asked her, little things here and there, occurred to her. Had Lorelei painted the unsigned still-life in the den, he had asked her when she returned from school one day. He had been intrigued when he found that Lorelei had occupied the room with the oriel window. She had seen him standing in the center of Lorelei's room later that day when she brought up Dee's laundry. He was taking measurements, he said. Maybe he was. Maybe all of his questions were normal. Lucy wasn't sure what renovating a house required. The Armstrong women hadn't paid any attention to such things. But she had seen him inside Lorelei's room again after that, standing at the window, looking inward at the room. He was definitely not taking measurements that day. And he'd always had such an interest in Summer, it seemed. Helping her with Megan. Not even a flutter of surprise or curiosity about her sexuality. That was strange.

And Dee. He was so solicitous. Was it out of sensitivity and consideration for Dee when he counseled her not to pursue admittedly drastic measures to identify the homeless man as Lorelei's murderer? "Who else could have done it?" he had asked her, as if she could possibly know such a thing. She tried to remember what his face had looked like when she'd agreed to give up the idea. Had he seemed relieved? Was it out of kindness that he'd offered to donate a sizable amount to the police force in Lorelei's name? Who was he? The only thing she knew for sure was that he had lied about his lack of familiarity with Glendale. That was the inescapable truth.

What exactly was she looking for tonight, anyway?

A ripple of shivers coursed through her body. She was probably just letting her imagination run away with her. How had that happened? She wasn't the one with the imagination. That had always been Lorelei. She cleared her head. She would put it all to rest right here, right now. So far, she hadn't found anything incriminating. He was solitary, evasive, that's all.

One last file cabinet and she would be done. Her hands shook. She couldn't wait to get out of Clarkson's room and back to her own territory, her daisy chain wallpaper, her soft carpet. The way the 'Glendale construction' drawer rumbled as it slid along its track made her jump. She found the same general assortment of bills and receipts that his earlier files held. She closed it. 'Current projects' was largely empty, with a folder for the new restaurant and a separate one for Al's funeral home renovations. In the front was a manila envelope marked Armstrong. She opened it. Inside was the real estate survey from her family's house. How had he gotten that, and why? Probably he needed it for his renovations. She looked at it for a second and decided to put it back. She picked up the envelope. Something else was inside. She reached in and pulled out something. It was a photograph. Of Lorelei.

Lorelei was smiling, her head thrown back, her fingers spread so the first prize medallion she won that day in the Arts Festival in Pittsburgh was clearly visible. Lucy had taken the photo. Later, she and Lorelei had helped Dee press it into the photo album they kept on the shelf under the side table in the den.

Lucy held Lorelei between her shaking hands.

Chapter 40

Clarkson exited the pine double doors from The Huntsman's Inn. His meal had been outstanding, venison sausage stew with dried apricots and a rich chestnut gravy, heightened by a chilled vodka before and a heady port after. He got into his car, started it and drove the familiar winding road through the woods. He was grateful for the solitude. At the bridge over the creek, he turned up the hill. The road to his place hadn't been cleared, of course, but he knew the terrain well. He guided his car through the snow and pulled into the space next to his cabin, his slant-roofed refuge. As soon as he opened the door, the welcome scent of pine forest hit him. His feet sank into the soft snow as he crossed the clearing. He unlocked the cabin's front door and turned on the lights. His breath formed visible puffs. He switched on the radio. The classical station was in the middle of a familiar Schumann piano concerto. He smiled.

He craved some time alone. No Armstrongs or their hangers-on. Especially no Lucy. He had made sure to tell Megan that he would not return to Glendale tonight. She would tell Lucy, he had no doubt. That way, Lucy would not wait up for him when he returned later.

The woodshed roof needed repairing, so he had canceled last week's cordwood delivery. He took off his scarf and coat and grabbed a handful of newspapers to start a fire. He appraised the stack of wood piled in the corner. Just as he expected. It wouldn't last all night, but certainly long enough for him to unwind awhile, relax, avoid Lucy. He set to work and within minutes had a fire blazing in the hearth.

He rubbed his hands together and went into the kitchen. The bottle of vodka in the lower cabinet was full. He poured some into a glass and walked to his favorite chair. The heat from the fire pushed the chill to the corners of the room. He sank into the chair, closed his eyes and leaned back. The music carried him. He would wait for the Armstrong house to fall into deep and dark silence.

After a bit, he refilled his vodka, just a bare splash to sip before his drive home. He sat and watched the snow falling outside, frosting the branches. Now and then, he closed his eyes and let the music engulf him. He might have enjoyed playing the piano if his younger days had been different. If he had been from the sort of family whose children did such things. But he wasn't really from a family at all. And mostly, that might have been for the best. Look at the Armstrongs. Their privileged background had left them as clueless as one could imagine. If Lorelei had half an ounce of self-preservation, she would still be alive today. And Lucy was no better.

What to do about Lucy, he wondered. She was certainly the easiest path, if not the most desirable, to all he wanted. And she was available. No question about that. Already, the Armstrong house felt like home to him. Perhaps he would transform the front parlor into a music room, with a baby grand piano tucked into the corner. He looked at his hands. He had managed to master almost anything he had attempted. It wasn't too late. Why not learn to play the piano?

He rubbed his fingers together. The fire had stopped raging. Now and then a flame erupted and licked at the remains of the last charred log. How quickly the chill threatened the warm little circle around the hearth. He picked up his unfinished glass, and walked to the kitchen. He rinsed his glass and returned it to the cabinet. He turned off the radio and the lights, and locked the front door. The snow was new and powdery under his feet.

He got into his car, started it, and blasted the heat. He angled the air vents toward the steering wheel and tuned the car radio to the classical station. His brief respite from the Armstrong household was almost over.

What to do about Lucy, he thought again, as he drove back toward Glendale. Lucy was, in one way or another, the key to what was rightfully his. He didn't believe in fate, destiny, or any of that nonsense. But the longer he stayed in Glendale, the more sure he was that he belonged there. In fact, the town needed him, with its crumbling storefronts and inferior dining establishments. Really, he had always belonged in a big house on the hill, attached to one of the original Glendale families. His own family was merely a blip, a fleeting presence in his life. A mistake. Actually, the Armstrong family, frail and spent, almost required his help. And he was comfortable there. Left to the inept Armstrongs for another few years, that magnificent mansion would have continued its decline, this time into hopeless disrepair. He thought about the new crown moldings he had installed in the upstairs, the transom windows he had scraped clean of paint. The Haverton estate at the turnoff to Braden had more impressive gardens, perhaps, but the Armstrong house was certainly the jewel of Glendale. Already its grandeur had begun to reappear under his careful hand. He would make it sparkle again.

He turned off Route 22 and took the fork past the hospital and down Main Street. The storefront of Fox's Pizza on his right showed signs of his new venture in construction. Soon his name would be on Main Street, from one end to the other. Al had suggested that after the funeral home renovations were complete, their joint names, Dupree-Mancini, should be emblazoned on the awning. Clarkson liked that idea.

He glanced at the clock in his car. It was late, but perhaps not late enough. Would Lucy be awake? Had she dallied in the kitchen, hoping he would show up tonight? He pictured her, dressed in one of her wool suits, round-toed heels, makeup caked slightly around her eyes. What if she were still awake?

He preferred not to risk an encounter tonight. The car was deliciously warm, the roads deserted. A detour seemed in order. A very special detour. He passed the Armstrong house on his left without turning into the driveway.

Tonight, he would indulge his curiosity and return to the lowlands. He had avoided them almost since his return. At first, he hadn't wanted to be seen there, but it probably didn't matter now, what with Lucy's utter capitulation. He drove along the hill to where the road descended in a curved path to his former territory. He rounded the last bend and the familiar landscape lay before him. The snow had turned the low brush lining the road into mounds of white. The gnarled remnants of vines were a lacey network.

He drove as close as the road allowed to the thicket where he had first met Lorelei. He cut the motor, got out of his car and stood. The blanket of snow wrapped everything in a profound silence. For a brief moment he sensed Lorelei in the soft quiet. It must be the night, he thought, as he watched the snow waft through the air. Or the vodka. He wasn't one to indulge in such fantasies.

He could see Lorelei with perfect clarity in his mind, though, her upturned nose, her wide eyes. In fact, her face was clearer to him than Lucy's. Strange, he thought, the way sometimes our most fleeting encounters are the most powerful. Beautiful, vulnerable Lorelei had provided him with everything he now had. She had beckoned to him, laid her gifts before him and then offered herself up. He had seen his opportunity and taken it, the way he always had in life. It puzzled him how others failed to embrace such a simple strategy.

He looked up past the whiteness of the hill that rose beyond the thicket. Far up on the hill, he could see the streetlights of Glendale. As he watched, rare headlights passed, but the houses on the hill blended into the darkness. He envisioned the Armstrong house, his house, really, with its carved wooden doors, crystal chandeliers and leaded stained glass, the beveled panes in the transom windows, the arched opening into the parlor, the polished baseboards. Yes, he belonged there, up on the hill. The house was as good as his. The peace he found in this realization was solid, unshakable. The lowlands no longer claimed him.

He stamped the snow from his feet and got back into his car. It was late. Lucy would surely have given up on him by now. He followed the road that snaked upwards along the hill, up Main Street to the fork where it met Sycamore, and pulled into the Armstrong driveway. Quietly, he let himself in the side door. The first floor was dark and still. He exhaled and relaxed his shoulders. He had a little space tonight, he thought, while he planned what to do about Lucy.

She would marry him, he was sure, and that way the house would certainly be his. It satisfied him to think that he could soon absorb the historic Armstrong family into his name. He would have a stonecutter inscribe 'The Dupree House' on a boulder, maybe a pinkish marble stone like Lorelei's. He would install it in the front garden where Main Street met Sycamore, for passers-by to see. He would surround it with peonies in the summer, pink, magenta, and white, and russet chrysanthemums in the fall. Yes, he supposed he could marry Lucy. He played with the thought as he mounted the staircase. Yet, there were other ways to deal with her. There were always options.

His footsteps were quiet as he stepped into the carpeted hall. Before he passed Lucy's room, he stopped. Her door was slightly ajar. That was out of character. He halted outside and slowed his breathing. He peered in as he walked past. Through the narrow space, he glimpsed the edge of her bed. Was it empty? He stopped and pushed on her door, ever so slightly, widening the crack. If she awoke, he could say he just wanted to see her again, make sure she was all right on this cold snowy night. The covers were tousled, Lucy's bed vacant. He looked to the bathroom door down the hall. It was open, the room dark. Megan's door was closed, no light under the door. Dee's as well.

At the staircase to his room, he paused and removed his shoes. He crept up the wooden steps, shoes in hand. The vestibule was dark. He passed through the archway. His room was undisturbed, but a light shone under the paint-stripped door that led to his half-finished office space that lay beyond.

He put his hand on the doorknob and quietly turned it. Inside, Lucy sat cross-legged on the floor. She held something between her long, polished nails.

Chapter 41

"Lucy," Clarkson said, unsurprised. She jumped.

"Clarkson." He noted the hint of panic in her voice. She slipped what she was holding under her knee. Clarkson set his shoes down, unbuttoned his coat and unwound his scarf from his neck.

"I'm surprised to find you up here at this hour. Perhaps I can help you with whatever it is that you're doing," he said.

Lucy froze.

He draped his scarf over his arm and brushed snowflakes from his coat. "It's really coming down out there," he said.

Her eyes tracked his movements. She wore only a nightgown. He could see her breasts through the thin cotton. She adjusted the folds of it over her knees.

"I came up here because..." Lucy paused. "I was hoping to find you." Her voice wavered a bit. She shook her hair, the way he knew she did when she was upset. She scooted herself to try to cover what she'd been holding.

"Didn't Megan tell you?" Clarkson asked. He kept his eyes on her as hung his coat and scarf on a hook in the corner. "That I planned to stay at the cabin tonight?"

"Yes, oh that's right, yes, of course, she did."

"I see," he said. "It was terribly cold. No firewood."

"Oh," Lucy said. The color had drained from her face.

Clarkson took a few slow steps toward her and stopped, his toes almost touching her knee. He folded his arms. On the floor next to her was the real estate survey of the Armstrong house from the courthouse. He glanced at the drawers in the cabinet by the wall. One was partly open, another had the bent edge of a paper sticking out.

"Looking for something?" he asked. "Or, actually, it seems that you've already found it." The edge of Lorelei's photo stuck out from under her nightgown.

Lucy rubbed her knee through her nightgown. She shrugged her shoulders. "What have I found?" she asked. Her voice was low and quiet. Her eyes were wide and he could see that her body trembled. He was surprised at her bravery. That she spoke at all. He tilted his head.

"I'm not sure what you mean." Clarkson focused his eyes on the edge of the photograph under her knee.

Lucy pulled out the picture of Lorelei. Her voice sounded small, fearful. "I came across this. Accidentally. It seems strange that you have it. In your room, I mean."

"She's a part of your family. I'm a bit of a historian," Clarkson said.

"A historian," Lucy repeated. She brought herself to her feet. "Is that what you are?"

"Do you have an issue with that?" Clarkson frowned, as if her very presence confused him.

Lucy shook her head. "I'm just confused. Wondering."

He shrugged his shoulders and then threw up his arms. "Ask me what you want to know," he said. "Shall we go into the other room, where it's more comfortable?" He put a hand on her elbow. It was stiff under his touch. He guided her through the unfinished doorway and closed it behind them.

"Here, sit down," he said and patted the bed. She sat. He took the photograph of Lorelei from her hands and set it on the marble window ledge.

"Well?" he asked. He leaned against the ledge and faced her. "What is it you want to know?"

Lucy's eyes met his for a moment, and then broke away. "I guess I don't really have any more questions," she said.

"I think you do."

Lucy opened her mouth as if to speak and then closed it again.

She was agitated, Clarkson thought, a good sign. He wondered how far she had dug into his personal correspondence. So, she had seen the photo of Lorelei and the deed to the Armstrong house. Neither of them were conclusive evidence of anything. Nothing else she may have found could incriminate him. From the day he had incinerated his home, his father's body and his entire store of childhood memorabilia, he hadn't saved a scrap of a personal memento. He had only kept files for his various business deals, along with a few required forms and documents. Throughout his life, his belongings had never included a photo album, a diary, not even a saved Christmas card or a love letter. He didn't have a single picture of himself from his younger days. From any days.

"I know it's painful for your family, but someone needs to assemble the story of your family," Clarkson said. "It's a labor of love."

"I see," Lucy said. Her voice was flat.

"Glendale is a town of history," he said.

Lucy looked down at her feet.

"And your family played an important part in it."

Lucy was silent.

"I've never had that," he said. "I'm not a part of anyone's history."

Finally, Lucy looked up at him. "Everyone's a part of someone's history," she said.

"I suppose, in some way," Clarkson said. He sighed. "Things were hard for me. I don't know if you can understand that."

She looked away from him.

"Why do you know so much about Glendale?" Lucy asked. She kept her eyes averted.

"Oh, I've read some, studied a bit. I don't know that much, really."

"Pete's Meats? Chockey's?" Lucy put a hand to her forehead. Her lips had whitened. Her hands shook. Her voice became very quiet. "Why were you in the cemetery that day, when we met?"

Clarkson was practiced at appearing unfazed. He hadn't realized he'd mentioned Pete's Meats, but he must have. Obviously, that had been a mistake. And Megan must have told her about Chockey's. He shouldn't have counted on Megan's obliviousness. What did she mean about the cemetery? How deep did her suspicions go? After a minute, he nodded. "I used to have ties here," he said. "Long ago."

"What ties?"

"Nothing important. I was young. Hardly enough to mention. Not like your family," he said.

Lucy said nothing.

"The Armstrongs have taught me something about history. If I hadn't met you, I would still be wandering. Rootless."

"What is so dark about your past that you can't even tell me how you know Glendale?" Lucy said the words slowly, halting altogether at times.

Clarkson gave a little laugh and shook his head. "My past? The past doesn't matter, Lucy," he said. "Can you understand that? Not one of us has a past that can stand up to the scrutiny of others. Didn't Jesus himself make that clear, 'let he without sin cast the first stone'? All that matters is that I've found something special in Glendale. I've found you." He registered the slight movement of her head at his words, the sudden sharp intake of her breath. Good, he thought.

Lucy looked at him and nodded, as though she were trying to put it all together.

"It's the truth, Lucy," he said. "We can ask questions forever, but some things don't matter. We've found each other now. That's all we need to know."

He sat on the bed next to her and put his hand on the nape of her neck. For a moment he wondered if he could strangle her, the way he had Lorelei. She would be gone and whatever she had pieced together about his past would disappear with her. But the problem with dead bodies was that they didn't simply disappear. If he could get her into his car and drive her out to his cabin, he could kill her there. But there would be evidence, tracks in the snow, witnesses. Megan might come bouncing out of her room at any time. He let his hand slide down her back. She wore nothing beneath her nightgown. He stroked her back.

"Oh, Lucy," he said. "If only you knew." She didn't shrink from him. He saw the catch in her breathing, the rise of her chest. She responded to his touch. Despite what she may have figured out, she was attracted to him. That's all he really needed to know.

"Lucy, can I ask you to trust me?"

She sat without speaking for a moment and then shrugged her shoulders.

"I don't think so. Maybe. I don't know." She shook her head. "I just don't know," she said.

She looked to be on the verge of tears. He put his hand on her cheek and she closed her eyes.

"You can, Lucy. Look at us. We're meant to be together."

She opened her eyes. He took her hand in his. "We're both alone, Lucy. No children. We have no one," he said. "Who do you have? Summer has Megan. You have Dee, I guess."

"Dee?" Lucy shook her head, "I have no one." The sadness in her eyes gave him the opportunity he needed.

"Lucy, if we can't trust each other, who will we have in this world? We've both been alone for so long. Far too long."

He let the tear that spilled over her lower lash slide halfway down her cheek before he brushed it from her face.

"I never want to see you sad," he said. "I never want to see us sad." He reached for her. She allowed him to pull her into his arms. He stroked her back and let her cry. "Everything will be all right," he said when her body was finally still.

She unburied her head from his shoulder and looked into his eyes. "It will?" she asked.

"We'll make it all right," he said.

Gently, he pushed her backwards onto the bed and traced his hands over the thin veil of her nightgown. She didn't protest.

He pulled her nightgown up slowly over her knees. He watched her face. Her eyes were locked on his. He pulled it higher, up over her waist. She trembled, but still, she lay there. He stood back. She didn't move. He unfastened his belt and undressed. Her eyes met his as he took both of her hands in his and pulled her to a sitting position. He slipped her gown over her head. Her breasts were full. He lifted them with both hands. She let out a little sound. Again, he pushed her back onto the bed slowly.

"It's all right, Lucy," he said.

She shook her head. "Maybe it isn't," she said. He climbed on top of her, ready. Her legs opened. With his hands he moved her underneath him. Her utter submission intoxicated him.

"I've never," she gasped.

"It's all right," he said.

He lowered himself over her and entered her. Her long nails dug into his back. She held onto him tightly as he moved inside her until he had finished. Her grip on him released, and he rolled from her. They lay beside each other, thighs touching. Her breathing was rapid and shallow for a long time. She shuddered and sighed. After a while, her breathing evened out.

"Are you okay?" he asked.

She turned toward him. "Will you answer a question for me? Will you tell me the truth?" Her words were barely a whisper.

"Ask me."

She looked at him for a long moment. She ran her hands through her hair.

"No," she said.

She got up and tried to slip her nightgown over her head. Her shoulders hunched as she tugged at it. He sat up and helped smooth it over her body.

She faced away from him, but he saw that her shoulders shook.

"Lucy, what is it?" he asked.

She was silent for a long time.

"You didn't kiss me," she said, finally.

"No," Clarkson said. "I didn't."

He could see her head nod in the darkness. They were quiet again. Her body was still.

"Shall I kiss you now?" Clarkson asked.

"Yes."

He stood up, still naked. He held her in his arms in front of the window. Glendale shimmered below. She tilted her tear-stained face toward him and their lips met.

"You can stay up here tonight if you want," he said.

"No," she said. She started to walk toward the doorway.

"Shall I walk you downstairs?" he asked, putting his leg into his pants as he spoke.

She shook her head, then turned and paused for a moment. She took a deep breath and approached him. Clarkson wondered if she had changed her mind, if she were about to climb into his bed and lie next to him for the night. Whatever she did would have to be all right. She stretched onto her toes, tilted her head back and kissed him lightly on the cheek. Her face flushed deeply as she turned away and hurried out the door.

He followed her through the vestibule to the top of the stairs. She didn't look back as she climbed unsteadily down the staircase. His breathing relaxed. He walked back into his room. He stood by the window for a long time. Snow still wafted through the air. The lit circles from Main Street's lampposts suspended the crystalline flakes in midair. The night was peaceful. He picked up the photo of Lorelei from the windowsill, looked at it, and set it back down. It no longer mattered what Lucy knew about him.

Chapter 42

Lucy gripped the handrail as she descended the wooden staircase. Her bare feet sank into the carpet at the bottom. The shadowed hallway ahead was a blur as she hurried past the closed doors of those sleeping peacefully. Those who deserved to sleep peacefully, she thought. She opened her bedroom door, closed it behind her and stood, paralyzed. Her bed, carefully made, pillows plumped and angled just so, seemed from another dimension. Sleep was out of the question. Everything was out of the question. What in the name of God had she done?

Did he love her? With everything else roiling in her mind, that's all she wanted to know. The realization shamed her. Was she simply evil? Had she always been evil, but never knew for sure until tonight? But mostly, did he love her?

She paced the room. What was Clarkson doing now? He had been inside of her. She could still feel his breath, warm on her neck and shoulders, his fullness between her legs. She was dizzy. She was changed. It was what she had wanted.

Before, when she had wondered if her virginity had set her apart, she had convinced herself that it hadn't. Sex was simply physical, like eating or sleeping or throwing up. Intercourse was really only an extension of masturbation, something she had done infrequently in her younger days, quickly and shamefully and then immediately denied. Sex was simply one of the many things that bodies did. It just hadn't happened to her. The same way she'd never had cancer, or gotten a tattoo. Tonight taught her that she had been wrong.

She leaned against the wall and closed her eyes. She could feel him, still. Another human had never claimed her so intimately, so completely. She was a part of him now. A part of him without really knowing who he was, what he had done. She sat on her bed before her legs gave out. Her bedroom vibrated with her guilt. The puzzle pieces of his evasions and denials began to interlock, forming an image she couldn't bear to see. She remembered their first meeting. Clarkson had said that he was a stranger to Glendale, merely jogging through the cemetery. He had lied.

What was he doing with Lorelei's picture? Could it be that he was no stranger to Lorelei? How could it not be? Lucy remembered her shock when she'd found the photograph, how her pulse had raced. His answers had soothed her. Seduced her. But now, in the quiet of her room, she knew that he had answered nothing. No, that wasn't true. He didn't need to answer. She hadn't asked. But she had known, even when she lay under him. The realization sickened her.

Her stomach lurched as if she might vomit, and things swam around her. Her fingers clutched the edge of her mattress. There was no way to make right what she had done. Her legs were rubbery as she stood. She slipped downstairs into the kitchen. She didn't really have a choice, she thought, as she opened the cutlery drawer and found the velvet-wrapped carving knife that had been her grandmother's. She untied the faded gold ribbon and unrolled the royal blue folds. There it was. Its ivory carved handle tapered into a blade that was thin, long and curved. Would it hurt? She put the knife in her purse. Almost as an afterthought, she remembered to throw her coat over her thin nightgown. She thrust her feet into her boots that stood primly on the mat inside the door. She was careful not to make a sound as she exited the side door. Hot, silent tears blinded her as she drove to the cemetery.

The angel gates rattled and the wind whipped Lucy's coat as she climbed the three snowy steps in the half darkness. She fought her way through the newly fallen snow toward Lorelei's grave. It had been a while since her last visit. She knew why.

Her eyes were swollen from crying, but she had no more tears for herself, for Lorelei, for anyone. She didn't know how to apologize for what she had done. No apology was possible. She felt inside her purse for the blade alongside her cosmetic case. She didn't know how one did these things, but she would figure it out. After all, Juliet had only been a child and she'd managed. But that was just a story. No matter. She was capable of more than she'd ever thought possible.

Lucy closed her purse. The snow had fallen all night, obscuring the path. She wove through the graves, the route familiar to her from so many afternoon vigils. Innocent vigils. A few months ago, the events of the past few hours would have been unthinkable. Maybe even yesterday, she thought. She had changed. She was no longer the prim and obedient Lucy.

Had all her responsible goodness been a sham? She hadn't thought so. Throughout her life, she had tried so hard. Always, she strived to make things right for everyone else. Even when she was the one hurt or angry or excluded, she had convinced herself that it was all her fault. Always, she was the one to grovel and apologize, make restitution for crimes she hadn't even committed.

Maybe that was her problem. She had erased herself a little more with each self-effacing act, until she allowed herself to teeter on the verge of invisibility. She knew now that invisible people were capable of terrible things.

Her feet picked a path through the frosted graves of the Seibert family. She was conscious of the knife, unsheathed and ready, in her handbag. Invisibility. Maybe it wasn't as bad as it seemed. She could have remained that way. It was easy to picture. She would have awakened this morning, showered, buttoned herself into the outfit that waited on her door hook, listened to the weather forecast as she drove to school, checked her wooden cubbyhole in the main office, taught, and cared for Dee. The days would have followed each other without complication. She would bring Dee her tea, wipe drool from her lips, tuck her into bed, until Dee's frail body drew its final breath. Then, she would plant Dee in the ground with the rest of the spent Armstrongs.

And she would continue to take out the garbage, dab moisturizer all over her face and body until her eyes failed and her mind faltered. Until she was alone in Dee's big house. The last Armstrong. She would have forgotten how to be lonely by then. And she would be blameless and spotless, and invisible until her own body failed and she joined the rest of them, the final corpse in Dee's cherished garden.

Now, that would never be. She dropped her purse in the snow, retrieved it and dusted off powdery flakes with her gloved hand. "Forgive me, Lorelei," she said.

Her legs ached as she tromped up the slope. The snow had drifted, deeper now, at the crest of the hill. She was happy that her legs hurt. Pain was what she deserved.

Lorelei's grave was just over the rise. Dawn fractured the grayness with ribbons of magenta. Within seconds, the pink marble stone would gleam before her. How should she do it? Should she spill her blood in a red river of contrition across the whiteness that blanketed Lorelei? Or should she kneel before Lorelei's grave, beg forgiveness, and then drive to the woods, alone. She could wander far into the wilderness, where she would already be half-forgotten when they found her. What would Lorelei have done, she wondered, if she had made love to her sister's killer?

She stopped. She wasn't sure what surprised her most. That she had finally put her suspicion into words, that Clarkson had murdered her sister. Or that she referred to what had occurred between her and Clarkson as making love. And even as she wondered, she knew the answer.

Had they made love? That was a curious way to think about what happened. No, love wasn't what they'd made. They had made something, absolutely. Even now, she felt the spot between her legs where he had entered her, moved, and gone still.

She carried herself differently today than yesterday. She was ashamed to admit it, but there was a power within her now. She loved him, but she hadn't a clue how he felt about her. She remembered his face, his hands. She remembered her legs opening to receive him. But, no, they hadn't made love. They had made each other whole.

She was surprised she knew that. That was the new power speaking, the power she acquired when he was lost inside of her. Before, she had thought of him as superior, in control. She was inferior under his steady gaze, too aware of the broken pieces that she hid inside.

Last night, his writhing body on top of hers showed her that he was looking for something, too. She had felt him explode and then shrink inside of her, soft and small. It had surprised her, touched her, equalized them in a way. But still, she knew that they hadn't made love. They were past love. And that was a pity.

Lorelei had been in love.

The grave was almost in sight. Did Lorelei rest there at Clarkson's hand? Soon, she would never have to know for certain. She could cling to a lingering doubt, and with one deft stroke, never have to wonder again.

She halted. There it was. The early morning pinkness deepened the rose marble. Snow blanketed the ground. It reached up and over the edges of the stone. The marker was hunched, rounded by the layer of white. Lorelei Armstrong, the engraved letters said. Lucy stood before it. She waited for the guilt and pain to hit. A crow flew overhead, squawking, and then was gone. Silence. Lucy waited. A sense of peace and finality descended on her.

She wanted to cry, but she couldn't.

"Lorelei," Lucy said out loud. "I'm sorry. I would take last night back if I could." She knelt, the way she supposed she should, but it felt false. She stood up. "I am more sorry than I've ever been in my whole life."

Even as she spoke, she knew those words, too, were a lie. She removed her gloves and took the knife from her purse. Her fingers traced the curved blade, glinting pink and purple in the sunrise. Still grasping the knife, she shook her coat from her arms and shoulders and pointed the knife toward her chest. Her hand shook and dripped with sweat. She closed her eyes and let the knife go. It dropped into the snow and disappeared. She stared at the spot where the snow had swallowed it. Only a slit marked its point of entry. No scar at all.

She didn't try to retrieve it. The truth was, she wasn't sorry enough to kill herself. Her life wasn't over. She wasn't finished with it. Yes, she had done something terrible, unspeakable. She had broken some commandment, she was sure of it. She and Clarkson. But she was past caring. Her former blameless existence seemed no better than what she had become at this moment.

"No," she said to herself. That couldn't be so. She remembered what it was to be virtuous Lucy, the person she was before she'd fallen in love, before she couldn't wait to see his face. She wouldn't choose to be that Lucy ever again, even if she could. The guilt took her breath away.

"Lorelei, I'm sorry," she said, and she meant it. Hot tears gushed. She collapsed in the snow before Lorelei's gravestone, now a deep rose in the widening bands of sunrise.

"I miss you, Lorelei," she finally said, her face streaked with tears. Lucy pictured her sister so clearly that she could almost touch her soft brown hair, hear her laughter. Lorelei had lived and loved. In her turn, Lorelei had embraced this world as fully as possible. At her funeral, everyone had said so.

And now, it was over for her. As it would be one day for Lucy. And Clarkson. Eventually, they would all join the mute garden of souls, their secrets irrelevant, their lives inconsequential. Lucy wiped her eyes. It was still her turn to live.

A shadow crossed over her. She looked up to see Clarkson. He leaned over, took her bare hands in his and pulled her to her feet. Her coat that she had left in the snow hung over his arm.

He shook it off and draped it across her shoulders. Her eyes held his gaze. A long silence stretched between them. Lucy's breathing slowed. Clarkson knelt. With both hands, he dug in the snow until the hilt of the knife was visible. He lifted it out and brushed off the blade. He straightened and tucked the knife inside his jacket. He held her coat open for her. She slipped her arms through the sleeves. They stood without speaking in the cold, muted cemetery.

"Let's go home, Lucy," Clarkson said, after a bit.

"Okay," she said.

He held his hand out to her and she took it. He guided her to his car, parked next to hers. They were silent as he opened the passenger door and helped her climb in. He started the engine. She looked out the window as they drove through Glendale, springing to life. Shopkeepers lit their festive windows, unlocked their doors hung with Christmas wreaths. They pulled into Dee's driveway. Clarkson shut off the ignition and turned to her.

"You didn't show up at school. People were worried about you," he said. "I told them you were fine."

Lucy looked into his green eyes. Was she? What was fine, anyway? She was alive. It's what she had wanted, she supposed.

"That's good," she said.

"I told them we were getting married."

He got out of the car, walked to her side and opened the door. She was grateful for his hand as he helped her from the car. Her legs shook beneath her. He kept his arm on her elbow as they walked to the side door of Dee's house.

"Yes," Lucy said.

Chapter 43

Dee was sad that the sunshine had begun to erode the crystalline artwork on the front parlor windows. It was cold outside, she could tell, from the way the hot air blasted from the radiator vents. She pulled her unicorn blanket up to her chin, the way she liked it. The designs on the window were lacey and swirled in parts, and then sharp and geometric. When she was young, someone had told her that Jack Frost fashioned those shapes while children slept. She liked that idea, that someone was hard at work while others slept.

Like last night. She hadn't been surprised this morning when Clarkson had announced that he and Lucy were getting married. Megan had screamed and jumped up and down, and hugged Clarkson. But Dee wasn't the least bit surprised. She had heard the comings and goings throughout the night, the furtive steps on the wooden staircase up to Clarkson's room, down from his room, more steps, a car motor revving in the early dawn. Dee wasn't sure exactly what they were doing, but Lucy and Clarkson had certainly been busy while others slept. And Dee had known for a long time that sex had been waiting to happen between them. Thank heaven, she thought. She hadn't thought Lucy had it in her, really. She wondered where Lucy had gone this morning. It had been too early for her to shop. Lucy usually shopped when her life veered from its normal path.

Dee had settled herself in the parlor early this morning. She knew that something was up and she didn't want to miss it.

Megan had taken the call this morning from Lucy's school, saying she hadn't shown, was she all right? Megan had been distraught, then frantic, racing around in her flannel pajamas with the Raggedy Ann face on the front. Dee had wanted to tell her that Lucy would be okay, that she had pattered around the house all night, up and down from Clarkson's room. That Lucy was probably sitting somewhere, waiting for the stores to open, so she could shop until she'd calmed herself. And that maybe, finally, Lucy had become human.

Dee hadn't worried about Lucy at all. She had listened while Megan called Summer and then clattered upstairs to summon Clarkson. Summer had wanted to call the police, but Clarkson had been calm. He had poured himself coffee and said that it was all right. That he would find Lucy and bring her back. That he and Lucy were getting married. And he had gone back upstairs to shower and dress before he set off to find Lucy and bring her home.

Maybe it hadn't happened exactly like that, Dee thought, but more or less. Sometime during the commotion, Clarkson had made her a breakfast of cinnamon toast and tea, just the way she liked it. He'd put his arm around her, shaken out her blanket and made it feel fresh as he tucked it back around her. She liked that. He knew how to treat a woman.

She worried about Lucy with him. Lucy was so odd. Ever since she was a baby. But then again, it might not have been Lucy's fault.

It wasn't hers, though. At least, not mostly. Dee used to wonder if it was, but how could a baby know things like that? And anyway, Dee no longer cared. Guilt and blame were the province of younger people. At a certain age, a person realized that life was just what it was. Still, what if she hadn't had those doubts about Lucy, all those years ago, the way she had?

Dee heard a sound and looked up. She knew Megan's boisterous footsteps before Megan entered the parlor and patted her on the head. Funny, Dee thought. Usually, Megan ignored her completely.

"Don't worry, Dee. Clarkson will find her," Megan said.

Dee nodded and smiled. If she weren't so tired of talking, if the words would manage to come out of her mouth in the right order, she would have told Megan that she wasn't worried. Lucy would never put herself in a position where dangerous things happened. Lucy was careful, watchful, a survivor. After all, Lucy had survived what Dee knew.

Dee drifted back to her own youth. She had been pretty. Everyone thought so. How she had ended up with Thaddeus was fuzzy in her memory now. Maybe it was because he never said anything. Just watched her. She had been young enough to find his silence intriguing instead of lazy. Or boring. Or plain old selfish.

Who wouldn't have grown tired of him? The first chance she had after the birth of Thaddeus, Jr., Dee went away with a few of her friends. "Just the girls," she had told her young husband. Who had watched little Thad? She couldn't remember. The girls had rented a cottage at the beach for a weekend. There had been four of them, counting herself. Marie who died ten years ago now, that blonde girl from Crestview, what ever happened to her, and another who they all lost touch with soon after. Dee had been ill that day, sunburned and waterlogged, and opted to stay behind in the cottage. The rest had gone to the beach. Later, Marie's brother had driven them somewhere. He and his friend had stopped at the cottage to check on her. What was the friend's name? She could still see parts of his face, his blue eyes, his clean-shaven skin, as he leaned over to kiss her. She couldn't remember his name. She knew it, of course. She had repeated it constantly to herself throughout the course of her pregnancy with Lucy. She had feared that she would utter it in her sleep and then awaken to find Thaddeus bent over her, his face twisted in shocked disbelief.

Charles. That was it. Was Charles Lucy's father? That question had floated through her mind every day, every hour it seemed, of her long pregnancy. It had been enough to drive her mad. How could she have almost forgotten his name?

Old age, probably. No, that wasn't it at all. It was because it didn't matter anymore. She never did know if Lucy had emerged as a result of that one evening with Charles. She used to study Lucy's face for signs of him, but as the years passed, his features weren't clear enough for her to decide. Lucy's blue eyes didn't look like his. Did they?

Throughout Lucy's childhood, Dee would examine her small body for traces of Thaddeus. When she grasped Lucy's hand to cross the street, she would catch herself checking to see if Lucy's fingers were short and square like his. Thaddeus had no clue. Dee had never even told Al about Charles. She'd never considered telling Lucy.

But Lucy always seemed to look right through her, as if she didn't quite trust her. Those watchful eyes. Of course, it wasn't Lucy's fault. But it wasn't really hers, either. She was young. If she had understood life a little better, she would have known not to marry Thaddeus, and not to have his son right after. And especially, not to enjoy an unrestrained day in a beach cottage and then wonder about that one day's aftermath for almost the whole rest of her life.

Almost. At a certain point, she had just quit wondering. When was that? Maybe it was when she was old enough to understand that life was so vast and imperfect that the enormous issues of her youth and middle age weren't the center of the universe. That, in fact, maybe nothing was the center. Yes, old age had taught her that. People who seemed to occupy the center of the universe dropped dead one day, got buried the next and were forgotten soon after. The relentless march of life closed right over the greatest triumphs and the worst wounds with surprising ease.

Look at Lorelei, Dee thought. Lorelei had been a light for her, the reason she hadn't gone mad with doubt and guilt when she was still young enough to believe those emotions had a purpose. Lorelei had been everything that Lucy wasn't—open, loving, adventurous. Lorelei had laughed. Dee had been able to squeeze Lorelei's chubby hands without wondering if her fingers were square like her husband's. With Lorelei, Dee had never had those soul-wrenching nightmares that a man would show up at her door one day, a man with an uncanny resemblance to her older daughter.

Dee thought that if she weren't so old, it would astonish her that she could recall Lorelei without doubling over in pain. She looked at her wrinkled hands. She felt the heaviness in her legs. She was that old. It wasn't so bad. She could think about Lorelei some mornings and then lick butter from the edge of her toast. She could smile. Still, it was a shame that Lorelei hadn't lived. Of course, one never got to choose such things. Her neck ached a little, so she snuggled into her pillow. She let her eyes close.

She was conscious of the side door opening. Two sets of footsteps echoed in the hallway. She recognized Clarkson's heavy, measured tread. Was that Lucy with him? She hadn't worn her heels, then. Her steps were soft.

They were in front of her, all of a sudden it seemed, the soon to be married couple. Lucy touched her shoulder and then turned away. Her eyes were puffy. Was that her nightgown bunching out from under her coat? Clarkson had his arm around her waist. Dee wanted to say something to them, but her eyes had to close again. She heard their steps retreat as if from very far away.

Dee wished Clarkson had fixed her blanket again, fluffed it up the way he had earlier this morning. She pulled at it a few times until it lifted from her lap. It wasn't the same, but it was a little better. She settled back into her chair and wondered if she would live long enough to see their wedding. For a moment, grandchildren crossed her mind, but that was silly. They were old. And anyway, it didn't matter, because it all went so fast anyway.

Chapter 44

Summer paused at the front door of the Armstrong house. The solid front of the mansion looked the same, the red brick faced with gray stone, the rows of tall windows with their old, wavy glass, the date set into the arch over the door, but it seemed somehow transformed. She reached into her bag to pat the edge of the crushed velvet fabric with her gloved fingers. She rang the bell.

"Summer!" Megan flung open the door and hugged her, rocking back and forth. "I have everything planned for tomorrow. Everything."

"That's great," Summer said. She gave Megan's shoulder a squeeze and extricated herself. Would Megan's relentless enthusiasm ever fail to surprise her? They walked to the front parlor together. Megan bent to plug in the Christmas tree lights, stopped, then stood and wiped flour-dusted hands on her jeans. "I'm a mess. I was in the middle of making an engagement cake for tomorrow night's dessert. I think I might have gotten flour on your coat. Here let me get it."

"No, that's okay. I'll just brush it off." Summer set the bag at her feet. "Dee's asleep, I see," she said as she wiped away the fine white dust from her lapel.

Megan shrugged and bent over again. She plugged in the tree lights. The parlor glowed. Dee stirred a little in her chair by the window.

"Dee's asleep? When isn't she?" Megan stood back to admire the tree. "That's better. We needed some holiday atmosphere. What's in the bag?"

"Oh. A dress. For Lucy."

"Lucy has more clothes than she can wear if she lives to be a hundred."

Summer laughed. "She does. I don't know if she wants this one or not. It's sort of special. I thought maybe she'd want to wear it to dinner tomorrow."

Megan wiped her hands on her jeans again, opened the bag and pulled out the folds of soft velvet. "It's pretty," she said. She stroked the ivory lace ruffle that ringed the off-shoulder neckline. She ran her fingers along the back, where rows of ivory lace cascaded down to the hemline in an upside down V-shape. "I'm not sure it's Lucy's type, though. Oh, I hope I didn't hurt your feelings. It's just, you know, Lucy has a kind of usual look or something."

"No. You're right. Actually, it belonged to her sister."

Megan's eyes widened. "Lorelei?"

Summer nodded. "It's definitely Lorelei's style. You didn't know her."

"I feel like I did sometimes."

Summer wasn't sure why Megan's remark made her blush.

"Is Lucy here? I told her I would stop by today."

"Upstairs in her room probably. You know how she's been ever since the engagement." Megan rolled her eyes. "I thought engaged people were supposed to be happy."

"Maybe it's stress," Summer said.

Megan shrugged and picked at something under her fingernails. "Maybe. I'll get her for you," she said. "I wanted to run upstairs and grab my iPod anyway. When you're done talking to Lucy, come into the kitchen and I'll show you what I've made for tomorrow. But don't let her see. You know, it's kind of a surprise."

"I will, and don't worry, I won't let her see."

Megan skipped from the room. Dee stirred, opened her eyes and closed them again. Summer arranged the shimmering velvet folds on her lap. If Lorelei never had the chance to wear it, at least Lucy might. Summer remembered the day Lorelei had brought the dress home, how excited she was. Her coldness that day still shamed her.

She slipped the dress into the bag, stood and walked to the window. She wondered if Lucy would be her old self when she came downstairs. Megan was right. Lucy's engagement hadn't made her a happier person. Love should be much easier.

"Hello Summer."

Lucy seemed to materialize before her. How had she not heard her footsteps? "Lucy," she said.

"I'm sorry. I'd forgotten you were stopping by." Lucy ran her hand through her hair.

"That's all right. I only came for a quick visit."

Lucy pulled at the tie of her robe. She looked down at her slippers, as if just noticing them.

"I can come back another time," Summer said. For Lucy, it was the equivalent of walking into the room naked.

"No, it's fine." Lucy's smiled seemed forced. "Shall we sit a minute?" Lucy lowered herself into the chair across from Summer. "I guess Mom's napping."

Summer searched for something to say. A crash and the loud banging of pots and pans clattered from the kitchen.

"Sounds like an avalanche," Summer said, privately thanking Megan for her klutzy tendencies.

"Yes, it does." Lucy didn't turn toward the direction of the sound.

"I wonder if she needs help," Summer said. The sounds settled into a managed cacophony. "Sounds like she's got it under control."

"Yes," Lucy agreed.

"You know that Megan's working on a special engagement dinner for you and Clarkson tomorrow evening."

"That's very sweet of her."

"I talked to Al and he said he wouldn't miss it for the world."

"No, not for the world," Lucy said. "He's very fond of Clarkson."

"Lucy, he's very fond of you, too. He's known you forever."

"As much as any of us know each other," Lucy said.

Summer tilted her head. The last few times she'd spoken with Lucy, she had been this way, cryptic, evasive. Summer wondered if she should forget the dress completely. "Lucy, is there something you want to talk about?" The words slipped out before Summer could stop them.

Lucy's eyes widened. Her lips parted. "I'm not sure," she said, after a pause.

"Lucy, if you're not sure about something, about anything, please, say so. No one can force you into something you don't want to do." Summer stopped herself. She wished that someone had forced her into acknowledging her love for Lorelei when she had the chance. She wished that Lorelei were about to wear the blue velvet and lace dress. "Or, understand that sometimes in life, you don't need to be sure. You just go with your feelings."

Lucy nodded.

"Is it Clarkson? Do you want to marry him?"

"Yes," Lucy said in a soft voice.

Summer took a deep breath and smiled. "Well then, don't worry. I know this is a real change for you, but true love works wonders."

Lucy raised her eyes to Summer's. "Yes, it would, I guess." Her eyes broke away again. "A wedding. We've never had one in the family."

"Here, I brought you something," Summer said. She pulled the dress from the bag and held it up. The reflection of Megan's multi-colored Christmas lights on the sheen of the velvet made it look like something from a fairy tale. "I don't know if you want it or not. It's for tomorrow's dinner. If you want to wear it, it's yours."

"It's lovely," Lucy said.

"It was Lorelei's."

Lucy touched it and then sat back, hands in her lap. "I never saw her in it."

"No. She bought it for our official announcement party. The one we never had."

"Oh, Summer." For a moment Summer thought Lucy would hug her or cry, but she didn't. Summer leaned forward and folded the dress into Lucy's arms.

"Thank you," Lucy said.

"As I said, you may have already decided on something else to wear. I know how you are with your clothes."

"I'm not sure yet," Lucy said.

"Whatever you want."

Lucy's fingers traced the lace edging at the neckline.

"Yes, well, that's all," Summer said. She rose. "I promised Megan I would look in on her before I left. I'd ask you to join us, but whatever's going on in there is a surprise until tomorrow."

"She's so thoughtful."

"Especially if Dee's kitchen survives. I'll see you tomorrow night."

"Summer?"

"Yes?"

"Just thanks for everything."

"Of course. No problem. Oh, I just remembered. When she picked out the dress, Lorelei called the color 'Lucy blue.' She said it matched your eyes."

"She always said blue was my color. You know how she was about such things."

They faced each other. Summer considered hugging her, but Lucy seemed contained, as if an invisible fence surrounded her. She touched Lucy's shoulder. "I'll see you tomorrow, Lucy. At the celebration feast."

"Yes. At the feast." Lucy fidgeted with the ring that encircled her finger.

Chapter 45

The voices that drifted from the parlor made Megan smile. When she had peeked in a while ago, Al and Clarkson were deep in conversation about some business detail, but Al's green suspenders embroidered with little red ornaments were unmistakably festive. The celebration of Christmas Eve and Lucy and Clarkson's engagement on the same night couldn't be otherwise.

Megan sliced the carrots and tossed them by handfuls into the steamer. She hadn't been surprised to spot Dee already in the parlor, in her usual chair, but she'd done a double take at the sight of her. Dee's sparse hair was teased into a white bouffant. And she must have dug the pink silk blouse she wore from the depths of her closet. It hung around her in a drape of shiny folds, gathered into a frilly tie at her neck. She was awake, for a change, and someone had smudged glittery silver powder on her crepey eyelids. Megan thought she looked like a time-ravaged Barbie doll, maybe a special edition Holiday Hospice Barbie. She'd immediately felt a little bad, and smiled extra-nicely at her. Lucy hadn't made her appearance yet, but Lucy was fussy. She was probably battling some invisible strand of misbehaving hair. Megan plucked a bean from a bubbling pot and tasted it. She turned the heat down a notch.

Summer entered the kitchen and slipped behind her to grab the silver canapé tray from the counter. Her black tunic over tight black leggings made her seem to float as she bustled from the kitchen to the parlor. Megan watched her elegant stride, the way she leaned over at the waist when she bent to sniff a dish on the stove. She liked to think that the longer she hung around Summer, the more she would resemble her. After all, she was her daughter.

So far, everything was perfect. Those years of standing next to her Virginia mother had paid off. That's what she'd taken to calling the woman who raised her. She'd shadowed her Virginia mother for her entire childhood it seemed, assisting as she chopped and stirred and basted, churning out wholesome spreads for her dad and her brothers and scads of cousins. Megan envisioned her mother's fleshy, capable hands, the prominent capillaries in her cheeks, flushed from the heat of the stove. Her Virginia mother had taught her more than she'd realized. She would tell her that, the next time she called. It would make it easier when she broke the news that she wasn't coming home anytime soon, that she had found her place in the world at last. Already, she imagined the tearful voice on the other end. Megan picked up the crystal bowl of red carnations and holly sprigs and headed for the dining room.

She set the flowers in the center of the table. The empty table held such promise. Megan had polished the Armstrong family silver until it glinted under the crystal chandelier. She had washed and ironed the linen tablecloths that she found in the old mahogany sideboard. The grand table with the curved legs, set with Dee's Haviland china and Austrian stemware seemed other-worldly. She wondered what her mother would think of this house.

Life back in Virginia seemed so ordinary to her now. Funny, her childhood home had always seemed special. Even though its boxy colonial shape was identical to all the others in the subdivision, it had stood out with its fire engine red door and shutters. The Brandons next door had black and the McGills across the street a dull blue. She frowned. The image of her former neighborhood had faded a bit, now a hazy impression of low ceilings, two-car garages, stainless steel cutlery and polyester tablecloths. She patted the solid mahogany sideboard as she headed for the kitchen.

The timer beeped. Megan grabbed Dee's potholders and opened the oven door. Sizzling juices jumped and spat. A cloud of steam stung her eyes as she lifted the pan from the shelf and set it on the counter. She wiped her face with the kitchen towel and smiled. The filet roast was fragrant, browned but not burned. She would let it rest before carving, just as her Virginia mother had. Megan brushed her hair from her face and walked to the parlor.

"Okay, you guys. Dinner is served in a heartbeat. Well, maybe a heartbeat and a half. And it looks really great even if I do say so myself."

"It smells divine," Al said. He followed Megan to the kitchen. "You put the champagne in the refrigerator, right? Let's get that open for our toast to the newlyweds-to-be."

"Megan, let me help you get things to the table," Summer said.

"Clarkson, it's time to get Lucy down here," Al called over his shoulder.

"Yes, she is taking her time, isn't she?" Clarkson said. He disappeared down the hallway.

"Dee, you're all dressed up," Megan said, as she intercepted Dee navigating her way to the dining room table. The corners of Dee's mouth curled upward a little, changing the pattern of wrinkles around her lips. Megan helped Dee into her chair and handed her a goblet of water. Summer hustled back and forth with baskets of rolls and hot platters of mashed potatoes, green beans with almonds, glazed carrots. Al popped the champagne.

Megan brought the roast from the kitchen and set it on the bronze-footed trivet, next to the flowers. She lit the candles at either end of the table. They all sat, leaving two empty chairs, one at the head of the table and the other next to it on one side. The bustle of activity and exclamations over the food fizzled. Megan wished she had dinner music. Her Virginia mother hadn't bothered with it, but she'd seen an ad last week on the food channel for 'Best Enchanted Eating Songs.' Right now, they could be listening to some of that fancy classical dinner music instead of the faint ticking of the clock from the kitchen.

"Shall I see what's keeping them?" Summer asked, when the silence and the empty chairs became overwhelming.

"No, I'm sure they'll be down any moment," Al said.

Megan's cheeks felt hot. She could feel the pink spots erupting on her face, itching down into her neck. Where were Clarkson and Lucy?

Chapter 46

Lucy sat at her dressing table and avoided the mirror. Her face didn't interest her at all. She knew the lines too well, what worked and what didn't. Age, and of course, recent events had changed her. But no matter what life handed her, she managed to hold up. What was the name of that insect that skidded on the tops of ponds and puddles? It had a round body and legs that stuck out from its center like rays from the sun. It had no substance, just all those legs that held up nothing. That's me, thought Lucy. Neither she nor the insect had chosen their fates. It was the way life had shaped them.

Her guests were waiting. The smell of meat wafted into her room and mixed with the lavender scent on her neck and wrists. She touched the velvet folds of her dress, Lorelei's dress. The velvet was soft, but unlike her, it had substance. Maybe the dress would work its magic. From the outside in, she would absorb its weight, soak it up until it marinated her whole body, heart and soul, in what she lacked.

She couldn't describe what it was that she lacked. But it had left a hole right through her center. Had she been dispossessed from birth, or disenfranchised somewhere along the line? That was a good question. She fished in her jewel box for her long crystal drop earrings. Once in her hand, they seemed obscene. The weight of her diamond ring was enough. She let the earrings fall, opened a white velvet box and unpinned two tiny diamond studs from their backs. She had to turn them in her palm to see them shine. That's all she wanted tonight, a fleeting glimmer like fireflies on a summer evening. If she could for once create a genuine spark, it would be just like that, the briefest flash. She would be happy with that.

Happy. That was a strange, impossible word. Happiness hadn't played much of a part in her life. Would she be happy now, with Clarkson? Or, would the weight of what she didn't quite know crush her more with each passing day?

Maybe he hadn't killed her sister. She had no absolute proof, only evidence that grew in the dark of a sleepless night, and shrank in the light of his company. Perhaps it was all right to have that secret between them, her suspicion and his knowledge of the truth, with neither of them ever choosing to settle the matter, for good or ill. She imagined that there were plenty of husbands and wives with tremendous secrets between them. The relationship between her own mother and Al, for one, must have hung suspended between her parents' marriage even if Thaddeus had no clue. And what about Summer and Lorelei, disrupted by the secret existence of Megan? But look what happened there. Did secrets always leach their way out, the way water managed to seep through openings too small to see? Or did they sometimes lie deep and still and sink to the bottom of one's awareness, rarely stirred by time's passing?

But back to that question of what made her able to compress herself into almost nothing, so that whatever befell her was okay, because she didn't really matter, anyway? It hadn't transpired overnight. When did she lose herself? Was it when her mother had retreated into the sadness of her own life and left Lucy to sort things out for herself? No, it was before that. Well before that.

She had always been an accessory to others. She was an accessory to the bright light that was Thaddeus, Jr. Dee had rarely used her name when she was a child. If she called for Thaddeus, then Lucy knew to follow. Lucy thought her own name too thin to speak. She was happy when Dee named Lorelei, a bold name, chosen for a person worth the gift of life. Lucy picked up the hairbrush. Why was she the one left? It made no sense, as if the sun and moon had fallen from the sky, leaving only the lackluster pinpoint of a disappointing star.

The noises from downstairs sounded lively. Happy. Lucy brushed her hair from her face, rolled it into a twist and pinned it in place. She slipped the diamond studs through the holes in her ears and squeezed on the gold backings. She stood up from her dressing table and smoothed the folds of Lorelei's betrothal gown.

She meant to head downstairs, but thoughts of Lorelei overwhelmed her. They could do without her for another minute. She crept down the hall and opened the door to Lorelei's room. She lifted one ivory heel and then the other, across the threshold, a flash of pearl-varnished nails visible through the peep-toes. She closed the door behind her.

Lorelei's presence inhabited every corner. Lucy leaned against the door to guard against a sudden wave of dizziness. When she knew her legs would support her weight, she edged away and circled the room. She ran her fingers across the wooden surface of the tilted desktop where Lorelei had sat for hours, drawing and painting her pictures. The tortoise shell hairbrush on the dresser reminded her of a young Lorelei sitting cross-legged on the bed while Dee worked to tame her cloud of brown hair. Lucy picked up the hand mirror next to it, almost surprised to find her own face peering back. She set it down. She paused to look out the oriel window, through the shadows of pines, and upward into the night sky, too dark for her to distinguish a hint of moon or stars. She turned away.

The chintz bedskirt brushed the floor with a soft sound as Lucy lowered herself onto Lorelei's bed. In her heart, she wished that it were Lorelei instead of herself pausing in the hushed upstairs, about to descend the grand staircase in a velvet dress.

Above the bed hung Heinrich Heine's Lorelei poem, the stanzas translated into English and written in fine calligraphy, the border cross-stitched with images of a golden comb, a listing boat, a mermaid tail. It had been a present at Lorelei's christening. The poem told the story of the maiden turned mermaid who lured sailors to their deaths beneath her rocky perch. Her father used to tease Lorelei. "All those poor, lovesick men, dying just to get a glimpse of you." He would tickle her and she would laugh.

Lucy pulled out the top drawer of Lorelei's nightstand where Lorelei once stashed her treasures. Inside was a folded page. She opened it to find a poem typed single-spaced on a plain white sheet. The poem was a Sylvia Plath piece, also called Lorelei. Lucy had never heard of this one. She read the whole thing. She wasn't good at understanding poetry. That had been Lorelei's thing. But a few lines from the text struck her: "Sisters, your song /Bears a burden too weighty/For the whorled ear's listening." For a fleeting moment Lucy felt a sense of their shared weights.

Funny, she thought, how everything that had occurred since Lorelei's murder had made her aware of how different she and Lorelei were. From the moment she had looked into Lorelei's waxy countenance, then away to the painting propped against the lid of her coffin, its curly signature afloat in a strange sea, she had been oddly conscious of the separateness of their lives. And over the past few months, the gulf between them had only widened. The Lorelei of her past dissolved a little more each day. Lucy touched the folds of her dress.

But they had been sisters, first, before they became strangers. Lucy remembered hoisting Lorelei onto the back of a white pony at the Glendale Fair when Dee wasn't looking. The two of them had laughed about it for years. It was true that Lucy hadn't known that Lorelei loved Summer, but she knew that Lorelei adored strawberries and that she imagined that lilies were stars fallen from the sky. And that Lorelei had once told her third grade teacher that she would probably grow up to be Cher. Lucy folded her hands in her lap. There were still a few pieces of Lorelei that belonged to her. Maybe that's the most one could expect.

She poked around again in the drawer. There was a birthday card signed by their father and mother, a certificate that commemorated Lorelei's appointment as official artist of the sixth grade. And a ticket stub from the Ice Capades performance in Pittsburgh that Lucy had taken her to, after their father's death. On the way home, Lorelei had hugged Lucy and promised that some day she would grow up to be just like her. Her arms had felt small around her neck. Lucy had answered, "You already are, silly. We're sisters."

There was a light knock. Clarkson opened the door and stepped inside. "Lucy?" He said her name as if it were real and large and important. "What are you doing in here? We're all waiting for you downstairs."

Lucy looked into his eyes for signs of what he felt about her. His face was the same as always, controlled. Had she been wrong to read into his expression that flicker of desire that had set her heart racing? Looking at him now, his eyes gave nothing away. "Lucy?" He reached for her hand and smiled at her with cordial coolness, a rootless smile. For a fleeting moment, in the center of Lorelei's room, his eyes seemed marbled, reptilian. And then the fan of lines around his temples spread to his cheeks, and she reached out for him. His fingers were warm.

How could she know for sure what he felt, with so little practice in her many years? And what did it matter? She only knew how she felt. That was all anyone could know. It would have to be enough. It was enough.

"I'm ready," she said.

Chapter 47

Finally, creaking on the stairs sparked a wave of relief at the table. Megan hoped her spots would begin to fade. She glanced around the table one last time.

"Oh, no," she said. How could she have forgotten? She had found it when she was cooking—a carving knife, half wrapped in royal velvet in a drawer. She grabbed the serrated knife next to the roast, raced to the kitchen and traded it for the new one. It was a work of art, its thin blade razor sharp, its inlaid ivory handle both substantial and delicate.

"For the occasion," Megan said, as she hurried back to her seat. At that moment, Lucy and Clarkson entered, arm in arm.

"Oh, my goodness," Lucy exclaimed. Her eyes lingered for a moment on Megan.

Megan was happy for Summer's sake that Lucy had worn her sister's dress. For some reason, it had seemed important. And Lucy wore it well. The lace that edged her low neckline softened her. The diamond studs in her ears sparkled.

"You look beautiful, Lucy," Summer said. Megan saw the tears that welled in Summer's eyes and wondered if she would cry herself. She had never known that she could love anyone the way she loved everyone at the table at that moment. In her Virginia family, she had felt suffocated, pigeon-holed into her role as the adopted one, always a bit apart. Here, they were all the same, adults, respectful of each other. Maybe they weren't perfect, but they were a family of love.

Why hadn't she thought to order that background dinner music CD? The quiet in the room was almost unbearable as Clarkson helped Lucy into her seat. He seemed so gallant, and Lucy so fragile. The rest of them could only watch. His strong hand encircled Lucy's thin fingers, her nails long and shining. He placed a champagne flute in her hands. The way Lucy looked right into his eyes sent shivers through Megan.

"We need a toast." Summer's voice came from the end of the table. "Al, would you mind doing the honors? But first…" Her voice broke for a brief second. She cleared her throat. She seemed to struggle for composure. "But first, let's take a moment to remember our Lorelei. To Lorelei. My friend. My soul-mate." She raised her glass and focused her eyes on Lucy. Megan followed her gaze to see a flush of red creep from Lucy's bare shoulders to her neck and up to her cheeks.

Megan turned back to Summer. For a moment, she glimpsed something new in her. A humanity. It reminded her of when she'd spotted her Virginia mother, lumpy and overweight, hurling herself into a pile of autumn leaves, laughing, more person than mother for once. Megan was overcome by the change in Summer, her softness, her intimacy. It was an opening.

"To Lorelei," Lucy said in a soft voice.

They clinked glasses. Megan felt the power of the silence that followed, the strength of Lorelei's invisible presence as it bound them all together.

"Al?" Summer said.

Al stood up. "Okay, sure, if I may have the honor." He tugged at his left suspender that had migrated too far from his pouch of a belly. "To another Christmas Eve," he began.

"Yes," Dee said. She sipped her champagne.

Al smiled at her, then continued, "But this one is different. We can't any of us forget what tomorrow is—that little baby in the manger and all. But tonight, we're celebrating an engagement of two of our own." He cleared his throat. Megan worried that he wouldn't find the words to continue. Dee twirled the stem of her champagne glass. He continued, "Some of us are lucky to find love for a lifetime. Some for just a little while. But whenever love comes our way, it's special." His voice wavered a little. "Here's to love, whenever it happens. And all of us here couldn't be happier for Lucy and Clarkson. Let's all raise our glasses to our guests of honor." He held his flute high in the air. "Health, happiness and love to both of you."

"Here, here," the voices around the table echoed, followed by the music of crystal on crystal.

Megan raised her glass along with the rest of them. Bubbles popped and tickled her nose. The awkwardness that had surrounded her throughout her life seemed to melt away. She looked at Al, his soft silver hair, his bushy eyebrows knit into one. Next to him sat Summer, pale and aristocratic, her thin arm holding her glass delicately as she brought it to her lips, her new vulnerability only enhancing her fragile beauty. Anyone would be proud to have her as a mother. Next to her sat Dee in her haphazard finery, gripping the stem of her flute with both wrinkled hands. And of course, Lucy. Her blue eyes shone above the velvet dress, her head tilted toward Clarkson. His strong arm steadied her glass as she lifted it. Each one of them had become unbelievably precious to her. Clarkson set his glass on the table and reached toward the platter. Before he could touch it, Megan pushed her chair back and stood up. Clarkson drew back his hand and turned his attention to her.

"One more toast," Megan said. "I need to thank everyone here for making my life complete at last. For becoming my family. Here's to family," she said, and held her glass high, the way Al had. She drained her champagne and sat back in her chair. The prism chandelier, the candlelight, Lucy's velvet, Summer's mane of black hair shone through the blur of her tears.

The clink of crystal on crystal again filled the room.

Clarkson picked up the knife.

"To family," he said. A slice of roast, its fleshy center pink and juicy fell under his deft stroke. He lifted it with the edge of the blade and nodded to Lucy. She raised her plate to him.

Epilogue

Lucy awakened in her childhood bedroom before dawn. This was it. Valentine's Day. Her wedding day. Clarkson had been aggressive in setting the date, insisting that a quick ceremony was in order so that Dee could still participate. He'd spent the night at his country home at Lucy's request. Her plea that she needed one last night on her own seemed to surprise him.

But Clarkson didn't understand. The stream of events over the past month and a half had brought more changes to her soul than the static pool of the many preceding decades. She knew herself now, a bit more with each passing day. And it wasn't only herself. She knew more about everyone, it seemed. At long last, she'd learned to pierce the aura of polite civility that most people wrapped around their darkest secrets. She'd acquired the radar of a bat, another sense altogether.

And that sense told her without doubt what she had done. And what she was about to do. Once she opened her legs to Clarkson, her heart and mind had opened as well, and she saw the world from a new vantage point—from its gritty trenches filled with pain and guilt and tombstones, to its lofty summits, with whooping orgasms and shared pots of tea. She saw everyone and everything anew, especially the calculating Clarkson as he wrangled his deals and sweet-talked his hangers on. Lucy was stripped of her flighty world of silly fantasies. She was newly anchored to a twisted world.

It was invigorating, it was tragic—it was real. She no longer had the luxury of shrouding herself in doubt. When she looked at Clarkson's hands, she saw them for what they were, the hands of a murderer who had sucked the life from her sister. No obfuscation or evasion on either his or her part served to mitigate the truth. There was no going back.

She lay in bed and regarded her sparkling wedding dress hung with its scrim of a veil, neatly arranged on her door hook. She wanted the marriage. It was the only antidote to her many years of bland servitude. She deserved a time to shine. She knew all too well the way the years flew by with maddening urgency. She rose from her bed and brushed past the dress with only a glance, then doubled back and lifted the veil from its packing. She threw it onto her dresser chair. A veil wouldn't be necessary today.

She crept to the door of Lorelei's room. So much had happened since the last time she'd visited this room, on Christmas Eve, before her wedding announcement. She had to return one last time. She had only one peace left to make before she ate her last breakfast as the prim Miss Armstrong.

She opened the door slowly. "Lorelei, it's me. Again," she whispered, and crossed the threshold in bare feet. The room seemed to vibrate in silent response. "I'm sorry it's taken me so long. We need to talk." Lucy stood in the center of the room. Was Lorelei here at all? Certainly here as much as anywhere, alive in her drawings, her letters, everything her small pale hands had once touched. It didn't matter, anyway. What Lucy needed to say was all that mattered.

"I've come to explain myself," she whispered. She focused her eyes on the oriel window. "I've tried so hard not to see the truth, but it's too clear to pretend otherwise. No one else knows, and I'm not telling them." Lucy bit her lip, turned and surveyed her surroundings. The cheerful chintz spread was frozen in tight creases. The chair at the drawing desk was pushed in. But all of Lorelei's possessions were still under the command of her departed soul.

"I know what he did to you."

Lucy leaned forward so the blood rushed to her head.

"But try to understand. I can only imagine your part in it. For God's sake, you could have learned an iota of self-preservation somewhere along the line. But you didn't." Lucy straightened and brushed her hair from her face. "You always acted as if any speck of common sense would pollute your artistry, would ruin you. Any child knows better. So it isn't just my fault. You helped bring about this day. You and all you stood for."

Tears streamed down Lucy's face. She got up, walked to the window, and traced the loopy outline of frost along the windowpane.

"I can't apologize. I shouldn't have to. I won't." The tears wouldn't stop. "But you're my sister, part of me. I've loved you since you were born. The best I can do is make you a deal. A promise."

Lucy drew in her breath, turned, and steadied herself. The tears stopped. Once she promised, it was set in stone. Not just in stone, but in granite, as pink and leaden as Lorelei's gravestone, the same immovable granite as the stone that Clarkson had placed in the front yard of the Armstrong house earlier in the week. The etched block letters said "The House of Dupree" in a brave and masculine font. It was his wedding gift to her.

"You see, the problem is, I love him, Lorelei. I know that's vile. Incomprehensible. But love isn't rational, is it? It's sweet and strong and feeds me in a way I hadn't even known to imagine. And maybe Clarkson has changed. People can. Look at me. And he's been kind to me. To Dee. To Summer. To Megan. He's rescued the rest of us, Lorelei. If things had gone otherwise, maybe he would have rescued you as well."

Lucy turned back to the window. "But he may not love me. I'm not a fool, although I've tried to be. Right now, you must see me as a traitor. If I am, a traitor is better than the husk of a human I was until Clarkson came into my life." This was the utter truth. The fire in her soul was a blessed relief every morning. The lift in her gait was something she hadn't even known to expect, cherish, or miss.

Still, there was something sinful in her newfound joy, and she knew it. "If I find out that he doesn't love me even a little, if he ever reverts to the monster only we both know he was..." The sudden sickness in her stomach was testimony to her resolve. "I swear to you, I will avenge the violence that he inflicted on you, on our family, on our name. I give you my word as a sister. If that happens, I will strike him down and set us both free."

Lucy fled from the room and almost barreled into Dee.

"Why, it's Lucy," Dee said, the bewildered look on her face slow to disappear. "Good morning." Her thin arm reached out and grabbed Lucy by the wrist.

Lucy wiped her eyes with the back of her free hand.

"Good morning, Mother," she said.

Dee stared at her long and hard. She released her grip. In the early morning brightening, Dee's dull eyes glowed with a whitish fire. "We're having a wedding today, you know," Dee said. "We all needed a wedding."

"Yes," Lucy said.